JOKER'S Fool

a SATAN'S DEVILS novel

MANDA MELLETT

AUTHOR'S NOTE

In reading order *Joker's Fool* comes number eight in the Satan's Devils series, but there's a difference to the other works. It's an M/M romance. If you like M/M, great, if you don't, the book can be missed from the series. If you like M/M, but not MC Romance, again, good. You can read this book as a stand-alone.

If you're new to MC books you may find there are terms that you haven't heard before, so I've included a glossary at the end to help along the way. I hope you get drawn into this mysterious and dark world in the same way I have done—there will be further books in the Satan's Devils series which I hope you'll want to follow.

If you've picked this book up because, like me, you read anything MC, I hope you'll enjoy it for what it is, a fictional insight into the underground culture of alpha men and their bikes.

Road Name	Role/Status	Other Name
Drummer	President	Rick Felis
Wraith	VP	Scott Remington
Heart	Secretary	Dale Norman
Dollar	Treasurer	Todd Bishop
Peg	Sergeant-at-arms	Ronald Rinter
Blade	Enforcer	Jack Sharples
Joker	Road Captain	Josh Wilkinson
Mouse	Computer expert	Tse Williamson
Adam	deceased	
Beef		
Bullet		
Buster	deceased	
Dart	transferred	Colin Lowe
Fergus	Prospect	
Hyde		
Jekyll		
Lady		Scott Flintstone
Marvel		
Matt	Prospect	
Paladin	(was Marsh)	
Roadrunner		
Rock		
Slick		Jeff Andrews
Shooter	(was Spider)	
Tongue		
Truck	Prospect	
Viper		

Cast List of Characters

Old Lady	Children
Sam	Elijah (Eli)
Sophie	Olivia
Marcia	Amy, Jacob, Isabel
Darcy	Noah
Carmen	
Alex	Tyler
Becca	
Ella	
Sam	Elijah (Eli)
Sandy	

CONTENTS

CHAPTER 1

Three years ago

Satan's Devils Vegas Chapter

Hey, Fred! Grab us a beer, will you?" Keys, leaning against the wall, shouts across to the prospect standing in front of the bar while rubbing chalk on his cue.

Walking around the table, I eye the position of the balls. Going for the blue one is probably my best option, though he's not left me much to play with. Even that's a tricky shot, a fraction to the left and the white will bounce off and shoot down the pocket. I lean over the table, line up the shot, pull back the cue… And totally miss.

Keys barks a laugh. "Fuck, Joker. What the hell's gotten into you?" Stepping up he wastes no time and seizing his chance, proceeds to clear the table of balls, as well as emptying my wallet.

Stoically I pass over the cash, knowing there's no way on earth I can tell him the truth and admit what had distracted me.

Grinning, as though he can't believe his luck, Keys' eyes widen as he looks past me, nodding in understanding as something catches his eye. "It was that fine ass, wasn't it?"

What? Fuck! "What ass?" I keep my voice nonchalant. *Nothing to see here. Move along.*

"Pixie." He jerks his head in the direction of the bar, where the sweet butt has appeared next to the prospect.

Swallowing fast to stop myself sighing aloud with relief, I give a self-deprecating grin. "Must have been," I admit, giving him a wink. Yeah, Pixie's ass was responsible for giving me a hard-on. I'll go with that. Following his lead, I watch as the sweet butt shares a laugh with Rosa, then disappears out back. Nevertheless, even though she's now out of sight, I decline when Keys offers me the chance to win my money back, knowing my concentration has been shot to shit.

Instead I take my keys out of my pocket. "Time to do some work."

Keys glances at the wristwatch he's wearing, tapping the screen a few times. "Oh, yeah. You're going to that new joint, aren't you?" His fucking watch displays our planner. It makes me think back nostalgically to when such instruments just told the time.

I dip and raise my head. "Yeah, Prez wants me to check it out. Seems someone's been putting a squeeze on them."

"Want company? I hear there's a good looking broad runnin' it." Keys looks optimistic, but I shoot him down.

"Nah, I can handle this one." I jerk my hips suggestively. At this point, the thankfully diminishing but still undeniable bulge in my jeans helps me get my message across.

Keys barks a laugh, at the same time shaking his head. "Fuckin' sure you can, Brother, fuckin' sure you can."

Making my way across the clubroom, I smack Fox on the back as I pass, and nod to Titch, the old timer who I'm sure sees more than the rest. Down to experience, I suppose, though sometimes I worry he observes far too much. I'm almost at the door when a heavily tattooed arm snakes out halting my progress.

"Church. Don't be late."

I've got a couple of hours until I need to be back. "Sure thing, Prez. Going to check out that restaurant you wanted me to. Shouldn't take more than a minute."

"Yeah? Okay then. Well, if there's something for us there, bring it to the table." After I raise my chin in confirmation, Red's attention switches elsewhere.

Stepping out into the fresh air, I take a moment to breathe in deeply. For what is far from being the first time in my life, I wonder if a bullet to the brain would provide a solution. Permanent, maybe, but perhaps better than the half-life I live now. Always feeling on the outside looking in, as though something is missing. I know only too well what I'd need to do to fix it, but that would be impossible. Nah, I'll continue to suppress that side of myself. Wouldn't do any good coming clean. I'll just take each day as it comes and hope the next will be better. Being a member of a one-percenter outlaw motorcycle club, maybe the bullet with my name on it is already heading my way and wouldn't need to be self-inflicted.

I half turn, my head cocked to one side, listening to the voices coming from inside the converted warehouse behind me. *My brothers are in there. Brothers who all have my back.* Or they do, for now. They wouldn't if the truth ever came out. For a second I see their faces filled with the disgust I'm certain I'd be able to read there if somehow they learned my secret, then I shake my head to clear it. *Just keep yourself doing what you do. Put one foot in front of the other and live each day as it comes. Gotta be careful, that's all.* Fuck, if I haven't had enough practice at that. I'm almost perfect. Except for those times when my body shows me up. *If Keys knew… Or even suspected.* He doesn't. Thank fuck for that.

My feet carry me across to my Harley Soft Tail. I sit astride, pausing again before starting the engine, another glance back to the building I've just left. Light and laughter spilling out from the doorway. Just one more family I'll eventually end up disappointing, as I've done all my life. Fuck, I've got to keep my shit under control. *No one must ever find out.* I can't allow myself to get distracted again. I'd gotten away with it this time.

The wind in my hair and pavement zipping past beneath my wheels means the short ride helps clear my head. My cock once again under control, I'm more settled and in business mode by the time I arrive at my destination. The restaurant had been easy to find. I take a moment to examine it. Recently opened, it's in a good position on the outskirts of town. Eyeing it expertly I note the location is well placed to attract passing traffic, a good enough financial prospect to attract unwanted attention. As I back my bike against the curb and switch off the engine wonderful aromas assault me. If the food here tastes half as good as it smells, the broad Keys had mentioned won't have much problem making this eatery a success.

The outside of the restaurant is freshly painted, the brand-new sign promising delicious delights. The only thing spoiling it is the boarded-up window taking up half of the frontage. Hmm. Tossing my keys in my hand, I stare at it for a moment. It doesn't take a genius to work out what's gone down, nor why the Satan's Devils have been approached.

At last, opening the door, I step inside, pausing to consider the decoration. There are booths around the side, and a number of tables in the centre, giving the options of privacy or eating in the open. The lighting is good, sufficient to see what's on the plate in front of you, dim enough to create a good atmosphere. Someone either knew what they were doing, or employed an excellent interior designer. It's a place that would immediately tempt me to sample the food, were I not here with a different agenda.

I've timed it right, it's late afternoon, the evening rush hasn't yet started. Only a quarter or so of the tables are filled. There's the odd single person presumably refuelling after their day at work, along with a couple of families eating early with young children. The place has a family vibe.

"Table for one?"

I smile at the waitress who's approached me. "Nah, sweetheart. I'm here to speak with the owner. Ms Kennedy?"

I'm clearly expected, as after a moment's scrutiny, there's a slight downturn of her mouth, she tilts her head toward what must be the kitchen. "Oh, yes. Erika's out back. She's expecting you."

"Thanks. Shall I?"

"Yeah, go on through."

Following the wave of her hand, in a moment I'm transported into a different world, one composed almost entirely of stainless steel lit by harsh overhead lights. All appliances recent purchases if I'm not mistaken. The atmosphere in the restaurant out front might be calming, but here I find a bustle of activity. There's a woman wearing chef's whites, and a kid barely out of school following instructions. Bending over, squeezing some vegetables, is the woman I suspect is the one I've come to see.

"The zucchini seems a bit soft." She speaks over her shoulder to the chef.

"Shit! All of them?" Turning, enabling me to see she's a pleasant, slightly chubby faced woman, the chef doesn't look pleased.

"Most. Try to use them today, okay?" the person I've assumed is the owner instructs.

"Sure, I'll get Regan to push the ratatouille. Second time this week we've been palmed off with out of date stock. I think we ought to look for a different supplier."

Having heard enough about their culinary issues, I cough. Both women swing around, and two pairs of eyes narrow. "Ms Kennedy?"

After she peruses my cut, the woman who'd been checking the veg steps across, her hand held out politely enough, but the lack of a smile suggests a little reluctantly. "Erika Kennedy."

"Joker," I respond.

"Know any good ones?" The chef laughs from behind us as though it's the cleverest thing she's ever said. It might well have been, had I not heard it a hundred times before.

But I oblige. "Why did the chicken cross the road?" When she grins and shrugs, I continue, "Who the fuck knows?"

"We can talk in my office," Erika offers, and without waiting for a response, turns. A woman who doesn't want to waste time. I can respect that.

Following her I step inside the smallest office I've ever been in. A desk and a couple of chairs fill it leaving barely no other space. She sits behind a computer and peers over the top of the screen. I move a pile of paperwork from the second seat, then make myself comfortable. Mindful my time is limited if I'm to get back for church, I dive straight in. "You came to us for help?"

Sighing, she leans back on her chair, folding her arms across her chest. Taking a second to examine her, I see while her forehead is lined, she seems younger than I'd thought at first. While her hair is tied professionally back into a tight bun, and her cheeks reddened by the heat of the kitchen, it doesn't detract from her none. Keys was right, she's a looker. My dick stays dead in my pants.

"Brice Harper advised me to come to you."

I nod. Partly in acknowledgement—word of mouth together with our reputation is how we get these jobs—partly to encourage her to continue.

"Been open a month. Got a visit last week from someone selling insurance." Her mouth thins. She seems lost in thought.

It's not difficult to fill in the gaps. "Only it wasn't insurance, was it? You pay a hefty fee, as a result your business doesn't get bothered."

Another rise and fall of her head. "You've got it in one. I didn't agree, of course. Couldn't afford what they wanted."

Turned it down out of principle too, I'd imagine. This isn't my first day on the job. "Your window being broken isn't a coincidence."

Now she shrugs. "Nope," she pops the p. "They made sure I knew that too."

"Who?" I ask, but I already know. We come up against them a lot.

"They didn't introduce themselves, but they were some kind of gang. Had a strange tattoo on the back of their hands. A cross with a symbol going through it."

My turn to nod. Yeah, just as I expected. Bunch of mother-fuckers preying on the weak. But we can't complain, it keeps us employed.

"Brice said you could help, and at a fraction of the cost." She frowns as though she finds that hard to believe. "What I want to know is, what makes you different? You?" she waves at my cut. "You're in a gang too."

This isn't my first rodeo, so I start my practiced spiel. "We're not a gang. We're a motorcycle club. There's no similarity at all. Cunts like them just want to do damage. Don't raise a fuckin' finger to do an honest day's work. Pay up or else they destroy your business, that's what they told you?" I pause for her unnecessary confirmation; I know how this works.

"But I shouldn't need to pay. Them or you." Her eyes flash. "Have you any idea how much it costs to start up a new business? I factored everything in then cut it all to the bone. I pay for buildings and liability insurance…"

Leaning forward, I interrupt a story I've heard tens of times before to appraise her of some facts of life. "Sure you do. Reality is, lady, that if you don't do something, you won't have a business to run." I take a deep breath. "You don't pay, they'll destroy you."

"But that gets them nowhere…"

I don't know where she's come from, but she's got no street smarts. "Sure it does. Sends a powerful message to the next person who tries to start something up. They don't give a damn about you, whether you prosper or fail. They just want to intimidate, smash a few heads and get paid for doing it."

"They'd turn physical? Violent?"

I stare at the woman who's probably got a business degree, chef's qualification perhaps, but clearly no knowledge of the way the world works. "You've got a small parkin' lot out back, noticed it on the way in. You do nothing? Then it might be you, that sweet waitress, your chef, or the pot boy out there. Even a customer. Yeah, something will happen if breakin' your windows doesn't get your notice. You'll lose staff, lose customers. Not to say gain a reputation you don't want. You've got families eating out there. Who would bring kids to a place where they might get hurt?"

The lines on her brow become even more pronounced. Then her eyes narrow in suspicion. "So where do you come in? I pay you instead of paying them? I'm still out of pocket with nothing to show for it."

My elbows are now on her desk, my hands clasped together. "Satan's Devils aren't the same thing at all. You take our services? This is what will happen." I raise one finger. "First, we check your security system, make sure it's up to scratch. We'll put in remote monitorin'—we've already got that set up for other businesses around here, Brice's for example. First sign of trouble, Devils come runnin'." I chuckle. "More effective than the cops, I can assure you."

I've caught her interest. "Next," I hold up another finger, "We'll frequent your establishment, and judgin' from the food I saw, that won't be a problem. Let it be known you're under our protection. To start with, we might be around a lot, once the gang's got the message, we can start backin' off."

"You want free food?"

Well, it would be nice, but… "Not what I'm sayin' at all. Look, lady. We know you're probably at your bottom line already, ain't going to push you further into the red."

"How much?" She goes straight for it.

"Less than the gang wants. But it needs to be costed up. I'll need to see what security you've got at the moment, times you're open, shit like that. Once I know more, I can put together a proposal. All you've got to say is that you're interested, and I'll start. Doesn't commit you to anything. You don't like what I'm suggestin'? Just tell me it's not what you want. You won't be bothered by us again. We're not that gang, or like them in any way."

"Hmm." It's not just the tone of her voice, it's the tension in her body. She's still suspicious. "How do you know you can stop the gang breaking the place up, or heaven forbid, attacking someone?"

I sigh. "Because we know them. They're just a bunch of juveniles who think the world owes them. Once they realise Devils are involved, they'll back off. We've knocked a few of their heads together before." I go for the kill. "Half of my club are ex-services. We're not a disorganised street mob. Those motherfuckers are nothing."

Her eyes have brightened as I've given my explanation. "You?"

"Marine," I tell her, taking no pride in it. That's all behind me now. Not the type of experience I care to reminisce on. "Lady, here's the bottom line. If you don't do anything, you're going to get your business destroyed before you have a chance to get going. What will you do if they come back tonight to take out the rest of your windows? Or if they molest one of your staff or customers?"

Her eyes grow dark once more. "You're threatening me now. Pushing me into a corner."

Again, I sigh. "Not at all, Ms Kennedy. We don't take kindly to these protection rackets. You give me the word, this is what will happen. Oh, I'll have to take it back to the club, but I'll be proposin' you get our protection while you're makin' up your mind." I smile, "Try before you buy if you like. Give our boys a couple of plates of that food you're sellin', that will be enough for now. When I get the written proposal to you, you can see whether you want to take us up on it or not."

A shrewd look, then a disbelieving laugh. "You'll offer protection for free?"

"In the short term. A day or so, yes."

Her lips purse, then her words are exactly what I expect. "I don't see how I can refuse. If, as you say, there's no commitment."

That's the point. She can't. The gang broke the window last night. They'll be back today to amp up the pressure. As she's probably found out, the cops are next to useless. They can't spare men to provide protection, nor seem very enthusiastic about tracking the gang down.

"Call me Erika, please. Ms Kennedy makes me feel ancient." It's the first time I've seen her smile.

Yeah, she's certainly much younger than I first thought. Pretty, curvy figure, expressive face with all the features pleasantly placed. *A nice enough package that does fuck all for me.*

I stand and hold out my hand. This time she takes it more warmly. "Someone will be here later tonight," I promise her. "Just to see what's happenin' and make sure your other windows stay intact."

Chapter 2

Taking my place at the table, I nudge Cuff in the ribs, "Hey man, wanna hear about my dick?" I pause for a split second before finishing, "Nah, don't worry, it's too long."

Rope glares at me, Cobra laughs, and Titch grins snidely. "You fuckin' wish."

"Hey, old man. What would you know? You've been watchin' me in the heads?" He couldn't. I avoid using the urinal if anyone else is around, preferring to do what I need to in a stall. A practice ingrained from youth.

"Nah, too busy trying to hold my schlong with both hands." Titch raises his enormous mitts as though to prove the point.

"Alright, alright. If you've all finished comparin' the size of your junk, can we get this fuckin' meetin' started?" Red bangs the gavel hard. As I open my mouth, the prez's eyes zoom in on me. "Not one more fuckin' word, Joker."

Imitating the action of zipping my lips shut, Twister, the enforcer, laughs. Then stops abruptly at a glare from Red.

"Okay. Let's get started. Got a beer and a whore with my name on it."

"Tramp stamp," I whisper to Keys who's on my other side.

"Shut the fuck up, Joker!"

Red's a decent prez, but he can be scary when he wants. When those green eyes flare, it's best not to push it. He stares around the table, checking all attention is firmly on him, then his gaze lands back on me. "Okay, Joker. How did it go with the Kennedy broad?"

I stay quiet. Not even opening my mouth.

"For fuck's sake, Joker! Christ, this isn't a fuckin' motorcycle club, it's a fuckin' kindergarten. *Joker…*"

As Red growls, I know I'm pushing my luck but make a show of unzipping my lips, then before he can admonish me further, I give my report. "As expected. Street gangs pushin' in. Said we'd cost up her protection but provide some bodies to help out in the meantime. Free food on offer, boys."

A few hands immediately shoot up.

Crash, the VP, is first to jump in. "Don't mind going myself. It's one of those gourmet restaurants, isn't it?"

"Food smells fuckin' good," I add as encouragement.

"They do burgers?" Sarge asks, looking perturbed.

"How the fuck should I know? Didn't stop to look at a menu." I pause, remembering what I'd seen in the kitchen. "They're doing something with zucchinis tonight."

"Fuckin' veg. I need meat." Fox slowly shakes his head. "But Tiff could do with a night out. Don't mind going along, Prez."

Red's head is in his hands. He raises it slowly. "Okay, VP, you go check it out. Yeah, Fox, take Tiff. Show this Kennedy woman we're a family friendly club. And Sarge, go investigate whether they do burgers. You okay to stay overnight?"

Sarge nods. "Sure."

He won't mind. His PTSD means he finds it difficult to sleep. He's often the one who volunteers for night shifts.

The new restaurant sorted, we move on to discussing the state of our businesses. We run an auto shop, a tattoo parlour, a strip joint—usual things for an MC—but it's our security services that bring in the most bank. After Drummer, the president of the mother chapter in Tucson, declared Satan's Devils would earn their money clean, we got out of the drug and gun running trade. We've got enough to keep us amused and in the black. I grin when I hear our personal take will be up this month. I've got my eye on some new pipes.

I'm just thinking about the new exhaust, the purchase of which has now unexpectedly been brought forward, when Indian, our sergeant-at-arms, raises his hand. "Want to talk about Fred. He's been here fourteen months now. Thought we could discuss giving him a space at the table."

Oh fuck. His words bring me back to the meeting with a start. Fucking Fred. It's bad enough I have to put up with him being around the clubhouse. Bringing him to the table? Making him a member? Having to sit opposite, or heaven forbid, beside him? Before I can stop it one word's escaping my mouth. "No."

I've said it so loudly all other conversation stops. Red and Indian are staring at me, Indian with disgust. It's him who snarls, "We all know you've got a problem with him, Joker, but fuck knows why. Fucker's given his all to this club. He's been here well over a year, puttin' up with all the shit we've thrown at him. I haven't brought it to the table earlier as I'm well aware you've got something against him. Apart from you, I ain't had any complaints. I don't see your objection, *Brother.*"

Red's more patient, holding up his hand after Indian's long spiel. "Let's get this out in the open. Might be something we need to discuss. What don't you like about him, Joker? You know something we don't?" Then, without giving me a chance to respond, his eyes go around the table. "We all know the score. Got to be unanimous else he's not gettin' voted in. Anyone with a say should speak up. Time's now, Joke, to let us in on what you know that we apparently don't."

What the fuck do I say? I shrug, offering weakly, "Just don't take to the fucker. Don't exactly know why."

While there's snorts of derision around me, Red leans forward, elbows on the table, his chin resting on his hands. To give him his due, he's nodding as though I've made a valid point. "Okay. Let's break this down. You don't trust him to have your back?"

I can't say that. Because I've kept my distance, I don't really know the man. What I do know is that I'm being unfair. I'm denying someone who's worked their butt off for the patch just because his presence unsettles me. Have I got that right? I cast glances at my brothers, trying to read the expressions on their faces. *Will they all vote yes?* If they do, can I really hold out? Deny a man the brotherhood he so clearly wants, just because of my fucking feelings and fucked up life?

"Just something about him, Prez," I suggest, again, inadequately.

Red closes his eyes briefly, then opens them again. "We've heard what Joke's said. Anyone else got any doubts? I have to remind you, we've all prospected, all taken the shit, with one fuckin' purpose in mind. To be able to call the men around this table Brother." He waits for that to sink in. "Now Indian's brought it up, we've got three options. Give him the patch, show him the door, or give him more time." Again, he considers me. "You've been a member a few years now, Joker. You're our Road Captain. Don't think I don't give merit to what you have to say. But would givin' him more time change your mind?"

I stare at my hands, trying to think. Red's asking if we let Fred continue to prospect, would he be able to prove himself to me? *Prove what for fuck's sake?* There's nothing he'd be able to do to make me come to an alternative opinion. But how can I explain that every time I see him he brings things to the fore I prefer to keep suppressed? *Perhaps I should leave, hand in my patch. Take that bullet...* I can't fuck up a man's life. Not when it's me who's inherently at fault.

Finally, I look up. I can't fuck up a man's chance at brotherhood because of the effect he has on me. "Don't know how to explain it, Prez, but time won't change anything. You're right," I nod at the sergeant-at-arms, "he's done his time. If everyone else is happy to give him his patch, I'll vote him in."

Red sighs heavily. "Don't like thinkin' there'll be discord among us. You sure that's the way you want to play it, Joker?"

No. I'm not sure. I'd rather not have to face the fucker at all. Still, if I find it too hard I can always walk away from the club. I've got that option. Or take that bullet. It's not as though I'm able to tell anyone the real reason. I clear my throat, take a deep breath, then seal my fate as I say firmly, "I'm sure, Prez."

Red stares at me for a moment, his eyes slightly hooded. Then he raises his chin and starts the vote with Crash. As he goes around the table there are no other objections, well, there wouldn't be. Fred hasn't fucked up, everyone else likes him. He's not a youngster, served a few tours in the Army before seeking a new type of camaraderie. It's only me that hasn't taken to him.

When Red gives the final 'aye', Fox, our treasurer and secretary, records it officially.

"Road name?" Hammer's enquiry, accompanied by a wide grin, brings me out of my thoughts.

Rope laughs. "With those baby features of his? Pretty Boy. What else?"

"He's already got a road name," I grumble. "Why not keep using Fred?" Man's called Scott Flintstone, I know that much about him at least. Boys started calling him Fred from the first day.

"Only used it to rile him up," Twister admits.

Fox is scratching his head. "Alright calling him Pretty Boy now, but what about when he's as old and ugly as Titch?"

Titch predictably shows him his finger.

"Way he attracts all the ladies, how about Lady's Man?" Crash suggests. "Once the fucker's patched in we're not going to get a second look."

"There is that," Shadow agrees, running his hands through his long hair. "I quite like that handle."

I do too. It might just help me remember what he really is. I raise my hand. "Lady's Man is a good choice."

Red throws me a quick look, seeming to be surprised at my contribution, then chuckles. "Okay, that's settled then. Let's get him in and tell him the good news."

Normally I enjoy this part. Knowing after all these months a prospect will be half hopeful, half despairing. An unexpected summons to church, and he might end up with a patch or get kicked to the curb. Or just be receiving a mundane instruction. There's a certain pleasure in seeing a man squirm, and being the fuckers we are, we make the most of it. Trying to forget it's Fred we're discussing, I attempt to push my feelings aside, but it's tough. The part I usually look forward to is tinged with darkness for me today. Fred, *Lady's Man* getting his patch might result in me handing mine in.

To everyone else, nothing's different about today. The prospect appears, is kept waiting, all eyes glaring at him, until Red finally lets him off the hook. Man, didn't expect it, his watering eyes a sign I was right to give in. Despite everything I get a burst of emotion myself at seeing his undisguised euphoria, reminding me of how I'd felt when I'd been in his place standing at the end of the table. He flinches a little at his new handle, then ruefully grins pulling back his shoulders. He takes the patches, holding them tightly as if afraid they'll be snatched away.

Meeting over, we rise to our feet. As each man passes, they slap our new member on the back. Wincing, I do the same, a hasty pat hardly anything more than a tap. When he turns, I look away to avoid catching his eye.

"You stayin' for the party?" Cuff asks as we're walking out, me hurriedly, wanting to put distance between myself and the man who disturbs me so much. "Well?" Cuff prompts when I'm too lost in thought to reply.

Stay and watch the hangarounds fawn over the new member? The sweet butts vying to be his first choice? Not fucking likely. "Nah, man. I've made plans." I pull myself together enough to accompany my comment with a wink.

Cuff grins knowingly. "You got a lady in town?"

I bump my fist against his. "Too fuckin' right, man. Fine piece of ass. I'm going to be tapping that."

I interpret his hearty slap to my back as encouragement.

Sixteen years ago

As always, I stare down at my plate, toying with my food while trying to avoid eye contact with my father.

"What you up to this weekend, Son?"

A direct question. My eyes flick to Mom who nods in support. I've already told her my plans, can't change my story for him. "Going to the mall with Bella and Gina tomorrow…"

My voice tails off as my father rolls his eyes.

Mom, oblivious to the undertones in the room, chuckles. "Our son's a great hit with the ladies." She grins at me and winks.

Dad doesn't share her enthusiasm. His gaze is considering as he looks at me. "Boy's too young to be thinking about girls. What about your other friends? Why aren't you hanging around with that, what's his name, Bart, anymore?"

"Brett," I correct automatically. "Don't see much of him nowadays. He's on the football team." We've got nothing in common. We had when younger, but recently we'd grown apart. The things he enjoys I have no interest in.

Dad thumps the table. "That's what you should be doing. Playing football, not shopping with girls. For fuck's sake, Millie. We brought up a fucking pansy?"

As he speaks I just look on in horror. The truth is, I like the female company. I like shopping for clothes, giving the girls my comments when they come out of the changing room. I'd rather be giggling, watching as they try on new makeup, than kicking a football around. In my gut, I know I'm different. I'm just not ready to admit, even to myself, just how.

"What's that mark over your eye?" Dad's still studying me. I'd hoped he wouldn't notice.

"Got in a fight." That, I know, will impress him. That's the way I'm supposed to act. I won't tell him I'm the target of bullies. He'll only ask why.

His eyes narrow. "What's the other guy look like?"

I force a laugh, "Worse," I lie. He got away without a scratch. Well, it was two against one. I've other bruises but I'm careful not to let him see them.

Dad looks at Mom and raises an eyebrow, then as parents do, seems to have seen through my untruth. He slaps his hand on the table. "Well, that's settled. We need to toughen you up. We'll go to the gym tomorrow. Get you punching a few bags. You need to get some muscles on you. Kid of mine wins when he fights."

The last thing I want to do is go to a gym, be surrounded by hot, sweaty, grunting bodies. But, of course, I go. Because that's what normal boys do.

Thing is, I already know I'm not normal.

Chapter 3

"Alright, alright. Break it up now."

Shadow and Sarge have technically come to the end of their third five-minute bout but continue to grapple in the middle of the ring, neither wanting to admit defeat. Indian climbs up, followed by Twister, and physically they pull them apart, the pair still struggling, their eyes shooting daggers at each other.

Glancing at Cobra, I shake my head. Shadow and Sarge are so evenly matched no one bothers betting on them anymore. Red, Crash and Titch have been doing the scoring, giving both men ten points in the first two rounds. There's nothing I've seen to put between them in this final one. No one's surprised when a draw is announced, though that doesn't stop Sarge putting his fist in Shadow's stomach as he's climbing down.

Shadow retaliates, and the fight starts up again on the floor. Red, unfazed, just signals to Indian and Twister to break it up once again. Twister's our enforcer for good reason. He's not known for being particularly gentle. This time once they're apart, they still glare at each other but start to calm down. A few choice words from the enforcer has them shaking hands. No one in their right mind wants to upset Twister.

Red looks around, his eyes fall on me. "Joker, you up?"

Yeah, I got this. For an answer, I swing myself into the ring, then wait patiently while Indian wraps my hands, wondering who Prez will give me as an opponent. It will be a member, prospects are allowed to fight, but only each other. I don't care who it is, I'll give anyone a run for their money. It's not often I lose…

"Lady's Man," Red calls out.

Fuck. My eyes widen as I swing around to face him, knowing Prez has to have done it on purpose. The first member Lady's Man gets to fight is me. My gut sinks as the one man I've successfully managed to avoid for days, weeks, *months*, jumps nimbly into the ring. For fuck's sake, it looks like a light breeze could blow him over. I'm angry at Prez, rage rising at being placed in this position. *Close enough to touch.* Too close. *And he'll be touching me…* I can't refuse an opponent Prez has announced. I haven't a choice.

Once his hands are wrapped to Indian's satisfaction, Lady's Man starts bouncing on his feet, banging his fists together. His eyes meet mine almost tauntingly, looking eager to get started, pleased that at last he's able to fight with the members now his prospecting time is behind him. Ready to show what he's made of.

Fuck it! Let's get this over with. He's not going to last one round. We might be matched in height, but I've got weight and muscle on him. Fractionally lowering my shoulder, I charge.

He's gone. My momentum takes me to the edge of the ring where Twister's waiting and gets me turned around.

Lady's Man's fucking quick, suddenly he's to my front where his punch to my stomach takes the wind out of me. Then he's back the other side, his fist raised in the air as though in triumph. *Fucking asshole's got speed and strength.* Realising I might have underestimated him, I start taking more care.

This time I make no subliminal sign to signal my intentions. I raise my fists as though to protect myself, then, as he advances, I turn, crashing him down on the ground. Quick as lightning he responds, somehow rolling me so he's the one on top. This time I get a punch to my jaw.

Enraged, I growl, and jump up, my leg already swinging in a chop designed to take him back down.

Red rings the bell. Five minutes has gone all too quickly, the judges deciding Lady's Man has won the first round.

I'm a fighter. I know what I'm doing. From the age of fourteen my father insisted I concentrate on sports which were particularly male oriented. I fought to keep him happy. Eventually succeeding when I started to bring home MMA trophies. I went into the Marines to prove to him I was something I'm not, and had my share of fighting there too. Fuck my life, I did. I had them all fooled when I excelled. By sheer determination. I'd built up my body together with the knowledge how to use it. In a fight muscle memory takes over, my brain sends an instruction, my limbs do the work. I've hidden that I lack any real competitive spirit, have no desire to win at all costs. I'd never admitted it, but the thought and feel of flesh meeting flesh for sport fills me with disgust.

Today something changes. As I hold that bottle of water to my lips, a rage rises inside me.

I don't get angry. I've a reputation for keeping my cool, normally making a joke about a situation to defuse it. I'll stand and defend my brothers, but it's mechanical, every move considered. Looking at Lady's Man, though, I can barely see him through the red mist that's now covering my eyes.

When the bell rings, I don't just come out fighting, I come out ready to annihilate the man who's responsible for bringing such discord to my well-ordered world. I had everything where I wanted it, everything in its place neatly packed away in locked boxes. *Until he brought the key and opened the lock.*

With a roar, I throw myself at him. Taking him by surprise I sweep his legs out from under him. Once he's on the ground, I fall on top and start pummelling. Uncaring my fists are landing on his face, the only thought in my head to take out the enemy.

He's fast. Far stronger than he looks. Almost immediately turning the tables, using brute strength to push me off, and in one smooth move he now has me on my back. He straddles me, raising his fist then his eyes widen as he stops, hand held mid-air.

The position he's in, sitting over my cock with only the flimsy material of our shorts between us means I'm unable to hide I'm getting an erection.

Fuck no. Not now. Not like this. Ignore it, it's nothing, please ignore it. As his lips start to curl I know my silent pleas are unanswered. *No. Fuck it. No.* Reacting automatically, it's my turn to take him by surprise. Half pushing, half slivering away, the words spewed from my mouth as I shout, "Fuck you!" then jump the ropes and exit the gym at a run, pushing past people left and right, leaving a roomful of stunned men behind me.

This is it. They'll all know. Lady's Man won't waste a second outing me. That smirk on his face, I know he's not going to let me get away with it. Fuck! Why did it have to be him? Why did Red want me to fight him? Why did Prez do that to me? Lady's Man's probably laughing about it right now. *He'll tell them all. He fucking knows.*

Sixteen years ago

"Josh! Oh, Josh. What's happened to you?" Mom comes running across the kitchen as I appear in the doorway, my father's hand on my shoulder. She stops dead with her hand to her mouth.

I'm struggling to keep back the tears. My whole body seems to hurt, my back, stomach, and as for my face... Well, I've literally just been used as a punch bag and know I look like it.

"Leave the boy, Millie. He doesn't need mothering. He needs to learn to defend himself."

Come to the gym, Dad had told me. Hit the punch bag a few times, he'd said. Although I'd much rather have gone out with the girls, what Dad wants, Dad gets. What I hadn't expected was for him to throw me in at the deep end. Put me in the ring with a much more experienced boy. A boy who was dancing on his toes with glee, his grin widening with every punch he landed. I got none in of my own.

Next time, Dad said. Next time you'll know better and get in a few hits.

It wasn't the next time, or the one after that. By the time I learned how to hold my own, I'd broken ribs, lost teeth, even once, had my arm broken. A brutal method, but gradually self-preservation took over and I absorbed enough information to defend myself, and then how to land punches of my own.

"You're becoming a man," my Dad had said proudly when I took my first prize.

Yeah, if being a man meant I could hold my own in the ring. That was his definition. I think even then he knew my heart wasn't in it. But forcing me to man up was his first attempt to change me.

"What the fuck got into you yesterday, Brother?"

My uneasy sleep being interrupted by a knock at the door isn't particularly unusual. That my visitor is the prez, certainly is.

My face burns red as I remember the evening before. I look steadily at the wall, refusing to look at Red as I wait for it. Wait for him to scorn, laugh, warn me away from the club. Knowing Lady's Man had to have been mocking me, telling everyone what had happened. They'll all know why, and this time, me, Joker, will have been the butt of the joke. I don't speak, just wait for what I know will be coming.

Red moves closer, dragging the chair from my desk nearer to the bed and sitting on it. Regarding me thoughtfully, he starts, "I'm not going to apologise for pittin' you against each other. But I want to know why the fuck you dislike Lady's Man so much. Fuck, for a moment there I thought you were gonna kill him. You wanted to. Hell, I saw it in your eyes. We *all* fuckin' saw it. Luckily he's shown he can hold his own. If it had been another man you might have succeeded. What the fuck is it, Joker? Am I going to have to warn him to watch his back around you from now on? Huh," he scoffs, "not that he'll probably need that advice."

What is there for me to say? Armed with nothing to defend myself or my actions, I remain dumb.

Red's shaking his head. "You voted him in, Brother. Need to put whatever shit there is between you to one side. I don't need to remind you that brothers are supposed to be prepared to die for, not kill each other. Need you to talk to me, Joker. What is it between the two of you?"

Terrified of the answer, I bite the bullet. "Have you spoken to him?" *Has he outed me?*

"Yeah," Red snorts. "Got about the same reaction as I'm getting from you. He won't say a fuckin' word either."

Some of my tension leaves me. So, Lady's Man kept quiet. For now. Does that mean he's going to use the information to taunt me? He could bring me down, destroy everything I've got with a few choice words. *Why hasn't he said anything? How's he going to hold it over me?*

Red's face reddens. He growls, "I can't have this, Brother. Can't have the two of you at each other's throats, you hear me? You fuckin' get things straight between you."

I flinch at his poor choice of words, but give him what he wants to hear. "I'll sort it, Prez." Fuck knows how, but Red's right. I can't communicate with my fists every time I see him.

"Yes, you fuckin' will. You've been a member for longer, but Lady's Man has been brought into the fold, and looking from where I'm standin', he hasn't once stepped out of line." He sighs, tugging at his short red beard. "Look, tonight you're on shift at the restaurant. Lady's Man will be there workin' with you. This is your chance, understand? I'm not asking you to become best buddies, just not leave me a body to bury, you hear me?"

Fuck! There I was hoping to avoid him. But what else can I do? Seeing Red's face is set, any protest would be futile. Not without good reason, and there's nothing I can admit that would give him that. He's waiting for an answer. What can I offer, but, "I hear you. You got it, Prez."

Red stares at me a moment longer before scooting the chair back a few inches and standing. "No bloodshed, Joker. I'm fuckin' trustin' you. You and Lady's Man. Whatever this crap is between you has got to stop. Today. You hear me?"

He leaves my bedroom without waiting for me to respond, I'm wondering whether he's given Lady's Man the same message. But it wouldn't be necessary. By now, the new member will know exactly why I've been avoiding him. Which means there's no way on this earth he'll want to be anywhere near me.

Scared of being laughed at, jeered at, I'll admit to being a coward, hiding out in my room all day, only making a trek out to the kitchen when hunger drives me there. I'm embarrassed to bump into any of my brothers, knowing they won't be able to resist a reference to my unusual behaviour last night. Knowing they can be worse than old women at times, it's probably been the main topic of conversation ever since. They're all well aware I've never before lost my temper, never even shown I had one. I'm the peacemaker, not the instigator. They'll have no idea why I tried to kill a man, *a brother,* in front of them.

It's my lucky day though, the clubhouse is quiet. I come across no one in the few minutes before I scuttle back to the safety of my room, a plate of food I doubt I'll taste in my hands.

No longer able to put off the inevitable, at eight pm I wander downstairs to find Lady's Man waiting for me by the bar, his raised eyebrow his only greeting. Inwardly I grimace when I see him. He's got a cut over one eye, the other blackened, a swollen jaw and a bruise on his cheek. Not so unusual after a fight, but my frenzied attack hadn't been normal. *I should apologise.* Fuck, if I do, he might mention my, er, reaction. I'll keep my mouth shut. *But I can't get through the whole night without speaking.* Is it too much to hope he'll ignore what happened? Probably. All I want to do is crawl back to my hole and never have to confront him, or indeed anyone, again.

"Ready?" Lady's Man breaks the awkward silence.

"Yeah." At least my voice still works even if it's a little husky.

Taking the lead, I go out to where the bikes are parked, leaving him to follow in my wake. Starting my engine, I zoom out through the gate without even waiting to see if he's ready. Well, if he can't keep up he knows where we're going. It's only a moment before he draws up alongside.

There are many benefits bikes have over cages, one of them being that at seventy miles per hour you can't have a conversation with your companion, which suits me just fine. When we get to the more populated area, I lower the speed, Lady's Man now forced to slot in behind me as the road narrows. The journey's far too short, and all too soon we arrive. We back up until our rear wheels touch the curb and dismount in silence, then walk the final steps to our destination still without exchanging a word.

I enter to find the restaurant is busy, almost every table filled with smiling faces, the loud sound of various conversations filling the air. Having taken to Erika the first time I met her, I'm pleased to see she's doing a roaring trade. As can be expected at this time of night, business is starting to wind down. Most customers have desserts in front of them, or coffees. Regan's busying herself clearing plates and there's two other waitresses who seem rushed off their feet. As soon as we enter, Erika appears from the kitchen.

"Joker!" Her quick smile indicates she's pleased to see me. The suspicions she'd previously harboured of the Satan's Devils the last time I was here seem to have disappeared.

Nodding at the now fixed window, I reply, "Looks better than it did last time. Did you get the estimate?" I'd sent her our quote the day after I'd been here.

Her brows knit together. "Yes, I did, thank you. More than I wanted to spend, but most of it was on the security system that I've been advised to install."

"It would be a wise investment," I stress. Yeah, it would be an expensive outlay, but she needs it.

Her arms fold across her chest. "Yes, I know. I have to admit, the costs for your men aren't as high as I feared."

"We're not about extortion," I explain. "Just about keeping the gangs under control. As you know, we already cover the neighbouring businesses, so the cost reduces the more we bring on board."

Her forehead creases in the same way I'd noticed when I was here before, but only for a second, then she's smiling again. "I've got the corner table reserved for you. Regan will bring you some menus…"

Shaking my head, I save her the bother. "Don't go to any trouble. Just give us a plate of something you've got left over."

"Steak and fries?"

Hell, that sounds good. Or would if my companion's presence hadn't ruined my appetite. "Works for me." I cast a look over my shoulder.

"Yeah. That will do nicely. The name's Lady's Man." He shows no embarrassment at using his new handle. He even accompanies his introduction with a wink. And fuck me, Erika blushes in response. I swallow hard to suppress the growl that comes to my throat.

While a slightly flustered Erika returns to the kitchen, I lead the way to the table she pointed out. There are only two chairs positioned kitty corner, both of them with their backs to the wall. Good, we'll be able to keep an eye on anyone coming in. Nice to pretend we're working while enjoying a free meal. Judging by the happy people around me, it's probably going to be pretty tasty.

Having seated ourselves, I pull the menu over, feigning interest in the type of food they serve. But I'm not given long. Soon a hand comes over the protective barrier I've placed between us and pushes it down. I glance up to see dark brown eyes gazing at me.

"Are we going to address the elephant in the room, or just let this silence continue?"

I could pretend I don't know what he's talking about. I could tell him I'm not one for small talk. I could, but, "Look, Lady's Man. I don't know what got into me last night. I lost it, okay? And as for… as for… I don't know what caused that. Too much fuckin' testosterone in the air or something."

Lady's Man studies me intently. "Or something," he repeats. He wipes his hand over his face, it draws my attention to the bruises I'd been responsible for, making me wince. *He'd done nothing to deserve those injuries.* No, that was all on me. I watch as he closes his eyes briefly, then opens them again. "Look, Joker. You might want to avoid it, but I'm not going to pretend I don't know what the problem is between us."

He knows? I shrink down in my seat. "I don't know what you're talkin' about." I try to sound unperturbed, while internally my stomach rolls.

"I don't have a problem with who or what I am," he informs me.

Well, he wouldn't. He's one hundred percent heterosexual. Though as a prospect he hasn't been near the whores, his reaction to the hangarounds who come to our parties bore evidence of that.

I glance up at Regan gratefully as she interrupts our conversation by placing two plates containing delicious looking large lumps of meat and a pile of fries in front of us. Along with steak knives. Giving my hands something to do, when I cut into the steak I discover the extra utensils are superfluous. I could have eaten it with a spoon. Although I wasn't hungry, the way this meat has been prepared and seasoned gets my juices running. I only hope Lady's Man is finding it just as good and will concentrate on eating rather than continuing our discussion. I'm to be disappointed.

He chews a mouthful of meat and swallows. "I get it, Joker. I do. You've been in the club longer than me, so you probably know how the brothers would take it." His eyes slightly glaze over. "I've worked hard for my fuckin' patch, earned my place around the table. I've longed to be a part of the brotherhood since I've been back stateside. Lost something when I did my last tour, found it here. Don't want to fuck it up. So, I'll take the lead from you."

With my eyes half closed, I shake my head. "Don't know what you're fuckin' talkin' about, Brother." I put down my silverware, my appetite fleeing as fast as it had returned.

Lady's Man's not so affected, continuing to eat until his plate is empty. Almost hypnotised by the repetitive movement of his fork from steak to mouth, I hope again the conversation has been concluded, thinking of ways we can work this tonight and keep well out of each other's way. But no, he gives me only a brief reprieve.

"You gonna finish that?" he asks, pointing and gazing hopefully at my plate.

I push it over to him. He takes a mouthful of the fillet I couldn't stomach, chews, swallows, then looks up. "Last night…"

"Just fuckin' leave it," I snarl.

Another morsel goes down. Then those brown eyes fix on me again. This time he lays down his knife and fork and sits forward. "Joker. Let's get this cleared up. Bring it all out into the open. Tell me, why have you kept your distance in the whole fuckin' year and two months I've slaved for this club? In that time, I've got to know all the brothers. Except you. You wouldn't even give me the time of day. Left the room when I appeared. Why? Prez wants us to clear the air between us, but unless you admit what's botherin' you about me, we don't stand a fuckin' chance."

Sitting forward I hiss, "I just don't take to you, *Brother*."

"Nah," he says, thoughtfully, "It's more than that. You know as well as I do what it is." A quick grin comes to his face. "Takes one to know one, Brother."

"I'm not…" I start, then snap my mouth shut.

His eyes narrow, and the corners of his mouth turn down. "I wonder. Are you tellin' yourself that or me?" He closes his eyes briefly as though in pain, while his head moves side to side. "Not quite sure which is worse."

I'm sitting, wondering whether we're talking about the same thing. Hoping we're not. Hoping he's not telling me what I think he is. Knowing I can't ask outright in case I'm wrong, and if I'm right, well, I don't want to know. He's correct in one thing. Keeping the patch is the only thing that matters.

"Joker?"

Her hurried approach and the frantic tone of Erika's voice instantly gets me heaving myself out of the chair.

"The gang's out back…"

CHAPTER 4

Lady's Man is on his feet only a split second behind, and trailing me as Erika waves us through into the kitchen, then indicates the back door.

"Lock it behind us," I throw over my shoulder as I rush out into the night air, just in time to see one of the gang members about to swing a bat at a car parked in one of the bays marked 'Customer Parking.' Wrenching the weapon out of his hand I continue his swing, but this time bringing it down on his arm. From his screech and the way his limb's left hanging, it looks likely I've broken a bone. *Good.*

Checking around me I see about half a dozen others. One's got a knife and he's going for Lady's Man. With no second thought, my brain quickly analyses the angle and distance and I use the appropriated bat again with another swing. This time I've done less damage, but at least the knife's dropped harmlessly to the ground.

Standing back to back with my brother, we carefully watch the half dozen gang members circling around us. "Shall I smile for the camera?" Lady's Man jokes with a pointed nod upwards.

Yeah, those cameras the boys fitted will be letting the club know precisely what's going down, and help will be saddling up and riding. All Lady's Man and I have to do is hold them off until the cavalry arrives.

"Whatcha doing here?" One of the gang members comes to stand in front of me, out of range, but still his eyes warily eye the bat.

"Protectin' our business," I inform him. If he misinterprets that we own this place that's on him. We do, in fact, have a financial interest.

"Look, we're in the same racket…"

"Not even close," I refute. My eyes go from him to a youth standing behind him. He barely looks adult, then I notice his hand twitching toward the inner pocket of his jacket. Bats and knives I can deal with. Don't want any bullets flying here. I'm certainly not a fan of being shot by a pimply faced kid who looks barely out of diapers.

The man, who I take to be the leader, seems to realise we won't be walking away. I can almost hear him thinking it through. There's six of them, if you discount the one who I put out of action, and only two of us. What he doesn't realise is he's dealing with the Devils, and Devils don't walk away from a fight. Not leaving anyone else left standing. He looks at me, then back at his crew. I watch him carefully, seeing the precise moment he makes his decision.

Lady's Man might be many things but he's not stupid. As the gang launch at us we're both ready with fists and legs flying. I personally send two knives soaring over the wall. Two men are down, a third holding his wrist. Now a fourth has dropped his bat, taken to his legs and is running. Two left. We approach, they step back warily.

Then pimply face draws his gun, but before he can fire Lady's Man is there, twisting it out of his grasp.

The distant sound of bikes approaching reaches me. When I grin at him, it's clear the gang leader's only too aware what that means. He backs off as I approach menacingly.

I offer him a smirk, *we've fucking got this*. Not going to need our brothers' help after all. This one's mine. I take another step forward.

"Joker!"

As Lady's Man's screamed warning reaches me I swing around to see that the one I thought I'd disabled has picked up the bat that had been discarded. There's a stinging blow to my ribs, then, nothing.

"What the fuck happened?" Carefully, pressing down on one hand, I pull myself up, my other arm wrapping protectively around my ribs. Once on my knees, I gingerly probe the huge lump growing on the back of my head.

"Fucker got a couple of lucky swings at you. Fuck, thought he was out of the game. Should have had my fuckin' eye on him." Lady's Man's brushing his hair back with both hands, then repeating the action. "Fuck, sorry, Joker. Fuckin' should have had your back. I couldn't get there in time."

I'm alive, aren't I? "I think you did." He's got nothing to feel guilty about. I hadn't given the downed man another thought either. "Where are they?" Belatedly, and tentatively considering the pain throbbing through my head, I look around and see half a dozen of my brothers, but no sign of the gang.

"Most took off. The fucker that hit you? He'll be back at the compound by now."

"Joker!" A woman's voice sounds worried. "You alright?"

"Yeah, how you doing?" Red's deeper voice booms in my ear as he crouches down by my side.

"Cracked a rib, I reckon." I should know what that feels like. "I'll heal."

"Nah, don't get up. You were out of it for a bit there. Got Petty coming back with the truck. Gonna get Doc to have a look at you." Prez's voice is gentler than usual.

"There's no need for that." I pull my feet under me, leaning forward to take the pressure off my chest, and start to rise.

A firm hand presses down on my shoulder. "Gave you an order, Brother. Want you looked at."

I've had enough knocks in the past to know medical treatment isn't necessary, but once Prez is set on something there's no changing his mind. Whatever my opinion, it seems I'll be visiting the doctor we use who has his own practice. The grey-haired gent who receives a generous retainer to be on call at all hours. As far as I'm concerned, I'd do well enough just going straight back to the compound and to my bed, but there's no point in arguing. Red's a good prez, as long as you don't get him riled. His temper can be as fiery as his hair.

"I'm so sorry you got hurt. Are you sure you'll be okay?"

At a disadvantage as I'm still on the ground, I look up into Erika's concerned face, noticing she's wringing her hands. Knowing she'll be feeling responsible, I try to reassure her, "I'll be fine. Taken worse hits before." I'm more annoyed the fucker got the better of me.

She doesn't look convinced, but politeness wins out. "I can't thank you enough, Joker, Lady's Man." She turns to the prez, "And you, Red, for getting your men here so quickly. If my customers…"

Prez raises his hand. "Your customers are fine, Erika. You kept them inside without raising concerns, no one knew anything happened. Gave them drinks on the house, I understand?"

A quick smile for Red, "Can't take credit for that. It was Regan's quick thinking. Took our time calculating their tabs too." The corners of her mouth quickly turn down, as she looks around warily. "Do you think they'll come back?"

Red stands and pats her arm. "If they do, we'll be here waitin'. They'll eventually get the message they don't want to mess with us."

I let the conversation carry on without me playing a part in it. It's hard to tell which the greater pain is, the sharp throbbing of my ribs or the pounding in my skull. Knowing I wouldn't be able to ride my bike, I'm relieved when I see the truck pull up. At least I'll be able to sit down. I wouldn't admit it, but I am starting to feel a little dizzy.

As Petty jumps out and comes over, Lady's Man throws him his keys and instructs, "Take my bike back, I'll drive him to see Doc."

The prospect nods. "He's expecting him. Your key, Joke? Roller's come with, he's gonna ride your bike back."

Reluctantly, but knowing it's for the best, I push my hand in my pocket and take it out. "Tell him not to drop it," I growl. I hate anyone being on my ride, but know the person most likely to lay it down tonight would be myself in my current state.

As Petty tosses Roller my keys, the latter grumbles. "Like I'm gonna lay his fuckin' bike down on purpose."

"Less of the mouth, Prospect," Red snarls. Chastised, the two prospects go and get on their bikes, or rather, Petty on Lady's Man's and Roller on mine, and follow the rest of the brothers out of the parking lot. When they've gone, I realise Red's talking. "Sarge and Cobra will take over in case the gang comes back. You take Joker now, Lady's Man. Let's get him clear before the customers come out."

Yeah, not good for business to have an injured bleeding biker lying next to their cars. I wave off the help that really I could have done with, and choking back a moan, stand and walk as straight as I can to the truck. Following Lady's Man's example, I slide off my cut, then climb into the passenger seat. Sighing with relief I rest my head back, then bring it forward again fast. I'd forgotten that fucking lump.

"This is stupid," I tell Lady's Man. "Waste of everyone's time." I don't need medical treatment. A broken rib will heal on its own, my head's seen worse bumps too.

Lady's Man shoots me a quick look. "Maybe Doc will give you some happy pills. Fuck knows you could use them."

"Hey, I make the fuckin' jokes."

"Who said I was jokin'?" he comes back with fast.

He's made a good point though. I start hoping Doc will give me some of the good stuff to take the edge off this pain. Might be worth the inevitable prodding and poking.

Doc, though, isn't satisfied passing out pills. He's either thorough or likes to play with his new toys as he insists on x-raying my chest, brushing off my objections. Finally, he leaves the room, then shortly after returns holding a fucking iPad which he's examining critically.

"You've got a cracked rib." I suppress the urge to say I could have told him that, but he continues, his eyes widening. "How the hell did you get all these injuries? By the look of how they've healed, you can only have been a kid."

"Fuckin' hell, Joker. What's all this?"

It's only then I notice Lady's Man standing looking over Doc's shoulder. His mouth hangs open, his attention alternating between the screen and me. "Ancient history." I answer them both dismissively, hoping they'll let the subject drop. *Why the fuck is Lady's Man in here anyway?* That shit is private. Between me and my past.

Doc eyes me for a moment, then shakes his head, his eyes gentling. "Doubt I need to tell you what to do. You're obviously no stranger to a broken rib. Rest, take it easy, let it heal by itself. No heavy lifting."

"What about his head, Doc?"

Glaring at him, I snarl, "For fuck's sake, Lady's Man. Leave it. I'll live." *Right about now rest and taking it easy sounds fucking good.*

Adding insult to injury, the doctor answers him, not me, "I haven't got the equipment to check, but I suspect he's got a concussion. You know how to watch for that?"

"Keep him awake, or only let him sleep for short periods. Wake him to check. Pupils should react normally, any nausea, vomiting or anything unusual, get him to a hospital."

"He's right here," I grumble.

"You know what you're talking about." Again, Doc ignores me, addressing Lady's Man.

"Yeah, I know first aid," Lady's Man agrees amicably.

At last the doc brings his attention to me. "I'll give you painkillers, but he," he points to my companion, "is in charge seeing as he knows what to watch for. No arguments if he decides you ought to go to the hospital." His eyes sharpen as I go to speak. "No arguments, I said. From that look on your face you're going to give him hell. But that's one nasty lump on your head and your skull could be fractured. I haven't got the equipment to check." By the gleam in his eyes though, he's estimating the size of the retainer we pay him, and considering how long it will be before he can add to his collection.

"I'll make him see sense."

Lady's Man. Fuck. I glower at him, then remember we've been fighting side by side tonight. He held his own, it wasn't his fault I was blindsided. But that recollection doesn't stop my eyes narrowing as I watch him pocketing the painkillers. Hating myself as much as him, now feeling even more woozy, I do take his arm as he gently sits me up, then helps me off the examination table.

Fuck, but I hurt. Perhaps it's because I'm older. I was better able to shake off the lumps and bumps when I was a kid.

We don't speak in the truck on the way back. On my part because I couldn't trust myself to say anything. Nothing pleasant, that is. Lady's Man has already learned far too much about me tonight. I don't know what, if anything, he's going to do with the information. Keeping my distance while he prospected has now backfired. I know nothing about him.

I'm relieved when, at last, we draw up to the compound, driving inside when Roller slides open the gates. After Lady's Man has parked the truck in its usual spot, I open the door to see Red approaching.

"Verdict?" Fuck me, now Prez is addressing Lady's Man too.

Oh, fuck it. Let him update Red. Means I don't have to. All I can think of is getting into my bed.

"You'll stay with him? Let me know if he needs anything?"

"Sure, Prez."

It's time I butt in. "I'm okay, Prez. Ain't nothing that's never happened before." I just want to be left alone. *I don't need a fucking babysitter.*

Red doesn't look like I've done a good job of convincing him. "You'll keep yourself awake, will you? Watch out for signs of a concussion? Nah. Lady's Man is stayin' with you. You got hurt on his watch."

"He doesn't owe me nothing. Wasn't his fault, Prez." I might not like the man, but I'll stand up for him.

Lady's Man puts his hand gently on my shoulder. "Stop arguin', old man. You don't get a choice."

My scowl has no effect, likewise the brusque manner with which I brush off his hand, causing me a lot more pain than him. Then, waving off the concerned queries of the rest of the brothers, I make my way to the stairs, pausing on the first step. "The man who…"

"He's here," Red calls out. "He'll be waitin' for you in the mornin'."

Good. I don't think I'm up to doling out any punishments tonight. Fuck me, but I'm tired.

"Don't worry, Lady's Man. He'll be alright. Dude's got a fuckin' hard head. I'd be more worried about the bat."

Starting to move up the stairs, I show my middle finger to Keys.

"Nah, something's wrong. He hasn't cracked a joke about tonight." Twister laughs at his own non-joke. "You fuckin' die, man, can I have your bike?"

"Come on, let's get some painkillers into you." Lady's Man mutters something about leaving me alone, then he rests his hand lightly on the back of my cut to get me moving. Even through the leather, the touch feels like it's burning.

Reaching my door, I pull my room key out of my cut. Lady's Man takes it from me, turning it in the lock. Then finally I step into what's been my home for the last seven years. It's nothing much, but usually I feel at peace here. Doesn't matter what time of day it is, comforting sounds of my brothers' voices waft in from outside, along with the grunt of Harley engines. Our businesses tend to be open day and night, so there's always something happening. Tonight, for some reason, it sounds unusually quiet.

As Lady's Man comes in behind me, what's normally my refuge feels oppressive. I half turn, attempting again to get him to leave. "I'll be okay on my own."

He shrugs. "You want to tell Prez, or want me to?"

I narrow my eyes at him, wanting only to be able to lick my wounds in private. Wanting to lie down and hopefully get the hammering in my head to tone down.

But I'm unable to hide that I'm swaying on my feet. "Here, sit down before you fuckin' fall down." When I do, he takes a bottle of water from out of his cut, and then the tablets Doc gave him. I take them without looking, I'm not allergic to anything, just hope they're strong enough to take the edge off.

He eyes me thoughtfully. "Let's get you comfortable. Can you lift your arms up?"

Yes, if I'm careful, I can. Giving in is less arduous than arguing. So I raise my hands, grimacing when he jostles me, even though he tries to be careful as he slides first my cut and then my tee off.

"Lie down," he instructs.

That I can do, and gratefully, almost sighing with relief as my cheek meets the pillow, remembering at the last minute I can't lie my head back due to the fucking lump. My eyes close immediately, then snap open as I feel a fumbling at my belt.

"What the fuck do you think you're doing?" My hands protectively cover my groin.

"Making you comfortable. You don't sleep in your pants, do you?"

"I can take them off."

"What's wrong with you, Brother? You think in the state you're in, I'm going to take advantage? I'm a man, you're a man. I assure you, you haven't got anything I haven't."

I can't tell him I'm worried that his hands on me might cause a repeat of last night's reaction. But neither can I behave like a virgin bitch trying to protect my virtue. So I sigh, and give in. Hoping the pain will be enough to suppress any unwanted movement from my cock.

It's a strange sensation having a man undress me, but Lady's Man's actions are mechanical, and, thankfully, concentrating on the dual throbbing in my chest and head keeps my dick from misbehaving. Having removed my boots and socks, he undoes my button and zipper, and pulls down my pants. *Thank goodness I didn't go commando today.*

I do feel better. Less constricted. Lady's Man pulls the sheet over me, and I inwardly sigh. It felt wrong being all but naked in front of him.

"You can sleep now, Joker. I'll be right here. I'll have to wake you shortly, but I'm going nowhere." Lady's Man's voice sounds surprisingly gentle. "I'll be here."

CHAPTER 5

*W*e're seated around in a circle. The man I hate most in the world is shouting into the face of the kid sitting next to me. My hands curl into fists at my side knowing it will be my turn next. They never stop, never give us a moment. On and on and on. I've been here a month already. I'm getting to the point where I'm not sure how much longer I can last.

In the mornings, we have intense sessions where we're berated for our supposedly unnatural yearnings. In the afternoons, well, anything goes. I've had electric shocks to my genitals, beatings, been given drugs which make me sick when I'm faced with pictures of a naked man. Perhaps the worst is where they lay their hands on me, praying to God to make me repent my evil ways. Even I know their roaming digits are coming pretty close to themselves being abusive.

At first I tried to change. Tried to become the boy my parents and society wanted me to be. The picture tantalisingly dangled in front of me, of the future with a wife and children, rather than being a social pariah. I tried, God knows, or would know if I still had faith he exists, how hard I tried to change. The shame of my condition daily ground into me, the threats from my parents that they didn't want me home until I had rid myself of these evil thoughts, didn't even want to see me until I was normal, had made me acknowledge I was mentally ill and needed healing. Needed the devil driven out of me.

However much I concentrated, however I struggled to change, I couldn't bring myself to think or feel differently. The most I

"

could promise God and myself was I wouldn't ever act on my unnatural impulses. After the shock treatments, that probably wouldn't be difficult. I'd be surprised if I ever had the inclination to even masturbate again. A sexless, valueless person, that's what I've become.

That last session proved one too many for Grant. Later that evening, Grant killed himself. He was sixteen, only a couple of months younger than me, and was sleeping in the same bunkhouse. I was one of the first to find him. It didn't seem real, even as I stood watching his lifeless body gently swinging, unable to comprehend that my friend had gone. Then, when I understood it was only his body he'd left behind, my emotion became one of envy. Not only was I left to survive this camp, but a lifetime of shame and self-hatred. I could see how he took the easy way out. He wouldn't need to struggle any more. Each day a challenge to appear normal.

I've got a mental illness, but it's not one that this camp is going to cure. It's a curse I'll have to live with for life. But if I don't get out of here soon, I'll end up like Grant.

As the breeze moves the flesh and blood shell which used to house a person, there and then I make the decision that I'll do what I have to do in order to convince them to let me leave. Hallelujah, I'm cured. Then I'll go back home and survive. Until it all gets too much. Transfixed I watch Grant gently swaying. Yeah, eventually I can see myself taking the same way out. A coward's escape? Or the brave thing, ridding society of one more demon they don't want to contend with.

There's no place in the world or heaven, according to the folks here, for people like me.

"Josh. Tell us why you chose to be gay."

The next day. Another group session. It's a question that's been asked a hundred times before, in a hundred different ways. Now I don't bother to try to think back, to analyse when I made such a conscious decision. Did I wake up one day and decide I was going to torture myself for the rest of my life? Of course I didn't.

I lift up my head. "I didn't make a choice."

"Josh, Josh. You know you weren't born to live this perverted way. You, like any innocent child, were born in God's image. And he certainly isn't gay."

I bite back the question, how does he know? Anything seen as being cocky is punished fast. It shows individual thought, and after the weeks I've been here, there's not much of me left. Very little remains of my identity.

"Come on, Josh. When did you start having these perverted feelings toward other boys?"

I shrug. I've always known deep down inside. There wasn't a particular moment when I woke up and thought, I'm going to be gay. Rather a gradual realisation that that's how I've always been.

The camp leader, the worst of them all, is getting frustrated. "Was it when someone abused you?"

I shrug again. I've tried saying I wasn't abused, but they have to look for a reason. Otherwise I've just been born evil and they won't have that. Nurture, not nature, is all they blame.

"Who was it, Josh? A babysitter? Family friend? Relative? Who touched you when they shouldn't?" A pause which I don't fill. "Your father? Was it your father who abused you?"

I think of everything my father had done. His own methods to make a man of me. The broken bones I'd had from being thrown in that ring time and time again until I was forced to learn how to defend myself. Yeah, that could be classified as abusive behaviour. I give a small nod.

The counsellor throws up his hands. "Thank you, Jesus. At last. Now we have something to work on. Everyone! Josh can change. We know what made him this way. Say, I was abused, Josh. Admit it, and God will cure you."

I don't speak. He prods me. "Say it."

"I was abused," I mumble.

"Louder."

"I was abused." I increase the volume slightly.

"Louder, Josh. Louder."

"I was abused!" Tears start running down my face as I link my lie to the treatment I've been receiving here. "I was abused," I shout. Then, louder. "I WAS ABUSED! I WAS ABUSED. I WAS ABUSED." I repeat it until my voice cracks.

"Jesus has made Josh see the light. Let's all pray for Josh. Pray that he is cured."

"Joker. *Joker*. Wake up!" Someone's shaking my shoulder as well as yelling into my ear.

Slowly I open my eyes to find concerned darkened ones staring back. "What the…" I start to move but stop as a pain stabs me in the chest.

"Keep still. You were having a nightmare. Fuck, it must have been a bad one." Lady's Man steps back, sweeping his hair away from his face. "Christ, sounds like having a broken rib again must have dredged up stuff from your past."

Fuck. What have I been saying?

For a moment, I think he's returning to his chair, but all he's doing is getting something out of his cut, then he comes back. His hand reaches out, I flinch back. "Hey, I'm just going to look into your eyes, okay?"

It's then I see a small Maglite in his hand, and the events of the day before come flooding back. *He's checking for signs of a concussion.*

He'd have made a good medic. "How are you feelin'? Do you feel sick? Let me look, yeah, your eyes seem okay. Do you want more painkillers?" His business-like approach helps me to relax. *Maybe I haven't given anything away.*

"I'm fine," I tell him. "I *will* be fine. You can go to your room now."

"Nice try." The corners of his mouth turn up. "But I'm stayin' right here. You're not out of the woods yet. I'll put the light off and you can go back to sleep."

Sleep? That's the last thing I want. Not when the remnants of the dream are still hanging over me, the place I never want to revisit. The worst time of my life. "Leave the light on."

He looks at me closely. "Must have been one fuck of a bad dream. You got quite agitated there. Want to talk about it? They say talkin' it out helps lessen its hold."

I doubt there's anything that will do that. My nightmare has freshened my memory, taking me back to the time I want to forget. Those weeks when I was mentally and physically tortured. The time that's retained its stranglehold over the rest of my life, and will be with me until I die, the experience impossible to shake off.

Hooking his foot around the chair, he yanks it closer to the bed. "You can tell me to mind my own business, but how did you come to break most of your ribs?" He shakes his head side to side, "Fuck, man. Nah, you don't need to tell me. I've put it together myself. Your father abused you. That's what you were shoutin'." His hand waves toward my chest. "No wonder it's all come back to you with another broken rib. The pain's a fuckin' reminder."

My first response is anger that he's been party to my most private stuff, but the rage quickly recedes as my head can't cope with raised emotion right now. I sigh, bitterly, regretting that the pain, or the tablets, or a combination of both, have resulted in him having a hold over me. My glare doesn't work; he's clearly not leaving. His intense stare and tilted head shows he wants to listen.

Oh fuck it, I've apparently already given some of it away. He could be right. Talking might be better than sleeping. Don't want to slip back into that dream again. I might as well tell him the rest. Well, perhaps not everything, but what I can. "My father didn't abuse me," I disavow him of that. "Or not the way you were thinking."

"Then, how?" Again, his hand waves at my chest, and his eyebrow rises.

I inhale as deeply as I can, and filter my past. My ribs. I can tell him about that. "When I was fourteen I was a wimp. Dad wanted to make me a man. Took me to the gym to learn how to fight. Martial arts, boxing, wrestling, you name it."

His eyes grow wide. "You got your broken ribs at a fuckin' gym? Where the fuck was your trainer?"

I give a self-deprecating grin. "My dad *was* my trainer. He had particular methods. You see, I wasn't very good."

"You've improved." He touches the bruises on his face and mirrors my quick grin.

"I had to," I resume. "He'd just throw me in with a boy itching for a fight. Usually one that knew what he was doing, and loved nothing more than to show off his skills on the scrawny kid." Glancing at him I notice he's looking incredulous. "I broke my ribs, broke my nose. Lost a few teeth. Once my wounds had healed, he'd take me back, and it would start all over again and more bones would get broken. I was as pretty as you before, my bent nose gives me character, he said."

Lady's Man laughs. "Thanks for the compliment, I think. But fuck, Joker. *Fourteen?* You were a fuckin' kid."

He doesn't know the half of it. That time in the camp was far, far worse, even though no visible scars had been left.

"I survived," I tell him. "I learned to fight and muscled up. Enlisted in the marines on my seventeenth birthday with my father's blessing."

"You still in touch with the fucker?"

That's an easy question to answer. "No. They came to my passing out parade, all dressed up, proud and gloating about having a second son in the service. I returned when I was on leave over the next couple of years." Then the pretending would start all over again. Eventually it had become too hard, too difficult to avert their suspicions I hadn't really changed. "After that, I never saw them again. It was all a front. They didn't give a damn about me or what I wanted, just that I was living a life they could boast of."

"Second son? Was your brother treated the same way?"

Gently, I move my head side to side. "He's nine years older than me, and there was no need to. He was the son they wanted. He'd enlisted when I was eight, we rarely saw him again. I haven't seen him at all for eleven years. Had no contact with him since I left home for the last time."

"I'm sorry you went through that." Lady's Man stands and paces. "Makes me guilty I had it so different. I didn't have a dad, but Mom was alright. More than alright, really."

Another shrug. "Yeah, well…" I shut my mouth to stop the words *you're normal* slipping out.

His back is turned toward me, so I allow myself the luxury of feasting on the way his waist tapers to the jeans which hug his slim hips before showcasing his long shapely legs. Raising my eyes, I notice his tee stretched tight across his back. As I'm studying his body, I don't miss the way his shoulders stiffen, and look away quickly as he starts to turn around.

"Your father preferred you to get hurt rather than accept you were gay?"

What the… "What the *fuck?*" Holding my arm over my body, I pull myself up into a sitting position. I breathe in as much air as I can, and retort as dismissively as possible, "I'm not…"

He's by my side in a flash, fury sparking from his eyes. "Don't you dare," he hisses. "Don't you dare fuckin' try to deny it."

Equally angry I spit back, "I don't know what happened the other night, but I certainly didn't get a hard on 'cause you were sitting on me."

His anger fades as quickly as it had arrived. "You went straight there, didn't you?" He chuckles. "Joker, the reason you've stayed clear of me is obvious. And don't think I didn't catch you checking me out just now. Nope. Don't say a fuckin' thing. I saw you in the mirror."

He knows. I can still deny it. *He wouldn't believe me.* Would anyone, once he's told them all? *Can I ask him to keep it quiet? Pay him?* I start mentally running through my bank account, calculating how much I could afford to offer him.

"I don't know what the fuck's going on inside your head, but it isn't good, that's for certain." His hands smooth down his face, pulling down his eyes. "Look, I hate your father for what he fuckin' did. And messin' with your body was probably the least of it. He fucked up your mind as well, didn't he?" His eyes find mine, and he shakes his head. "The reason I'm so gutted for you is because my mom took it completely differently."

Wait. What? Is he saying what I think he is? *He could be laying a trap. Careful, now, Josh.* I need to be very sure. "Your mom took what differently?" I get out in a clipped tone, almost holding my breath for the answer.

Coming closer, Lady's Man perches on the edge of the bed. "I had no father. He was killed on a tour when I was three. I don't remember him at all. Mom brought me up by herself. I always knew I was different, I got on well with my mom, even from an early age our relationship wasn't the same as other boys my age. Christ, I used to advise her what clothes went with what. I think she had her suspicions, but I finally came out to her when I was twelve. Her reaction was acceptance. Her only worry was on my behalf, knowing life wouldn't be easy. She made no attempt to change me, just gave me the space to grow into the man I was to become."

"You're not gay," I tell him, sensing a trap. "I've seen you with the hangarounds."

He raises his chin. "I suppose the best word to describe me is bi. It's men that I like, but a woman can sometimes be a nice change to my hand. And, of course, it keeps the pretence up." He half turns so he's facing me. "I've watched you, I've taken my cues from you, Joker. I want to be accepted here, so I'm not going to rock the boat. If you think comin' out will mean havin' to leave the club, I'm not gonna risk it. I've worked too hard to get my patch."

I inhale. This is too much. To find the man that's got the interest of my cock is gay too? It's beyond my wildest imaginings. Still suspecting he's playing me for a fool, I start to pry. "So you stick to women here?"

"Have done, yeah. But you won't see me with them much. Just when the itch gets too bad. Sometimes I go into Vegas."

Me too. The brothers think I have a woman there, but instead I'll be finding a male prostitute for the night. I always return feeling dirty and ashamed, and I admit, not far from being suicidal resulting in me going on a bender for a couple of days. For years after the traumatic and unsuccessful treatment, I'd had no sexual desires at all. But gradually they returned, and when it gets too much, well, I know exactly what scratching that itch means.

"Have you ever been in a relationship?" Now he's opened up, I want to know more. He's so easy in his skin. So different from me. How does he cope? *How does he live with himself?*

"Nah. Never trusted anyone enough. Never liked someone that much. Sure, there was someone I saw regular for a while before I started prospectin', but it was more of a convenience, you know?"

I think I do.

"What about you?"

He's being honest with me. Can I, with him? I purse my lips, his head tilts to one side, and I find myself saying, "I thought if I ignored it, I could live without sex."

"But you couldn't." He's turned away, now looking into the distance, and not at me at all. "Seems we've got a lot in common when it comes down to it. I'll tell you this, Brother. I noticed you soon after I started prospecting. Wanted to get close to you. Become friendly. But you didn't give me the time of day. I had my suspicions why. Hopes really."

Hopes? A bubble of excitement churns within me that the man I find so attractive, so sexually appealing, wants me too. Then it bursts almost as quickly as it arose. *Nothing can come of it.* If anything, we've got to keep even further apart.

Lady, well, mentally I've dropped the rest of his handle, now knowing it doesn't suit him at all, Lady's watching the various expressions crossing over my face. While I'm thinking of how we can reasonably keep our distance from each other, it seems he's thinking on very different lines. "Fuck it, Joker. You're attracted to me. I'm attracted to you. So, what about it? You and me? Want to give it a try?"

It's impossible. "No," I reply, adamantly shaking my head. "You said it yourself. Red or the brothers get wind of it and who knows what they'll do? Never heard of gays in the club, not in any chapter. They'll never accept it."

Lady looks at me strangely. "They might. On the whole they're a good crew."

"No," I repeat. Memories of that godawful camp come back to me. The shame and disgust I've never rid myself of. The abhorrence of my parents, the knowledge there's no place for people like us in society. Although my broken rib protests, I pull myself into a sitting position, staring at him intently. When my silent appeal doesn't work, in desperation I plead, "Promise me, Lady. No one must ever find out our dirty secret."

Another strange look. Then a strangled laugh. "Dirty secret? That's what you think this is?"

Chapter 6

irty secret?" Lady repeats, rolling his eyes. "It's no one's business but ours what our sexuality is. We can't help it; it isn't a choice. I'm with you that some of the brothers might have been brainwashed and would look at it differently. We are in an all-male club. Might worry we're going to try to turn them or such shit. But most of them would accept it."

"You can come out if you want to. I'm certainly not. I've lost one family, don't want to lose this one as well."

His brow creases. "Is that why you make jokes all the time? To deflect?"

I've never really thought about it. "Could be." Yeah, maybe making people laugh, showing a shallow side of me stops them looking at me too closely.

Suddenly he's flopped down beside me on the bed. Not touching, but I can feel heat emanating off him, can smell his perspiration mixed with deodorant, and an underlying musk of a man. I've never had a man so close to me before, well, not other than for the few moments of a paid sexual encounter. My cock twitches, telling me it likes the idea. But even if my rib wasn't paining me and my head still throbbing, I'd not take him up on it, if invitation is indeed what he's offering. We can't afford to get close, fuck it, definitely not as we're both in the same club. Any attraction might be just that, because we're the only two queers for miles. I didn't even like him before today. *But that was because I didn't trust myself around him.*

"Your gaydar is broke, you know?"

"What?"

"I suspected you were, but you had no idea about me, did you?"

I hadn't. He doesn't need an answer, so I don't respond.

"Last night," he continues, "What you didn't notice, is when you got hard, I did too."

What? Had he? In all honesty, I hadn't stayed around long enough to find out.

His hand crosses the gap between us. He takes hold of mine and squeezes it. I expect him to let go, but he doesn't. His fingers tighten then he raises my hand to his lips and kisses it.

I freeze. No man has ever shown me affection before. The last person to kiss me *anywhere* had been my mother a very long time ago.

"You've not had it easy, have you?" His voice has softened. "I'm, what, five years younger than you? I'm far more comfortable with myself. But then, I had my mom's support. Without anyone in your corner, you've gotten used to keeping what you are hidden."

I don't pull my hand away. I should, but his simple tactile gesture has done more than any words could to make me lower my guard. It slips out before I can stop it. "That's what conversion therapy will do for you."

His grip tightens. He pulls himself up and leans over me. His dark eyes open wide, the amount of white showing suggests they're filled with horror. "Fuck, Joker. No. When? How old were you? Oh, fuck, Joker."

"Sixteen," I admit through gritted teeth.

"Was it as bad as they say?" his voice has quieted, any lightness gone.

"Worse," I admit. *Don't ask me to talk about it. Don't ask me to open that door. Once was enough tonight.*

Another squeeze of my fingers as he lies back down. "Fuck. That's what you were dreaming about."

"Yeah."

"Oh, babe. Babe. I don't know what to say. Shift over, I want to hold you."

I freeze, undecided. It would be madness to start something we might not be able to stop. Something that would mean creeping around behind our brothers' backs. I've worked my whole life to get people to believe that I'm straight. Is he worth risking all that I've achieved? I barely know him.

"Babe. You're hurt, nothing's going to happen tonight. Possibly never will. Be nice to have a friend at least, someone who understands. Getting together would mean lyin' to everyone else, and I don't want to go there unless we know there's something between us. Something important enough to take that risk. But fuck, you've been through so much. Shit, I don't want to even imagine. Let me just hold you."

A stronger man might have been able to resist; a stronger man might have told him to get lost. But the chance to be held in Lady's arms suddenly seems too good to pass up. Slowly, I start to move closer.

"Hang on, hold up a minute." He sits up. "Have a painkiller then perhaps you can go back to sleep."

Yeah. Like I want to risk dreaming again. But obediently I take the tablet, downing it with water. When he lies back he opens his arms invitingly. With one arm under my neck, carefully avoiding the bump, and the other draped over me, I snuggle into his side, now able to breathe in more of his scent. Which is wrong. I suspect I could become addicted to it.

Gently he kisses the top of my head. "Go to sleep, babe."

I should have been restless. I shouldn't have been able to relax being held in another man's arms. But again, doing what

I'm told, I close my eyes and know nothing more until a voice is telling me to wake up.

I struggle with the process, too warm and comfortable to move.

"Joker, Brother. Come on." There's mirth in the tone. "Wake up."

"Whatdya want?" I grumble.

"To check you out."

"Beyond a joke, Brother." Nevertheless, I open my eyes, allowing him to check that I'm not in the process of dying. Now that I'm awake I'm aware of an urgent requirement. "Need a piss."

I immediately miss the feel of the arms which drop away, allowing me to slowly slide out from under the sheet and pull myself to my feet. Then I am aware I'm only dressed in my boxers. I feel eyes burning into me as I carefully reach down to pick up my jeans.

"Don't mind me." He chuckles behind me as I feel my face flush red, as pulling my pants up I'm only too well aware my cock has decided to bounce into life. Shirtless, I quickly leave the room to visit the heads down the hall.

"You okay, Joker?" Hammer's coming in as I'm going out. He's just wearing underpants and is scratching his balls.

Ignoring what he's doing, and that he's just let out a loud fart, I respond. "Sore and fuckin' angry the fucker got the better of me."

He scowls. "You'll get payback in the mornin'."

"Too fuckin' right," I reply, zipping up before walking back to my room.

I hesitate before opening the door, suddenly embarrassed by the memory of finding it so natural to sleep in Lady's arms. *Should I tell him to leave?* Fuck, if I'm honest, I'm enjoying his company. *Enjoying his touches.* I'm still undecided when finally I open the door.

"Was about to come to check up on you." Lady's sitting on the bed, leaning against the headboard with his arms folded over his chest.

"Bumped into Hammer," I explain, knowing full well it was my indecision which delayed me.

"Hmm." He seems to be able to see right through me.

"Lady," I move to the bed, sitting down before continuing, keeping a distance between us. "I'm okay, I think you should go."

"That's still to be seen, and no, I'm not leavin'." Unfolding his arms, he sits forward and draws up his knees, clasping his hands around them. "No one's going to give a damn that I've been in here all night. It was Red's instruction."

It's not just that. The longer he stays, the more difficult it will be to part with him. I already know that. Whether it's him, or whether he's given me comfort for the first time since I was a kid, I'm undecided. There's one thing for certain though. "This, you being in here. It can't happen again."

Lady's eyes burn into me. "Why should we care what anyone else thinks? I don't give a damn who stays in whose room."

I sigh, "We've been through this. We could be expelled from the Devils."

"There are gay motorcycle clubs, you know."

His reminder takes me by surprise. Of course I know, but I've never given them a second thought. Now, for a moment, I do. *What would it be like to ride with like-minded brothers? With men who see no shame in being attracted to each other?* I hadn't considered there was another option.

But that would mean admitting to the world who and what I am. My dirty secret I've kept hidden from the day I left that damn camp. There's not a single doubt in my mind. "I can't come out."

Lady's brow creases. "Why the fuck not?"

Pointing to him, I sneer, "You don't exactly go around announcin' it yourself."

His shoulders rise and drop. "I wanted to be a Satan's Devil from the time I first heard about them. There was a man I served with who rode with the Colorado chapter. We got close," he gives a quick shake of his head, "not like that before you say anything. I'd always loved ridin', already had a Harley. When we were on duty together he'd pass the time tellin' me about what it was like. About the brotherhood. Got me hooked." He grins briefly, "Guess you could say he brainwashed me into thinkin' there wasn't a club that could come close."

"He know about you?"

A roll of his eyes. "Don't ask, don't tell, remember? Even after that shit was over, it wasn't easy to tell the truth. Nah, he didn't know. But the pictures he drew of the Satan's Devils gave me something to hang onto for when I got out." He inhales sharply. "Then, when a roadside bomb took him out, I kinda felt I owed it to him to join up."

That the two men had been close is obvious. "I'm sorry."

"Yeah, he didn't deserve that." Lady's quiet for a moment. "Thing is, I don't think my sexuality is anyone's business but my own. But I was brought up so differently from you. My mom never even suggested it was something to be ashamed of. She went out of her way to let me know she was proud of me, what-ever I do, whoever, *whatever* I am."

For a moment, I wonder what it would have been like to have had such support growing up. Then I realise it's impossible to even imagine it.

His eyes are on me again. "How long did you have to undergo conversion?"

Putting my elbows on my knees, I rest my chin on my hands. I've never spoken to anyone about it before, only relive it in my nightmares, try not to think about it during the daylight hours. After all these years, the effects linger on. I have a moment of indecision, then decide to answer. "Until I was cured."

A quick look in his direction shows one eyebrow has risen.

"Well, that's what I convinced them anyway. It was either that or kill myself."

He pales, then his cheeks glow red. "From what I've fuckin' heard, they don't turn people straight, but they make them sexless."

I bark a mirthless laugh. "Electric shocks to your groin will do that."

A sharp intake of breath, a quick disbelieving look at me. "I thought that was banned in the early nineties."

"It was," I agree, "but the Pray out the Gay camp used whatever methods they wanted, the ones they thought would work best."

He cocks his head, "So, what…?"

I know what he's asking. "They'd show us porn. Each time we got an erection, we'd get an electric shock."

"Christ! I'm surprised you can get it up at all." His hands are moving uselessly as if he doesn't know what to do with them.

I've started, so I'll carry on. "For many years, I couldn't. No mornin' wood, nothing. Didn't bother me. Actin' straight became a habit. Easy with no sexual inclination."

He sniggers. "It's workin' fine now, if the other night was any indication."

"Luckily, only with you," I say without thinking.

"Yeah?" His grin widens.

I resume gazing ahead at the wall. "Doesn't matter. I'm not going there, okay? This club means too much to me to jeopardise my membership."

"You could be doing the brothers a disservice."

"Don't want to put it to the test. It's too risky." That's my decision, nothing will change it.

His lips narrow. "So that's why you acted as though you disliked me? Because you had the hots for me?"

I swing around, too fast. My rib protests. I give it a moment to settle, then go to refute his suggestion. Instead, I decide to be honest. "Yeah."

He leans forward and bumps his fist against my arm. "You're not so bad yourself." Then he grows serious. "Look, I'll respect your decision. Won't be any improprieties between us. I won't do anything to make you uncomfortable, I respect you too much for that. But we can be friends, support each other. And fuck, Joker, if you need to unburden yourself, well, I'm your man."

For a second I wonder what it would be like if he really was my man. Then shove the thought out of my mind fast. We, *I*, can't afford to go there. There's too much to lose.

Chapter 7

The next time I wake, I'm alone. My first reaction is to reach my hand to where Lady had slept, feeling the chill on the sheets, but notice the pillow still has the indent where he had lain, proving the whole night hadn't been a dream.

I miss him. Miss his non-sexual touches, his comfort, his compassion and understanding. How he'd allowed me to unburden myself in such a way no one's ever sanctioned before. I permit myself a moment to remember, to relive how it felt to be held in his arms before reminding myself just what's at stake.

It must never happen again.

At least he had the sense to remove himself before I awoke. *Nothing amiss here, folks. Move along.*

I find the bottle of water and pain tablets next to the bed. His thoughtfulness makes my mouth curve, until the necessity of keeping him at arms-length from now on slams into me. Knowing our attraction is mutual, it's possible just a look could give us away. He might not feel it as deeply, but outing myself is something I can never see myself doing, for his sake as well as my own. He obviously didn't grow up exposed to the antipathy directed at gays. Didn't have to see the revulsion in his father's eyes. Hadn't seen how sickened people could be. Nah, he doesn't know what he'd be letting himself in for. He's been lucky enough not to know how people will react should the truth come out.

I grit my teeth, unable to stop the "oof" of pain that escapes as I go to sit up. My head's beating a rhythm, the ache in my ribs keeping time. *I've had worse than this.* Breathing shallowly, moving carefully, I need more time than usual to dress. After a visit to the heads, I use the support of the banister to walk downstairs.

"Joker. How you feelin', Brother?"

"Good, Rope." I refrain from supporting my ribs with my arm.

"You look like fuckin' death," Cuff informs me, walking up and putting his arm around Rope's shoulder. He playfully tries to place a kiss on Rope's cheek.

"Get off me, man." Rope slaps his hand. Everyone knows these two are straight. They just play together in one of the BDSM clubs in Vegas. It's no wonder they're close.

"Joke! Here, Brother." Crash is waving at me. "Got your man in the basement. He's strung up waiting for you. Thought you'd like to play." As I approach him, he's able to get a closer look. "Or just watch," he corrects.

Watching I can do. Swinging a fist is perhaps beyond me today. I follow him down the stairs.

Indian's hovering, Twister laying out pliers, a blow torch, a saw. *Jack hammer?* What the fuck is he going to do with that? I smirk at the man I last got a fleeting glimpse of behind me picking up a bat. His eyes are flicking between the various tools in absolute horror, and it looks like he's already wet himself. *Twister's mind fuck is obviously working.*

Red's eyes meet mine. "You feelin' better, Joke?" Then to no one in particular he calls out, "Someone get our brother a fuckin' chair."

"Sore, Prez." I thank Sarge, then park my ass in the seat, grateful to sit down.

"Lady's Man told us you survived the night." As Fox mentions his name, I see Lady on the other side of the room, raising his hand in salute. Somehow managing to convey that's all he had told them.

As Twister continues to get ready, other brothers start surrounding me, all with the same desire, to find out how I'm feeling. Never one to like being the centre of attention, I purse my lips, then start, "Knew a man once. Owned a submarine."

My words, as intended, stop the polite enquiries.

Fox's growl encourages me to continue.

"Got complaints it was too loud. So he fitted a muffler." I leave a space until I reach the finale. "After that he became known as the muff diver."

A collective groan. "That's bad, even for you, Joke."

Hammer nods at Sarge. "Well, he did get a blow to the head."

"Yeah, once he says something to make us laugh, we'll know he's alright," Shadow agrees.

"I'll try harder." I grin at them. This. This brotherhood. This is what I live for, and is exactly what I can't afford to lose.

"So, Joke." Prez steps closer. "You were the one hurt. What d'you want to get out of this?"

Another case in point. If I say I want him dead for coming at me from behind, they'll do it and bury the body without a second thought. Who could even think of jeopardising friendships like this? When Red raises his eyebrow, I know I must answer. "Let him live, Prez, but hurt enough it sends a message not to mess with us."

"Aw, shucks. You spoil all my fun, Joke. I had a great plan for taking him out." Twister grins over his shoulder.

"Let's get on with it. Got better things to do with my time. All yours, Twist." Red leans back against the wall behind him and crosses his arms. He looks bored.

"What's your name, punk?" Twister asks, approaching with a wooden baton.

"Chris. My name's Chris."

"Chris." Twister turns around again facing the rest of us, chuckling as though he's heard a good joke. Then he swings back around, using his momentum to strike the baton at Chris's legs. I hear the snap of a bone.

I hate watching this. One thing to deliver retribution when it's him or you, but not when your opponent is unable to fight back. Had too much of that in my past. I grit down on my teeth, hold back my vomit, and stoically watch as Twister breaks his other leg, then for good measure, both his arms.

Chris is alternatively crying with pain then begging for mercy. I wince as the baton hits his ribs, my arm protectively going around my own. At last it's over, and the prospects are called to take out the trash.

I catch Lady's eye in time to see his grimace.

"Okay for you, Joke?" Twister's in front of me now, carefully wiping blood off the baton for when he'll be using it again.

"Yeah. Good job, Twist."

He places his hand on my shoulder. "That's what brothers are for. To have your back."

It is. Another thing I can't give up. I resolve to treat Lady as I would any brother. No longer with animosity, but will pay him no special attention. Things said in the dead of the night to be forgotten, and never referred to again.

Taking his cue from me, Lady keeps his distance. Polite, respectful, but not over friendly. As the days pass, I begin to breathe easier as the fear of exposure recedes. If I ever steal a look and feel a pang of regret that things can't be different, I've only to remind myself of how much I have to lose to stamp down on that shit.

Experience has taught me how best to let a broken rib heal. Following my own self-imposed rules, the process goes smoothly. In a few weeks, I'm back to full fitness again. After making sure Lady's nowhere in sight to distract me, tonight I'm to be found at the pool table with Keys. I've long since won back my money, and usually find him easy to beat, but right now he's making me work for it.

Biting my tongue between my teeth, I eye up my next shot. It's perfect, that ball rolling into the hole just as I'd planned it. Then the next does likewise. When the final ball, urged by the gentle touch of my cue, drops into the pocket, Keys looks rueful. "Thought I had you there. Tricky shot, that last one."

It had been. "Nah, easy, Brother."

He swears under his breath as he hands over the money. As I take it, I spot Red leaning against the wall. How long he's been watching us, I've no idea. Taking a cue from the stand he starts to rub chalk on the end. "Want to play the master?"

I laugh as I'm meant to. "Sure thing, Prez. Your money's as good as anybody's."

We toss, he loses, I make the break, downing two balls as I do so, then miss the next by a hairsbreadth.

As he lines up the next, he says casually, "Nice to see you and Lady getting on better. Don't like brothers being at each other's throats." Yeah, it might not be just me that dropped half of his handle. Lady's Man proved a bit much. The man himself didn't seem perturbed.

I watch as Red pockets one ball after another. "Lady's not so bad once you get to know him."

"I like the brother myself. Got a good head on his shoulders."

Thank fuck he's missed one, and I'm back in the game. "Yeah, interesting man." *Yes!* Got the shot I was aiming for. And the next. Now just the last ball… *Damn it!*

"Bad luck." I've left the balls positioned perfectly for the prez. He pots the shot easily, turns and holds out his hand, his fingers waggling.

Opening my wallet, I take out the money I just won from Keys and pass it across to a grinning Red. *Easy come, easy go.* Red pockets the notes, then nods. "Don't like bad feelin's among brothers. Pleased you've sorted it out." Seeming to lose interest in both the discussion and me, Red swivels, looking for another victim.

Spying Lady's back and leaning against the bar, I go to join him. *Just catching up with a brother. No harm in that.* "How's your day been?"

"Good, yours?"

"Would have been better if I'd beaten Red," I say, ruefully.

"Not often anyone does," he replies, chuckling. Tilting his head to one side, he asks, "Want to go for a ride tomorrow?"

I throw him a look. "No."

He sighs. "Brothers ride out together all the time. Ain't gonna be no one raising their eyes."

For once, he's got it wrong. My lips curl as I remind him, "Got that ride out. Aren't you coming?"

He bangs the heel of his hand against his forehead. "Clean forgot. Yeah, of course I'll be there. Want any help?"

A club ride is something I could never not remember. I'm the Road Captain. It's my job to plan the route, make sure we get any permissions we need from other clubs, or, if the circumstances warrant it, from the police or counties we'll be travelling through. I ride at the back of the pack making sure there's no stragglers. Not that there often are unless someone's got a problem with their bike, we're too well practised at riding in formation. The help Lady's offering is stopping traffic at junctions if necessary, but there's only about ten of us on the ride tomorrow, so that won't be a problem.

"Doubt it, but you'll be close by in case. Appreciate the offer." As a newly patched member Lady will be riding only just in front of me.

Rosa, the old lady of our president who died last year, finishes her conversation with Titch and walks behind the bar. "Beers?" She's always lived for the club. After Prez got taken by cancer, she stayed on to be a mother hen to 'her boys'. We're all glad to have her.

When Lady and I both nod, she puts two bottles in front of us. I turn around, amused to watch Red winning more money off Cobra, and, only half paying attention, reach behind to pick up my drink. I misjudge it. My hand touches Lady's who's going for his at the same time. His fingers stroke a brief caress across mine, and the skin where he's touched tingles.

Looking back in time to see him wink, I pick up my bottle and take it to the other side of the room. Kicking out a chair I seat myself at the table next to Hammer and Fox. "What's up, Brothers?" Soon I'm deep in conversation about bikes. Shortly we're joined by the sergeant-at-arms, who sneers when we start expounding the virtues of Harleys.

"Nah, an Indian has them beat every time."

His observation heats the conversation.

Inputting a few contributions, including a couple of put downs for Indian, I watch Lady out of the corner of my eye. When Pixie puts her arms around him, I feel like I've been punched in the gut.

"What? Oh sorry, yeah. Got my belt drive swapped for a chain a while back. Makes a fuck load of difference." I try to concentrate on the discussion, while a myriad of thoughts go around my head. *Is he going to go off with her? Fuck her? Let her touch him, let her suck his cock? Touch her?* Each question I'm unable to answer leaves me feeling worse. My hands grow sweaty.

"You alright, Joke?"

"Yeah, I'm fine," I snap, annoyed that I'm letting what Lady's doing get to me. There can't be anything between us, so why should I worry what the fuck he's doing? I force myself to look away from the man who's tying me up in knots. Before long I realise I'm not taking in a word that my brothers are saying.

Giving an exaggerated yawn, I stand. "See you tomorrow bright and early, assholes. I'm going to get some shut eye."

In my room I slam the door shut, and take a deep breath, only then allowing myself the luxury of wondering what it would be like to act on my attraction toward Lady. Then for a second I allow myself to actually consider it. But the shame washes over me again. *You're not normal. You're an aberration.* The thought of my brothers, hell, everyone looking at me with disgust and repulsion is overwhelming.

I'm a thirty-year-old man, enough years behind me that I can think for myself. Theoretically I know it's the conditioning I went through that's warped my mind worse than my sexuality. Other men come out with no problem. Although I only have to open a newspaper to see the difficulties they face. Sure, men and women can marry the same sex nowadays, but they still face the stigma of not only being different, but unnatural.

I've pretended for far too long to be something I'm not, to change now. Even knowing happiness could be within my reach, mentally I'm just not strong enough to acknowledge my true desires, even to myself. Except for those moments of weakness which drive me into town. It would have been easier had my libido stayed dead.

A knock on my door has me realising I'm still standing in the middle of my room, lost in my thoughts. I take a deep breath in an effort to cleanse my mind, then automatically I take the two steps necessary before I have my hand on the door knob and am opening it.

Lady pushes his way in, his eyes flaring. He places one hand on my chest, using the other to shut the door behind him. "I didn't go with the slut." His voice is monotone, as though he's fighting with some emotion. Anger? Arousal? I'm not sure which.

But his intention becomes clear when he wraps his hand around my neck and pulls me toward him. He barely gives me a moment before slamming his mouth onto mine, as if unable to hold back any longer.

I've never felt another man's lips on me. Anyone's, for that matter. Stunned, shocked, my initial reaction is to pull away, all my senses screaming *this is wrong*. But Lady is strong, as I try to jerk back he holds me pinned against him. He softens the contact, his mouth moving over mine so gently and temptingly as if sensing my inner turmoil.

I like it. Our faces so close I'm breathing in the air he's exhaling. *It's not right.* But oh my God, *it's good.* I become less rigid, though one part of me is hardening, my body reacting even though my brain wants to switch off. When his tongue licks where my lips are tightly pressed together, I automatically open my mouth, a silent permission for his invasion, not knowing what to expect, or what is to come.

Our tongues touch. He angles my head, nips at my bottom lip with his teeth, then, when I open wider, thoroughly explores my mouth. Then he retreats. Beginning to feel drunk on his taste, I follow his lead, now it's me pressing forward asking for more. Again our tongues meet and dance. He tastes of beer, his flavour like nectar for a starving man.

My arms rise. Hesitantly I place one around the back of his head, pulling him closer to me. Instinctively knowing I can't get enough of him, can't get near enough. Our groins touch, two hard cocks meeting, starting to grind together. I prevent the moan coming out of my mouth. Christ, I'm on a hair trigger. He's aroused me so fast, so much. Sensations I've never experienced let alone enjoyed before.

Using all my strength I push him away, the back of my hand wiping over my mouth, my eyes wide and staring, my cheeks flaming. *What have I done? What have I allowed him to do?*

Lady steps forward, I take a step back, incapable of forming words, I simply shake my head.

"It's alright, Joker." His eyes soften. "It's alright," he murmurs as though comforting a child.

At last I find my voice. "It's not alright, Lady. It can never be right."

"You like me, I like you. Fuck, it's a lot more than that. How could you think I would go off with the whore when my mind, hell, my body, is fixated on you?" His brow creases.

I swallow before finding the strength to answer with the right words. "You should have gone off with her. I've got nothing to offer you. You've proved your point, Lady. My body responds to yours, but fuck it, that's not where I want to go. Ever, you got me? Never come into my room again." I drop my chin, then raise it so I can look straight in his eyes. "What if someone saw you?"

"What if they did?" he challenges. "Brothers go into each other's rooms all the time. No one thinks anything of it."

Turning around, I walk to the other side of the room, resting my elbows against the wall and dropping my head into my hands. *If I was braver… If I hadn't lived my fucking past…* Lady roused such feelings inside me I'd never felt before. When I'd had my dick sucked or stroked by a male prostitute I'd felt dirty, disgusted with myself. Not with Lady though. With Lady, my reaction felt natural, as if I wanted to explore more. To know what it was like to have a lover in my bed. *To take things further.* I'm not even sure how I'd had the strength to pull away, but if I hadn't, I'd probably have done something I'd regret.

I want to tell him to go before I weaken and change my mind. But that's not enough. Somehow I have to make it clear that there can never be anything between us, however much we both want there to be. Not here, not in this club.

I hear feet moving, feel him at my back. "Joker…"

"Lady," I interrupt. "I don't know what you want from me. A fling, a relationship. Fuck, who could predict where it could take us?"

"Joker, I like you. A lot…"

"I like you too, Lady. Too fuckin' much. Always did. Even when I was denyin' it to myself. But we can only be friends, nothing more. No benefits to be had." I swing around to face him. "What if we start something, and find out it works? Won't take long before we give each other away. Then where would we be?"

"Who the fuck knows or cares?"

"*I care.*" In my mind, I see the disgust on the faces of my parents. The people at the church, and as for the camp, the words they used to describe my perversion echo in my head. I can't go through that again. If that makes me weak, so be it.

I haven't said anything more, but he must read something of my thoughts on my face. Raising his hand, he places it gently on my cheek. "I'm not going to pursue something you don't want, Joker. What you're not ready for yet. It will be fuckin' hard stayin' away from you, but if that's what you need, I'll give you space." He stares into my eyes until I can no longer meet the gaze of those all-seeing dark beautiful eyes. Then he's gone, leaving me feeling I've lost something essential. I watch his back as he walks to the door. He turns before opening it, giving a sharp nod. "When you're ready, I'll be waitin'."

CHAPTER 8

So there's this man. Sees a pretty girl in the bar and offers to buy her a drink. She accepts, but tells him he won't get anything in return." I break off, looking around to check faces are tilted toward me. "Yeah, he thinks to himself, she might say that now, but give it time. So he tells her that's okay, and offers to buy her another. Again, she tells him he won't be receiving any payment. She's beautiful, gorgeous, tits out to here," I indicate what I mean with my hands as my brothers listen rapt. "He tries again. More drinks bought, more consumed. Eventually he thinks he's plied her with enough alcohol so he invites her to his apartment. But still she turns him down, telling him there's no point." Another glance around, yup, they're leaning toward me. I lay it on. "Did I mention how fuckin' beautiful she is? Ten doesn't do it, she's an eleven, maybe a twelve," I pause. Like puppets, they're all nodding. "He's thinking he can't let this one go, his dick is throbbing like hell, so he thinks, what the heck? I'll go the whole fuckin' nine yards. 'Darlin', he says taking one of her hands in his. 'You're the most beautiful woman I've ever seen in my life. Come home with me, please.' When she goes to shake her head, he reaches up his hand, caresses her cheek and goes for broke. 'Come with me please, I want you for my wife.' Her eyes widen. Grabbing her purse, she immediately jumps down off the stool, turns her captivating blue eyes on him, gushing breathlessly, 'Why the fuck didn't you just say that in the first place? I'd love to fuck your wife.'"

Cobra guffaws, Sarge slaps me on the back. While I'd been speaking, practically the whole club had gathered around.

"Got any more, Joker?"

Titch is nodding enthusiastically, so I think fast. "What do bitches and fuckin' search engines have in common?" I allow a brief pause before providing the punch line. "Neither will let you finish a sentence before interrupting."

"True that," Keys is nodding. "Fuckin' true. Hey, what does the baby computer call its father?" He pauses, waiting expectantly. When no one answers, he finishes triumphantly with, "Obsolete." Our go-to computer guy isn't upset, just shakes his head when conversations restart without even a chuckle. He walks away mumbling, "Fuckin' wasted on you lot of assholes anyway."

I'm not surprised to see Lady standing at the bar, watching me with hawkish eyes. He pretends to be absorbed in picking the label off his bottle when he sees he's been caught. It's only fair turnaround, I spend time observing him too. It's been two weeks since that life changing kiss. I've been unable to forget the feel of his mouth on mine, and admit I want more. But even when my resolve falters, I force myself to remember how wrong it was, how we can never repeat it. I can't give in, can't be tempted again. It would be far too dangerous. One more taste of him, and I doubt this time I could walk away.

"Hey, stop ogling Lady's ass, you fuckin' perve." Rope's amused words hit me like a bucket of cold water. I glance at him quickly, his mouth is curved up showing it was a joke, but fuck, it was a warning. I've got to be careful. It's as much what I do unconsciously that will give me away as any overt activity.

"You've got some fuckin' nerve callin' me a perve," I shoot back, thinking fast. Cuff and Rope are so named because of their proclivities which they don't try to hide. They're both straight, but they don't give a damn we all know what they get up to. If you want advice about restraints or floggers they're your go to men. As he laughs and walks off, I wonder if he'd actually be sympathetic. He must come across all sorts in the types of places he goes to.

At the next church Red has something different for us. "Tucson chapter need our help again."

Sarge groans. "Fuckin' assholes. Never can handle their own shit."

Tucson's got problems. Week or so back, they lost their prospect. Killed by a club called the Rock Demons. Most of the Vegas chapter attended the funeral, I stayed behind, my broken ribs not up to such a long journey as yet. Red made a pledge to help them should they need it.

Prez glares and growls, "This time *their* shit is heading in our direction. You could say we were given a heads up."

Sarge and Hammer tilt their heads, while Twister nods. "We're listening."

"Got Rock Demons coming our way. Drug running. Need a crew to go out to handle them." When all hands go up, Red points around the table. "I'll be going along with Indian, Twister, Sarge, Hammer and Cobra."

Not me. Like the others not picked, I shrug. That's the way it goes. Mustn't read anything into it.

With a chin lift at Sarge, Red adds, "Tucson have called for a few more bodies to help them with the remaining Demons. Crash has agreed to go."

"I'll take Cuff and Rope with me." The VP twists his head so his gaze falls on the two men in question. Both nod. It's agreed. "We leave in a couple of days." Again two heads dip then rise.

The first part goes smoothly. As I would have expected, our boys get the drop on the Rock Demons easily, taking them out before they get anywhere close to the city. We all cheer when the team walk back into the club without a scratch on them.

Now we're just waiting for news from Crash. It never sits well with any of us, having men in a fight without the rest of us close to have their back. But again everything goes without a hitch, down to the good organisation and planning. After assisting in blowing up the Demons' clubhouse in Phoenix, the VP updates Prez, who informs us. All safe and well, now on their way back home again, having decided to make the journey straight from Phoenix.

It's while we're waiting to give them a warm welcome that the clubroom suddenly goes quiet. AC/DC's 'Can't Stand Still' cuts out mid song. A rumble of protest has me standing, and in case of a threat my hand's already on my gun. But a shout from behind has me turning.

"Brothers!" My eyes, and all others, go to the prez who's standing outside his office, his hand smoothing over his red beard. He's shaking his head, an immediate sign that what he's got to tell us won't be good news. "Fuck, I'm sorry to have to tell you this. Got word from Drummer. Brother called Adam from the Tucson chapter has been killed."

"Thought Crash said they took out the Rock Demons with no casualties?" Titch shouts out.

Red's face glows. "They did that alright. Found everything had gone to shit when they got back to their clubhouse. It was the fucker who was after their VP's lady. No other fatalities, just Adam."

A few cries ring out of, "He was a good fucker," or "Fuckin' shame."

"We going to the funeral?" Twister asks loudly.

"Too fuckin' right," Red replies. He catches my eye. "Joker, can you get the shit organised? It's next week. We'll all be going to show our support."

I nod, following it up with a verbal confirmation. "Sure thing, Prez." Half of me is devastated that we've lost a brother, might not be from our chapter, but a Devil all the same. The other half is already thinking of everything I need to do, starting with making sure all the bikes are checked out. It's a seven-hour ride with a good wind behind us, eight or more if not. Don't want any breakdowns to slow us down.

"We going down to fight?" Indian wants to know what we're facing.

"Not this time," Red answers our sergeant-at-arms. "They've got it handled. This is just about showin' our respects."

With that, Red's finished his announcement. As he goes off with Indian, both shaking their heads, Lady comes over. He pulls out the chair beside me. "You know this Adam?"

"Yeah, met him a few times. Good solid fucker. Man you'd want on your side."

"He was that." Fox, overhearing, comes over to join us. "Tucson crew havin' it bad down there right now."

"Just what I was thinkin'." I raise my chin at him. "Two members down in just a few weeks." The prospect who died had been patched in posthumously.

"Adam." Lady scratches his head. "Didn't he get a road-name?"

Sarge sits down, chuckling. "That *was* his handle." He grins at Lady. "Had a big fuckin' Adam's apple. First thing you noticed about him."

"He liked to play on the gaming machines. Mostly I remember seeing his back." I recall what I knew of him.

Sarge laughs. "And the swearin' when he didn't win."

"Remember that time," Shadow kicks out a chair, "when we met up for a ride out? Fucker swerved to avoid a rattler. Darn near laid his bike down right on it."

Slowly more brothers gather around. Crash, Rope and Cuff return, grab drinks then come over to join us. The stories get longer; the reminiscences get fonder. Whatever chapter we're in, we're all Satan's Devils. We will mourn the loss of one of our own and ensure while he might be gone, our brother will forever be remembered in the tales that will be told about him.

Lady, who may have met Adam at the prospect's funeral but clearly can't place him, just listens on. At one point my eyes find his, mine narrow slightly as I send a silent message. *This is what I can't afford to give up.* In response, he closes his briefly.

While I let the conversation wash over me, a chilling thought hits. What if one day we're sitting around talking about Lady? What if he gets shot, or fuck, just comes off his bike? What if he's injured or killed? I know one thing. My life would have a damn huge hole in it.

When the evening winds to a close, brothers making sure the sweet butts, Pixie, Jinx and Angel are being well used, I take myself off to my room. Hearing footsteps behind me, I pause before opening my door. Looking back, I see it's Lady.

"You're not comin' in," I say brusquely, allowing for no misinterpretation.

"Joker, I just…" His eyes flick up down, then left and right as he shakes his head. "Fuck it, Joker… If anything happened to you…"

He's been thinking along the same lines as me. I try to be cruel. "You knew what this life was like when you signed up. We play hard, we die hard." Sometimes on my part I still think, the sooner the better. Even more lately.

His eyes flare. "Don't you give a damn?"

His words bring back the thoughts I was having downstairs. "Of course I'd care. Don't want anything to happen to you, or any brother. But shit happens."

"Yeah, shit fuckin' happens. And you'll, what? Sit sharing stories? Pretending you couldn't care less? That you don't give a fuckin' damn? Or, when you're standin' next to my coffin, are you going to finally admit your feelin's? 'Cause that would be a fuckin' waste, *Brother*, to come out after I'm gone."

I move fast, slamming him against the wall, thumping my fist into the brickwork beside his head. "I give a damn about everyone in this club. Of course I'd be sad if anything happened to you. Same as anyone."

"Sad? Fuckin' sad?" Lady's voice rises. "You'll be fuckin' sad? You're a fuckin' liar, Joker. Lying to yourself as well as everybody else. Well, I'm fuckin' done waitin' for you to come to your senses…"

"What you going to do, Lady?" I snarl. "You threatenin' to out me?"

"I wouldn't do that. I like you too much. Respect you too. But I'm not gonna remain faithful to a jerk who doesn't deserve it. You had your fuckin' chance, Joke. Now you've blown it!" He raises his hands, plants them on my biceps, and gazes into my eyes. "I'll give you this to remember me by." Then, with no further warning, his lips crash onto mine. He leaves his mouth closed as if teasing me with what I'm missing.

"Like that, is it?" A loud voice sounds by my side.

I jump back, wrenching myself out of Lady's hold. A sharp breath in, then I swivel to meet Crash's censorious eyes. Fuck. I'm lost now. It's over. I try to deny what he's seen. "It's not what you're fuckin' thinkin', VP."

His eyebrows rise.

"I'm outta here." Having given his parting shot in a voice full of disgust, Lady storms off down the corridor.

Crash says nothing. I don't feel like trying to fill the silence. My fists clench and unclench. I'm poised to jump to my defence and to Lady's. But I get no chance. After a moment, he simply continues on to his room, shaking his head as he goes.

I enter my own, sinking to my knees with my hands over my face. I'm shaking. When the tears start to leak from my eyes, my hands are trembling so badly I can barely wipe them away. *This is it. What I've been dreading. My brothers finding out. Was that disgust I saw? Or disappointment on the VP's face? Is he going to out me right now? Or wait until morning. What will happen to Lady?*

I could pull my gun out of my cut, use a bullet to end it. If I can keep my hand steady enough that is. *But Lady…*

If the shit hits the fan it will land on him too. Whatever he thinks, I do care for him. More than I've cared for anyone in my life. I owe it to him to wait and face whatever's coming our way. One thing's for certain. There'll be no joking my way out of this.

Resolution made that I won't selfishly be ending my suffering tonight, I drag myself up, stagger to the bed and lie down fully clothed.

How's Lady taking it? Is he, like me, lying worried, and yeah, I admit, scared? Frightened of a future without the club. *Perve, Rope had called me.* He was right. Now the VP's borne witness to it.

I don't sleep, I just lie awake, going over the options in my head. Not that I've got many. *Join a gay club like Lady had suggested?*

Various thoughts constantly swirl around, circling then coming back for me to take a second look. Could I stay? Try to fight my way out of it? Make the brothers accept it. Nah, that's a stupid idea. If I, myself, believe it's so wrong, how could I convince others that what I feel for Lady isn't disgusting but natural?

I don't sleep. Every fucking time I close my eyes, Crash's disgusted face appears to me, his expression burned onto my brain.

When the sun starts shining through the blinds, without a knock or waiting for an invitation, my door opens and Lady steps in.

I sit up fast. "You shouldn't be here," I hiss.

He shrugs. "Damage has been done, hasn't it? Now we've got to look at damage limitation."

"How the fuck do we do that?" I growl. If he hadn't come after me last night. If our argument hadn't gotten so heated… if he'd gone away when I'd asked. This is one hundred percent down to him. Everything I've tried to be, the person I projected to the world has been destroyed by his impulsive action.

Not seeming anywhere near as upset as I am, he leans back against the door. "If anything's going to happen, we'll deal with it. Side by side. Or, if they kick only one of us out, you know that will be me. Last in, first out and all that. I won't have the loyalty of the brothers you have."

"They wouldn't want me here." I'm certain of that.

"Nah. I was the one kissing *you*. Crash didn't see you respond, because you didn't. You could complain, accuse me of harassment. Say you always suspected something was off with me, hell, you were threatened by me. That's why you didn't want me patched in. They'd throw me out in a flash. Or, even if Crash says you were into it too, they just might not want their faces rubbed in it. If one of us goes, problem solved."

I don't want him to go. I want everything to go back to normal. Oh fuck, what's normal, anyway? I run my hands through my hair, tightening my fingers until I get a welcome bite of pain from my scalp. I don't even consider dropping him in it to protect myself. "I'm not throwin' you to the lions. We face what's comin' together."

A moment to glance my way, then, "Look, I'm going down to get some breakfast. Rosa's cookin' up a storm. Come down with me."

"Not hungry," I mumble.

"Puttin' it off isn't going to help. Frontin' it out, might."

"Fuckin' off right now before the inevitable happens might work too." I glare at him. Then shake my head. "I'm not a coward. I know what this is going to be like, remember? I've lived it all my life. I feel sorry for you; you'll have to face up to being a monster in their eyes."

"They can say what they like. Call me names, give me a beat down, I don't give a fuckin' damn. I know who I am and I'm damn proud of it. Who I'm worryin' about is you. You've had it rough and deserve better. Hidin' or runnin', neither of those is the answer."

He's right. It's not. It's the coward's way out. But one that appeals. I pace my room, he gives me time. "Okay," I say at last. "I'll come down on two conditions. One, we keep our distance from each other, let it be known last night was a one-time thing. Nothing happened, and nothing will be happenin'. And two, you go down first. Give me a moment."

"If that's the way you want it." He straightens his back, his scowl letting me know it wasn't what he wanted me to say. One last lingering gaze, then, without another word, he opens the door and steps out.

Chapter 9

It takes me ten minutes to pluck up the courage. Six hundred seconds during which I'm tempted to pack my saddle bags and get the hell out of town. It's the thought of leaving Lady in the lurch that stops me. If I run, there'll be no one to take what's handed out but him. I can't do that to my friend, or to anyone. Whether I'd personally taken to them or not, I stood up beside any of my brothers when I was in the Marines.

With a heavy heart, I descend the stairs. Lady will have done what he said, he'll have stepped into the kitchen, which today, to me, feels like the lion's den, or a sea with sharks circling, sensing blood. As I take each step downward I wait for the cries of derision, for the complaints and remonstrations. But all I can hear is laughter interspersed with the sound of cutlery on plates.

Crossing the clubroom, I take a deep breath before stepping in. There in the middle of the table sits Lady, a stack of pancakes and bacon in front of him. He even snatches a piece of bacon off Petty's plate saying prospects shouldn't be allowed to eat with everyone else. Crash is laughing at something Twister's telling him. He catches sight of me, sends me his normal chin lift, but does nothing else. He doesn't react differently at all. He clearly hasn't said anything. No one's treating me, or Lady, other than they'd would normally.

Maybe he's waiting to speak to Red?

Sarge comes up behind, slapping me on the back. "You're blocking the doorway, Brother. Make your fuckin' mind up. You going in or out?"

"Got a plate with your name on it here, Joker." Tiff, Fox's wife who's helping Rosa, calls out.

I lift my leg and make my feet move. Now I'm given no option but to proceed as I've done every day for the past six years since I was patched in, I take the loaded plate from Tiff, thanking her with the best smile I can summon, then take the seat Titch has just vacated at the table. It puts me next to Shadow.

"Bad fuckin' news about Adam, yeah?" he starts, then there's a gap as he chomps down on the perfectly crispy bacon. "Want some help organising the run?"

The question helps put me into business mode, shifting mental gears, taking my mind off Lady. "Need to find out what Hellfire and Snatcher are doing. Snatcher might want his boys to break their journey here. Will be a big group if they join us."

"Could meet up with the Colorado boys at Rio Grande."

I nod at him. "I'll talk to Red, see if he knows what they're arrangin'. If there's a big group of us, at least part of the way, it will need to be carefully planned."

"The cops will be preparin' for the funeral anyway. They know we'll all be there."

"Don't want any trouble we can avoid, Shadow. If we can head it off before it comes to us, the better. Drummer's probably already told the dom club we'll be movin' through, but I'd like to check for ourselves." I've always liked Shadow. He's got sharp eyes and has alerted me to trouble more than once. If I could no longer be Road Captain, I'd recommend him for the job. If anyone gives any weight to the opinion of a fag like me, that is.

Red appears with an empty plate which he passes to Rosa. He sees me talking to Shadow, guesses what it's about, and gives me a chin lift. Then he beckons at Crash. "You wanted a word, VP?"

My appetite flees. With difficulty, I stop myself from looking at Lady. Balancing a hand on the table, I push myself up. "I'll see you later, Shadow. I'm going to the shop to have a word with the mechanics about prioritising our bikes."

It's a valid excuse for me leaving. I've spoken loudly. If Red wants to talk to me after his chat with Crash, I won't be hiding. Anyone here will know where to find me.

During the morning, I agree with the mechanics that the bikes with belt drives should be prioritised. Chains are more reliable, they just need oiling and cleaning. The belts which can easily be damaged by stones or grit might need changing. Oil needs to be checked and topped off, as well as those important brakes and tyres given the once over. Mostly we keep our bikes well maintained, but I'm determined there'll be no mishaps on our long journey. Especially if we end up riding with another chapter. Taking preventative action where we are able. Don't want to end up with egg on our faces in front of another crew.

After an hour, I've stopped looking behind me every time I hear footsteps. By lunchtime I'm starting to breathe easier again. By mid-afternoon I dare show my face in the clubhouse, finally plucking up the nerve to go see the prez.

"Ah, Joker. I thought you'd be coming to see me."

I give Red a moment, but when he waits for me to speak first, I wonder if he's giving me the chance to admit what Crash must have told him today.

"Well?" he prompts.

"I, er, I…" *Spit it out, man.* "I wanted to ask whether you've heard what arrangements Hellfire and Snatcher are makin'."

"I have." His grin suggests he's pleased he pre-empted my enquiry. "Knew you'd want to know. Hellfire's obviously going direct as you probably have guessed. Snatcher is going straight there too. You only need to factor us in."

"That makes it easier. Shadow's offered to help. He's got an instinct for this." Might as well give him a heads up that the man would be a good replacement.

Red nods. "Thanks for that, Brother. Good to know if you're ever indisposed. But hope you'll be in the role for a very long time yet."

Crash can't have spoken to him. Perhaps I should come clean. Get my side in first. But my nerve fails me; I say nothing at all. Don't want to see Crash's disappointment reflected in Red's eyes.

With so much to think of and sort out, the rest of the week passes quickly. I start breathing easier each day that goes past, and no one says anything. I begin to find it easier to concentrate on business, making sure the mechanics are on top of their jobs. While brothers take good care of their bikes, a few parts need ordering in, and the crash van has to be stocked up with all likely replacement items we could need on the way.

As Titch watches the last bike being wheeled off the ramp, he steps back, brushing his hands on a rag. "All done, Joker. I can't see anything that would give us a problem."

"You mind that you're drivin' the crash truck, Brother?"

"Nah." He flexes his hands. "Got a touch of arthritis. Eight hours is a fuckin' long ride nowadays. Would do it if I have to, but tell you the truth, I don't mind steppin' up and going in the cage."

Unable to leave the compound unprotected, it's already been arranged the prospects, Petty and Roller, will be staying behind.

Thanking him again, I leave to make sure the brothers have remembered to top their tanks up. While we'll have to be stopping fairly frequently as a couple are riding with the smaller three gallon tanks, I don't want to have to call a halt before we even get out of Vegas. Yes, that has been known. As I make the rounds checking—yeah, there's one, Hammer admits he's running on fumes already—I ponder again how Crash can't have said a word. Maybe it doesn't matter to him? It could have been worse were it someone else who'd interrupted us.

It sucks that I can't talk to my friend. Well, not any differently to any of the other brothers. I've suffered my fears alone, sleepless nights when I just wanted to talk to someone, but didn't dare approach him. I'd opened up to Lady in a way I never had to anyone before, and still don't regret it. From time to time I've seen him, having a laugh with the brothers, or with his arm around one of the club girls. Each time it hurts knowing it was me who pushed him away. Given his way, he'd have stood by my side and worked it through.

As if he can read my thoughts, he's coming toward me. His fist bumps mine. "All set, Brother?"

"Yeah," I confirm. "Think Shadow and I have thought of everything. Fuckin' lookin' forward to gettin' going now."

"I hear you." He raises his chin toward me. The gleam in his eyes shows he's on the same page. We're both thinking of nothing but the wind in our faces and the pavement flying by under our wheels. Freedom. A chance to blow all my fretting of the last week away.

"Likin' the idea of the journey, not so much why we're going. Still, we'll give Adam a good send off."

"That compound's going to be crowded."

"They've got the space." I might not have gone to the Tucson compound for the prospect's funeral, but I've been there often enough over the years and watched it gradually being built up from a burned-out hulk to something that most clubs would envy. Their spot in the desert is spectacularly scenic too.

That night, I sleep surprisingly well, my mind apparently sufficiently satisfied I've done everything I need to. The next morning, we get going early, stopping to top up—both our tanks and our stomachs—around the halfway two-hundred-mile mark. Then it's back on the road again. So far so good.

There's a big eighteen-wheeler in front of us. The road is straight and clear, so I'm not worried when I see Red zoom past, followed by Crash and Indian, then by Twister and Fox. Two by two the brothers go around it. The truck driver must be having a bad day or he's got something against bikers. He's alternating between pulling on his horn and thrusting his middle finger out of the window. I start to smile as I see Cobra pulling out, twisting his throttle so his front wheel almost leaves the ground, Keys keeping pace beside him.

Fuck! Cobra's bike suddenly starts swerving. He misses Keys by an inch, twisting those bars hard to get free of his brother, *too damn hard.* Now he's heading straight for the truck. All I can do is watch, seeing it happen as though in slow motion as Cobra fights to keep the bike upright. Almost laying it down as he swerves across the road, over the centre line and into the opposite lane. *Thank fuck there's nothing coming.* At last the bike's slowing, Cobra's still shiny side up, it's still losing speed. He's fucking stopping it, now he's stopped, his left leg crashing down to support it. I let out a breath I hadn't realised I'd been holding.

Bikes up ahead are reducing their speed, riders who, having seen what's going on in their rearviews, are pulling over, letting the truck pass, then parking up the median and running back. Keys, and the brothers riding behind him who somehow managed to keep out of his way, have already halted. Like me, they're all breathing fast. Riding close in formation, that shit is scary. If he'd gone down, he could have taken someone else out too.

"Fuckin' spoked wheels," Cuff sneers with disgust, as he crosses the road eyeing the damage.

Cobra's still sitting astride the stricken machine. His lungs are heaving, and I don't blame him. Having a spoke break and go through your tyre at what must have been ninety miles an hour isn't a fun thing to experience.

"Fuckin' had to show off, didn't you?" Keys kicks at a rock.

I shake my head at the computer guy. Yeah, it was a close call, closest for him, but Cobra hadn't done anything anyone else hadn't done.

Red walks back, says nothing, just lays his hand on Cobra's shoulder. It's taken as a sign for us all to spring into action. Titch drives ahead, does a U-turn, then brings the crash truck up alongside the stricken bike. Shadow and I go to the back, get out the jacks and spare wheel. At last Cobra dismounts. Being well versed in what we're doing, it's not long before he can get back on his ride.

Time's getting on. Red and the front runners walk back to their bikes, then having mounted up, Red gives the signal and we're back on the road, riding in formation once again. All in a day's work. A brush with death again avoided. Cobra's now laughing, riding off with his middle finger held up.

With the unexpected delay it's late afternoon by the time we arrive at the Tucson compound. The sun is still shining down, but having lost some of the ferocity of its midday heat, it's a nice temperature. One of the Tucson prospects, Marsh—their only prospect now, I find out later—is directing us as to where we can park. Once organised, our engines switch off. Now we're able to hear shouts and hollers all around us.

The air is filled with the smells coming from grills which are cooking out behind the clubhouse. Bikers are milling around, dark leather-clad men as far as you can see in every direction. There's a cute little girl being chased by a woman, presumably her mother who's wearing a property cut. The kid is laughing as she tries to evade the adult's hands, and not looking where she's going, she runs straight into my legs. Picking her up, I right her, and get ready to hand her over. When the woman catches up I can see she's the Property of Heart.

"Thank you," she gasps out. "I'm Crystal. Heart's my man. There's food and beer around the back if you're hungry or thirsty."

"Joker," I smile down at her. "Thank you, ma'am."

A slap on my back, I turn with a grin, then frown as I see Lady. A quick shake of my head, then I'm walking forward to catch up with the rest of our boys who've heard Crystal's invitation. Whatever Lady had to say will stay unspoken. Can't afford any slip ups. Not now.

It's things like this, getting together with other chapters, calling every man brother even if you've never met them before. That's what being in an MC is about, and what I don't want to lose. It's more important to me than anything. *Any. Fucking. Thing.*

I drink, eat, obviously don't fuck, but no one would worry about that, the club girls are in high demand. Even if I was so inclined, the only thing available would probably be my hand. Later in the small hours of the morning I find myself a spot, lying down with my head on my jacket.

The funeral is the same as others I've attended, an escort of Harleys lining the driveway to the graveyard. I'm just one anonymous biker amongst the rest. No blinking light above my head to make me stand out as different. There, alongside these men, any of whom I'd fight to protect, I'm proud to be part of the send-off for Adam. We bow our heads, feel a moment of regret for his death, then it's back to the clubhouse for a celebration of his life.

The next morning, we set off to go back to Vegas, many nursing sore heads. As we leave, I give one last lingering look at the Tucson compound. *Fuck, this is a nice place.* Brothers have got it made here.

Chapter 10

Thanks, Fox. Good to know the dollars are coming in." Red raises his chin toward the treasurer who's just given his summary. He scans the faces around the table. "Anyone got any questions?" After we all shake our heads, he nods. "Good. Just wanted to mention Joker did a great fuckin' job organisin' the run to Tucson. Sad reason to go, but fuckin' good ride and good company."

Verbal thanks and chin lifts come at me from all directions. I shrug them off, in a 'weren't nothing' gesture. Embarrassed as I was just doing my job.

"Would have been easier if Cobra could control his fuckin' bike," Keys snarls.

"Shut the fuck up," Cobra shows him his finger. I smile to myself. Those two have been at it ever since we've been back.

Red glares at them. "Get in the ring together. Sort it out there," he suggests. "Fed up with the pair of you." After chin lifts showing they agree with his suggestion, Prez continues, "Carryin' on with the Tucson theme, I've been contacted by Drummer. As you're aware, the Tucson chapter have faced more than enough trouble recently, and lost a couple of good men. A member and a prospect." Red pauses as we confirm we do indeed all know. "Those troubles, I'm assured, are over, but it's left Drummer short. He's openin' up the mother chapter to any member who's a good fit, and who wants to transfer there."

My head tilts. Well, fuck me. I like the compound, it's in a great position. Good facilities there too. I haven't seen the rooms the brothers live in, but I've heard talk. If I transferred, my problems would be solved. No one would have an inkling what I am, the other plus being I wouldn't be tormented by seeing the man I can't have every day. Hmm. I won't make any hasty decisions, but it's an idea to think on.

"You got anyone in mind, Prez?" Hammer asks.

"Yeah, who do we want to get shot of?" Cuff laughs.

Red allows us a moment, then when we've all settled down, begins, "I don't want to lose any one of you, let's get that straight up front. But sometimes a brother can do with a change of scenery, so I'll understand if anyone wants to go. But be warned, Drummer is going to be picky over who he takes in. Last fucker who transferred tried to rape his VP's woman. They don't want to transfer in another problem."

"That's you out then, Titch. You're a fuckin' problem."

Titch responds to Twister with his middle finger.

"On the other hand," Red continues as if no one had spoken, "no pressure's gonna be put on anyone. No one wants to step up, no one has to."

With no other business, the meeting wraps up. As we walk out to get a beer, some brothers are discussing making a move. I find myself wanting to discourage them. Red probably wouldn't allow more than one man to jump ship, otherwise he'd be left in the same position Drummer's trying to fix. Shorthanded. The more I think on it, the more it seems to be the answer.

"You're not seriously thinking about it, are you, Joker?"

I raise my beer, wondering if he can read my mind while thinking how to answer Lady's question. "Might be. Might not."

"Don't do it, Brother." Lady sounds worried.

Casting my eye around, no one's taking any notice of us. Subtly I move down the bar, Lady follows. We're now out of earshot. Even so, I lower my voice. "Would solve things. Crash might not have said anything, doesn't mean he's not going to.

Maybe he's waiting to see if we'll slip up again. I go, you stay. We'll both still be brothers. Problem sorted."

Lady closes his eyes letting out a deep sigh. "Problem's all in your head, Brother. If it comes out, we've already talked about this. Might not be the end of the world like you're thinkin'."

"Can't take the fuckin' risk," I snarl, still keeping my voice low. "You know how I feel."

"I know how I fuckin' feel, Brother. That's that I don't want you an eight-hour fuckin' ride away."

"If I go, I go. You'll survive." But hell, how will I? I'll fuckin' feel I've left something behind. Something important.

He stares at me until I meet his gaze. "You don't think I'd miss you? Fuck, I miss you and you're standin' right here next to me. I've never felt like this before, about anyone. I just wish you'd give us a chance, Joker. You're throwing what could be the best thing to ever happen to either of us away. Please reconsider. Give us a chance."

As he ends his plea, I wish I could tell him how much I'd like things to be different. But I can't expose what I am. Just can't. It's at that moment my mind's made up. If I can, I'm going to transfer to the Tucson chapter. Staying in Vegas, living in such close proximity to Lady will do me in. I don't want to leave him. Much as he thinks nothing will change if we come clean, I'm equally convinced we'll be out of the club. Maybe worse for denying the truth for so long. While I couldn't care less what they do to me, I don't want Lady to suffer. No, he'll be better off without me. This is what I have to do.

"What are you two boys chatterin' about? Thinkin' of transferrin'?" Twister comes over and slaps his hands on each of our backs.

"Nah. What? Give up this place for a vacation resort and a swimmin' pool? Think I'm fuckin' crazy?" I jibe the enforcer. "You?"

"Nah. Got my position here. Same as you. Wouldn't want to go back to being one of the grunts." He waggles his eyebrows at Lady, a said grunt, a patched member without an officer position.

Though Twister alluded to it, being Road Captain isn't much, certainly doesn't get you sitting at the top of the table. Or not in our club, at least. It wouldn't bother me much giving it up.

"Anyway. Wanted to come find you. You up for a shift at Erika's tonight? You too, Lady? Rope and Cuff want to drop out."

I smirk. "They going to be tied up, later?"

"Doing the tying up, actually. They're going to be givin' a Shibari demonstration."

My eyes open wide. "What the fuck is Shibari?"

Lady laughs. "Don't get yourself wound up in knots worrying about it," he tosses at me, making Twister laugh. Then to the enforcer, "Yeah, sure. I'm game."

What can I do but nod and agree?

Two hours later I'm pulling up outside the restaurant. It's just before closing time, but Erika's got plates ready as soon as we walk in. Fuck, I'm glad I don't pull this duty often, I'd be as fat as a pig with the food she serves.

"Joker!" She puts her arms around me for a brief hug, then pulls back. "You okay?"

"I'm fine, darlin'. Healed up good now." I realise I haven't been back since the night I got injured. Since the night Lady admitted having a reciprocal liking for me. "How's business going?" I ask, partly interested, partly to get Lady out of my mind.

"It's going great. The gang hardly comes around anymore. You giving me personal attention tonight?"

"Nah, you don't need it. Lady and I are coverin' the block. But our phones are set up to your security system so we'll be there in a second if anything sets it off."

"But you've got time to eat, first?"

"Sure have." Lady's eyeing the plates that Regan's just put on our table.

"I'll leave you to it, then. It's so good to see you again, Joker. I'm glad you made a full recovery. Had me worried there for a bit." Erika pats my arm as I follow Lady to the table.

He sits, picks up his fork and prods at some sort of chicken dish. "Brings back memories, doesn't it?"

Of him lying beside me in bed. Watching over me, caring for me. Yeah, it sure does. I shake my head to clear it. "Of me getting a baseball bat to my head and a boot kicked into my ribs. Yeah, great times."

He points his fork at me. "Wasn't thinking about that. But what happened after."

I shrug as if that night hadn't meant anything to me, not wanting to admit the number of times I'd wanted to repeat lying in his arms while I slept. I try a mouthful of the food, it's tasty, but I've got no appetite. I vow one day to come back without Lady so I can at least stomach the food and enjoy it.

Lady has no such problems. Half his plate's gone, I've barely touched mine. "So, Tucson. I can read you like a fuckin' book, Joker. You're going, aren't you?"

I give up the pretence and put my silverware down. "It will solve everything."

His head moves negatively back and forth. "Doesn't solve anything. You gonna go through your life runnin' from this?"

Shrugging again, I tell him, "I've done okay so far. Me, the club, my bike. All I want."

"Fuckin' liar," he says, partly under his breath. Then adds more loudly, "What if I asked you to stay?"

"I couldn't. As long as they'll have me, I'm going." The more he speaks, the more made up my mind becomes. "Unless Crash says anything, can't see why they wouldn't have me. I've kept my nose clean."

"And they haven't got a Road Captain."

That's useful to know. But, "Did you ask?"

"It came up for some reason while I was there. I was talking to them about their officer structure."

"Perhaps they can do without one."

Lady shakes his head, "Don't think that's it. Might mean they'll jump at the chance to take you, rather than a lowly member like me."

"Shadow can step up here. I won't be leaving the club short."

"You don't mind leaving me short, though. I'll fuckin' miss you, Joker."

I'll miss him too.

Just like last time, he finishes my plate. Luckily that's where the similarity ends and we have a quiet night, the gang not putting in an appearance. He gives up on trying to persuade me to change my mind. In fact, we barely speak much more at all. We've said all there is to be said.

The next morning, I grab a few hours' sleep, then go down to Prez's office. I'm lucky to find he's there, and alone.

"Joker. What can I do for you?"

I take the chair he indicates and sit down, splaying my knees and resting my elbows on them. "I'd like to transfer to Tucson."

"You too?"

Me too? "Who else wants to go, Prez?" I'm quite heartened at the thought one of my brothers might be coming with me. I don't know any of the Tucson crowd, so someone who's familiar could be good to have with me. On the other hand, they might only want to take one of us.

Red shakes his head. "Not sayin'. Drummer will have the final say, don't want the brothers to know who hasn't been selected if it comes to it."

"D'you know what he's lookin' for, Prez?" Until he'd said that, I hadn't seriously thought I might be turned away.

"He's short of a Road Captain, I can tell you that." Red tugs at his ginger beard. "Trouble is, if you go, I'll need someone to fill that position."

"Shadow," I offer without hesitation. "He's good. Knows as much as me. Helped me out often enough."

"That's good to know." Red narrows his eyes. "But why do you want to leave, Joker? Aren't you settled here? One of the brothers botherin' you?"

If only he knew... "It's nothing like that, Prez. Got a sister in Tucson." I really don't like lying to my prez, but he's put me on the spot and it's all I can think of quickly. I had to come up with an excuse that would work. "Her husband's getting a bit handsy. Would like to be a bit closer if she needs me."

"Ah. Fuckin' family." Red frowns. "I didn't know you had a sister?"

"We're not that close. But as you said, family is family."

"Hmm. Well, if it's something like that it makes sense. Hope for her sake Drummer accepts you. I won't try changin' your mind if it's made up."

"Thanks, Prez. Er, how soon will I know?"

He sits back and folds his arms. "Drummer and Wraith are coming up in a few weeks. I'll be going through anyone who's put their names forward at that time. Keep your nose clean in the meantime and we'll see what they say."

"Always keep my nose clean, Prez."

"Know you do, Joker. Would it help if I said we'll miss you? Take some more time to think it through. Think what you're givin' up. Sin City which never sleeps."

I grin. "That makes the peace of the desert sound very attractive," I tell him, as I get to my feet. "Thanks, Prez. Hell, I respect the fuck out of you. Everyone at the club. I just think it's time to move on."

"And be close to your sister."

I have to work fast to catch up. "Yeah, my sister." Now I've got to get out fast before I slip up. Fuck. I start wondering how to avoid getting caught in the spider's web of my own making.

Chapter 11

It's only a couple of weeks before the Vegas clubhouse is visited by the Tucson chapter's—the mother chapter's—prez and VP. For a few hours after they arrive, they are holed up with Red. I wait eagerly for a summons I hope will come. I don't know why, but I'd cleaned my boots and made sure to wear a decent tee and fresh jeans, but in the end, I needn't have bothered. I'm not called to Red's office, and neither do Drummer or Wraith approach me when they appear later on that evening.

Visiting officers mean a party is in order, Red naturally wanting to show how the Vegas boys roll, hopefully impressing the national prez. For some reason, he's decided on a demonstration in the ring and pairs up Lady with Sarge.

Sarge isn't a big man, but he's muscular and solid. Lady, on the other hand, looks like a breath of air would blow him away. I grin to myself, remembering the time I was the one underestimating him. He might be slim and his muscles aren't impressive to look at, but he's fast with a powerful swing. Just thinking about it makes me rub my jaw ruefully. Then I remember what happened that night, and the next. *If I get my way, I'll be leaving Lady in my rear view.*

Half of me wants to go back to my room. Not to stay and watch. It's bringing forth reasons why I shouldn't go, and just how much he means to me. Perhaps he's right. I should stay, come out to my brothers. Would that mean I could have the relationship I want?

Then, as I look around me, I see the men I'd have to convince. Nah, it's better this way. I won't be exposing myself or Lady to any fallout. The least I could expect is to see revulsion on the faces of the men who currently call me brother. Coming out, bringing my sexuality and Lady's into the open, would sicken them. Just like it did those who are related to me by blood. These are good men; they wouldn't want to know there was an aberration in their midst. *Don't ask, don't tell.* Just like when I served. Keep that shit hidden well under wraps. The only way to ensure it stays that way is to remove myself from temptation.

Acknowledging the truth, knowing the only solution is to remove myself from Vegas, I find I'm unable to drag my eyes away from the men who are now bumping wrapped hands, and taking their stance in preparation to fight. Around me my brothers are betting on the outcome. I glance at the visiting officers who'll be judging along with Red. They seem surprised the bets are about even for each man. Yeah, Lady doesn't look like he'll be putting up much of a fight, but I know he's going to surprise them.

I've left it too late. It would look odd if I go without watching their bout. Then I also need to stay close in case Red wants to introduce me. *Fuck, I'm trapped.* But not for too long. Hopefully I'll be transferring shortly. For a second I wonder who's the other brother who's put in a request. It wouldn't be Rope or Cuff, they wouldn't leave that club they go to. Fox is too settled here with Tiffany, and in any case, Red wouldn't let an officer go. Sarge? Could be putting on a show for Drummer and Wraith. Perhaps. Not Titch, he's too old to start over. Keys too indispensable. That leaves Cobra or Hammer. Either would have my back. Come to that, can't think of a man who wouldn't, well, in all matters but one.

The bell rings, my gaze snaps to the ring. *There he goes.* Sarge, over-confident, rushes in with the first punch. I almost laugh at the look of astonishment on his face as he hits only air. Lady bounces away from him, delivering a sharp kick to his back. More cautious now, Sarge takes his time considering where to lay his fist next. Lady takes advantage, then they're both on the floor and I feel a moment of envy as Lady's arms surround his opponent. My cock twitches at the memory of his weight on me. Purposefully I allow memories of that camp, the electric shocks to return, and immediately I've brought myself under control.

Lady wins the first bout. Sarge puts up more of a fight in the second, the score will be closer but I still reckon Lady's got the edge. *Oh fuck.* Sarge has grabbed hold of Lady's hair. Twister, the referee, calls a halt. *Was it a deliberate foul?* They have a discussion, and in the end, agree it was an accident. Sarge, caught off balance, had just put his hand out. *I'm not so certain. I think he's getting desperate.*

I catch Lady's gaze, see the grin on his face. *He's got this.* Whether Sarge did it on purpose on not.

Twister starts the clock again, and they're back fighting. *No. Sarge has got Lady on the ground.* But Lady does that twisting thing again, and now he's, *fuck me,* got Sarge in a submission hold. *How the fuck did he do that?*

Sarge taps out. It's all over. Money changes hands from Sarge's supporters to Lady's. Equal amounts of frowns and grins surround me.

Yes! Indian and Twister are getting their hands wrapped now. The sergeant-at-arms and the enforcer are going to show the Tucson brothers exactly how it's done. All thoughts of leaving flee me. I want to stay to watch this. Undecided, I place my money on Twister.

Less than twenty minutes later and my wallet's fifty dollars lighter, my voice is hoarse from screaming, and I'm going away with a few lessons learned I'd like to try to put into practice. *Have they a ring in Tucson?* Someone mentioned a gym, but I don't know if they have fights there. Wouldn't stop me going if they hadn't, but I'd like to keep my hand in.

We move upstairs to the clubroom where loud music is already playing. The sweet butts are ready and waiting. Jinx makes a beeline for the visiting prez, Drummer doesn't waste time disappearing into the room he's been given for the night. Angel tries to interest Wraith, but he turns her down. *Ah, yes. He's recently taken an old lady.* Idly I wonder how long it will last, and whether next time he visits, he'll be taking up the offer of her services. Unless she's particularly special, I've seen enough bikers not practicing fidelity.

Angel isn't left alone long. Indian, hyped up from winning his contest, wraps his hand around her arm and pulls her away with him. Oh, there's Pixie with Shadow's cock down her throat. Cobra's hanging around, clearly the next in line.

Another night I might have been heading into Vegas, but not now. If I've got a chance at getting out of this city, I'll hang around, see if I can impress the visiting VP. *Should I approach him?* He seems deep in conversation with his counterpart, Crash. *Fuck. What could Crash be telling him?* The air comes out of my lungs in a whoosh remembering what Red had told me. *Drummer and Wraith will be choosing who they let transfer very carefully.* If Crash is being questioned about me, exactly how far will he go with his disclosures? *It was only once. He saw nothing of significance. He's kept his mouth shut up to now.*

It is me they're discussing. It has to be. Wraith just glanced over at me directly. I meet his gaze with a chin lift which he returns, then his attention's on the VP again. I'd give my right arm to hear what they're saying.

"You still set on going?"

Inhaling sharply, I turn to face Lady. "Yeah." *Fuck. I don't want Crash and Wraith to see me close to Lady. Not right at this moment.*

"When do you think you'll find out if they'll take you?"

I want to get out of this conversation now. "Dunno. When they want to tell me." I see Indian has finished with Angel, and as I expected, Cobra has taken his place. "Gotta see Indian," I tell Lady, lamely.

Escaping him quickly, I go over to the man who's got a satisfied smile on his face. "You ever gonna get a proper ride?" I start, knowing this will begin a long and probably heated conversation. As expected, the sergeant-at-arms starts extolling the virtues of the Indian he rides. We're soon joined by Titch, who reminisces about bikes that he's had. That soon descends into him talking about past members, and draws a crowd all willing to hear a good story. We drink, laugh, slap backs, touch fists. It's a good evening. By the time I extricate myself, Wraith's disappeared, and neither Drummer or Pixie are in sight. Nor Angel, come to that. But what girl is going to turn down a handsome, visiting president? Drummer wouldn't be turning away any of them. It's how he got his handle. He bangs everything in sight.

I drink enough to fall into oblivion when I lay down on my bed, but not enough to stop me waking in the early hours, my body drenched in sweat and shaking. My breath's coming in pants as though I'd run a marathon. Mercilessly the dream stays with me, not fading or weakening. I picture every detail of Grant's body swaying in that bunkhouse. The boy who'd rather die than live with what he was. I've seen dead bodies enough over the years, have been responsible for taking a life more than once—justly deserved of course—but he was my first. The reason he took his own life too close to be comfortable. Making me question how I can live with myself.

Shaking my head doesn't clear the image from my brain. I sit up, pull my legs over the side of the bed, get up and stretch, then after pulling on my jeans, exit my room and go to the bathroom for a piss. Not because I need one, but to try to fully wake up, not wanting to risk sleep again. *Another beer. Maybe something stronger. That's what I need.*

Something to take me over the edge into a dreamless rest. Still rattled, I pass my brothers' rooms, walking quietly so as not to disturb them. The lights are still on over the bar. As I head toward my destination, I see a figure sitting, a bottle of tequila on the table in front of them. When I see who it is, I almost return to my room.

I don't. Instead I grab a glass for myself and go over.

"I'll miss you," Lady rasps out as I approach. "I'll fuckin' miss you, Brother."

I'll miss him too. But I don't tell him that.

"Couldn't you sleep, either?" he asks when he sees I'm not going to respond to his impassioned statement.

"I slept. Then woke up. Needed a drink." It's the short answer, and all I'm going to give him.

His eyes look tired, red-rimmed. "Are you thinking about tomorrow? Speaking to Red? Finding out whether you're going to Tucson or not?"

"That's part of it," I admit. I down my shot then take another.

"You're hoping the answer is yes." It sounds like he's hoping it's not.

"Been through this, Brother. Not wantin' to get into it again. You know my reasons."

"And you know my feelin's," he snaps. "At least I acknowledge mine."

I inhale sharply, then sigh. "It's not my feelin's I have trouble admittin', but it's the actin' on them is where I can't go. Just leave it, Lady. You won't change my mind." More liquid goes down my throat. It's smooth, he's grabbed a good make. Deciding to change the subject, I grin. "You took down Sarge alright."

"Yeah."

"Everyone underestimates you."

He looks at me sharply. "Always expect surprises from me," he says enigmatically. My eyebrows rise, but he doesn't expand.

I'm worried. "What are you going to do, Lady?"

He puts down his empty glass, regards it for a moment, then reaches over and squeezes my hand. "Nothing for you to worry about, Joker. You've made yourself quite clear." Then places his hands on the bar, using them to lever himself up.

I watch him walk across the room, feeling the warmth his touch had left on my skin fading slowly as he disappears from sight. He doesn't turn back, or bid me goodnight. *I'm leaving him.* Well, hopefully I am. But is it hope I feel or despair? Helping myself to another drink, my nightmare returns to my mind. Had Grant appeared to me as a suggestion? A final exit instead of a transfer? Have I really thought through all the implications of leaving Lady behind?

CHAPTER 12

"Joker. Come in, sit yourself down." After waving me to the chair, Red reaches over to his printer and takes off a document he'd printed out. He glances down at it, I give him a moment to read it. It's not long before he looks up. "Well, you got what you wanted." I tilt my head wanting to be certain we're both on the same page, which is confirmed as he resumes, "Drummer's agreed on your transfer to Tucson."

I roll my head back. This is just what I wanted. Isn't it? A fresh start. No one who's caught me in an awkward clinch with another man. No one who'll have the slightest suspicion about me. All I need to do is stay out of trouble, make sure to play it literally straight down the line. *New brothers. A new family.* It's up to me not to fuck it all up.

"Have you had second thoughts? You know I'd be happy for you to stay." Red's eyes narrow, it's then I realise I haven't responded.

"Nah, no second thoughts, Prez. This is just what I wanted."

"To be closer to your sister." He frowns as he says it.

Does he suspect? I should have come up with a better excuse. Liked the fucking area or some such shit. Don't like that I'm leaving my brothers here on a lie.

Avoiding mention of my fictitious relative, I simply ask, "When?" Now it's decided, I want out of here as soon as possible.

"Drummer's expectin' you next weekend."

That soon? The image of Lady comes into my head, I shake it, as though it's that easy to dismiss him from my mind. Sooner is better, maybe I'll stop thinking about him. Out of sight, out of mind.

"Too fast?" Red's frowning. He's mistaken my gesture.

"No," I rush to correct him, "That will be fine. Just thinking of what I need to do in the meantime."

Prez taps the paper in front of him. "Here's the transfer document. Just needs your signature." He raises his eyes, looking straight at me. "Sign this, you're no longer part of this chapter."

That's putting it starkly. Making it all come into perspective. My year of prospecting and the six years I've been a patched member play like an old movie through my head. Red's giving me the time I should take to make this momentous decision before finalising it by scrawling my name on that piece of paper. Finding I'm staring at it as though it's an animal I'm not sure is yet tamed, I raise my chin and lift my eyes to him. "Got nothing against this chapter. Be sad to leave it. But I don't have much choice. I'll sign."

"Your sister." Red notes again.

I nod, but don't utter any words, unwilling to expound on the lie.

He pushes the paperwork over the desk. I skim through it, see nothing unexpected, noting both he and Drummer have already added their signatures. When I look back up he's handing me a pen. Taking it without hesitation, I scribble my own on the line left empty. I fold the paper before handing it back. "Thanks, Prez."

He barks a laugh and shakes his head. "Not your prez any longer," he informs me. "You answer to Drummer now."

I startle. During my internal discussions rationalising that distancing myself from temptation was the best move I could make, I hadn't thought about what else I'd be leaving behind, or just how much hearing those words out of Red's mouth would hurt. I've been in the Vegas chapter since I was a prospect. Lived on the compound for seven years. Served under two Vegas presidents. Having signed the paperwork, this isn't my home any longer. Suddenly I feel adrift. Lady comes back into my fucking head as though he's haunting me, along with his voice telling me, *we can make this work*. No, we can't. The only result would be to ensure we're not only evicted from this chapter, but from any chapter of the Satan's Devils.

Red's watching my every expression. "I can tear this up…" he suggests.

"No," I reply quickly. "Just seems a big fuckin' step, that's all."

"A fresh start. New chances and opportunities. Up to you not to fuck it up." He passes a palm over his forehead. "It doesn't work out? You can come back. But I'll be makin' Shadow Road Captain, so you wouldn't get that position back."

"Understood." One way or another, I won't be coming back. There's always that bullet if things get too much.

Red stands and comes around my side of the desk. He holds out his hand, grasping mine firmly when I place it in his. Then he slaps my back, and I slap his too. "Fuckin' good to have had you beside me all these years, Joker. I'll probably be sayin' this again before you leave, but I wish you all the fuckin' best. Here's to your future. May you find what you're searchin' for."

Five days. That's all I've got. Five days to pack up seven years of a life. After leaving Prez's office the hours pass as if in a whirl-wind. Red's been good, arranging for the prospects, Petty and Roller, to follow me down in the van with the belongings I can't get in my saddle bags. They won't be hanging around, just going straight back. That's why they're both coming along to share the driving.

As I'll be leaving on Saturday the brothers are planning a leaving party for Friday night. But their plans get altered, and my celebration is cancelled when a job comes up for Petty and Roller on Saturday, bringing my move forward by one day. I'm not too bothered; having made the decision I just want to get gone. On Thursday, in a fairly low key affair, I say goodbye to my brothers, have a drink with them—not too much, I want a clear head for the long ride ahead.

Friday I wake early, alternating between brimming with excitement and debilitating sadness. Lady's stayed clear of me for the past few days. He'd said he was busy with some shit, but I think he's been avoiding me. Half longing to see him, half pleased he's staying away, I do hope he's at least there to see me off. I'll miss him. Terribly. But I won't be changing my mind. I can't stay here. Can't fuck up the rest of my, *our*, lives.

We're leaving at the ass crack of dawn in order to allow Petty and Roller to have a chance to get back again on the same day. It's the thrill of the unknown, the anticipation of stepping into a new life, that has me showered in seconds flat and dressed within minutes. Then hesitating as other emotions hit. The fear of not knowing what's ahead, whether my new brothers will become as close as those I'm leaving behind. It's the thought of the one I'm going to miss the most that has me reluctantly picking up my keys, chaining my wallet to my belt and finally, closing the door to my home for the last seven years. *Today's the first day of the rest of my life.* Moisture pools behind my eyes as I walk down the corridor for the final time.

Descending the stairs, I pull back my shoulders resolving to let no negative thoughts intrude. It's time to move forward without looking back. Leave everything of the past seven, no, more than that, thirty years behind me. Make a complete new start. That's what I need to do. Not think of what I'm leaving in my rearview. *Don't think about Lady.* For fuck's sake, *don't think about Lady.*

It's five-thirty am. Time to get a quick coffee then go outside to my bike. I've agreed with the prospects we'll grab breakfast on the road.

I hear voices as I open the clubhouse door for the last time as a member of the Vegas chapter. *Fuck me!* It looks like everyone's risen early to see me off. There's Red with his arm around Jinx, leaving me to suspect she spent the night in his bed. There's the rest of the officers, Shadow, and even Titch who's got his hand over his mouth to stifle a yawn.

Keys is looking bright eyed for some reason, Rope and Cuff both looking like they've just dragged themselves out of bed. Cobra's here, and Sarge and oh, there's Hammer. Sarge is looking as though he'd had a few more after I'd gone upstairs last night, Fox and Tiffany are looking half asleep.

My eyes search out the man I want to see most, while at the same time hoping he doesn't turn up. But he's not here.

I have a quick word with Petty and Roller, then go to my bike which gleams in the early morning sun. Then it's back slaps and goodbyes. Everyone wishes me well. The last person I speak to is Red. When I eventually get on my ride, I furtively have to wipe tears from my eyes, before covering them with my sunglasses. Just as I'm about to turn and give a final wave, I hear another bike starting up.

There's only one man missing. He now comes into sight. Fuck. It's Lady on his ride. *What the fuck is he doing?* Is he going to escort me to the outskirts of town? Fucking hell. That's not going to hide there's something special between us. *Shit.* What's the man thinking? Still, it's him who's got to live with the fallout, not me. Not my fault. Nothing on me.

Lady parks his bike alongside me and winks. Then he kicks down the stand and gets off. I watch in amazement as he walks around, shaking everyone's hands, the air echoing with slaps on leather as he receives the same treatment as I just have. A man hug from Red, then he's back with me. His face splits into a brazen grin and once again, he winks.

Then he leans over, speaking quietly so only I can hear. "Didn't think I'd let you go off by yourself, did you? You need someone to keep you in line."

"When was this fuckin' decided?" I hiss.

"Same time as you. Asked Red to keep it quiet. Told him I was still makin' my mind up. Only told the brothers when you took yourself off last night."

"Well, you can fuckin' change it back."

He smirks. "Nope." He pops the p deliberately.

"Then I'm stayin'."

"No, you're not."

"You two going, or what?" Petty's hanging out of the truck yelling at us.

How can I get out of this? If I turn around and go back, what message will that send to my brothers? Oh, a couple of months ago they'd have understood, they knew I'd hated Lady. But they also know in the meantime we've patched our differences up.

There's hooting from the truck. Lady raises an eyebrow.

Oh fuck it. Seething inside, all my plans for a fresh start demolished, I start my engine, kick the stand up, and without checking to see that Lady is ready, select first gear. I'm off.

The gates have been opened in readiness. Lady's right beside me, his long hair flowing out from under the helmet we're required by law to wear in Nevada. First stop in Arizona, and I'm taking mine off. I'm so angry I'm pushing the speed limits. Lady easily keeps up, his machine the equal of mine.

The summer day's already warming up, but I'm used to riding in hot weather. Sun on my face, sufficient wind blowing past to keep me at a comfortable temperature, pavement rushing by beneath my wheels and a good long ride ahead. The breeze seems to blow my bad mood away, or at least, lessen it a bit. By the time we make our first stop, I've realised I'm enjoying Lady riding by my side, his movements so well synchronised to mine. One of my fears about walking into a strange club, knowing some people by sight but having no knowledge of what they're actually like, has lessened. Lady and I will just have to be careful. I'll make it clear to him. He might have thrown in his lot with me, but we won't be starting anything up. We're heading into a new beginning for both of us. That means we'll be strictly hands off.

He parks alongside me when we pull up. As I take off my helmet and slide my sunglasses into my cut, he gives me a long look. "You come down off your high horse yet?"

In the sunlight, I squint at his face. "We need to have words."

Shaking his head, he tells me. "No need. I already know what you're going to say, Joker. I might not like it, but I understand it."

I'm puzzled. "So, why come along then?"

"For fuck's sake," he growls. "Maybe I can't have you the way that I want, but I'll have your back, Joker. Always. I'll always have that."

I look down at my bike, just to take my eyes off the man who has me so confused I don't know whether I'm coming or going. That he's following me to a new chapter, hell, a new city, expresses without words his depth of feeling for me. I'm unable to put forward any arguments that I don't feel the same.

Petty and Roller have got out of the truck and are staring at the offerings displayed on posters in the window. "Filling our stomachs or topping up your tanks, first?" Petty calls out.

Lady looks at me. "Stomachs," I pronounce.

As the two prospects walk away, I raise my fist, offering it toward Lady. He lifts his and our bunched fingers touch together. "To new beginnings," I tell him, accepting the future will hold what it may.

"A fresh start," he agrees.

CHAPTER 13

We arrive at the Satan's Devils Tucson compound just before three in the afternoon, having made good time. The prospect, Marsh, slides open the gate, letting us inside what is to be our new home. It's scary to accept this is quite possibly where I'll spend the rest of my life. This strange place where I've only been an infrequent visitor until now.

"Prez and VP are out on a ride," the prospect informs us. "But you're expected. If you go on up to the clubhouse, there'll be someone there to show you around."

We need to know where to put our stuff so the Vegas prospects can get back on the road. We ride up to the clubhouse. The first thing I notice is that there's far fewer bikes here than I've seen before. When I've been here previously, finding a space has been hard. But of course, it's only the Tucson boys here today. My boys. My new brothers. Avoiding the spaces closest to the door, Lady and I back into spots at the end of the line. As I kick down the stand I wonder how long it will be before I feel a sense of belonging here.

I glance at Lady who seems to be waiting for me to take the lead. Shrugging, I walk toward the clubhouse, push open the door, and am greeted by an almost empty room. When I was here last there'd been standing room only. Now, for the first time, I'm able to get a good look around. Chairs and tables are mis-matched and old. The whole place could do with a coat of paint, but it's tidy and clean. The bar is untended, but my dry mouth starts salivating at the thought of a drink, so I head in that direction.

At that moment, a child toddles out of the kitchen. It's déjà vu when, giggling, looking behind her and not where she's going, she slams straight into my legs.

"Whoa, there, sweetheart," I chuckle, then seeing her mother coming up to us, search my memory to dredge up her name. "Crystal, isn't it?"

"I'm Crystal, yes. Heart's old lady. And this here," she picks up her daughter, "imp is Amy. You must be Joker and Lady. We've been expecting you."

"I've met the imp before," I smile. "At Adam's funeral."

Her face creases at the reminder, but she seems a sunny faced woman who doesn't stay down for long. "I remember now. Hey, Amy. You'll have to stop bumping into…?"

"Joker," I supply.

"Oker," Amy gets out, then giggles again.

A woman walking with a slight limp comes through the doorway to the right of the bar. I recognise her as Wraith's woman. "I thought I heard strange voices." She comes up alongside Crystal. "I'm Sophie," she introduces herself. "The VP's old lady. Wraith said to take you up to your suites if you got here while he was out. But you must be parched as well as knackered after your journey. Want a beer first?"

I glance at Lady. He mouths, "Knackered?"

Sophie giggles. "Tired," she translates. Her accent gives away that she's from the UK.

"Er, Joker. We'll just have a cold one then get on our way," Roller suggests.

Crystal, still carrying Amy, has gone behind the bar, and is already expertly one-handedly opening four bottles. We take one each. After raising our bottles together, we start drinking. It's welcome after the long ride.

"Do you want to bring those with you?" Sophie asks.

I nod. Sooner we get our stuff unloaded, sooner the prospects can get going and we can start settling into our new home. Going back outside, I grab my saddle bags, while Petty and Roller get a couple of boxes out of the truck. Sophie, seeing we're ready, starts walking.

"We both up that way?" It's easy to catch up with her, she's moving quite slowly, definitely favouring one leg. Hasn't she got a fake one, or something? Think I heard someone say. But no need to pry now, I'll be here long enough to find out in time.

"Yeah, you're both in together."

I stop dead. Lady bumps into me. Sophie notices. "In together?" I query.

She laughs, a pleasant tinkling sound. "Oh, not that way. I don't mean you're sharing. You're in two suites next to each other. We've given you one of the new blocs which has just been restored. You know this was an old vacation resort, don't you? There's two suites in each bloc, each with its own bath-room. The men all have one each, well, except for Peg."

"The sergeant-at-arms?" I think I'm right. Got to get all the names and positions straight.

"That's him. Well, the story goes no one wanted to share with him, so he got two to himself. He's converted one into a living room and kitchenette."

As we've been talking we've reached the top of a small incline. Not very steep, but enough that Petty and Roller, carrying the heaviest of the boxes, have started to sweat. Sophie indicates the bloc beside us, pushes open the main door, then produces two sets of keys.

"There. This is you. Up to you which you take, left or right. You've both got the same view from the balcony."

Balcony? I cast a sideways look at Lady to see by his expression that he probably thinks he's died and gone to heaven too.

He moves to the right; I go to the left. Sophie sorts out the correct keys then hands them over. Without delay there's two keys turning in identical locks opening up two identical rooms.

Not wanting to gloat too much in front of the Vegas prospects, I simply check he's carrying one of my boxes, and then wave Petty in. Roller carries his next door. Then, without being told, they go back down to start bringing up the rest.

Sophie looks on in satisfaction. "Well, I'll leave you to get settled in. Wraith and Drummer shouldn't be long; they've just taken off to clear their heads. Come down to the clubhouse when you're ready. Oh, and if you didn't know, it's church tonight. I expect you'll be invited. But obviously, being a mere woman, I don't know about stuff like that." Her easy smile softens her words.

Lady and I exchange glances as she walks away. I don't know about him, but I'm not daring to talk, just in case it shatters this daydream I must have strayed into.

I might be an ass sometimes, but even I'm not going to make Petty and Roller bring up all of my shit, so I start walking back down the incline, unsurprised when Lady catches up to walk alongside.

I've lived in the Vegas compound longer than Lady, so I've got more shit to unpack. We've finished bringing his few boxes up before mine, but he continues to help. When we've finished, the prospects chug down the last mouthfuls of beer. We shake hands, slap backs, wish each other well, then they take off. For a moment I watch the truck disappear, hoping to fuck I've done the right thing. Part of me wishing I was in the truck with them, heading back to what's familiar, instead of standing here in very unknown territory.

Carrying the last of my boxes into my room, Lady follows me inside. Without invitation, he goes to the patio door and slides it open, stepping out onto a balcony which must be the same as his. There's even a table and two chairs out there. As he leans over the railing, I stand behind, admiring the same view. It's possible to see for miles, down across a valley and out over to a range of mountains. Looking to the right, mountains rise up high in that direction too. It's so fucking beautiful it's breath-taking. Words are inadequate to describe it.

Lady turns and raises an eyebrow. "Think this will do?"

As accommodation, it couldn't be better. "It'll do." I start opening my mouth to say something else when he swings around, getting up in my face.

"Don't say anything else, Joker. You laid down the ground rules, I'll do my fuckin' best to respect them. But look at this. Two rooms. Two men who're already brothers. We sit out here havin' a beer, ain't going to be anyone to question it. You come into my room, I come into yours. Who's going to say anything?"

He's right. But give in to that, we might take things further. Then start slipping up in front of our new brothers. I've got to put the brake on his thoughts now. "Yeah, we can share a drink. But you ain't comin' into my room after dark, Brother. Everything I said still stands."

His brows draw together, then his shoulders slump. A few moments later his back straightens. "Okay, Joker. Have it your way." He holds out his hand for me to shake it. "Friends."

Lady disappears into his room. After pausing a moment, staring at his closed door, I pull mine to, then turn to begin tackling my boxes. There are drawers by the bed and a closet to hang stuff. Not much different to the set up in Vegas, so I soon have most of my clothes and shit sorted. The boxes of books, mainly Harley manuals and magazines I've picked up over the years, can stay where they are for now.

The luxury of having my own bathroom only really dawns on me when I take a much-needed piss. No more having to visit the heads, pushing past drunken brothers. Well, not here in my suite anyways.

I've just flushed when Lady knocks at my door.

"Thinkin' of going to the clubhouse, seeing what's up. Don't know about you, I could do with another fuckin' drink. First one hardly touched the spot."

Yeah, I can work with that. Sooner we show our faces, sooner we get to know people around here. Start getting accepted.

On the way back down the slope I feel like pinching myself to make sure this compound isn't a dream. But then, it's not the surroundings that are important, it's the men who eat, live and breathe here. If I don't get on with them, if they don't take a liking to me, well, it won't matter none that the scenery is beautiful and the facilities beyond my imagination.

With that thought in mind, it's with a little trepidation that I, this time, follow Lady into the clubhouse, noticing by the set of his shoulders that he's probably feeling much the same. Fuck, it's like being the new kid at school all over again.

The prospect who let us in is now minding the bar. Lady nods to the couple of men sitting at a table, then, getting the priority right, heads straight for the bartender. "Two beers," he demands. His manner makes me grin. Prospecting isn't far back behind him; he'll still be relishing he's moved on from that.

I've just taken my first sip from the bottle when two men I recognise come in. Nudging Lady, I give him a warning. "Drum... Prez, has just come in."

Prez makes a beeline for us, his lips curling up slightly as he nods at the bottles in our hands. I put mine back on the bar as he holds out his hand to be shaken. Grasping mine he pulls me in and slaps me on the back, then does the same thing to Lady. "Welcome, Brothers. You got your shit settled? Accommodation to your taste?" It sounds a genuine welcome.

"Yeah, thanks, Prez." It seems I speak for both of us. The title sounds odd on my lips. It's going to take time to get used to addressing another man as Prez.

"Hey, Peg. Come 'ere." Drummer beckons to one of the men sitting at the table I'd noticed on my way in. When the tall bearded man comes over, he introduces us straight away. "This 'ere is Joker and Lady."

Peg eyes me up before offering a quick nod, then his eyes narrow as he turns to the man at my side. "Lady, eh? That's one fuck of a handle." I cast a glance Lady's way as though seeing him for the first time. Christ, he's so beautiful. My gut churns. In Vegas we'd never given a thought to what we'd called him, but with that name, his good looks…

Lady shrugs and grins. "Started off as Lady's Man, got shortened," he explains. "I've got used to it now." Sweet butts are coming in, Lady makes a point of staring at them, watching them walk across the room moving their hips in an exaggerated way.

Peg lets out an audible breath, then starts asking about our rides. As I answer automatically I realise his reaction, his wariness, confirms how right I am that Lady and I have to be careful here. Being sergeant-at-arms Peg's opinion would hold a lot of sway. He was clearly suspicious about Lady's handle. Hopefully Lady's said enough to reassure him. *Nothing to see here. Just two normal men having a drink.*

Having introduced us to at least one person, the prez saunters off. I see him stop to talk to the VP's woman, she's smiling broadly at something he's said.

The clubroom starts to get crowded. Thank fuck everyone has a flash with their road name on their cut, I'm never going to remember all the handles, well, not for another couple of days at least. Heart seems a good man, clearly thinks the world of his old lady from the way his eyes follow her across the room. Dart is a laugh a minute, and in the looks department almost gives Lady a run for his money. Tongue's got a stud which catches the light as he talks, and he's not shy telling us how the ladies love that he's got it.

Blade, the enforcer, I'm cautious about for now, and he with us, but then, Lady and I have got to prove ourselves before we get fully accepted. Shooter is young, and immediately is deep in conversation with Lady, both finding common ground having only recently been patched in.

A loud roar from Drummer summons us into church, to which we are indeed invited. Hanging back, I wait until everyone's seated, then Lady and I take the two spare chairs placed at the end of the table.

It's a different dynamic from that in Vegas. A similar agenda, but it's clear why Drummer is the prez of the mother chapter, he takes no shit, clearly not as easy going as Red.

I listen, but don't contribute. Being new, I've nothing to say. Just lift my chin as we're given an official welcome. When the position of Road Captain is mentioned, Peg explains he'd been doing that role, and is relieved he's now got someone to pass it onto. When invited I give a bit of a spiel about my approach to the position. I seem to have said the right things, the vote's taken to endorse it, and Heart, who seems to be the secretary, records it.

When the meeting ends, there's a party in our honour, but as they usually party after church I doubt there's much more to it. Except we're the centre of attention. The camaraderie we're offered goes a long way to making my mind easier. *A new set of brothers who I'll have to get to know the peculiarities of, but they seem friendly enough.*

I watch and learn. Soaking up how everyone is acting just as much as what they're doing. Wraith and Drummer are giving the prospect some shit, so nothing much different there. I catch

Lady grinning as he sees it. There is a second prospect, I'm pleased to see. A man called Roadrunner. He appears to be new, an addition since I was last here for Adam's funeral.

When the VP leaves after a quick word with me, I return to people watching, observing a club girl approaching the prez and getting the brush off. Then her eyes sharpen as she finds Lady.

In the looks department, I come nowhere close, attracting female attention or not has never been a worry for me. But I'm not surprised when she comes directly over, audaciously putting her arm around my Vegas brother.

"Hey, you're new. Want to come get better acquainted? I'm Pussy, by the way."

Lady's eyes flick to mine, there's a wealth of questions contained in that one glance. I force myself to shrug, and turn in the other direction, making myself think that it's better if Lady can convince people he's straight. Then there'll only be one of us avoiding the free pussy, but hopefully they'll just think club whores are not to my taste.

I push down the wave of jealousy that burns inside me as I watch him walking away, Pussy's hand clinging onto him possessively as though she doesn't want to risk losing him to anyone else.

My fault. Down to me. I pushed him away. Made it clear there was going to be nothing between us. My fault. Down to me.

CHAPTER 14

ice bike. You really restore it yourself?" I wander around looking at it. If a man had done the work on it, I'd be in awe of the attention to detail.

"I did," the woman who introduced herself as Sam confirms. "Rode it here from Washington too."

That's some feat for anyone, let alone a woman. I'm genuinely impressed. Vincents are a devil to handle, takes a fucking good rider. She goes up in my estimation. While I'm examining it, asking her about where she sourced her parts from, I catch sight of the prez entering the shop. His eyes flare when he sees me talking to Sam. I might not have a man's natural impulses, but I can read jealousy when I see it. Knowing it's important to keep up the pretence, I think fast.

"She's beautiful. Just like her owner."

As Sam blushes, I get a slap around the back of my head. "Enough of that, fucker," Drummer snarls.

I stand, grinning, holding my hands up in submission. "Didn't know you were there, Prez." My eyes flick between the woman and man, sensing there's something there. So I do the smart thing and move on, leaving them to get on with whatever they have to discuss.

My first full day on the compound I occupy myself with looking around and familiarising myself with the setup, including the dynamics of the people who call it home. Viper, who I saw getting a blow job from a whore last night, apparently has an old lady. Guess he gets here what he doesn't get at home.

I wonder what Sam, his newly found daughter, thinks about that. None of my business, of course.

Apart from Wraith and Heart, Bullet and Viper are the only other men with a ball and chain. More old ladies than in Vegas, but not so many as to make it uncomfortable. The benefit is, as I've already found, Crystal's an ace in the kitchen, the food even better than Rosa's. Heart's wife seems a fixture in front of the stove, so far there's not been a time when she hasn't been standing there or by the sink. Carmen and Sandy live off the compound, but come to the clubhouse with their men.

Amy, her two-year-old daughter, takes a little more getting used to, resulting in me starting to look down at my feet instead of around me. If I'm not stepping on toys, I'm inadvertently walking into her. Little minx gets into everything from what I've seen. But all the brothers seem to tolerate her well enough. Not having had anything to do with young kids in my life, it surprises me that I find myself laughing more than swearing at her. The blonde-haired and blue-eyed kid just seems to be a bundle of joy with a way of making people smile.

Prez and Sam have gone out riding, I don't see anything unusual in that. How they return, however, is another matter. They come in hot, the gates flung open and as quickly closed behind them. I'm not surprised when we get a summons into church.

I haven't seen Lady this morning, don't want it to seem like I'm glued to his side, and in truth I can't face him after last night. Seeing him go off with the whore, well, that comes under the heading of things I wish I hadn't seen. *My fault.* I remind myself. *He owes nothing to me. I practically pushed him into her arms.*

As I take my seat, unable to face Lady, I look around instead, slowly absorbing the rising levels of adrenaline around the table. "Seems like we joined in time for the action," I say. "It always this hot down here?" If it is, it makes sense Drummer needed more members.

"Before we had trouble with the Rock Demons we'd had it quiet for years," Prez answers me reassuringly.

I hear a clicking of fingers beside me as Lady puts in, "Looking forward to having some excitement."

His view isn't shared by our new brothers, but then, in recent events, they have lost two good members, even if one was only patched in after his death.

Discussions abound, but no one has any ideas who was gunning for Prez and his woman this morning. He'd clearly been impressed by the way she could ride. Church ends without anyone knowing more than they did to start with.

Prez gets a call then disappears with the VP and sergeant-at-arms to meet with someone called Devil to get more information. I join in the conversations where everyone is discussing what went down this morning, partly to try to get myself up to speed with exactly what potential enemies the Tucson chapter could have. Certainly sounds like life's not going to be boring here. *Fuck me.* Vegas was quiet in comparison. Perhaps getting involved in the action will take my mind off what I can't have. Yeah, I think I've made the right move.

In Vegas, apart from the club whores, there'd only been two old ladies, Rosa and Tiffany. Here there's five if you include Sam in that number—if I'm reading Prez right, that's the way he seems to be heading. Sophie is a barrel of laughs, and enjoys playing on her English accent and using words us Americans don't understand. When Dart, Slick and Viper join the women at a table, I gravitate over in the spirit of forming new bonds. Quite as a coincidence, I end up in the seat next to Sam.

When Drummer returns I start making a promise to myself not to get close to his woman again when for the second time that day I'm clouted around the back of my head.

"Ow!" Rubbing my posterior lobe, I swing around. When I see who it is, I jump up quickly offering him my seat. "Sorry, Prez."

As he glares at me I realise I'm doing myself no harm if he mistakenly thinks I'm lusting after Sam. All part of the front I want to put up. Yeah, I'll just keep this up. A few slaps to the head is worth it if I can fool my new brothers. From a safe distance, I eye Drummer curiously, noticing how he acts with Sam. What was it? Just a week ago he gave no signs he had a woman, living up to his name and enthusiastically going off with the sweet butts in Vegas. *Sam's only just ridden here from Washington*, I remember. Damn, Drummer seems to have been hit hard and fast. It will be interesting to see if she can really tame him, or whether he'll be back to his man-whoring days soon enough.

In Vegas, most days followed a similar pattern, life wasn't boring, but depending on the day of the week, you could normally tell where to find any brother, and predict what he'd be doing. That Tucson is different, I've already had a small taste of. The very next morning though, I'm eating the whole fucking meal.

One-percenter clubs don't abide by government rules, and as such, we're mistrusted, hated. Since they first came into existence, citizens have wanted us shut down. The best result, in their eyes, is to haul all the members in under a RICO charge. It might only be one member who'd committed the crime, but under that act, all members could end up facing a twenty-year prison sentence.

When fucking feds flood in through the front gates without warning the following morning, I fucking wish I'd stayed in Vegas. As they round everyone up, my thoughts of spending the best part of my life behind bars makes me want to scream in frustration and anger. As Lady and I stand handcuffed, staring on with our jaws just about touching the ground, I'm crushed by my burden of guilt. *If I hadn't denied him, had come out, he wouldn't be looking at going inside.* A chill runs down my spine. If they can make that RICO shit stick, we could both become prison bitches.

Fuck this. We transfer clubs and end up in the pen. Risking a look at Lady, guilt slams into me. *He's only here because I came. He could be safe in Vegas.* I don't much care what happens to myself, but him?

As if he's aware of the thoughts running through my head, he shakes his head quickly. But it doesn't stop me blaming myself.

The feds start sorting themselves out, finding they've got a warrant for everyone, with the exception of us and the prospects.

For a moment, I stand holding my breath, not sure how they're going to handle it. But then they check the paperwork once again, then undo our cuffs. *Fuck, being new here, we've gotten away with it.* Doesn't mean I'm not concerned for my brothers who they're rounding up to take away, but at least here, on the outside, there must be something I can do to help.

But once again my jaw drops as they start impounding the bikes, sorting out which rides belong to the brothers being arrested. It seems with a RICO warrant they can take anything.

Trucks roll out with the confiscated bikes on them, men are taken away in other vehicles. The compound sounds quiet when the noise of the engines eventually fades.

"What the fuck do we do now?" Lady, like me, is staring after the dust cloud, the only thing left to suggest our brothers were ever here. As silence settles around us, I realise I have no immediate response.

When Sam steps out of the clubhouse, I'm still standing bemused, never having been in such a situation before. We've been here less than two days, and now the club we've joined is no more. That thought is fucking hard to handle. As the senior member of the decimated Tucson chapter, I do the only thing I can think of. I pull out my phone.

I wave it at Lady. "I'm gonna get on to Red. Fuckin' unbelievable. We transfer to a club that's under a fuckin' RICO indictment."

We're the only two members left. I'm not surprised when the prospects exchange worried glances.

"You gonna walk out on the club?" Marsh asks, sounding disgusted.

For the first time letting his anger break through, Lady kicks at a stone on the path. "There ain't no fuckin' club!" he shouts. "What the fuck d'ya expect us to do?"

"Hang around until Drummer and the others get back." Marsh is nearly pleading. "The feds didn't find nothin', so they got nothin' to hold them on."

I exchange glances with Lady. He looks as shocked as I feel. We transferred to another chapter expecting life would go on much the same, just in different surroundings. Now look what's fucking happened. *There is no club.* Everyone taken away. Though the prospects are hopeful, I can't see Drummer and the rest being released. Or not for the next two decades.

Misinterpreting our silence, Marsh steps up. Prospect impresses me when he says, "Oh, for fuck's sake. I'll ring the ol' ladies, tell them the news. There's no point them comin' to the compound." He seems to think someone has to take point if Lady and I are going to bail. Not saying we're doing that, he just needs to give us a minute to get our heads straight. And get some advice. What's happened here is well above my paygrade.

Roadrunner gives me a disdainful look, then, ignoring us, turns to Marsh, and seeming to have written us off for now, seeks his counsel. "The businesses?" he asks. "I could cover the strip club. Fuck, once this gets out who knows what panic there'll be or what staff we'll lose."

"Sandy manages the restaurant; I'll tell her to keep on with that and perhaps give you a hand with the strip club?" The two prospects nod in agreement with each other.

Fuck me, now Sam steps up. "I'll keep the shop going. It'll be slow, but we want something for them to come back to, can't get too far behind and let the work pile up." I look at her sharply. She seems positive they'll be released, but then I put that down to optimism. She's a strong woman, she's not going to roll over and give up.

Although my audience is depleted, I keep up with the persona of the person I've decided to portray. I eye Sam up with a leer on my face. "Of course, there is one benefit, there's three sweet butts and Sam. I like those odds."

"I'm Drummer's woman," she replies firmly.

Again I look her up and down. "There's prison rights, you know?"

Giving a shake of her head, she rises to the bait. "And what the heck are they?"

Lady grins. "When an ol' man's inside, the other brothers can see to his ol' lady's needs if you get what I'm sayin'?"

"Oh no. You…"

"Messin' with ya, darlin'," Time to end this now. I'm not aiming to worry her; just convince her I've got the same needs as everyone else. I grin. "Just foolin' around tryin' to lighten the mood." Then I try to set the prospects at ease. "Look, I'm not plannin' to jump ship, but I'm out of my depth here. We all are. As I said, I'm going to speak to Red. Get some advice. Fuck, this has been one motherfucker of a mornin'."

"Think we're lucky to be fuckin' breathin' free air," Lady puts in. "Hate to think of our brothers chained up in cells."

"We need to get protection on them inside." I'm all seriousness now. "They won't be safe without. Red can help get that shit organised."

Sam says she's going to the shop to sort out what needs to take priority now she'll be virtually the only mechanic. Road tells her he'll be along in a minute. While they're sorting themselves out, I place that call to Red.

It goes about as expected. Red's shocked as hell, but says he'll get onto discovering where they're being taken, start getting them some cover while they're inside. As well as instructing the club lawyer—I hadn't thought of that.

Now I've taken charge, Road's looking at me for direction. I nod and point down to the shop, releasing him to go help Sam.

Lady's talking to Marsh. "Blind leading the blind here. You've not sat around the table, and we're so brand spankin' new we ain't got a clue what's going on. You're right that we need to sort out the businesses." He pinches the bridge of his nose. "Need to get to talk to Dollar as soon as possible."

"Red didn't suggest it, but maybe we can get some brothers here from Vegas and the other chapters," I contribute to their discussion. "Can't keep things going without manpower."

"They may get out. They might not be able to hold them."

I slap my hand on the young prospect's back. It's down to me to keep their spirits up. "You're right, kid. That's what I hope. But it's best to plan for any contingency. That's what…"

The sound of a shot cuts me off.

Lady's gun's in his hand before the echo fades, as is mine.

"What the fuck…"

"Marsh, stay here." Christ. If someone's coming gunning for us, he might end up being the only man left. It's then I remember the sweet butts. Prez had told them to keep their heads down low while the feds were here. They need someone to direct them. "Look, update the girls with what's gone on, okay? Get them to stay away."

"Crystal's here in her suite with Amy. Sophie as well."

Damn. "Keep them out of sight, yeah?"

His eyes are flicking left and right, his mouth dropping open as he gets my meaning. Without giving him a chance to say anything more, Lady and I start making our way in the direction the shot had come from. The shop. Where Drummer's woman and Road are working.

The gates are wide open. The prospect is lying in a pool of his own blood. Lady starts shouting for Sam and running into the shop. But she's gone. Fuck. Fuck. Fuck!

I'm on my knees beside Road. "Lady," I yell out. "Go ask Marsh who they call on for medical help here." Christ, I'm so new, I haven't even had a chance to ask. Well, you don't expect to be faced with a man very possibly dying in front of you the second day after you've joined a new club.

"They took Sam…"

Road's come to. His face is deathly pale, his voice barely above a whisper.

"Who?"

I don't want to pressure him, but any knowledge he's got is best said before he stops breathing.

"Jackson. She knew him from Washington. Set up…" Then he passes out again. Fuck, he's not the first man I've seen bleeding out, but the prospect's got a future in front of him. He doesn't deserve to die like this.

"Hang on, man. Hang on."

"Marsh has called a man named Doc. Medic apparently. He's on his way." Lady's hand comes down on my shoulder, his fingers give me a squeeze. Then he speaks to Road, "Hang in there, Brother. Help's comin'."

I notice he's given him the honorific only reserved for patched members. But right now, I think he's right to. The prospect's life is on the line.

While we're waiting on the medic I take off my shirt and try to plug the hole where blood is pouring out. My medical knowledge leaves a lot to be desired, but I'm sure that's the right move at least. I continue applying pressure to the unconscious man.

When Doc arrives, an ex-Army medic he tells me, he checks Road over, then asks Lady and I to carry him up to the clubhouse. Marsh hasn't done a very good job of keeping the old ladies out of sight, they're now all waiting, worried, in the clubroom.

Sophie rushes over as soon as she sees Road. "Road!" Her hand covers her mouth. "Is he...?"

"Give me a bit of room, Soph," the gruff medic spares her a quick reassuring smile. "Let me see what I'm dealin' with here."

Thinking fast, she leads him into one of the crash rooms at the back of the clubhouse. I give the doc some space to treat his patient, figuring Sophie can assist where needed. Then I look around me. Crystal's eyes are reddened as she tries to keep Amy occupied. From her face I take it Marsh has explained what happened this morning. Can't keep that quiet with all the men gone. Knowing instinctively Lady would be better at dealing with distressed women, I decide it's not here that I'm needed.

"You stay here," I tell Lady. "I'm going down to get those gates closed."

He nods, distractedly looking in the direction they've taken Road. Something about him worries me. "Hey, man. We'll get through this, okay?" I risk putting my arm around him. A quick hug as I'd do to any of the men. Though no other man would cause my body to tingle. "Brother. We've got the other chapters at our back. Just need to get through today, okay? I'll speak to Red again later. We'll be okay. We *will* be okay."

"Could have been you, Joker," Lady says quietly. "Could have been me."

"But it wasn't." I wait until he turns to face me. Fuck, I've been in the club longer than he has. Haven't seen shit quite like this, but enough that I'm better able to cope. "We have to let the cards fall where they will, Lady. Just focus on the fact that for now, we're okay."

"You reckon they got what they wanted? Or will they be coming back?"

"From what Road managed to tell me, they wanted Sam." For a second I worry about who's going to be breaking that news to Drummer. First though, we need to find out where he and the rest of the brothers are being held. *Fucking feds. Left us wide open.* Their fault Sam has been taken.

"What should we be doing?" Lady swings around to face me. "If we're the only ones here, it's up to us to find Prez's woman."

It is. Right now I don't have a fucking clue where to start. Hell, I'm only a Road Captain, know about planning routes, know shit about locating a kidnapped woman. "I'll speak to Red, get him on board. Keys can start investigatin'." Jesus, I thought I'd left the Vegas lot behind. "Need to get access to Drummer. Don't know shit about Sam 'cept where she's come from and that Viper's her dad. Need to know more to get tracin' her." Fuck, I don't even know her full name.

"Go get that gate closed." Lady seems to have snapped out of it. "Don't want any more visitors today."

When I've slid the gate shut and locked it, I spend a while looking around in case I can find any clues. Of course, I find nothing. Tyre tracks, yes, a plenty. But with the visit from the feds earlier, it's hard to tell which are fresh. No one's conveniently dropped a calling card. Without knowing more about this club's business, I haven't a fucking clue where to start.

But hold on. There's a car coming up the track. For a second I slide my hand into my cut ready to take out my weapon. Until I recognise it. *Shit.* As if I haven't enough to deal with. *More fucking women.*

I open the gate but go to the driver's window. "Carmen, Sandy," I nod at them.

"What the fuck's going on, Joker? Crystal rang…"

Fucking women can't keep their mouths shut. "You can't do anything here, Sandy, best you go back…"

"Go back when we don't know what's going on? Not fucking likely," Carmen huffs from the passenger seat.

Defeated, I raise my hands up and step back to let them through, realising I've as much chance of getting them to turn around as of stopping the tide coming in.

Nothing more I can do here. Making sure the gate is again locked and secured, I make my way back up to the clubhouse. Entering I smell the odour of freshly brewed coffee and find Crystal's in the kitchen pouring cups. She turns, barely before I've put my foot over the threshold. "What's going to happen to Heart, Joker?"

Of course she must be worried out of her mind. Knowing there's nothing I can do to reassure her, I try my best, the words *twenty-year sentence* running around my head. Fuck, Amy would be a full-grown woman before her dad got out. But no need to plant that thought in Crystal's head just yet. "We'll have to wait and see, sweetheart. Got no idea at the moment." I lean my back against the counter. "Been in touch with Red though. He's getting the club lawyer involved."

Putting the coffee pot down, Crystal waves her hands in the air. "I feel so useless. I don't know where to start to try and help. Don't know who to call." Her eyes go to her daughter, playing happily under the table, unaware of what's going on. Her mother takes a deep breath. She's trying to keep it together, when I can see she's on the verge of breaking down. There's no doubting the love Heart and Crystal have for one another. If he goes away for a long time, it will destroy her.

"Hey, don't look for trouble before we know what's going on. Red will get it handled," I try to raise her spirits.

"He could go inside for life." *Ah, so Crystal isn't as oblivious as I thought she was.*

Fuck, I know what she's thinking, that she might never see him this side of a prison wall again. "Hey, don't get ahead of yourself." I firm my voice. "Let's find out what they got on them first. Keep doing what you do best, Crystal. Heart needs you to be strong for Amy."

As she straightens her back, I realise I might have been wrong in my first assessment. When she gives me a sharp nod, I see not a weak woman, but a strong biker's old lady. Then she turns and places several coffees on a tray.

Carrying cups I return to the main room and pass them around, finding Lady having a similar conversation with Sophie, while Sandy and Carmen are hanging on his every word. I don't miss the plea for help he sends me. But fuck me, comforting the women isn't something I do best.

I try though, but don't know if I help much. I doubt anyone would appreciate a joke right now. It's a waiting game for all of us.

It seems an age before Doc finally appears, at least he's got good news. "Road's going to be alright. It was a through and through. I've managed to stop the bleeding and sewn him up."

My brow creases. "The bullet?"

He shakes his head. "Not in him, thank fuck."

Which means it might be down by the gate. If I find it, there's a remote chance it might provide a clue as to who took Sam. Probably not, but it's an excuse to get me into the fresh air. There's nothing I can do here except sit around waiting, trying to second guess what's going on.

As I once again leave the clubhouse, I notice lightning flashes down Tucson way and pause for a moment. Someone it seems is getting one hell of a storm. But here is dry, with only the sound of distant thunder. There's a good chance the storm will be heading our way. If I'm going to search for that bullet, better get to it before any rain comes.

The blood drying on the ground shows me the exact spot where Road fell, so I have a good look around there first. Finding nothing, I extend my search, trying to follow the trajectory from how he appeared to be hit. Thunder comes again. Sounds like the storm's getting closer. Only… as the roar grows louder, I realise what I'm hearing is not thunder, but bikes. Lots of bikes. *Red?* Nah, he couldn't get here that quickly. *Another club?*

Fuck! What if I'm faced with the Tucson chapter's enemies? All by myself. They're coming up fast. No time to go warn Lady. It's only me at the gate. *Nah, Lady's best where he is. Safer for him if I try to take out as many of them as I can before they can get to him.* He'll hear the shooting, he'll be prepared. Sliding my gun out of my pocket, I check the gate is still secure, then stand firm. Maybe it's today I'll be facing that bullet. My face is grim as I realise for the first time in my life, I wouldn't welcome it.

I widen my stance. The bikes draw closer. They're in sight now. *Right, how many am I dealing with here?* I start to count them up.

Hang on. That's… It can't be. I'm imagining things. But, fuck. It fucking is. My gun's back in its holster and I'm running to open the gates. Gravel spits up around me as Drummer, Wraith, Mouse and some of the other Tucson members shoot past me, not stopping as they ride up to the clubhouse.

I might not know why or understand it, but all I can think is, *thank fuck.*

<h1 style="text-align:center">Chapter 15</h1>

I follow the bikes up to the clubhouse, so shocked my hands don't feel steady. One minute I'm ready to face down an enemy, the next I'm staring at brothers I never thought I'd see on the outside again. *What the fuck is going on?*

Entering, seeing at least half of my brothers there, I stare at the prez as though he's an apparition, unable to process what's right in front of my eyes. *How the fuck?* If the feds were going to hold anyone, it would have been him. Something's going on.

Drummer doesn't wait for me to come back to my senses. "What's the news on Road?" he snaps. Then when I don't immediately answer, continues, "Well, man?"

Giving myself a mental shake I repeat what Doc had told me. His mind eased on that score, he follows Mouse into his office.

Fuck. What the hell is going on?

"Joker?" Wraith sees me brushing my hand over my head and comes over. "You okay, man?" He puts his hand on my shoulder. "Laid a lot on you today but couldn't warn anyone…"

"He doesn't know," I rasp out, suddenly remembering what will be important to Prez. Shrugging Wraith's hand off I start to take a step in the direction Drummer left in.

"Who doesn't know what?" The VP's arm shoots out, holding me back.

"I've got to tell him, Wraith. It's Sam, she's been ab…"

"Abducted. Yeah, we know. It was part of the plan. But it's all gone to shit," the VP updates me with a scowl.

The plan? What the fuck?

"Yeah, she's fuckin' gone." I swing around at the sound of a loud crash. Viper's picked up a chair and thrown it over the bar causing bottles to smash. "She's fuckin' gone!" he repeats, screaming at the top of his voice.

I'm standing looking on in horror. Momentarily I'd forgotten Sam was Viper's daughter, but now there can be no mistake. Man's on a mission to destroy the place. Lady's corralling the women out of the range of his blind temper. Wraith disappears after the prez. I go to try and calm Viper but only just avoid a fist in my face. He's completely out of control.

Sandy stands and approaches her husband, but whatever she says doesn't go down well. "You don't understand shit!" Viper starts yelling at her. "Don't pretend you know how I'm fuckin' feelin'."

"For fuck's sake man, calm down." Wraith must have warned Prez as he's appeared and puts himself between Viper and Sandy. "Shut the fuck up and listen to yourself. It's not down to Sandy she's gone."

Viper's eyes burn into his. "No, that's on you! You fuckin' set her up." As they stare each other down, Viper's shoulders slump as the rage starts to leave him. When he speaks next, he all but whines, "What's happenin' to her, Prez? What the fuck is that bastard doin' to her?" Oh fuck, now he's got tears streaming down his face. *Poor fucking man.* What can it be like to find your daughter, only to lose her?

What could I have done? Why had I let her go down to the shop with only the prospect with her? Should I have gone myself? What the fuck is happening here? What plan had the VP alluded to?

As Drummer takes his arm and leads Viper to the bar, I exchange a glance with Lady. He's looking equally perplexed as he shakes his head, mouthing clearly, *What the fuck?*

Once Viper's quieted, I need to speak to Drummer. Come clean. Take the blame for fucking up. Leaning over, I tell him quietly, not wanting to wind Viper up all over again, "I didn't know what the fuck was going on, Prez. Thought the feds had taken you, thought it was a RICO indictment or something." I pause. "It's on me. I let Sam go to the shop. Should have made her stay here…"

His cold grey eyes stare at me. "You did right, Joker. That was what we intended to happen. Just went to shit after that. That's on me and no one else. Look, I know you were, and still are, in the dark. We'll have church in a few and fill you in."

Thank fuck for that. I start to get annoyed. *Why weren't we in on this plan everyone keeps mentioning?* Prez starts to move, but there's more he needs to know. "I called Red," I tell him quickly. "He's started getting you protection, which, as you're standing here, you clearly don't need. He also is contacting the lawyer."

Prez's cheeks hollow as he inhales a deep breath. "Thanks, Joker. You did what you thought was best. But now, looks like I've got a call to make to stop Red getting the cavalry mounted up." He slaps my back as he walks off to his office.

At least he understands I did the right thing, even if it wasn't necessary. That annoyance starts to turn into anger. *Why were we kept out of the loop?* Do our Tucson brothers not trust us?

"What the fuck d'you think's going on?" Lady comes to join me. "Can't make sense of anything I'm overhearing." His face is drawn. "We knew no more than the fuckin' prospects. Starting to think we're not in favour here."

"You and me both." I grab a couple of unbroken beer bottles that escaped Viper's wrath and open them up. "Don't like this, Brother. Don't like it at all." I look around. "And where are the rest of the fuckers? There's only half the club here. Are they still being held by the feds?"

Lady doesn't get a chance to respond as Drummer suddenly appears and roars, "Church! Now."

"Guess we're about to find out." I raise my eyebrows at Lady.

I stomp into church, kick out my seat and take it. But as I listen, my rage starts to fade, as I comprehend Lady and I had had it easy. That fed raid? Well, seems my brothers all thought it was for real. Thought they were facing decades in the pen. Fuck.

A set up? From beginning to end? Prez offers his apology, not only to us, but to the whole of the club. I listen carefully, trying to make sense of what I'm hearing.

Sam, fucking brave woman that she is, had volunteered to let herself be abducted in order to break a slave trafficking ring. Satan's Devils had been working with the feds, although most of us didn't know it. As Prez goes through that plan at last, I nod my head. *Yeah, should have worked. Should have been easy.* Feds emptied the club to allow Sam to be taken without bloodshed. *Failure one. Road got hurt.* Prez is continuing. I'm relieved when I hear the other brothers are free, but still chasing those traffickers.

Failure two was that things didn't go down the way they should have done. They've lost track of Sam and now have no way to trace her. *She's been fucking bought. As a sex slave.* I glance at Lady; his eyes are wide. Hell, no wonder Viper's so angry. As Prez explains how she was driven away by a stranger, I see Viper tensing all over again.

Viper interrupts the prez. It's understandable, all he wants to do is be out there searching for his daughter, not sitting around the table discussing it. But Prez has a good point. She could be anywhere in the state, or out of it by now. We need more information before we go running off like headless chickens.

I nod when Drummer offers the explanation Sam's father finds so hard to accept. "Agree with you, Prez. We gotta do this smart." I earn myself a sharp look from Viper. We might have a bead on the fucker who's taken her, but there's no telling where he is. He's got countless properties under his name.

Half the meeting seems to be taken up with calming Viper down. From what they're saying they know Sam's abductor isn't going to waste time before he starts molesting her. *Raping her.* We can't spend days trying to find her. We've got to narrow the location down. *I hope we can find her before he touches her.* I like Sam. I wipe a bead of sweat away. I'm all on board with this now. My eyes fix on Prez, noticing that beneath that steel in his face, there's anguish he's barely able to hide. My suspicions are, while his words say different, he'd actually prefer to be taking action like Viper wants. Doing something, anything, to save the woman I suspect his feelings run deep for.

Beside me, Lady's tense. He, too, appreciating the urgency. I watch Prez. It's clear to see he's worried sick about his woman, but he, at least, is keeping his shit together. Christ, I'd be beside myself if it was Lady who went missing. Would pull out all the stops to find him. My reaction would be more like Sam's father's…

Hell, why am I fooling myself I could look at Lady like any other brother? I can't. He means something. Means something to me. I risk a glance in his direction, only to find him watching me with a similar expression to the one that must be on my face.

Then I feel a squeeze on my knee. A barely there touch. A gesture of comfort. *Needed that.* His hand moves away as quickly as it had settled on me. It was enough.

At last Mouse appears with information. He's got a good lead. Not guaranteed, but fucking better than we've had up to now. It's not only Viper who's anxious to get going. As only half the Tucson members are here, leaving Drummer short, Lady and I are both on our feet. Don't want to be left out of it this time.

In moments we're on our bikes, Drummer leading, Wraith and Blade behind him, then Viper and Beef. Lady and I ride at the rear, followed by the crash truck being driven by Mouse. Throttles are twisted all the way as we break speed limits to get to our destination as fast as we can. *Gotta save Sam.*

When we find the house and approach, I start to feel less of an outsider. Devils are Devils from whatever chapter; we seem to fit in with the team as though we've always worked alongside them. We help search the house, until eventually, after despairing that despite everything we've come to the wrong place and Sam must be somewhere else, we find a basement. That's where we find her.

Just in fucking time. It was close, but the fucker's dead and she's rescued. I shake my head in wonder as Sam goes up in my admiration all over again. Having faith Drummer would find her, she put up one hell of a fight and did what she could to save herself. I just don't like to think about what would have happened had we arrived any later. She's hurt but walking wounded.

Did I ever think life in the Vegas chapter was boring? I can't remember doing so, but that word certainly doesn't apply to Tucson. But never once does the thought of bailing enter my mind. As it turns out, rescuing Sam isn't the end of it.

Lady and I haven't been here a week but we're thrown right in the thick of shit neither of us would have ever dreamed of being involved with. Alongside our new brothers we find ourselves preparing for an influx of trafficked women. That's enough by itself, but then we discover the club is being used as bait by the feds to catch the traffickers.

Having no option, I go with the flow, doing what I'm asked to. With almost no time to catch my breath, I fall into bed each night and drop into a dreamless sleep. Maybe this was what I've always needed. So much action I have no time to contemplate anything.

When the trafficked women appear on the compound, I'm assigned along with Beef and the prospects—Road refusing to be kept out of it even though he's injured—to keep them safe. The feds, having purposefully let slip where the women were hiding, are leading the traffickers straight to us. But not providing any support to take them out, their view being the loss of a few one-percenters is just collateral damage. The rest of the club will be facing off against the ring who took Sam, possibly with cartel support. While I'll be safe babysitting women.

I hate being separated from Lady, especially as he'll be on the front line. But I'll do what I've been assigned, can't do anything else. Can't explain why I'd prefer to be near him, can't tell anyone I trust no one else to have his back.

No, I can't come clean about my reasons.

I try to take my mind off the danger he's in by doing my best to comfort the scared, traumatised women, reverting to my usual backstop, being true to my name. They've been through some fucked up shit, and I slip easily into the role of making them laugh. Strangely enough, they sense I'm harmless, even when I make jokes full of sexual innuendo. While I'm playing the clown it helps hide my concern about Lady. I've got the cushy job babysitting, Lady's putting his life on the line. So I joke and laugh, make others relaxed, while I know part of me would die were he to be killed. That bullet might come into play after all.

It's not just the rescued women we're protecting here, all the old ladies and sweet butts have taken refuge in the house too. It's crowded, but broken laughter rings out as I act the fool. Beef's playing along too. Some of the less traumatised women are giving as good as they get. Sophie, well, the VP's woman goes up in my estimation. She's egging me on, and I see her assessing the mood around us. I nod, letting her know I'll take my cue from her. Beef winks by my side, he's playing along too.

Suddenly she lets fly with a scrunched-up paper cup. "You cretins! You wankers! What the bloody hell made you say that?" The cup misses me, but Sam, just entering, has to duck to avoid it.

I hold out my hands in supplication. "She asked me how big I was…"

"She meant how bloody tall you were, you tosser! She didn't want you to offer to show her your dick!" Sophie's hands are on her hips.

A muffled giggle comes from a pretty twenty-something with auburn hair, with her hand over her mouth unsuccessfully trying to smother her laughter. The other women range from a slight quirking of their lips to outright grins. Sophie now winks at Sam letting her know she's got a good handle on the situation.

I'm enjoying the very English insults thrown my way. What Sophie's saying doesn't upset me. Neither does it make me contrite.

"Look, I can show you the goods and prove it." My hands go to the zip of my jeans.

Cries of 'no, put it away' and 'oh god, not that' come from the women, and a few more give an actual laugh. I'm putting on a show for them, at the very least taking their minds off their predicament.

Sam, however, decides to call an end to it. If I'm honest, I'm relieved. "Even in the unlikely event I'd like to see your cock, Joker, I think Drum would cut it off if he knew you'd been waving it around."

"Fuck, Sam. Didn't see you there." I pretend to do up the zip I never actually took down and remove my hands smartly. "Prez would have my balls." *Phew. For a second I was wondering how far I'd have to take it.*

As Sam takes over, I, at last, have a moment to myself. Wandering into the kitchen for a drink of water, it dawns on me I wouldn't have been able to have found my place here without Lady, or be able to deal with all the shit that's been thrown our way. His silent support, his discreet touches when no one's looking. The heated stares he gives me behind people's backs.

We've never spoken about that first night on the compound, but since that day, I've not seen him anywhere near a whore. But that doesn't mean he hasn't been using them.

What's he doing now? Surely if he'd been killed I'd know it? My joking with the women had been for me too. Now alone for a moment, I feel crushed by the weight of my worry. I return to the main room, just for company.

Thunder crashes, lightning lights the darkened sky. Time drags. *Lady. Where are you, Lady? Are you safe? Don't you dare fucking die.* Just when I'm about to run out of jokes, Dart appears. He looks tired, rainwater's dripping off him, but there's a light shining in his eyes. Crossing the room fast, I approach him, my eyebrows raised in question.

He grins. "It's done."

"Anyone injured?" Beef's at my side, asking the question I'm reluctant to hear the answer to. *Don't let Lady be hurt.*

"Tongue took a bullet to the leg, but he'll live. Prez got a graze to his arm," he replies. Seeing Sam approaching, his voice lowers as he relates how Drummer's been hurt. "One of Red's men got shot, not sure who, but it's not serious. We're celebrating down at the clubhouse. Your old prez is here, Joker. In with Drummer at the moment, but you might want to come down and show your face."

"Red? Who's with him?" I'm quickly wondering who of my old crew was injured, while feeling a huge sense of relief he hadn't mentioned Lady.

"Didn't stop the fuck to ask," Dart replies.

"Is it safe to leave them?" Beef eyes the women.

"Yes. Prospects can stay until Prez lets them stand down."

I don't need any more persuading. I'm out of that house before Sam corners Dart and hears the problems are over for herself.

Instead of going straight to the clubhouse, I detour into my suite, needing a moment to pull myself together. I stand with my back to the door, wondering why the fuck my eyes are leaking. Then I lean forward putting my hands on my knees. *Lady's okay.*

The last few hours have been all but intolerable. *I should have been fighting at his side. Should have been in a position to protect him.* But I'd been given a job to do by my prez. I'd done what I could, kept up the spirits of the women, while being as worried as any of the old ladies about their men. I've never been in that position before, never had to worry about someone I had feelings about, being safe myself while they were in danger.

Someone I had feelings for.

Fuck it! I pull myself up, wiping my eyes on the bottom of my tee. *Feelings for Lady.* Damn the man for following me here. Damn him for going off with the sweet butt. Damn him for making me jealous, for making me worry, for knowing my whole fucking world would fall apart if he were no longer in it. Damn him for fucking existing.

Fuck it. *Fuck him.* And damn it, fuck me. It took this situation to make me admit the depth of emotion I feel, that it's more than just as a brother in the club. But I've blown it. I pushed him into the arms of the whore. *I* told him I wasn't interested. In suppressing what I am, I pushed my only chance of happiness away. How can I stay here? How can I take another situation like this? Worrying myself sick about him, but him never knowing.

Pressure at my back tells me someone's pushing from the other side. Someone trying to come in without knocking. Swinging around, I pull open the door.

Lady's outside, his face tense. "Wanted to check you're okay. Expected to see you down at the clubhouse. There's a drink with your name on it. Red's here, he's in with Prez at the moment, but Crash, Twister, Hammer and Sarge are asking where you are. Came to get you."

"Who's hurt?" I ask, just as tersely.

"Hammer. But he'll be fine. Doc's patched him up, then he headed for a beer saying it was the best medication."

Yeah, sounds like Hammer. I should go down and meet my old brothers. I shouldn't be hiding up here. I shouldn't be staring at Lady, my eyes sweeping from his head to his toes, checking for any injury I haven't been told about. His clothes are wet, his hair dripping. But Dart was right. He's not hurt.

I feel dizzy with relief, now I can let go of my fear that I wouldn't be seeing the man now standing before me alive again. *No more of this. No more wasted chances. No more lying to myself, or to him.* Closing the distance between us, I stand only inches apart, then rest my forehead against his.

For a minute that's the only part of us touching. *It's not enough.* My hand moves seemingly of its own volition, and curls around the back of his neck. He tilts his head slightly, my mouth finds his. A gentle meeting of lips, hesitancy on both our parts. Mouths softly moving against each other, until his opens, and my tongue probes in. Exploratory movements, unsure of my welcome.

But he responds, our tongues advance and retreat, our lips caressing. After a moment we move apart, our actions synchronised.

Lady stares at me searchingly. "Was fuckin' worried about you, man. Knew if they got through you wouldn't have the manpower to stop them."

I huff an incredulous laugh. "You were worried about me? Fuck, it was you facin' danger head on. Fuckin' killed me, Brother, not being with you."

His hand comes up to cup my cheek. "What do you want to do, Joker? What is this?"

I lean into his touch, "Fuck if I know. My position hasn't changed. Ain't gonna come out in front of the brothers. But I can't keep this inside anymore." I cover his hand with my own. "Need you, Lady."

"Scott," he says softly. "When we're alone. Call me Scott."

"Josh," I introduce myself almost formally.

"Like that. Like your name. To me, you're no joke."

It's as though a spell has been woven between us, neither of us wanting to break it, but both hesitant to do more. Lady looks almost nervous, but from all the times I've been giving him mixed signals, I can understand why. He'll be wondering if I've pulled him in, only to push him away again.

"No more," I try to reassure him. "Not again. I'm in this, Scott."

He still looks uncertain, his eyes fixed on mine. "We'll take this slow, Josh. All new to you, isn't it? Slow and steady. No need to go fast. At your pace, Brother. As slow as you need it."

"Taken the first step," I reply. For me it's a big one. Starting a relationship with a man, allowing myself to enjoy a man's closeness, is admitting I'm gay and embracing it. No longer hiding or trying to change.

"We can be us here. In private. No one needs to know, Josh. I'm down with that. Whatever this is, wherever this goes, it's just between us."

"Here. In private," I confirm. Then admit, "Don't know what I'm doing, or how to do it."

"Together. There's no rule book. No right or wrong way of doing things. It's just us, and what feels right."

I thought I'd be horrified, I thought I'd hate myself. This is the one thing I've tried my hardest to avoid. To be attracted to another man, and to act on it. Well, I may be going to hell, but right now I feel like I've reached out and grabbed my own piece of heaven. Something feels this right? How can it be wrong?

"We're expected at the clubhouse," he reminds me.

I indicate the state of him. "You ought to put some dry clothes on while you've got the chance."

"Get out of my wet things?" Something flashes in his eyes. When he shrugs off his cut and his hand shoots up to the back of his neck to swiftly pull his wet tee over his head, I recognise what that spark was. *A challenge.*

He's perfect. Lithe and slim. Muscles ripple on his chest with the movement of his arms. One brow rises as his hands move to the zip of his jeans. *Oh fuck, is he…?* He is. He unfastens the button, starts to lower the zip. There's a bulge in the denim, and fuck, my cock's growing too.

Then he smirks. "I'll just go next door and put some fresh clothes on."

My mouth drops open, but whether in relief or with disappointment I'm not certain.

CHAPTER 16

Scott takes only a minute or two to change. In no time he's back, dressed in a fresh black tee and dry jeans which hang low on his hips with his Satan's Devils cut completing the ensemble. Even with his damp hair loosely tied back into a bun, he's a sight to see. *What the fuck have I just agreed to?* My hands shake. To stop them I clench my fingers into fists.

If I do this. If I go through with it. I'll be giving in to those base leanings, the ones I've successfully suppressed over the years. I can't do it. Then I look at the man striding confidently at my side as we walk down the track. *Can I take my chance? Christ, I've lusted after him for months. Can I give in? Can I accept myself and the way I am?*

Red's nowhere in sight when we enter the clubhouse. He's still in a meeting with Drummer and Snake, who's the San Diego prez, and the officers from Tucson. As Lady goes across to our old brothers Dart raises his hand, beckoning me across. Leaning over, speaking into my ear with a careful eye out that none of the old ladies or sweet butts are around, he updates me.

"Twenty bodies?"

"Yeah, thereabouts." He jerks his head in the direction of the rear of the clubhouse. "They're in a truck out there."

They were fucking lucky the police hadn't come searching. Twenty bodies. *Fuck!*

Dart nods again, this time toward the room where we hold church. "Guess that's what they're talking about in there." I'm still reeling. *Twenty bodies?* In Vegas we buried such remains far out in the desert, but only one, possibly two at a time. My mind boggles at the thought of so many. Dart's face grows serious. "Hope you're handy with a spade."

"Where do you hide them?" I hadn't thought to ask before. It's hardly the first question you ask when you join a new club.

"You? We, surely." Dart looks at me sharply, having picked up on the pronoun I used.

"God," I press the heel of my hand to my forehead. "Must be Red and the others being here. Sent me back, you know?"

A hand lands on my shoulder. "We know," Beef growls. "But you're a Tucson member now, right?"

I can make no excuses. I transferred good and proper.

"Anyway," Beef starts, "to answer your question, usually up in the woods behind the compound. But this number? Fuck. No idea how we'll handle it."

As I start silently running through options for disposing of the high body count, Lady appears from the direction of the rooms out the back. Following him are Crash, Sarge helping Hammer, and Twister bringing up the rear. Seeing they're heading this way, I raise my chin in greeting.

"Joke, you old fucker." Having propped Hammer on a stool, Crash slaps my back. "Come here, you asshole." He pulls me in for a hug. My other Vegas brothers treat me the same way. I'd hate to admit it, but I'm still more comfortable with them than the brothers here. *That's because you keep yourself to yourself.* Crash is right. I am an asshole.

"How's the leg?" I turn to Hammer.

"Fuckin' sore. But Doc got the bullet out and I can ride."

"No, you can't," Twister interrupts.

"Fuckin' can…"

As they continue to argue, I tune them out. "Dart, Beef, meet some of the Vegas fuckers." When they turn around, I make the introductions where they're necessary, then we've all got beers in our hands and are, of course, discussing bikes.

"Hey, listen up!" Drummer's voice cuts through all other noise and conversations stop dead. "Need some volunteers."

It's not necessary to ask what for. My hand, and everybody's, shoot up. Hammer's too, but Twister moves fast to grab his fist and tries to force it back down. The ensuing hustle catches Red's attention.

"Uninjured men only," my ex-prez shouts.

When I find out the plan for burying and hiding the bodies, my jaw drops open. But I'm game, fuck, yeah. I'm game. I slap Lady's back, seeing he too is grinning with amusement as alongside my brothers from Vegas and a few from San Diego—including a guy called Marvel who keeps asking questions about the Tucson club—we spend the next few hours digging a trench. Well, Viper's machinery does the hard work, the manpower's for carrying bodies and covering them up. By the end of the afternoon we've built an off-road trial bike track winding its way through the forest behind the compound.

Then, fuck me, someone's brought Road's trials bike up. Now my mouth's wide open again as Peg sets off around the track. His face almost splits in two with pleasure, now it seems no one wants to miss out on the action. One by one we all do our part to make the track look well used, and have a fucking good time doing it.

We start timing the runs which means it gets competitive. I find I'm a natural and come in the fastest. Lady's only behind me by a second. As I step forward, I notice Red beaming, and taking temporary ownership of us again as he shouts something about Vegas boys being the best.

But, well, I'll be fucked. Just when I thought I was going to be declared the winner, Sam steps up. *Bitch can't beat me, can she?* But that's exactly what she does. Christ, Drummer's old lady can ride. Who'd have expected that?

"Hey," Lady nudges me. "You reckon Prez will let her join the club?"

Not for the first time this afternoon, my jaw drops. "Fuckin' hope not."

Jeez. What a day this has been. Starting off with a war approaching and the tension that goes along with preparing for that. Then my fears when I was separated from Lady, my conversation with said man, and finally, after dealing with the unpleasant task, I've had one of the best times of my life. I made sure I was cheering for the Tucson boys, and laughed loudly when Crash, well, crashed.

My conversation with Dart and Beef, cementing things with Scott, and now the impromptu race have solidified my feelings for Tucson. When Wraith slaps me on the back and thanks me for keeping the women's spirits up, I realise it's only now I've mentally accepted the transfer. Notwithstanding, of course, the convenient accommodation arrangements.

My satisfaction with my new life, the grin on my face, stays with me until later that evening, and the party that had been interrupted then restarted is still going on. In deference to Hammer's injury the Vegas men haven't yet gone home. I'm standing alone by the bar, beer in hand, one eye on Lady who's giving me occasional glances of promise for the night to come, when Red chooses that moment to approach me.

"So, how you doing, Joker?"

"I'm doing good, Red. Good," I repeat more firmly. Perhaps, had he asked me yesterday, he wouldn't have gotten such a positive response.

My old prez turns around, his back against the bar, his eyes surveying the room. "And your sister?" he enquiries conversationally.

Shit. I try to think fast, but before I come up with a suitable reply, he swings around and stops me, holding up his hand as if to stop another lie coming out of my mouth. "There isn't a sister," he informs me, his sharp gaze burning into my face. "Keys looked into you on a request from Mouse."

I swallow hard. Not even bothering to deny it, I just ask, "Drummer know?"

I'm holding my breath, but the answer is what I dreaded, though suspected. "Yeah." Presidents don't keep secrets from each other. No, only people like me do that.

Putting down my beer bottle before my shaking hands drop it, I feel the blood drain from my face. "He gonna kick me to the curb?"

Red's quiet for a moment. "Had a conversation with him. Told him you were a good brother," his eyes flash, "for an asshole, that is. He said he'd seen that for himself."

That's one thing, but his response hadn't addressed the question I'd asked. I'd lied to not one, but two Satan's Devils' presidents.

Red rolls his eyes. "Fuck it, Joker. Leaves a bad taste that you left on a lie. Wish you hadn't felt it necessary. Drummer would have taken you anyway. You must have had good reason for wanting to jump chapters."

What if he asks me the reason? "I did," I confirm, hoping he doesn't continue to pry.

"I'd have let you go anyway, Joker. Don't know what you're struggling with, you never let anyone in. But have my suspicions."

Fuck! If I didn't go white before, I think I do now. *He can't have guessed, can he? Did Crash say something after all?*

"Jesus, Joke. You alright?"

Red's voice seems to echo through a long tunnel as I vaguely realise I'm falling, dropping to the ground. I've forgotten how to draw air into my lungs, my vision is blurring.

"Joker! Joker! You're okay, man. You're having a panic attack. Back off, Red. Let me see to him." I hear Lady's voice as he snarls at Red. *He mustn't be here right now.* Still struggling to draw air into my lungs, I gasp, but they seem to have forgotten how they work. "Slowly, Joker, slowly. Breathe with me." His tone is now gentle, soothing but firm, as I feel hands on my face, raising my head so I'm looking into his eyes. "Breathe. In, out, That's it. You're okay, Brother. That's it. That's good."

My lungs begin working again. Staring at Lady, I inhale and exhale in time with him, the oxygen working to clear my head. Somehow I manage to pull myself to my knees, embarrassed when I see the circle forming around me.

"Can we give him some fuckin' space?" Lady's glare and his words show he's noticed the same things.

"Back off. Nothing to see here," Drummer, who must have appeared while I was in my shameful state, roars out. Then he too crouches down. "You okay, Brother?"

I nod, not wanting to show weakness in front of the prez. Grabbing the bar I pull myself up, wishing instead I could simply curl into a ball and that the floor would open up and swallow me.

"You've had a panic attack," Lady informs me unnecessarily. I've had them before, but none as bad as this. None that have come up so fast without warning, leaving me unable to control my breathing.

"What triggered it?" Drummer, Red and Lady are the only three close now, though raising my eyes I see concern reflected in the faces of the brothers who might have moved away, but are still casting glances at me. Concern that I'll fall apart and let them down, I expect. I'm unable to answer the question, but as it turns out, I don't have to.

"PTSD," Lady snaps. "Obvious, isn't it?"

Red shakes his head. "You know the details, Lady?"

He won't… "Nah, but it's obvious, isn't it? He served."

Red clears his throat. Drummer looks at him. Red continues a conversation that though I'm here listening, I don't appear to be a part of. "I think he thought he was going to have to leave the club."

Drummer rolls his eyes and swears under his breath. "His sister? Or lack of?"

"Yeah," Red confirms. His face looks drawn as though he feels guilty for bringing it up.

For the first time someone addresses me directly. Prez. "Don't like being lied to, Brother. But you've proved yourself a loyal club member. Don't know why you felt you had to get your transfer based on untruths, but you did. It's done. That's that."

So easily? My eyes flick between Red and Drummer. "I needed to get away from Vegas."

The corners of Red's mouth turn up. "To come somewhere quieter."

Drummer barks a loud laugh, then his face grows serious again. "Is that what caused this, Joker? The business that happened today?"

Maybe that had been a part of it. But I can't admit that. "Look, Drum, it won't happen again…"

"Shit, man, not askin' you to make any promises you won't be able to fuckin' keep." Drum wipes his hand down his beard. "PTSD can't just be shaken off."

I need to give him something. "Red's right, Prez. Club means everything to me. Thought you were going to make me leave. Once the thought took hold, well…"

Lady speaks for the first time in a few moments, saying through gritted teeth, "Joker's right there, Prez. Nothing is more important than the club to him."

I try pushing away from the bar, and yeah, my legs do support me. "Sorry for causing a disturbance, Prez."

Red's hand shoots out, landing on my arm. "Stop right there, Brother. Look around you. A large percentage of these men served and if they didn't come back damaged themselves, they know people who did. Ain't no one here judgin' you."

"Not just the men," Drummer puts in. "Women too. I just wanted to know if there's a trigger we can avoid so it doesn't happen again."

"Don't threaten to throw him to the curb," Red suggests drily, raising his eyebrows toward Drummer.

"Can we talk about this later? Joker's done in. I'll take him back to his suite." Lady's glaring at both Drummer and Red.

"There's no need, Lady," I contradict. "I'm fine now." In truth, I feel like I've run a marathon, and my head's aching. But I need to prove to these men that while I might have had a debilitating panic attack, I can bounce back just as fast.

Drummer gives me a searching look, then waves his hand around the room, bringing my attention to the fact I wouldn't be the first to leave. The party's winding down now. No sweet butts are in sight so that means they're fully occupied. While we've been talking most of the Tucson brothers have retreated to their rooms, only Crash and Twister are still here from the Vegas Chapter.

"I'm going to join my woman," Drummer informs me. "Suggest you do the same. Well, not join me with Sam, of course. Get some fuckin' rest."

"I'm going to get some shut eye myself," Red agrees.

Seeing Lady is looking at me anxiously, and more than anything, wanting to escape before he says or does anything to give me away, I finally shrug. "Been a long day," I agree.

Drummer's hand lands on my back. "You got that right, Brother. You got that fuckin' right."

Lady lets out a long breath. "Come, Brother."

Our suites are adjacent to each other. No one's going to bat an eyelid if two brothers walk out together. Trying to convince myself, I follow him across the now almost empty clubroom, only a few diehards left, up to our suites.

CHAPTER 17

Lady goes into his room and pulls his blinds down, immediately turning on a light. I do the same, but my door pushes open a minute later, and he steps in.

"Not tonight, Lady." I can't take any more, not now.

Ignoring me, he pushes past and goes to sit on the bed. He leans back against the headboard, swings his legs up, crossing them at the ankles. Elbows bent, he places his hands behind his head. *Fuck me if he doesn't look right lying there.*

He might look relaxed, I'm anything but, as his sharp eyes examine me. "Understand you better now, Josh."

In response, I crease my brow.

"It *is* all about the club for you, isn't it? You fuckin' lost it when you thought you were going to be sent out."

I go over, perching awkwardly on the end of the bed, keeping distance between us. Splaying my legs, I put my head in my hands. "It's the only family I've got, Scott." Following his lead, I use his government name.

"You don't lie to family."

I round on him. "I thought I had to. I needed to get away. It was spur of the moment to make something up. Something that would explain why I wanted to switch clubs."

"You're lucky you got away with it," he replies. "Got to have lost some trust there."

I know. I'll have to do something to earn it back. I'll do anything.

"You're never going to come clean, either, are you?" Suddenly he sits up, pulling up his knees and wrapping his arms around them. "Tonight showed me the depth of your feelings, Josh. How much you fear losing all this. How it would destroy you if the club ever found out about us." He bows his head, then raises it again. "I understand. I do." His hands brush his cheeks. "Not gonna be easy, but I want this. Want *you*. I'm not going to give you away, okay?"

I know it's hard for him to understand. He doesn't have the demons I do.

"If there was a pill I could take, I would."

"Fuck, Josh. You're gay, not fuckin' ill," his voice snaps, drawing my attention to the red flash down his cheek bones. His gaze fixes on me for a moment. Slowly his tension seeps away as quickly as it had flared. "You ever had therapy?"

Now my own temper rises. "Fuckin' therapy? *Therapy?* You know I fuckin' have."

One hand waves dismissively. "For fuck's sake, Josh, I don't mean some shrink trying to make you straight. I mean someone who'll help you accept yourself for what you are."

I stay silent. There wouldn't be enough words in the dictionary for me to come to terms with that. Oh, I've given up thinking I could change, but be truly comfortable with who, what, I am? Never.

Lady, *Scott*, shuffles his way down the bed until he's close enough to reach out his hand and touch my face. That gentle caress gets me so twisted up I don't know what to do. Half of me wants to pull away, to remind myself I should be disgusted at the touch of a man. The other half wants to lean in, to take the physical comfort he's offering. My desires and fears are tearing me in two.

Suddenly he stands, my skin feels cold as his fingers leave my skin. "Get some sleep, Josh. We'll talk in the morning."

He leans down, his lips brush my hair, then he's gone. I clench my fists to stop myself calling him back.

I hear movement in the suite opposite, then it all goes quiet. Still I stay sitting just where he left me. The events of the day, of the evening and night, keep running through my head. I'm blowing hot and cold. I'm confusing the man. Christ, everything I want is within my reach if I just had the guts to reach out and take it. We could keep it quiet, have an illicit relationship which no one would find out about. Keep to the privacy of this bloc which houses our two suites. No one has to know what happens after the door closes behind us. To have someone to lean on? To share everything with? *To make love to.*

But what if we can't keep it hidden? A vision of my father's face swims up in front of my eyes, and the words of the counsellors at the camp roll around my head. *You're disgusting. You're not normal. You've got a choice, Josh.*

A choice? Why would I choose to be different? Why would I choose unnatural impulses if I could change? Why would I choose to be a social pariah?

Then I see Scott in front of me. So confident in his skin. So unashamed of his leanings.

My thoughts lead me nowhere. Eventually I go through the mechanical motions of getting undressed and sliding under the cover, but sleep evades me. Now it's my embarrassing panic attack which comes back to haunt me. To all but pass out in front of two club presidents? I can't let that happen again. Who'd want to trust their life to a brother who could collapse at any time?

Morning brings no relief, no answers to my dilemma. Over the next few days things are strained between Scott and myself. I don't know what to say to him and he can't read me. I told him I would commit to him, that there would be no going back, but the way my body reacted when I thought my membership of the club was being threatened has shown me, and him, where my priorities lie. Staying a Satan's Devil and being determined to do nothing which might threaten that.

It's easy to see that Scott is disappointed, but he doesn't try to get physical again, doesn't push me to do something I don't want. Fuck, who am I kidding? I want him as much as I want my next breath, but can't allow myself to do anything about it.

Days stretch into weeks. We both settle into the new club. Things have calmed down, no feds, no trafficked women. I'm slipping easily into my role as Road Captain, my experience already proving useful on a couple of runs. Though I was wary about speaking to him, despite having lied to the prez, he's mentioned nothing else about it.

Brothers here start to turn into friends, though the fact that I'm different keeps me slightly isolated. Everything seems to be ticking along until one evening in the clubhouse.

"Brothers!" It's not unusual for Drummer to appear and shout for our attention. But something about the expression on his face shows tonight isn't normal. Dart and I stop our discussion about mods to his bike, both pushing away from the bar.

"What's up, Prez?" the VP calls out.

"Heart and Crystal have had an accident. They're in the hospital."

There's uproar, confusion. All brothers talking and moving at once. One of our brothers is down. We're all going to the hospital. No one wants to be left behind. Though pressed, Drummer has no more information at the moment. Fuck. As I go to my ride I'm hoping Heart and Crystal are going to be okay. Heart, I've come to respect. Crystal? Her vivaciousness is infectious. She's almost always resident in the kitchen with her daughter, Amy, getting under everyone's feet. Their presence makes the clubhouse more homey. Christ, I hope it's not serious. *Fuck. Let them both be okay.*

When we return later that night, the atmosphere is sombre. "Fuck, Joker. Why?"

Lady sits beside me on a couch which has seen better days. It dips, making our bodies slide together. For once I don't move away. We've just received devastating news, it's only human to want comfort. We're not the only ones getting close. Beef's standing with his arm around Rock's shoulders. Peg's standing close to Blade.

I lean my head into my hands, at last addressing Lady's question. "Fuck knows why, Lady. Why was someone like Crystal taken? And Heart? What if he doesn't pull through? They've got a daughter, for fuck's sake."

"Club will be there for Amy. Whatever happens. But the little tyke's lost her mother. Nothing will make up for that."

I shake my head. "Might be better for Heart never to wake up. He was so in love with Crystal." The thought brings moisture to my eyes, and quickly I swipe it away.

"Crystal was one of the good ones, Brother. Why the fuck did it have to happen to her? We'll all miss her."

He couldn't be more right.

Since the first busy week after we arrived, things have been quieter, and I'd settled into a routine, but Heart's accident, or whatever it was, has turned that on its head.

When we meet in church it quickly emerges that there are a number of things that don't add up, shit we need to get clear. Life starts to heat up again. And so do my thoughts about my relationship with Scott. A brother lying close to death, the loss of his wife, makes me think again about wasted chances. But how could I start something when I've so firmly pushed him away? How have I the right to keep changing my mind?

I think about him constantly, even when I can't find the words to approach him. One evening, I'm relaxing back on the couch while he's playing pool, finding myself unable to take my eyes off his ass when he leans over the table to place a shot. Unable to look elsewhere, or stop inappropriate thoughts for this place and time running through my head. Around me, the sweet butts are in action, and for once I'm not worried about the swelling of my cock as it could have been a result of the live porn show going on around me. It's as if everyone is celebrating a life that Heart may not have much longer to live.

"Hey, looks like you could do with some help with that." A female voice interrupts my thoughts.

Before I can deter her, Pussy comes down on me, her knees either side of me on the couch, and proceeds to give me a lap dance. Lady, fuck, Lady looks up from taking a shot, having a clear view of what's happening.

He's fucking smirking.

Pussy's rubbing herself all over my cock which is hard for the man I've been watching. From the expression on his face, he sees everything I've been trying to hide. As my eyes meet his, he holds my gaze while Pussy reaches down to my zip, unbuttons my jeans and takes out my throbbing cock. I pretend it's him. His hand. His fingers squeezing.

He stares, his eyes fixed on my face. His hand moves to his crotch as if showing me he's hard too.

I'm transfixed. The stroking of my dick, his expression. He's licking his lips now, drawing my attention to his full mouth. *Could be my cock in there…*

My balls start to tighten.

"Gonna come for me, big man?"

Pussy's brash voice brings me back to my senses. My cock deflates as I push her off, the spell completely broken.

"What is it?" The sweet butt sounds puzzled, her lips purse.

"Not in the mood," I tell her shortly. Then I zip myself up and stand. *Gotta get out of here.*

I'm walking up to my suite when Lady catches up. "Thought you were making a point in there."

I don't answer him until we're at our bloc, then after going through the outer door, tug him into my room. Once inside I forcibly swing him around and push him up against the door.

"It was you flaunting your fuckin' ass that got me hard, not that fuckin' sweet butt."

"Yeah?" he asks, a wide grin on his face.

"Yeah," I confirm.

He gives another of his smirks that I both love and hate. "What you going to do about it?"

I move in close, allowing him to feel my once again swollen cock rubbing against his crotch. I'm met by his equally hard one. I'm driven by yearnings I can't control, for a moment can't find my voice to explain my desires. Then it comes out. What I wanted all the time Pussy was sitting on me.

"I'm going to do nothing. You're going to suck my cock."

The grin slides away and his eyebrows draw down. "Ain't one of those two bit gigolos you used to use, babe."

He takes me aback. Fuck. He's right. That was what I was trying to dismiss this as. A one-off urge to get my dick some relief. I start pulling away but he places his palms on either side of my face, then his lips are on mine. Our mouths clash together, teeth meeting. When he sucks my bottom lip into his mouth and gently nips it, I groan. His taste, it's like coming home.

Our tongues meet, glide together, diving deep as though neither of us can get enough. All the time our hips are moving, pressing together, our cocks grinding into each other.

Then his hands drop away. This time it's not a woman working my belt, but a man. It's Scott.

"Scott," I breathe into his mouth in desperation, easing my hips back to give him space.

With quick precise movements, he has my zip undone, my fly opened enough to take out my cock. His hand feels like a dream come true. Rough, calloused fingers, knowing exactly the pressure I like.

It's not enough.

Lowering my hands, I fumble with his buckle, my impatience making my movements awkward. Then I've got it undone, and copying his actions of a moment before, I soon have his dick extricated and in my hands.

He's long, hard as steel, with velvety skin stretched taut. My thumb slides over his slit, feeling the wetness that's his pre-cum. Experimentally I fasten my hand tight around him, my fingers able to encase him. Then I apply pressure, and slide my hand up, then down, just as if I was jerking my own dick, hoping he too likes the motions I enjoy.

His balls. Moving my other hand down, I cup one then the other. He moans loudly, his voice vibrating into my mouth where we're still joined.

Slow, speed up, tight, loose, then a rhythm that's sustained. I feel a tightening in my balls, the tingling in my spine at the same time as I feel him swelling. He's going to come. The signals enough to take me over at the same time.

Still linked with our tongues in each other's mouths, I gasp, he growls, and months of pent up frustration seem to shoot out of my dick as I come harder than I've ever come before. My legs feel weak and start shaking.

Lady's lips gentle on mine, then he pulls back, placing a tender kiss on each side of my mouth. His eyes, soft with dilated pupils, stare into mine. He pushes me back a little to give himself room to tug his tee over his head, then, as my gaze is transfixed by the beauty of his skin, he wipes first my hands, then his own, then cleans off our stomachs.

Still standing by the door, both our heads bend so our fore-heads meet.

"Felt fuckin' good, babe."

"Scott, I…"

His fingers grab hold of my hair. He pulls back my head. "Don't you fuckin' say it, Josh. Don't you fuckin' dare pull away now. You've given me one taste, and don't doubt for a moment that I don't want more. A fuck load more. So don't dare fuckin' back out now."

One side of my mouth turns up. "Was only going to tell you that was the best fuckin' hand job I've ever had. Couldn't pull back if I wanted to."

His arms are around me, my head on his right shoulder, as his is on mine. The same height, we fit together easily. "You will," he tells me softly, speaking into my ear. "I know it. Expect it. You'll have regrets. But we'll deal with them. Together."

Chapter 18

Will I regret this? At the moment, I don't see how I possibly could. But he's probably right. While my body's still humming, my blood still racing through my veins, the last thing I want is to lose this connection between us.

"Stay," I plead. "Stay with me tonight."

"Not pushing this fast. Gonna take this slow, Josh," Scott mumbles. "But there's nothing more that I want than to hold you all night. Lie beside you. Knowing you're close."

I've asked, he's accepted. Now I don't know how this goes. All of a sudden I feel self-conscious, already regretting my impulsive request.

But Scott understands without me saying a word. He gently pushes me back to give himself room, then bends and takes off his boots and socks. Standing again, he pushes down his still unfastened jeans, tucking his deflated cock back in his boxers.

"Alright to use your bathroom?"

He's giving me space. Speechless, I nod. My eyes follow him as he walks over and shuts the door.

Moving fast, before he comes back, I strip out of my clothes, like him, retaining my underwear, then slide between the sheets. Leaning my head back on the pillow I throw one arm up over my eyes, unable to prevent a small smile coming to my face. I've come the closest I ever have to having meaningful sex with another man *and I don't feel guilty*. Well, I frown, not yet.

It's only minutes before he's back. Now he's beside me. When he lifts his arm, I raise my head a couple of inches, allowing him to pull me into his side. His skin, next to mine, is warm. Tentatively I touch his chest, exploring the ridges of his strong muscles.

"Feels good, babe."

I don't let my fingers travel south, nervous, even after what we've just done, knowing I'm not ready for more. As his hand covers mine, moving it back up his chest, I know we're on the same page.

I suspect he's trying to put me at ease when instead of talking about our fledgling relationship, he starts a different topic. "Fuckin' hard seein' Heart like he is."

"I don't like sittin' with him, Scott. Watching those fuckin' monitors, fearin' they'll stop that incessant beepin'. Not knowin' whether he's with us or not. Fuckin' kills me."

"I hear you, Josh."

"Sam and Drummer are good with Amy."

"That they are. Lookin' after her as though she was their own. Poor kid can't understand why her mom and dad aren't there for her though."

"She's a tough kid, she's already bouncin' back." I've been pleased to see tonight she's been laughing.

He suddenly turns onto his side, his eyes peering into mine. "I want you to go to therapy, Josh."

This sudden change of subject takes me aback, and it takes me a moment to respond. When I do, it's with an excuse. "There's too much going on, Scott. I can't take time away from the club now. We've got the police hanging around, Heart in the hospital, who the fuck knows who gunnin' for us, and Slick's old lady's sister involved in a child groomin' ring."

"I'm not talkin' about startin' tomorrow, babe. But tonight, what happened between us felt so right, I don't want to take the risk of it hittin' you hard. I'm in this. All in. But you do need help. You're not the first I've known come through the conditionin' you went through with lastin' effects. And not good ones."

"Scott…"

"Let me have my say, huh?" When I nod, he continues, "It's vital we get the right therapist. Not someone who'll set you back. Let me do some research, look into it, okay? See who people recommend."

"The club won't know anyone…"

"Not talking about the club, babe. But there'll be groups for people like us in Tucson. I'll do some askin' around. Find someone who can actually help."

"I don't see how they can."

"You've been handlin' this shit alone for far too long, Josh. Let me in. Let me help." He blinks a couple of times, then asks, "You ever been to a gay club? An LGBT support group?"

My eyes widen, silently telling him not to be stupid.

"You ain't got a tribe, babe. No one to talk to. No one who understands."

"I've got my brothers," I object.

"All straight," he scoffs. "You can't talk to them as they wouldn't understand you. Imagine a group of people who all know what you're going through. The challenge of being something different to the norm."

"Social rejects."

Shaking his head, he tells me sadly, "We shouldn't be. Rejects is the wrong word. People who are generally misunderstood."

"I'm not going to a gay bar or club." What if the brothers saw me?

He pulls me to him again. "Just let me find someone for you to talk to, okay? With your past all bottled up in there," he taps me on the forehead, "you'll have it with you for the rest of your life. I want us to be together, but I'll tell you this, Josh. I can't take much more of you pullin' me in, then pushin' me away."

I go quiet. Right now I want him, am relishing being this close to him. But in the morning, what will I feel then? I know what I'll do. I'll dress, put on my cut, straighten my shoulders and go down to meet my brothers as though nothing remarkable has happened. Unable to admit I've just had the best sexual experience of my life with a man who I realise I'd be lost without. Worse, I'll ignore him. No little looks, no touching.

It's the threat that eventually he'll have enough that hits me like a blow to the gut, even though I always knew what I was risking. Tonight wasn't making love, making out more like. But it's whet my appetite for more. As much as I'm hiding my sexuality from my brothers, I'm hiding it from myself, trying to suppress it. That's not fair to Scott, and, being selfish, not fair to me.

I know how much damage that fucking gay conversion camp did, building on what had started at home. I could turn my back on it physically, but mentally it's with me every day, haunting my nights through my nightmares. I'm thirty years old, what choice have I got? Living how I am is killing me. If Scott walked away, maybe that bullet would be my only answer. I owe it to Scott to try. For the first time I start to think, I also owe it to myself.

Before I can change my mind, I let the words come out. "Set it up. I don't see how therapy can do any good. But I'll give it a go."

A long exhale as Scott gives a heartfelt sigh of relief. "That's all I can ask, babe."

Silence descends. I close my eyes, thinking he's going to sleep. Startled when he suddenly asks, "What do you make of the new prospects?"

"Jekyll and Hyde? Boosted the ranks, that's for certain." We've got four prospects now.

Scott chuckles. "Hyde's already fucked up."

That he has. "Slick's already saying he'll never get patched in."

Another soft laugh in agreement. When it goes quiet again, I hear him softly snoring.

No nightmares haunt me tonight. I wake in the morning feeling more rested than I have for years. And in a fucking great mood. A good morning kiss from Scott certainly puts a smile on my face.

My phone starts vibrating, then does it again. Putting it perilously close to throwing itself off the bedside table. Picking it up, I see a message from Drum.

"Shit. Church. Now. Something must have happened last night."

Wasting no time, Lady picks up his discarded clothes and disappears into his room to get fresh ones. After only the absolute necessaries in the bathroom, I join him outside. Before very long we find we missed all the excitement while we were having a quiet party for two.

Slick, Drummer, Wraith and a couple of others rescued Ella's sister Jayden, but only just in time to stop her rape by multiple men. After killing them, moving the bodies and burying them, they had fun in the storage shed with the one man they'd left alive. The one who'd groomed Jayden. Diego. Diego Herrera. While regretting that I missed out on all the excitement, I notice the name seems to strike a chord with the members who've been here longer.

Marvel, recently transferred from San Diego, together with myself and Lady, sit looking puzzled. Lady's the first one to ask, "Who are the Herreras?"

"A family who's got their hands in too many twisted fuckin' pies in Tucson. They breed like rabbits," Dart tells us.

"We should leave them the fuck alone." That's Peg, always looking to the club's safety. "If they find out it was us that shot them up last night, killed their punters and two of the family, they'll be comin' for the club. They've got their own fuckin' army."

Another discussion I can't be part of. May have been here a few months now, but there's still shit for me to learn about this new city I live in. Keeping quiet, I listen to them discuss the possible repercussions and fallout from the rescue of Ella's sister carried out the previous night.

Poor fucking little girl. Only fourteen and been through so much already. I know how hard it is to get over something that happens in your formative years. I feel so fucking sorry for her. I risk a look at Lady, the pain in his eyes shows me he's connecting the dots too.

Suddenly my attention is caught. Prez has made a suggestion that Slick violently objects to.

"If your answer's to send Ella and Jayden away, I'm going with."

Wow. Slick's been here a long time. He'd leave the club for his old lady without a backward glance? When I'm refusing to even think of doing similar to be with Scott. That gives me pause for thought.

When discussion reveals the Herreras could well find out who was responsible for killing members of their family, I exchange another wide-eyed glance with Lady. Seems the Tucson club is livening up again.

Prez raps his fingers on the table. "We could hide our heads in the sand, divorce ourselves from this shit. Send Jayden away and lose a good fuckin' member with it," he jerks his chin toward Slick, "and still end up in a fuckin' war."

Wraith's been quiet, and now has his say. "I agree. But at the moment we're going into this blind. We need to find out what we can about this family, and see if it's even possible to take them all out. It's gonna be one fuck of an operation. Fuck knows how many we could be up against."

It's time I made a contribution. "The way these gangs work, or how we've seen it in Vegas, is that their foot soldiers have no loyalty. Cut off the head of the snake, the ones who pay their wages, and they'll be too busy lookin' for other jobs rather than seekin' revenge."

Wraith's not sure. "Don't forget they're family. It might not be as simple as that."

"So we hit all of them." Slick glares at Wraith.

"It would make Tucson a lot cleaner." Rock tugs at his ear.

Drum wipes his face wearily, he looks tired. "We've got Heart in the hospital and are tryin' to track down who ran him off the road. And now we're proposin' to go up against a family with far more manpower than ourselves." Breaking off, he gives a little laugh. "And I was hopin' for a bit of fuckin' peace and quiet."

Peace and quiet seems not to be the norm in Tucson.

Heart. Yeah. We still don't know who's responsible for the accident that killed his wife, and will quite possibly take his life too. But we do have one enemy we can target. When Drummer calls a vote, most don't hesitate to say 'aye', and those that do, only for a second. The vote gets recorded. We're taking on the Herreras.

As we leave church Lady pulls me to one side and whispers in my ear, "Sure you don't want to join a gay club? Might be a bit of a smoother ride."

I bark a laugh, mock punching his arm. "Can't take the heat, Brother?"

CHAPTER 19

With so much going on in the club and members having to rotate to sit with a still unconscious Heart, Lady and I don't have much alone time together for a couple of days. Marsh, the prospect, gets patched in. He's given the handle Paladin, as young Jayden seems to think the sun shines out of his ass, believing he was personally responsible for rescuing her.

Drummer's ploy to impress on the Herreras the resources we've got at our beck and call means the other chapters all descend on Tucson. It's good to catch up with the Vegas members again, but chaotic and rowdy. When Drummer gives a speech rallying the troops, and members from all the five chapters begin chanting 'Ride Satan's Devils, Satan's Devils Ride Together', I feel a lump in my throat, proud to be part of this extended family. By the time I return to my room I'm drunk off my head, able to do nothing other than collapse onto the bed.

I vaguely remember Scott undressing me.

In the morning I wake with a banging hangover.

The other chapters have left a couple of men each to support us, so the clubhouse is crowded, all the crash rooms taken up. Drinks and conversation flow freely, and that first headache isn't the only one I have.

Only a day or so later, we have a do-over when the full contingent of the other chapters arrive once again for the very sad occasion of Crystal's funeral. Standing next to Lady I discreetly wipe moisture from my eyes as her coffin is lowered into the ground. I might not have known her long, but from the moment she greeted us on our arrival at the compound, I'd taken to her. It isn't fair how the good die young.

After the funeral even Crash, Sarge and Cobra, together with Lost, San Diego's VP and a couple of his boys become quieter, knowing they're here for a reason, there's a job to be done. The mood is serious, the clubhouse becomes quieter again, and without the additional encouragement, I'm better able to manage my alcohol intake.

In the Vegas chapter we had an uneasy relationship with the police, but as some were in our pocket, we didn't have raids unannounced on the club. Or cops turning up out of the blue. But that's what happens here. For some reason the cops, or one of them at least, wanted to help Crystal's mom—who a blind man could see in no way resembled a responsible adult—get custody of Heart and Crystal's daughter, Amy.

There are several meetings behind closed doors which leave me a touch uneasy.

Hearing Scott come up to the bloc, I open the door to my room. "Word, Brother."

"Josh." He pauses, his eyes raking over me. "You're a sight for sore eyes." Self-conscious, I don't know how to take his compliment. Just stand back to give him room to come through the door. "What's on your mind?"

I stand with my arms folded, speaking aloud what I've been thinking. "Do you get the feeling we're being sidelined?"

Giving me a sharp look, he crosses to the bed and sits down. "Kept out of the meetings and such?"

"Yeah."

"We're new to the area. Don't know the faces yet. Don't know the background of what's going on. These men have been brothers to Heart for years, Amy's grown up in the club. Slick's an old timer. Of course they'll rally around..."

"I don't think Drummer trusts me," I blurt out, interrupting him. "After that lie about my sister."

"And he doesn't trust me by association? Come off it, Josh." He sighs. "Look, I don't see Tongue, Shooter, Marvel or Rock, to name a few, playing a big part either. We get updates at church."

Updates, sure. They keep nothing from us, still, "I'd rather be doing something than just hearin' about it."

Scott tilts his head to one side. "See, I can more easily go along with it. Prospectin' ain't so far back for me, I'm still enjoyin' my seat at the table. In Vegas you'd been patched in, what, six years? You're used to being in the thick of things."

"Don't want to be treated like a prospect."

Another loud exhale. "You're not. But to some extent, we both need to prove ourselves. We're still an unknown quantity." Suddenly he grins. "Now, are you going to give me some lovin', or pout all night?"

It's been two nights since we brought each other satisfaction. Two nights since we slept in the same bed. As I gaze at him, see the perfection lying on my bed, wondering how the fuck I'm so lucky to have such a gorgeous specimen of a man interested in me, my skin tingles in anticipation of his touch, and my cock begins to lengthen.

He meets my stare, the grin slips off his face. His eyes become heated as he licks his full lips. He slides off the bed and approaches me, his expression becoming so intent I feel like prey being stalked by a predator. Tonight, there's no doubt he's in charge.

Close enough that I can feel the warmth of his breath on my cheek, his hands go to the back of my head and for a second he holds me securely in place. At last our lips meet. Gently at first, a teasing caress, a brush full of promise of decadence to come. A little more pressure, a swipe of his tongue has me opening my mouth allowing him to sweep inside.

He holds me tighter. Our lips now meeting with almost bruising pressure. I follow where he leads, mouths mashing together, our tongues duelling. My cock thickens under his onslaught, his groin presses close and as another hardness meets mine my hips make little jerks, a pressure building that will soon need relief.

I moan, he groans, or maybe it's the other way around. Our mutual arousal making us one being, our identities merging, our humanity almost forgotten as we press closer together, our cocks rubbing against each other as though we're animals in rut.

He pulls away, breathing heavily. My lungs heave in time with his. "I want you in my mouth. Want to taste you."

Fuck. That sounds so good to me. I want, need, the same thing. "Want to taste you."

He pushes my cut over my shoulders, gently throwing it over a chair, then pulls my tee up over my head. It gets stuck on my nose, I raise my hands, shaking with desire to help him. Then he lays his palms flat on my chest, rough fingers smoothing the skin, reaching my nipples and gently tweaking them, as if I need more stimulation, sending a tingling straight down to my balls.

Need him naked. I mimic his actions, but with more urgency. Ripping his cut off and chucking it on top of mine, then tugging at his shirt. He helps when it gets caught on his hair. This is no choreographed dance; this is our desperate need to remove all obstacles between us.

He unbuttons my jeans, as I take down his zip. Without words, we each start sliding down our own jeans, a brief moment of mirth when we both need to bend to the floor to remove our boots.

I toe mine off quickly, shrug off my pants, then, after a brief hesitation, slip out of my boxers.

I'm naked before him for the first time.

His intake of breath, the sharpening of his eyes tells me he likes what he sees. Reverently he reaches out, gently tracing my cock, the soft touch making it twitch and bounce up.

"You're fuckin' beautiful, Josh," he says huskily.

His veneration does the impossible, making me harden to the point I think I'll explode. Quickly I pull his hand away, placing the heel of mine to the base of my cock.

"Give me a second," I beg hoarsely, closing my eyes and willing the churning in my balls to subside. There's nothing I want more than to feel his mouth on me, can't peak to soon, but he's driving me close to insanity.

He's smirking, but his facial muscles are taut. *I'm affecting him too.*

"Get on the bed," he instructs.

With jerky, not quite in control movements, I obey. Following me down, he kneels over me, his legs either side of my head, and offers his cock to me.

As I take it first in my hands, then bring it to my mouth, he leans forward, placing his fingers around my dick. His tongue licks the inevitable pre-cum that's already leaking. I do likewise to his, the first time I've tasted a man's essence. It's salty, slightly bitter, but is like nectar in my mouth.

I groan around him as he places his lips around the head of my swollen appendage and copy his movements. The hum he elicits makes my hips jerk. As he bucks above my face the movement pushes him in further between my lips. I realise my actions are having the same effect on him.

I take him in deeper, my hands controlling how much I have in my mouth. I swallow, he growls and starts to pump, small movements forcing me to take more of him inside. I gag, he pulls back, I draw him back in again, trying to relax my throat against this unfamiliar but welcome invasion.

"Fuck, Josh. Babe, I can't last."

Neither can I. I massage his balls, tightening my hands around them, trying to take his whole length in my mouth. I swallow again, and feel him start to swell.

"I'm coming," he warns me.

"With you," I manage to stammer out.

I'm full of sensation. I don't know where I stop or he begins. The welcome, amazing relief as my cum explodes into his mouth and the warmth of his that I'm trying to swallow down. The pleasures I'm giving and taking combine. My eyes roll back as I see stars, for a moment everything goes black, then explodes in a kaleidoscope of colour.

I suck and lick as his cock softens between my lips, not wanting this to end, not wanting him to let me go.

Then he's lifting himself up, turning around, smashing his mouth down on mine. I savour the tang of me on him, he must taste himself in my mouth. We sample each other, and it seems so right. A perfect combination.

"Fuck, Josh…" he starts, then doesn't add any more.

I shake my head, there are no words to describe what just happened between us. It felt so right, so good. So unlike the prostitutes I'd let give me a blow job before. Such a technical description doesn't start to describe the mind-blowing experience I've just had here.

He rolls off me, pulling me into his side, pushing my face down into his chest, just holding me. It's what I need. I feel like I've come home.

I wait for the feelings of guilt to assail me. Wait to feel dirty. But what just happened can only be described as beautiful, not wrong at all. I grow angry at myself, and the world, for even daring to describe our coupling as unnatural, when it felt the most genuine thing I'd ever done. For the first time in my life, I feel honest.

No going back now.

Outside of this room I'll pretend to be straight. But here, with Scott, I'll be true to myself.

"I'll go to therapy," I mumble my reaffirmed promise against his chest.

"Babe…"

"No, let me get this out. I don't want to diminish what I've found with you, Scott. Don't want to feel it's wrong. Right now I'm feeling the best I've ever felt in my life, but I know my nightmares will continue to haunt me, and I'm still going to hear those voices in my head. Voices so loud they'll make me push you away whether I mean to or not. I don't want to hurt you, and I'm afraid that's what I'll end up doing. I need help. I'll be honest, I can't see it working, but I'll try anything if it means I have you."

"You have me, babe. You have me." He manoeuvres my head so he can look into my face. "I get you, Josh, I do. You want me *and* the club. We'll find a way to have both. Out there," he waves his hand toward the balcony, "out there, we're brothers. Christ, Rock and Beef are so close they share women together. No one's going to look twice at us as long as we don't walk around holding hands." He breaks off and grins. "Not that I wouldn't be proud as fuck for everyone to know, but I respect your feelings. But in here, in our suites, we'll be ourselves. It's no one else's business what we are, what we do, behind closed doors."

"Will you come with me?"

"To the therapist? Of course, if that's what you want."

I bite my lip, then tell him my reasoning. "You need to know everything, Scott. Need to know what a fucked-up son of a bitch I am."

He chuckles softly. "If you think that's going to put me off, you couldn't be more fuckin' wrong." He takes my hand, placing it over his chest. Underneath my fingers I can feel his heart beating. "Not going to name it, not even going to try. But you're in here, Josh. Taken me by surprise, never felt anything like it before. I'm here for the long haul. You've already tried to push me away, and I've always come back."

"I don't deserve you."

"Babe, you probably deserve more. If it's me that you want, it's me who's hit the fuckin' jackpot." He looks down and must see the frown on my face. "Talk to me."

"You went with a sweet butt…"

"It was just a blow job. Had to imagine it was you sucking my cock." He laughs self-deprecatingly. "Won't be going there again. I promise you that. Not when I've got the real thing in my bed."

"You're bi…"

"Okay, now. Fuckin' stop. You know how Drummer got his name?"

I nod, I do. Because he banged everything in sight.

"You think he'd cheat on Sam?"

Might not have known Prez long, but long enough to know that's the last thing he'd do.

"He can commit to her because he's found his one. That's the way I'm feelin' now with you."

"But you like women, won't you miss…?"

Again he chuckles. "Nah, I prefer men in any event. Now I've got you, I won't feel any loss." The next thing he says turns the tables. "And you, Josh? You gonna commit?"

"I'm all in. Don't want anybody else." I'm shocked he even asked me. I realise I've got to stop doubting myself, and my worth. If I know I can give my all to Scott, why can't I accept I can be all he needs too?

Because of your programming. Because I've got it locked in my head that if Scott can be with a woman, surely that would make his life easier? If he can deny one part of himself, shouldn't it be the one which society finds disgusting?

He's just told me I'm his one. He's not fighting the same demons as me. What would it be like if I could forgive myself for wanting him to be mine too?

I begin hoping therapy might help.

<h1 style="text-align:center">Chapter 20</h1>

Plans made in the dead of the night don't always come to a rapid fruition. Though I remain steadfast in my promise to seek help, it doesn't appear I'm going to be able to see anyone outside of the club anytime soon.

With Jayden in the sights of the Herreras, and the police trying to serve a custodial order on Drummer in favour of Crystal's mom for Amy, the women are all shipped off to Vegas to keep them safely out of harm's way.

Just in the nick of time too. Almost as soon as they've gone, the cops return with a warrant and turn the clubhouse upside down. Quite literally. Angry they couldn't find what they were looking for, it's like they've set out to destroy everything. The clubhouse, even brothers' rooms, are left in one hell of a mess, most of the furniture in pieces. The female cop looks disgusted with what her colleagues are doing, but clearly hasn't the power to stop them.

Wide eyed I stand next to my old VP, Crash, watching my new home being destroyed. Accepting silently his glance offering sympathy. When the cops eventually leave empty handed, Lady and I go to salvage what's left of our suites, Crash and Lost offering to clear the communal areas with their men.

Then later we're involved with a different sort of cleansing. Taking out members of the Herrera family who'd been involved in the child grooming ring. Five hits in one night. Lady and I are both assigned to Peg's team. It gets the adrenaline rising, but our hit goes off without a hitch. Slick is also leading a team, and he busts in on a party, surprisingly finding the reason why the cops hit us so hard. One of them is caught in the middle of raping a young kid. Slick loses it when Detective Archer admits to running Heart and Crystal off the road, and shoots him on the spot, Crash slitting his throat to finish him off. Prez isn't happy they killed a cop so indiscreetly, but I don't have it in myself to blame them. Would have done it myself if I'd discovered he was responsible for killing Heart's old lady, and for putting the man himself in a coma. As the days pass, hope slowly leaves us that he'll ever come round.

Riding with Crash, Sarge and Cobra, the brothers with old ladies go to Vegas to collect them, as with Detective Archer underground it's safe for them to come home. Lost leads his men back to San Diego. The clubhouse seems quiet with everyone gone.

"Just wanna hold you and sleep tonight." Scott puts his arm around me as we go into his suite.

The adrenaline rush having faded, that's all I want to do myself.

After a well-earned sleep, we walk down to the clubhouse the next morning, not even making it through the doors before someone calls our names. "Lady, Joker!"

"Hey, Dart. What's up?" I reply when I swing around and recognise him. *What the fuck's up now?*

"Gotta mount up and ride, man. You'll never guess what's fuckin' happened."

I feel Lady tense beside me.

What the fuck now? Haven't we been through enough?

"Don't look like that, Brother." Beef comes over, slaps my back and at last enlightens me. "Slick's biting the bullet. Setting up a surprise wedding for Ella in Vegas. We've all gotta go."

I look at Lady, he's grinning. It's no hardship at all to do that.

As Road Captain, I quickly get everything organised, and then everyone on the road. Fuck me, what a laugh. We collect Ella from a day of pampering, joking among ourselves as to how she'll be able to ride through Vegas behind Slick in that short dress she's wearing. Blade starts taking bets as to whether she'll show off her ass. She doesn't. Beef and Dart lose, but don't complain.

Slick rides his bike straight into the wedding chapel while we park up outside. I take a second to greet Hammer, Twister, Rope, Cuff and the rest of my old chapter I hadn't seen lately, sneaking a look at Lady doing the same, and then it's inside to watch Slick get married after a hasty proposal.

A fist bumps my arm. "What would happen if she'd said no?" Lady asks quietly, his eyes twinkling.

"Fuck knows," I laugh back. But knowing how much those two have come through together, a negative response would have been surprising.

The reception is good fun, a chance to catch up with old friends. Topped by the fantastic news that Heart has woken up. If we needed anything more to celebrate other than the end of our troubles and Slick's wedding, that update was all we could have hoped for. The party, which continues back at my old clubhouse, is even more rowdy as a result. I end the evening drunk, then go to sleep basically where I collapse.

Our return to Tucson is uneventful, giving us welcome space to come down from the highs in Vegas. While Heart's recovery is a cause for celebration, it's sobering when we have to cope with his more than understandable reaction to hearing he's lost his wife, and that she was buried while he'd been unconscious. As the days pass, his anger seems to increase rather than diminish. Acceptance will be a long time coming as he tries to cope with his grief.

Dart's just updating me on his mood today, which apparently has been particularly trying, when Lady walks into the club-house.

"A word, Joker?"

Lady and I have embarked on a tentative relationship. Tentative as I'm still wary of unintentionally outing myself. While we tend to gravitate together, in public neither of us give any sign that we're anything other than brothers who came from the same club. At night, Lady will come into my room, but something's holding me back from going any further sexually than we already have, and understanding my reluctance, he hasn't pushed me.

I nod at Lady, then excuse myself to Dart. "Sure. Catch you later, Brother." I go to the bar where I ask one of the new prospects, Hyde, to get us both beers. Jekyll, the other, is manning the gate.

"What's up?" Lady slides a piece of paper toward me. On it is written a time and a place. I raise my eyebrows in query.

He leans closer. "Therapist," he tells me. "She comes highly recommended."

Drawing back my shoulders, I raise my chin. I've made a promise to him, and myself. I'm not going to back out. But later that evening, when Scott knocks on my door, I turn him away.

"Not tonight, Scott." My eyes plead with him. Before he gave me that fucking note I was yearning to be close to him again. But therapy brings up such bad connotations in my mind, my dick is flaccid and isn't going to rise anytime soon. Memories of electrodes and those fucking 'therapy' sessions, the reminders of everything that I've tried to move on from, bringing me down.

He eyes me carefully, then reaches out his hand and touches my cheek. I flinch, I can't help it. "You going to be okay alone?"

I've been alone most of my life. One more night won't make much difference. I raise my chin.

"You need me? I'm right here. And, Josh. This is the right thing to do, you hear me? You've got to move on, put the past in a box and lock it away behind you."

I doubt seeing a therapist is going to help with that, but I've made my decision. "I hear you."

Whether it just happened that way, or whether, as I suspect, he's avoided telling me until the last moment, the appointment is for the next morning. I feel decidedly uncertain as we ride up to a nondescript building.

"You sure you want me to come in with you?" His eyes examine my face.

I am. The last time I had 'therapy' may have been years ago, but is still all too fresh in my memory. I don't want to be subjected to anything like that again. "Yeah. You know me, know what I need, Scott. You know to get me out of there if I start having problems."

"You won't," he reassures me. "I've been assured she knows her stuff."

I know he's been talking to like-minded people, and I know he'll have chosen someone who he believes can help. But that knowledge doesn't stop me becoming increasingly nervous as I walk up the steps to enter a fresh and bright looking reception. Scott deals with the formalities, and soon we're called in.

The therapist stands and holds out her hand. Her smile is welcoming as she says, "I'm Delia Harmon. Call me Delia, please."

"Josh," I reply, knowing I've got to face this as myself, and not hide behind my biker persona.

"Scott." Behind me, Lady takes his cue from me.

"Partner?" she queries, presumably to get things straight from the start.

I half turn, shocked by her direct question, and interested in his answer.

"Sure am," he replies firmly, and for me, there's a smile.

"Well, let's get ourselves comfortable." Her easy acceptance of our relationship helps a little to put me at my ease. *No judgement here. No look of disgust.* Despite Scott's reassurances, deep down that's what I was expecting.

We seat ourselves in comfortable chairs. When I look at her expectantly, she doesn't disappoint, wasting no time in asking, "Tell me what you expect to get out of our sessions, Josh."

"Can I just say something?" Scott interrupts. "I'm here for moral support. If there's anything you wish to say privately to Josh, I'll get out of your way."

Delia smiles. "It's not couples' counselling then."

"No, it's me," I admit. My mouth opens, but nothing comes out. I look down at my hands, then across to Scott, silently pleading for help.

He lifts his chin slightly. "Josh can correct me if I'm putting it badly. Josh is gay, but was brought up to think he wasn't normal. That conditioning is fixed firmly in his head. He's having difficulty accepting his sexuality, he prefers to keep it hidden."

As I'm sending him a nod of thanks for putting it so succinctly, Delia gives me a considered look.

"I'll take it that coming here today is a big step for you, Josh."

Again I nod. She's correct.

She taps at a tablet for a moment, then her attention is back on me. "The fact you've taken this step shows you wish to be comfortable with yourself. And that, at the moment, you're not."

Another dip of my head up and down.

"There's a continuum of stages when someone comes to accept they have a different sexuality. I'd like to explore exactly which stage you're at. Let's start at the beginning and see how far we get today." She glances down at her writing, then puts her tablet aside. Leaning back in the chair, she looks as relaxed as

I'm feeling tense. "Tell me, Josh. When did you first realise you were gay?"

My brow creases as in my head, I look back. "I think I always knew I was different. By the age of seven I knew I wasn't the same as my older brother, who then was on the verge of leavin' home. When we spent time together, he preferred physical games while I wasn't interested."

She doesn't prompt, doesn't question, just waits for me to go on.

"School? You know what school's like. Boys growing older, starting to talk about girls. About things they're not ready to actually do yet. Kiss a girl, take her out, fuck, er, sorry, make love to her."

"If you're comfortable with the term fuck, don't change it on my account. In my experience that's exactly what young boys talk and think about."

I spare her a brief smile, while beside me Scott chuckles. "I didn't want to do any of that." I glance at my companion, and cough to clear my throat. "I didn't like getting changed for PE, didn't like taking showers with the other kids. I was embarrassed when they started talking about which girls gave them erections as none of them did me. As I went through puberty, I knew it wasn't girls who turned me on."

Suddenly I can't stay seated. Abruptly I stand, crossing to the windows, barely seeing the quiet Tucson street outside. "I was thirteen, fourteen perhaps, when I found my dick did work. Embarrassingly so. I was watchin' a game of football when the school jock, a couple of years older, was playin'. I got my first real hard on. He was stunnin', lithe as he moved across the field. He was the sort of man all the girls lusted after. Huh." I break off and look at Scott. "The sort I apparently am attracted to. A real lady's man."

Scott grins at our private joke.

Delia doesn't object to me pacing the room, but her next question has me sitting back down and clenching my fists.

"Did you tell anyone? Friends? Family?"

"No," I snarl. "I was too busy trying to be straight. I wanted to be normal."

She stares at me for a moment. "Do you still want to be straight, Josh?"

Now that's the question, isn't it? I don't answer immediately. Before I met Scott I'd have had the answer at my fingertips. But if I was normal, I wouldn't have him. Wouldn't be sharing the things that we do. *I'd probably have a woman instead. Could be open about my relationship with her.* But it wouldn't be him.

After a short silence, I give my considered response. "Life would be easier if I was straight."

It's her turn to nod. "Life would be easier for a lot of people if they could change something. A visible scar, a disability, skin colour, their background. I could go through a long list. It's not just sexuality that can't be changed and has to be lived with."

I haven't thought about it that way before. She's right.

"So I've got to accept it?"

"Sounds easy, doesn't it? But if it was as simple as that, you wouldn't be here with me today. Let me sum up. You were a young teenager when you first knew. Go from there. What was, is, your relationship with your parents?"

"I haven't got one," I respond with a snort. "Dad saw I was effeminate." At her surprised look, I break off and huff a laugh, "Building muscles, growing a beard, concentrating on the voice. There are some things you can change if you're determined enough." My crooked nose also helps, of course. I frown slightly, remembering how I got it.

"Go on."

Here goes nothing. Then I explain to a stranger what went on in my life. I take a deep breath. "He made me fight in the gym, mixed martial arts from the start. I grew better, eventually could give as well as I got." Scott coughs, but I'm not expanding any further. Him knowing is enough. Without looking at him, I continue. "Didn't matter what he did. I could bulk up, change my looks, but not what was underneath however much I tried. Dad guessed."

As my voice trails off, her eyebrows meet. "He wasn't impressed?"

"I was dirty. Unnatural. An abomination to choose the lifestyle I was heading for."

"Did you choose to be gay, Josh?"

My eyes widen. "Fuck, no. Why would anyone? With the world set up for heterosexuals, why the fuck would anyone want to be gay?"

"What did your parents do, Josh?"

I don't want to tell her. Know it will lead to more questions, but I've made a promise to Scott that I'll try. And that means telling all my secrets. I inhale deeply, then admit, "When I was sixteen they sent me to a Pray out the Gay camp."

Her face falls. There's a brief pause as she wipes a hand over her brow. "I take it, it was bad?"

"Kid, a friend, killed himself while I was there. That's when I decided to get out. Convinced them they'd cured me, joined the army soon after when I turned seventeen."

"The camp gave you the full treatment?"

I don't want to go through the details again. "The full treatment. Aversion therapy, counselling. Yeah. They did whatever it took."

"You know that many states ban conversion therapy for minors?"

"Yeah, I do. And it should be all of them, not just a minority. For everybody, for fuck's sake." My face glows as I continue. "It doesn't fuckin' work. Just screws you up. Makes it so you're too scared, too conditioned, to even think about sex. Huh. You can't have sex, can't imagine havin' sex for long afterwards. Sometimes forever, sometimes for years like myself." I feel my cheeks flaming, overheating. My breathing speeds up as I continue my explanation. "Doesn't stop you being gay in here." I tap my finger to my forehead. "It makes you understand how people see you, a filthy creature little more than an animal who's made a dirty lifestyle choice. Dirty. Filthy. Disgusting. A reject. Abhorrent. Repulsive…" More words spew out of my mouth and I can't stop them, each one louder than the last. The conditioning ingrained them in my mind. "Despicable…" I'm conscious I'm rocking back and forth unable to do anything to stop myself. I put my head in my hands and still the labels used to describe me flood from my brain through my mouth. "Revolting. Nauseating. Wrong. Unnatural." I'm shaking, my body jerking forward as I spit out each word.

Scott's up and his arms are around me, physically stopping my automatic movements. "Shush, shush babe. Hey, come on. Stop it now." He grips my head to his chest, gently stroking his free hand up and down my back. "Shush, babe. Shush." It's only when Delia passes me a handful of tissues I realise tears are running down my face, and I'm blubbering like a fucking baby.

I'm vaguely aware that Delia has moved away to give us space. As Scott takes a tissue from the box she's left beside me, I realise he's crying too. *I shouldn't have let him come with me. Should have faced it myself like a fucking man.* Now I need to pull myself together.

I dab at my eyes and move myself away from Scott. "I'm okay," I mumble, trying to convince myself.

Scott blows his nose loudly, looking at me with red rimmed eyes. His intense stare burns into me. Suddenly words come tumbling out of his mouth in a rush. "Is that what you think of me, Josh? Is that how you see me? Dirty? Filthy? Disgusting?

Nauseating? Unnatural? What else was it? Oh yeah, despicable. Is that what a homo is in your eyes? Is that what I am?"

What the fuck? I hold my hands up to stop his tirade. "No, Scott. No. No, a hundred times no." Reaching out my hands I curl my fingers into his tee, jerking him toward me. I look straight into his eyes. When he attempts to turn away, I loosen one hand and pull his chin back. "You're the best fucking man I've ever met, Scott. Those words would never apply to you. You're a beautiful person. Inside and out. Nothing I said just then would even begin to describe you."

"Then why do you apply them to yourself?" Delia cuts into our conversation. "Either the words describe everyone who's gay, or they apply to no gay person at all."

I try to let her words sink in. My brain has difficulty computing them as she walks over and retakes her seat. She looks at Scott, then me. "I think that's where this session will end today. We've covered a lot of ground." She holds up a fisted hand, and pops up a finger. "There are six stages you need to go through to be comfortable with your sexual orientation, Josh. The first two were addressed before I met you, the third I think we're dealing with now. One is where you first came to know you had different feelings from other boys your age. The second is when you compare your feelings in comparison with others, identify what's different about you. That's when you slotted yourself into the label of being gay." She's holding up three fingers now. "The third is where you rebel against your sexuality. It's hard being gay in a world you see as straight. You've tried to conform, have been forced to conform, then when that didn't work, tried to hide your sexuality away." She waggles the third finger. "Your sexuality is part of you, Josh. It's what makes you tick, how you feel, how you react. It's a part of you that's in play all the time, it's not something you can turn on or turn off."

She pauses, and checks I'm still listening. I am. "What you've got to do, Josh, before I see you again, is to try to give yourself permission to be you."

"I can't come out." My eyes flick wildly to Scott's.

"Not asking you to do that." She shakes her head. "Too much too soon. You served, I see from your records. Well, you wouldn't go out to war without bullets in your gun, would you?"

Of course, I wouldn't.

"What I'm hoping to do here is to equip you so when you pick up your weapon it's ready to fire. You're not there yet. You might never want to tell everyone, but that's not what this therapy is about. Why is it anyone's business? Why should they know? No one walks around asking anyone if they're straight. What we're doing here is focusing on you being comfortable with yourself. If the time comes when you do want to admit to your sexuality, by then you'll be strong and comfortable enough with yourself to face any reaction head on. *That* will be your ammunition."

She turns her attention to Scott. "It was useful you being here today. I'd like you to come along with Josh next time."

"I will," he says without hesitation, though I might be having words with him about that later. *He cried for fuck's sake.*

Because of careless words that I said.

CHAPTER 21

Once again I find myself appreciating the benefits of riding a motorcycle. If we'd been in a cage, silence would have encouraged conversation. Right now I need some time alone to process the gruelling session on my own. Feeling emotionally drained, and strangely, physically tired, my one thought is to escape to my suite as soon as I return. I back my bike into what's become my usual space. It's when I'm kicking down the stand, I sense someone approaching.

"You okay, Brother?" It's Prez himself. Walking up he gives me a considered look, when he draws close enough he puts his hand on my arm.

"Fine," I reply, trying to summon a smile, wondering why he's come up to me, and why he's acting concerned.

He enlightens me with his next question. "You been to therapy?"

Fuck. What does he know?

As my eyes widen, he squeezes his fingers against my bicep. "PTSD is hard to get under control, Joker. Sometimes therapy just digs that shit back up. You look like you've been through the wringer."

"He has," Lady confirms from behind me, having got off his own ride.

"It will get better," Prez assures me. "Getting help is the best thing you can do. Though it might not seem like it at the moment." Another tightening of his fingers. "You need anything from me or the club, you just ask, you hear me? A few brothers here know exactly what it's like. They served, saw shit, needed support to get over it. No shame in that, Brother. No shame at all."

I'm reeling, breathing hard, having a hard time coming back from the notion that he might have known exactly what type of therapy I'm attending. The excuse he's given me is easy to go along with. The concern he's showing overwhelms me. It's not far from the truth that I saw some shit while I was a Marine, but that pales into insignificance measured against what else I'm dealing with. Nonetheless, I didn't expect the support he's offering. With a catch in my voice, I thank him.

"Lady," Prez addresses my companion. "I was hopin' to catch you. You gonna be okay to take the night shift with Heart tonight?"

Don't refuse, I mentally instruct him. *Don't do anything to give us away.* Don't give the impression I might need you.

It's one of the times he shows he can't always read my thoughts. "I wanted to keep close to Joker. It was pretty gruellin' today, Prez."

Shit.

Drummer turns to me. "You gonna need him?"

"Nah," I reply, injecting positivity into my voice. "Got a lot to think about. I'll be fine workin' it through by myself."

Lady's throwing me a look, but Prez just nods. "Got a whole club of brothers here for you, Joker. You need anything, we're only a call away. Like I said, number of them know exactly what you're going through. Brothers willing to help. All you've got to do is ask for it." He glances at Lady. "Know you came down from Vegas together, natural you should lean on each other as that's what you've always done. But you need to integrate into this club. This is your family now. We're here, for both of you. You get me?"

I get him. Loud and clear. *He's noticed us gravitating together and not joining in. Got to work on that. If he's seen it, everyone else will have too.* "I get you, Drummer. Still finding my feet."

He raises his chin. "Understand that, Brother. Not easy after havin' been so long with a different chapter. Takes a minute to find your place." That's his parting comment.

At last I'm free to go up to my suite, but I'm not permitted to go alone.

"What the fuck?" Lady hisses as he walks up the incline with me. "I wanted to be here for you, Josh. Not babysittin' Heart. It's you who needs me."

We're at our bloc. I wait until we're inside. "Scott," I say tiredly. "Apart from the need to keep up appearances, I've had a lot put on me today. It was hard hearing for you too. Got stuff in my head I'd prefer to work through alone. Didn't like upsettin' you like I did today. Don't want to do that again."

His eyes roll upwards then down again. He sighs loudly. "Fuck it, Josh. We're partners. We share everything. The good and the bad shit. But you've put me on the spot now. Jesus, man. I can't back out." He pinches the bridge of his nose. "What if it brings everything back? What if you have nightmares again?"

Then I'll deal with them, like I always have done. Alone. "You heard what Prez said, Scott. Plenty of brothers around if I need help. He's noticed you and I stay close. We've got to stop that, mingle more. Otherwise people will start to suspect."

"Suspect what? That we're doing things together they'd think are filthy? Disgusting? Would turn their stomachs? If that's what they fuckin' think I'm not sure I want to call them brother."

"It's the way of the world," I say sadly. "Can't deny that's the way it works. Look, I've got some reflectin' to do, and it's best I do that by myself. Have done enough talkin' and listenin' today.

Delia and you have given me shit to trawl through. Yeah, I fully expect the men around us would be repulsed if they knew what we are. Now I'm considerin' lookin' at shit differently. Yeah, I need to get to a place where I can accept what they think doesn't matter. Long way for me to go, Scott. Fuckin' long way."

Another loud exhale. He bows his head in defeat, then looks up. One thing about Scott is he's always thinking on his feet, doesn't let anything keep him down for long. The more positive tone therefore doesn't surprise me when he next speaks. "We've got church tomorrow," he reminds me, "and I got work to do on Saturday. But Sunday, get ready for a ride. You're comin' with me to Flagstaff."

My eyes crease in confusion at the sudden change of topic. "Flagstaff's a four fuckin' hour journey. Why the fuck would I want to go there?"

He grins. "'Cause that's where my mom lives. We're going for a visit. Pack a bag. We'll stay overnight."

It shows how little we know about each other. Apart from knowing his mom is a million miles away from being like my own in her character, I didn't know where she lived. But getting off the compound sounds attractive and, after today, something perhaps we both need. A long ride is something I can look forward to. Of course, I immediately start wondering whether the two of us going off together would be suspicious, but it's as though he can read my mind.

"Shouldn't ride alone on the road, Josh. You're the Road Captain. What would you say to someone else?"

Take a companion. Have someone there to have your back. And what better person than the one everyone knows you're most friendly with? Just this once can't hurt, can it?

He gives me a couple of hours' space. I lie back on the bed letting today's therapy session do a rerun through my head. I hadn't had any faith in a therapist being of any help, but even I have to allow she'd made a few good points. That fuckin' camp had conditioned me to think one way. Is it really all I have to do is turn that thinking on its head? I still have my doubts, but I'll go back and see Delia again.

After dragging me down for dinner and a drink in the clubhouse, Lady goes off to Tucson to keep Heart company, and I half-heartedly play a few games of pool with Blade and Viper which, not unsurprisingly, I lose. My head's not in it tonight. I hand over some dollars then take myself back to the suite.

Being honest, I do miss Scott, miss his warmth beside me in bed. My mind returns to churning through the session earlier today. *If I don't see Scott as something disgusting, why should I see myself that way?* I've met other gays. Seen them around Vegas. Men walking close together, sometimes even holding hands. *Are they revolting?* Nah, I'd envied them. *A minority. Misunderstood by the heterosexual majority.* Not the same as the rest, but nothing worse, nothing better. Just different. Which means I'm not abnormal, just a part of the diverse population.

I try to stay awake, wanting my positive thoughts to stay with me, not wanting nightmares to return and blast me back into the past once again, but feeling exhausted, my eyes soon close. Surprisingly I have a dreamless sleep.

Knowing Scott will have returned and be sleeping in, I don't disturb him the next morning. Around lunchtime Beef asks if anyone wants to go to the Harley store in Tucson as he wants to pick up some parts. Remembering what Drummer had said about getting close to different brothers, I volunteer.

It actually turns out to be a great afternoon. The weather perfect for riding, not a cloud in the early autumn sky. After Beef selects the parts he needs, we spend more time than we should have checking out the new models. I'm even conned into taking a test ride. When we finally leave, I readily agree to

Beef's suggestion that we stop off at a biker bar for a beer, ending up sitting outside in the sun.

Beef's good company while we drink our beers exchanging stories and jokes. But as he finishes off his drink, I find myself wondering what he would think if I came out and admitted I was gay. Would he continue to sit here and treat me as if nothing had changed? Would he look at me like something he'd want to scrape off his shoe? Or would, heaven forbid, he be suspicious and think I was coming onto him? The perennial fear of the straight man. In most states it's a legal excuse for hate crimes, given the misnomer, gay panic.

I don't say a word, of course. The risks are far too great. I can't predict how he'd react, but chances are, any consequence would be negative.

Losing track of the time, we make it back as brothers are already going into church. Lady's already seated. We just exchange nods.

We soon get through the normal business, then onto things that happened before my time in this chapter. The club who'd been responsible for killing the prospect and Adam had been the Rock Demons out of Phoenix. I already knew the Tucson Devils had been responsible for blowing up their club. What I hadn't been aware of was that two of the Demons had escaped. I also hadn't heard the full story about Slick's old lady, nor how that fucking club had raped her. Watching his face tighten during the discussions, I can see how affected he is. I'm not surprised that revenge is on the top of his agenda.

It emerges that one of the two Rock Demons who escaped has been spotted in San Diego. Snake, the San Diego Prez, has offered to help track him down. Although I've a soft spot for Ella, and all the women come to that, that I hadn't been involved in the main event means I'm not personally invested. I'll give Slick any help I can, that goes without saying, but I zone out when they get down to details, and it doesn't seem any tasks are going to be assigned to me. I add my aye when it comes around to the vote confirming the last remaining Demons will be taken out. Just tidying up history which doesn't really concern me.

"What's the latest with Heart?" As Prez moves to a new subject, I perk up, knowing Lady had been with him last night.

"He's not in a good place," Wraith replies.

"Can understand that." Viper frowns.

Lady puts up his hand, the prez gives him a chin jerk. I turn to watch him as he starts, harmless sounding words which put together give us a complete shock. "He's not plannin' on comin' back to the club." *What?* By the expressions on my brothers' faces, I'm not the only one to be surprised. Lady continues, "I was with him last night. Seems he's makin' plans to visit an ex-Army buddy up in Utah."

"If it's the one I'm thinkin' of, I thought there was bad blood there." As Dart frowns, I recall Dart and Heart are best buds. "He never agreed with Heart bein' in the club." *Does this mean he's turning in his patch?* I scowl, unable to understand how a man could do that. Even after all Heart's been through.

Lady shrugs. "Don't know about that, but the fucker's pickin' him up Sunday."

"He needs his real friends, his *brothers* around him," Beef snarls. Too fucking right, Beef. I raise my chin, a sign I completely agree.

I can't get my head around the fact he might not be coming back. Man's got responsibilities. "And his fuckin' daughter needs *him*. He takin' her with him?" I ask.

The shaking of heads makes it clear no one knows the answer to that.

"He comin' back when he's healed?" Dart asks, sounding concerned.

But Lady simply shrugs again, showing he's given us all the info he had.

Prez snarls out, "He doesn't quit the club without talkin' to me. And we don't take brothers leavin' lightly." Drummer's face has gone dark.

"Don't shoot the messenger, Prez. Just repeatin' what he told me."

Lady gets a chin lift while I think on Heart. Becoming a member of the Satan's Devils isn't easy, but once you're in, you've got brotherhood for life. *What could make a man want to leave that behind?* Sure, he'd be returning to a clubhouse where he'd lived with his wife. But every one of us here would do our utmost to make it easier for him. Man's got to do what he has to, I suppose. I hope he realises he's not in the right place now to make such far reaching decisions for his life. But he shouldn't be ignoring his daughter. She needs her dad.

The next day I go check out my bike. We've got a long ride tomorrow, I want to make sure there's no nails in my tyres or shit like that. I decide to do an oil change—it doesn't really need it, but fuck, I love administering to my ride. Then I clean the chain and give all the chrome a polish. It takes up most of the day.

When I eventually return to the clubhouse I find Dart, drinking himself into a stupor and swearing at everyone in sight. Lady, back from whatever he was doing, is already seated with their small group at the table. He's diplomatically trying to get to the bottom of what's upset the brother so much.

Dart's usually easy going, so his outburst is strange enough that I stay within earshot. As I loiter I'm able to hear the full story. It's that black girl Dart's recently employed at the strip club. Seems he went to see her today, and found out the reason she came to us for a job. She's stripping to get money together for an operation to save her son's life. Added to that, her violent asshole of an ex who she came to Tucson to escape, despite her confidence to the contrary, probably knows exactly where she is.

Poor bitch. That's one fuck of a lot on her plate. Dart's right to be worried, but ranting and raving won't fix any shit.

Prez has clearly latched on that her ex, who happens to be a cop, might be trying to find her. Having identified there's a possibility of blowback on us, he wants to have a conversation with Dart to see what the repercussions might be. He asks me to take Dart's place at the strip club tonight. I don't hesitate to agree. Not that seeing naked ladies does anything for me, but I'm happy to help out. I've already got suspicions Dart feels more for the woman than he's willing to admit. Man doesn't lose his shit for just an employee.

When it's time I leave the clubhouse, giving the brothers who make lewd comments about how I'm going to spend my evening a middle finger salute. Lady gets the same for his smirk. Most brothers enjoy pulling a shift at the strip club.

Intrigued by what I've learned this afternoon, I'm interested to meet Alex, and take to her as soon as I do. With all her trials and tribulations, I half expected a downtrodden woman, full of despair. But I find someone completely different to my expectations. Looking at her, you wouldn't believe she carries the weight of the world on her shoulders, and boy, despite her physique not immediately leading you to suspect it, she owns that pole when she dances like no one else could. I see the reason why Dart took her on, even agreeing that she didn't need to get completely naked. Watching out for her on behalf of my brother, when a man gets too close when she's on the stage, I give him a bloody nose.

With that exception, the shift passes without incident. The work's not gruelling, but it's late by the time I get back to the compound. Scott's door is closed, but he's left it unlocked.

Mindful of the hour, I open it carefully in case he's already asleep. He's not.

Shirt off, lying back on his bed in his normal manner, feet lazily crossed at the ankles, hands behind his head, he looks toward me with a wide grin. "Have you seen Peg's suite?" The question isn't what I'd expected to be greeted with, having been prepared to answer an enquiry about my night.

Rapidly rearranging my thought pattern, I lean back against the door. "Have you?"

"Yeah, he wanted to show me something."

Okay, right. He must be going somewhere with this. "So? What's he got? Gold plated commode or some such shit?"

His smile broadens. "Nah. Crafty old bugger that he is, he's managed to get both suites for himself. One's his bedroom, just like ours. The other's been turned into a living room, and the second bathroom's a kitchenette."

"Sounds nice." Sounds like a mini apartment.

"Yeah." His brow furrows. His expression matches the pensiveness in his voice. "Would be nice if we could do the same."

What? "You're not serious, are you? We might get away with sleeping in the same bed, but I think someone would notice if we converted the suite."

He sighs. "Yeah, you're right. But it's an idea. Something for the future perhaps? Would be nice to have our own place."

I've got to stop this right there. And now. "Not coming out, told you that, Scott." I recall my thoughts when I'd been with Beef the day before. "Can't do it." The only way we could mimic Peg's accommodations is to come clean with everyone. I repeat, "I can't do it."

Sitting up, he swings his legs over the side of the bed and scoffs, "You've really bought into this relationship, haven't you?"

Seeing he's concerned that I might again have had second thoughts, I raise my chin. "Told you I have."

An intense stare, then a quick nod. Then he continues, "On my part, I don't think there'd be much of a problem. And if they can't accept what we are, then maybe they're people I don't want to be around."

"But it's not just the brothers. Everyone's like that!" I snap. "That's what the whole world thinks of us."

His head shakes side to side, as the corners of his mouth turn down. "Nah, that's just your experience, Josh. There's good folks out there who don't give a damn. Who'd look at us as people without givin' us a label." He holds out his hand. "Come 'ere."

When I go over, he gives a tug and off balance, I'm forced to sit. "I'll give you what you want for now. But if this goes where I hope it will, we'll be visitin' this topic again. I don't like havin' to hide what I feel for you, Josh."

"That's where we're different. Exposin' my feelin's for you will just bring a whole load of hurt down. I want to protect you from that." That, to me, is the whole point. To avoid being a topic of conversation, to avoid those nasty looks sent our way. To avoid people showing their disgust or making snide comments.

"Ain't protectin' me from shit, babe. Though I'll accept you're not yet in a place where you can see that."

When his hand moves to cup my chin, gently stroking the stubbly beard, I see a change in his eyes, pupils dilating with desire. His thumb sweeps over my lips, my tongue snakes out to lick it. I hate disappointing him. I know he's wrong. I know the risks he wants us to take, but I know they're not worth taking. I could lose him, or the club, or God forbid, both. But I do want to show him, despite our differences of opinion, how much he means to me.

Taking the initiative, I push him back and straddle him, my fingers finding his nipples and pinching them lightly, then I follow my hands with my mouth, sucking and nipping until two small hard peaks form.

"Playful, are we?"

Yeah.

Sitting back, wasting no time, I undo his jeans. He lifts his hips helping me to remove them. He's gone commando, his cock bounces up, pre-cum already glistening. Leaning my mouth down, my tongue laps it up. He groans loudly. My own dick is pressing painfully against my zip.

Quickly I stand, stripping my clothes off fast, then I lie down on top of him, my weight held on my arms. As my mouth closes on his, our hard and ready cocks slide against each other.

Fuck, he feels good. Both our hips jerk as our tongues mate together. *Need him. Now. Need to feel his hands on me.* I roll to the side taking him with me, then place my hand around his cock. He takes hold of mine. Eyes open, we stare at each other, our breathing speeding up, our chests rising and falling in unison. Barely blinking, just moans and sighs coming from our throats, the smell of sex and male pheromones permeating the air.

Mouths so close I'm breathing in the air he exhales. We transcend our individualities, becoming one complete being.

It doesn't take long before we're coming together. Hard and fast. Stickiness coating our bellies. I press my lower hip against his to try to keep the mess off the sheets, then twist my upper body so I can reach for my t-shirt to wipe us both off.

"Fuck," I tell him. "Gets better every fuckin' time."

"Could be even better," he starts, raising an eyebrow and looking at me. "If you'd let me take that ass."

The next step. I lay back, arm thrown over my eyes. *What would it feel like to put my cock in him? Feel him in me?* In my warped mind, hands and mouths don't mean we're taking it all the way. Maybe there's a gleam of hope they aren't the acts that I'd go to hell for. Aren't the most shameful deed a man can do.

Shameful? It's only that if anyone knows.

"It's alright." His hand lies flat on my stomach. "I can wait until you're ready."

But how long will he wait? What if I'm never ready?

"Hey, if we don't get there, I'll deal. Come 'ere, let me hold you. Get those worries out of your head. Go to sleep, babe. We've got a long ride tomorrow."

CHAPTER 22

The next morning we leave early, having to suffer rain until we reach Casa Grande where we make our first stop to remove our cuts, placing them carefully in our saddle bags. Taking the opportunity to get out of the damp for a spell, we enter the restaurant where we eat a good and plentiful enough breakfast to set us up for the rest of the run. As luck would have it, the sun's out by the time we get back on the road.

I love long runs. Gives me the chance to relax, to just enjoy the feel of the wheels rolling over the tarmac and the wind rushing through my hair. The distinctive sound of my Harley rumbling from the exhaust pipes, my type of music and all I need. It's a long straight road, so I can stay in top gear, my hand steady on the throttle. Making it even more enjoyable is that I have Scott riding beside me, the pair of us in complete harmony. So much so, when I glance to my right and grin, he's already grinning back. I give him a thumbs up, he returns the gesture. All's good with the world.

I don't know what to expect from his mom. I know that she's always accepted Scott for what he is, but that could be because he's her son. *What's she going to think of me?* As we near our destination, more questions start running through my head. *Has he brought anyone home before?* Why hadn't I asked him? *Do I pretend to be straight? His biker brother?* Damn, I should have found out.

I grow more tense the closer we get.

He leads the way confidently down streets he's clearly familiar with, finally turning into a pleasant residential area. A few more turns, then he's indicating and braking, then backing up onto a driveway. I do likewise, parking up alongside him.

I open my mouth to get the answers to questions I should have asked earlier, but before I can say anything, the door opens, and a pleasant looking woman around fifty emerges at a run.

"Scott!" she yells excitedly, making a beeline for her son. She puts her arms around him, giving him a big hug and a sloppy kiss on his cheek that has him wiping his hand down his face.

"Mom," he admonishes her, but his eyes gleam.

Watching their reunion, I take the opportunity to examine her. I reckon it must have been his dad who provided the genes to give him his height, she can't be much over five foot. Which makes it easy for him to pick her up and swing her around.

"Put me down, you big oaf," she laughs.

He does, then glancing back, sees me standing awkwardly. Before I know what he intends, he's got his arm around my shoulders and is pulling me forward. "Mom, meet Josh. My boyfriend."

Her eyes go wide. *Oh shit, Scott. You should have kept that to yourself. She's going to freak. She…*

"Josh? Boyfriend?" Her eyes harden a little as she puts her hands on her hips and her eyes flare at Scott. "And why did I not know this?"

"Because it's fairly new," Scott informs her casually, seeming completely unconcerned. "But it's serious," he adds. And fuck me, he kisses my lips. In public. Right outside her house.

While I'm waiting to hear her objections, his mom's moving toward me. Quickly so I'm given no chance of escape, her small arms come out to hug me. When she lifts her face and taps her cheek, stunned, I obediently put my lips to her skin. She smells like lavender.

"Well, come in, you two. I want to know everything. How you met, where you're living. Are you another of those bikers, Josh? Come on in. I've got coffee on and I've made your favourite cookies, Scott. Or do you want to take your stuff straight up to your room? Or show Josh the bathroom? Or…?"

"Slow down, Mom," Scott laughs. "Come on, Josh. I should have warned you about my old ma. But then you mightn't have come."

His mom bats his arm. "Scott, less of the old."

Meeting Rachel, Scott's mom's name when I eventually find it out, proves to be a revelation for me. Especially when Scott goes outside to get our overnight gear from our saddlebags to bring it into the house. Her eyes glisten as she looks at me before saying,

"I'm so pleased Scott's found someone. Know you must be special, Josh. Scott's a fussy one. And he's never brought anyone to meet me before. He tell you that?"

He hadn't. I shake my head.

"You look good together. You serious about my boy?"

That's an easy one. "I am, yes." I suppress the niggle in the back of my mind that says, not serious enough to come out. I'm doing him a disservice, but I can't help how I feel. Behind her back, I frown.

I'm sitting at the kitchen table with a coffee between my hands and feel someone ruffle the hair on my head. "Glad about that, 'cause I'm all in too." It's Scott, of course. He overheard. My words, luckily, not my thoughts.

Rachel beams as Scott kicks out a chair and sits down, pulling the third coffee toward him while simultaneously reaching out to take a cookie from the plate in the middle of the table. He then pushes the plate toward me. The inclination of his head suggests I should try one. I do. It's good.

"Auntie Kathy's popping around later. Clint will be with her too."

"It will be good to see them." He nods at me then explains, "My aunt and uncle."

"Your grandparents wanted to come down, but I put them off. When you said you were bringing someone, I hoped, well, I hoped you'd found someone at last. I'm afraid I was selfish, wanted you to myself."

"They wouldn't approve?" I suggest.

Her jaw drops. "What the hell do you mean?"

"Mom," Scott jumps in. "Josh's family disowned him. He's never been accepted before. He's not come out."

"Oh my." She stands and makes herself busy refilling the coffee pot as though giving herself something to do. Then she swings around. "Oh, honey. That must be so hard for you. I couldn't think of sending Scott away, however he'd turned out." She takes a step toward her son. "I couldn't be more proud of him."

She's easy to talk to. Her manner so open, I find myself asking, "Didn't you mind when you found out? Did you try and change him?"

"Change him?" Her voice rises. Scott slides his chair back a fraction and sits watching us. A hand lifting his third—or it could be a fourth—cookie toward his mouth. Rachel takes her seat again, places her elbows on the table, resting her chin on her hands. "Change him," she repeats again, looking thoughtful. "Honey, when he first told me, I already suspected. Had seen he was different, but couldn't quite put my finger on how. Gave him the space to grow into whatever he was going to."

"Kathy spotted it first," Scott butts in. "Didn't she?"

"My sister had her suspicions, yes. Huh." She gives a short laugh. "She'd already started eyeing up boys for you." Growing serious again, she carries on, "But I gave you the space to talk to me yourself. You were young, so I told you, no pressure, just see what you become." She gives a small frown. "So no, I didn't try to change him. Scott's my son, and I love him unconditionally. The last thing I'd want to do is try and force him to be something he's not. I'm proud of him as he is."

Scott reaches out his hand, places it on hers, and squeezes it. "Josh wasn't so lucky. His folks sent him to a 'Pray out the Gay' camp."

My eyes flick him a warning, I didn't want him to say that. But Rachel's reaction smooths things over.

Her hands cover her mouth. "Oh my God, Josh. I'm so sorry. I've read about what goes on. They're terrible places. Shouldn't be allowed."

"No ma'am, they shouldn't," I find myself heartily agreeing. But hoping she doesn't ask for details.

Her eyes flit to Scott. "You helping your man?"

I answer for him, feeling brave enough to do something I never thought I'd do in front of another person. Being in her presence makes my next action seem natural. Reaching out, I take hold of his hand. "He sure is," I tell her. "He sure is."

With that, she thankfully lets the subject drop.

The rest of the day passes easily. Late afternoon his aunt and uncle pop around, then early evening, despite Rachel's attempts to keep them away, three of his grandparents turn up on the doorstep. His grandpa on his dad's side having passed away a few years back. To my astonishment, they all treat me like I'm already a member of the family. His surviving grandad having fun at our expense, asking who's going to make an honest man of who.

I go from feeling incredulous that these good people show no signs of discomfort having two gays in the house, to enjoying their easy acceptance. For the first time in my life, feeling relaxed in front of strangers, able to be myself. Not watching what I say, or how I look at Scott. My facial muscles hurt as I'm smiling and laughing so much.

When they get out the board games I settle right in, feeling probably the most at ease that I ever have. I lose gracefully to the expert—Scott's grandpa—which I'm assured isn't unusual.

The old folks start talking about leaving, when Rachel catches my eye, and says with a big grin, "You know, I think I'm going to adopt you, Josh."

"You can't adopt a grown man, Mom," Scott scoffs when he's finished choking.

She stands, hands on her hips, looking as ferocious as a tiny woman can. "Nothing to stop me if I want to."

I chuckle. "I'm up for that."

"That's settled." His grandpa gives a satisfied nod. "He's part of the family. No escaping us now, Josh. And that game there was close. You'll have to come visit again, and I'll give you a chance to get your own back."

Scott grins at his grandpa, but says sternly, "Pops!" then sits forward, his eyes narrowed. "If you adopt him, Mom, that would make him my brother." His eyebrow rises. "Something sounds very wrong with that."

"Shucks." She sits down again. "Hadn't thought of that. Well, do it another way then. Make him my son-in-law."

Now it's my eyes opening wide as I return Scott's horrified glance. *Far too early for us to be thinking about that.*

But he knows how to deal with his mom. "If we decide to take that step, Mom, you'll be the first to know."

She looks at me slyly. "Nothing to stop you calling me Mom in the meantime, though, is there? Nobody's business but ours."

Fuck me if that doesn't get me right in the feels. Moisture pricks at the back of my eyes. Luckily Scott makes an abrupt change of subject when he starts telling his uncle about his bike.

When the visitors at last go home, I'm surprised to find that Rachel's been busy while they've been here, an explanation for her brief absence now provided. She's changed the sleeping arrangements, giving us her king-sized bed for the night, herself prepared to sleep in Scott's room. Just one more thing that shows how easy it is for her to accept we're together.

We hold each other through the night, but there's only innocent touches. His mom is only yards away after all. I lie awake for hours, the incompatibility between his family's behaviour and my own opening my eyes. *Not everyone thinks gays are dirty.* What would it have been like if I'd had supportive people around me when I'd been growing up?

For one thing, I wouldn't be trying to hide my relationship with Scott. I might even be tempted to join a gay club instead of pretending I'm straight.

Scott's family's so welcoming, we're persuaded to stay an extra night, giving him a chance to show me around the area where he grew up. I've appreciated the time together. There were no public displays of affection out of the house, a step too far for me to take. But in this place where no one knows us, I don't feel eyes burning into my back as if people can tell what I am just by looking at me. Not having to pretend to be something I'm not seems to take a weight off my shoulders. Maybe one day, if it all goes well with Scott, we'll start somewhere new, start over, come out and be ourselves. No more pretending. *Maybe.*

When we leave on the Tuesday, Rachel hugs me like the mother she now says she is to me and makes us both promise to visit again soon.

Fuck going to see Delia. Seeing his family, being accepted by them, has probably been the best therapy I could have had.

CHAPTER 23

The weather holds up as we ride back to Tucson. I settle back and enjoy the ride. It's lucky in that we have a clear trip, a good straight run apart from stopping for gas.

As when we get back to Tucson, my new-found peace is immediately shattered, the compound in uproar. Dart, Slick and Mouse had gone to San Diego to flush out Slick's Rock Demon, Dart going along with the intention of finding Alex's ex and setting him right on the ways of the world. Yeah, that was the plan. But it had all gone to shit. While Dart was happily riding to California, unbeknown to him, Alex's ex had come to Tucson and taken both her and her kid. I'm astounded when I hear. I've taken a liking to Alex, and Tyler? Well, he seemed a bright kid. No way I'd like to see harm come to either of them.

There's little we can do here, not knowing the area, the San D club are best placed to search for them, but it's obviously the only topic of conversation. Beers are consumed, tempers are fraught during the frustrating couple of days before we have word Dart's found Alex. When I hear the state she was in and that her ex had left her to die a lonely and painful death, it makes me feel sick. *What bastard can do something like that to the mother of their child?* At least she's alive, as Scott reminds me. Knowing my brother, if Dart has any say in the matter, she'll stay that way. He's just got to get his head out of his ass and admit what we can already see, that he wants to claim her.

There's a collective sigh of relief once she's found. A feeling of getting back to normal. Time is what Alex needs, and that's what Dart will give her. People start laughing again, pool games get played once more as days pass by without further excitement.

Until Drummer gets a call from Tyler, Alex's six-year-old fucking kid, of all people. From the sounds of it, Alex, Dart, Slick and Mouse have been abducted. Tyler was pretty adamant Snake, the San D prez, was behind it.

What the fuck? While Drummer, Wraith, Peg, Blade and Road the prospect prepare to get moving pretty damn fast, I offer to go along with them preferring to help rather than sit on my hands, but Prez asks me to stay on standby at the compound. If they need more help, they'll call on the brothers left behind.

I hate waiting for news. But looking around me, I'm not the only one with a sense of feeling useless, not understanding what's happened—whether the young boy's mistaken or not—or what threat there is to the club. None of us can believe a chapter president has gone rogue. Tyler's only six. Maybe he got muddled up with what's gone on. Fact is though, we already know neither Dart, Mouse or Slick have been answering their phones. We try to keep the news from Ella, but she cottons on fast something is wrong. Something that made the officers go tearing off to California. She's not stupid. Dollar comes up with some story that we've lost touch with Slick and they're just checking things out as a precaution. It doesn't help her feel better. Paladin, shit, that lad's grown up fast even during the time I've been in the club, takes it on himself to support both Jayden and Ella.

Once again no one can relax, all on edge hoping for an update. Then amazed when it comes in. Turns out nine of the bastards in the San D club had tried to enact a coup, led by that fucker Snake and his sergeant-at-arms Poke. To say the news stuns us is an understatement. Shit, it was only a few months back that Snake and his boys were helping to protect the mother chapter. That they've turned against us is unbelievable.

Fang, the Demon Slick had been chasing, was tied up in the mess. He now is dead, along with Gator, one of the traitors. The other seven, names I hadn't known before but which I soon know by heart, Shark, DJ, Crow, Rattler, Tinder and Bastard had been sent out of the club in bad standing. So many, and all at once.

It's shocking. Distressing. There's no doubt they deserved it for what they had done, but hell. One day to be a brother, the next with a reputation which means no club would have you? Out bad. The two words a brother never wants to hear. All the discussion about how those men will be feeling right now brings home yet again how essential it is to keep my sexuality, and Lady's, under wraps. Listening to their fate described in stark terms warns me how I'd never want to be placed in a position like that. This club is everything to me. To be sent out with no one behind you? Knowing you'd lost the brotherhood, that you'd never find anyone else to take you in? I'd rather be dead.

I don't think any of us have completely come to terms with what's happened, even when Dart returns to Tucson bringing Tyler, Alex and Mouse with him. I'm pleased to see Alex looks like she's recovering well, and as for young Tyler, well, every member takes time to shake his hand. All of us impressed like fuck that at six years old, he'd managed to get a warning to Drummer. Watching him shrug off the thanks as though he'd done nothing, bemused by all the attention, I reckon he'd make a good brother when he grows up. Then pull myself up. According to our by-laws, the colour of his skin prohibits it. I wonder if anyone's thought about that?

Soon after, Drummer gets back, bringing the traitorous president and sergeant-at-arms with him. Guess it's not going to go down well for Snake and Poke. I doubt I'm alone in thinking I'd rather spit at them than talk to them. My other brothers return with Drummer, along with Lost, the San Diego VP, who keeps his head down, as though nervous about speaking to anybody.

Thanks to Prez's warning, we're prepared for the other visitors coming in. Red arrives with Crash shortly after Drummer returns, Hellfire and his VP Demon from Colorado aren't far behind, Snatcher from Utah's the last to arrive with Thor. While they accept drinks and food on arrival, it's clear to see they're all in a serious mood, none of the usual joviality when brothers from other chapters meet. Well, they would be sombre. It's not often a president of an MC turns bad. Thank fuck. It's a situation Satan's Devils have never had to deal with.

Once the visitors are fed and watered, at last we're summoned into church. This is a meeting I think we're all both eagerly anticipating and part dreading. With extra chairs squeezed in, there's hardly room to breathe. Heart's chair, still left empty, is pushed to the back of the room. We're crammed so close in together I'm almost sitting on Lady's lap, but that's not going to cause any raised eyebrows, Shooter's all but sitting on mine.

We then have one of the gravest meetings I've ever been involved in, one like I hope never to be part of again. Most of the Tucson chapter stay silent, offering their votes when the time comes, but not saying much else. Awed in the presence of four club presidents and five VPs.

It's my old prez, Red, who suggests the solution. I reckon Drummer set it up so it wouldn't be seen as him, the president of the mother chapter, forcing the decision. The idea of killing Snake and Poke is not one which is going to be taken lightly.

"Ain't got no option." My eyes flick to Red who starts, his gruff voice heavy with emotion. "Can't leave them alive. Out in bad standin' is far too good after what they've done."

The other presidents only put forward more good reasons. It comes as no surprise when it's decided Snake and Poke will be dispatched to meet Satan. If only half of what they're supposed to have done is true, they fully deserve it.

As I'm thinking they'll be getting to that immediately, Lost, the San D VP, wants a word. And fuck me if he doesn't open his mouth to put himself in the firing line. Suggesting we put him out bad as well, as he hadn't seen what was going on.

This is heavy going. I risk a look at Lady, his eyes are wide open as he listens and watches the proceedings. I've been a member far longer than he has, but even for me, this is way outside of my comfort zone.

Words go back and forth until Drummer states his opinion that Lost should keep his patch. I breathe an inward sigh of relief. Satan's Devils have already lost too many members in the last few days.

But Snatcher disagrees. *What the fuck?* There's gasps all around the table. Dart, in the middle of lighting a cigarette, pauses with the lighter burning, but only half way to his lips. Everyone sits frozen. Until the Colorado prez continues, suggesting he becomes prez of the San D chapter instead.

There's loud sighs of relief from all around. Of course, that decision can't be ratified here, that's down to the members left in San Diego. But it sounds like a good idea. Now another change is proposed. That Dart goes back with Lost as his temporary VP. Well, fuck me. Wouldn't have predicted that in a million years. I throw him a chin lift in support. *Good on you, Dart. Seems you proved yourself in Cali.*

My mind's fixed on the drink I need badly after all this shit, when Prez announces there's another problem. My jaw drops when he points out the exact thing I was thinking before the meeting. Dart's claiming Alex as his old lady, which leads Drum to question what happens if Tyler wants to join the club. In an important, far reaching decision, all clubs agree to change the by-laws opening it to everyone if they're a good enough fit. Whatever their skin colour. Oh, and as long as they're male. The thought of females is a big step too far. That suggestion, quickly and to my mind rightly dismissed, brings the only moment of light relief.

We must break now. But no. They're talking about Tyler, about how to raise money for the operation he needs. Drummer mentions the poker run which I know of already, Lady and I have discussed it before. I know Lady's going to volunteer to help as he'd been involved in organising one in Vegas. At the time doing it as one of his prospect tasks.

It slowly dawns on me there's still no drink in sight or likely to be any time soon. When the meeting finally comes to a close, all the Tucson chapter—excluding the prospects—are required to go to the storage room alongside the visiting officers. Most of us are here just to watch, not to take part. It wasn't necessary for Drummer to enforce it, but something as serious as this? We all need to be there. Taking the life of a Satan's Devils prez and high ranking officer needed to be approved by all chapters. This is fuckin' grim shit.

Snake's going to be no great loss, I think as I watch him try to persuade everyone to get into drug running. I feel glad he was never my prez, that the option of transferring to San D had never come up. I just don't take to him at all. Well named in my opinion.

Marvel's standing just in front of me, his shoulders slumped. I touch my hand to his shoulder, a brief touch of support. Having heard his views, he's not sorry Snake hasn't long for this world, he's more annoyed he was ever taken in by him. Like Lost, he believes he should have seen indications that Snake had turned on what the Satan's Devils stood for.

Watching Snake being stripped of his patch is tough. It's the worst thing that can happen to a member. Bile rises into my throat. I swallow hard to prevent myself puking when Blade lights the blow torch and methodically burns Snake's Satan's Devils back patch tattoo off. Christ, the air smells like a pig grilling. *Can't show myself up.* I swallow again, feeling my Adam's apple rising and falling rapidly. Lady's eyes meet mine, his face pale, but he draws his shoulders back.

Next we're all invited forward to show our own disgust. By the time everyone's planted their fist on him, I don't think Drummer needed to waste that bullet, Snake must already be dead. I suppose it's part symbolic. The mother chapter president taking the final shot.

Then it's Poke's turn. Now I'm expecting the acrid odour and am better prepared for it, I watch stoically. He deserves it, I tell myself over and over again. His protests and pleas beforehand, then the screams as his tat is burned off, the air growing thick with the stench makes my ears and nose sting. There's no escape. All I can do is keep my eyes and expression steady as he takes his final and terminal punishment.

When it becomes too much, I turn my gaze away from the man being tortured, scanning the audience. My brothers are mostly standing, feet apart, arms folded, faces expressionless, though some have paled like me. *This is what happens to anyone who betrays the club.*

It's then a chill comes over me as my eyes find Lady. *What if we're found out? What if we're sent out bad for keeping our secret? For essentially lying to the club. Would they burn our tats? Could I stand seeing that done to Lady?*

I couldn't.

The risk is no longer just seeing disgust on their faces. Retribution may be much harsher than that. *Who knows how far they'll take it?* I harden my resolve. *No one must ever find out.*

Nah. Can't take the chance. Me? I don't really give a damn about myself. But Lady? The thought makes me even queasier than I was already.

Finally, it's over. When I'm back at the bar I no longer want beer. Without me asking, Lady hands me a brandy.

Chapter 24

Always turns my stomach," Scott says quietly, as he enters my suite later. We'd stayed as long as we had to, then I'd left first knowing he'd be following soon after.

I don't have to ask what he's referring to. "Yeah. Same. Never get used to it." My brow creases. "Sometimes I wonder if what I am affects my reaction, you know?"

Scott huffs. "That's got nothing to do with it." He walks into my bathroom, I hear water splashing in the sink. When he comes out, he's rubbing his face with a towel. "I fuckin' threw up, Josh. Went around the back of the storage shed, couldn't hold it in any longer. And I wasn't the only fuckin' one."

My eyebrows rise.

"Between you and me, Brother?"

I narrow my eyes, *why does he even have to ask?*

He gives it a moment, then nods. "Blade."

Blade? The enforcer? He lives for this shit, doesn't he? Relishes the torture he inflicts. That he's made physically sick by the work he's asked to do for the club puts a different slant on things, and it makes me start to see him in a different light.

"He doesn't want anyone to know, Josh."

I can understand that.

"What he did," Lady continues. "What *we* did." He shudders. "That was some sick shit."

"They deserved it." Snake and Poke couldn't have lived. Their deaths made an example to anyone else who was thinking of betraying the club.

"Deserved to die, yes," he confirms, "but having that back patch burned off first?" I pat the bed; he comes to sit beside me. "Josh, you know you worry about being turned out of the club? Do you reckon they'd do that to us? Is that why you're so careful about us not coming out?"

I rub my hand over my chin. "Fuck knows. I'd have said no." I think for a moment, remembering that thought I'd had while sitting at the bar that afternoon with Beef. "This club is as het as they can be. For all I know, they could have a case of gay panic." I tilt my head, waiting for his nod, seeing by the narrowing of his eyes he's already getting where I'm coming from. "Fuck, Scott. If most of the states still permit the gay panic defence as a plea toward mitigating or commuting a sentence for murder, let alone violence, what might it mean to an MC?"

"Most lawyers advise against using it. And even judges are against it being a valid excuse for a hate crime."

"We're not in a court of law, Brother. We're in an outlaw motorcycle club." My words seem to hang in the air.

Scott bites his lip, then sucks it into his mouth. "The other traitors were just told to get their tats inked out. Would our *crime* warrant our patches being burned off? Or killing us?" He breathes out a breath. "Do we really think so little of the men we call brothers that they'd be so threatened by what we are?"

"We're hiding from them, lying to them. In my case, for the second time. Who knows what they'd call it? Betrayal? Or would they hate us so much they'd…"

His eyebrows draw together. "I like my skin. I like my life. Don't want to lose either. Reckon you're right, Josh. If we're staying Satan's Devils, we have to be fuckin' careful and not let anyone know."

"Maybe we should think about joining a gay club, like you suggested."

He's quiet for a moment. "Not sure what that would look like. I like the brothers here. Might not be able to predict their reaction if they knew about us, but I like them for all that. So I say, not yet." He pats my hand. "Not until we have to. Though I'd love to be able to live as myself, I'm happy here. Never a dull moment, so to speak."

After the meeting we'd had followed by the unpleasant aftermath, he's got a good point. "Life's certainly not boring in Tucson, Scott." My lips thin, "But no looks, no touches. We make friends with the other brothers," I warn him.

"Yeah. Got that. We've been through that before. I reckon today's been a warning of what we could face if we slip up." He nods, then after a moment, changes the subject. "Hey, talking about brothers. Felt fuckin' sorry for Marvel."

I had too. "Feel you there. Couldn't quite read his expression, whether he was more disgusted or guilty."

Scott purses his lips. "Doubt he's got anything to be guilty about, unless it's by association that he was a member of a rotten club. Man's good to have at your back."

I agree. There's nothing he's done that's shown us otherwise, but if I'm not mistaken, Prez might look at him suspiciously for a while. He could have been a plant feeding info back to Snake. It's highly unlikely from what I've seen of Marvel, but Drummer's a man who likes to be careful.

"What about Dart, then?" Scott murmurs. "He's stepped up, got a VP spot now."

"Only temporarily. But I reckon he deserves the shot."

There's a sigh close to my ear, then arms pulling me down on the bed. "What a fuckin' day, week, it's been, Josh. I'm sorry, but I just want to hold you and go to sleep."

He'll get no argument from me. Violence and death turn some men on. Luckily that applies to neither Scott or myself. Not that we shy away from it, we wouldn't be members of a one percenter club if we did. Men deal with it in different ways. Some fuck, some drink, and me, well, I'm finding there's nothing better than snuggling up to Scott.

Early next morning I'm disturbed by a knock on my door. *Oh fuck*, the handle's turning. Luckily, it's locked. A voice calls out, "Joker? You in there?"

Scott wakes with a start. Not wanting to speak I point to the bathroom. Silently he slides out of bed, grabs his clothes, quickly checking he's left nothing behind as I pull on my jeans. "Comin'," I respond to the voice outside as I spy Scott's cut and throw it at him.

When Scott slips out of sight, I open the door, my hand over my mouth to stifle a genuine yawn. "Dart?"

He smirks. "Wake you?"

It's so obvious, I don't respond. It would have been so much worse if I'd forgotten to lock the door and he'd caught me awake with Scott's hand on my junk.

"Sorry, Joker. But I'm off to San D now. I just wanted to ask, well, you looked out for Alex at the club. Can you keep an eye on her here? I don't like leavin' her, and I know she trusts you. It would make my mind easier."

"Of course, Brother. You didn't have to ask. You still expectin' trouble?"

He frowns. "Her ex is still breathin', so yes."

"No worries. I'll do what I can. And good luck to you too, Dart. Sounds like you'll have a lot on your plate down in San Diego."

"That I have, Brother. You're not wrong there. Fuck knows what Lost and I will be walkin' back into."

"Lost seems a good sort."

His face splits into a grin. "He is. I think we'll make a good team as long as we get the rest of the brothers on board. I'll do what I can to help him get his feet under the table, then I can come back home." He indicates the door opposite. "I couldn't wake Lady. Know where he is?"

"No fuckin' idea. I'm not his keeper." My voice is sharp as I lie.

Dart shrugs. "Oh, well, I know he volunteered to help plan the poker run with Alex. Just wanted him to be on the alert for trouble as well."

"I can pass that message on. I know he likes Alex, and young Tyler."

For a moment a shadow crosses Dart's eyes, I doubt it's too far a leap to assume he's thinking of the kid's health issues. Then he steps back, says goodbye, and leaves. At fucking last.

When the outer door slams shut, Scott comes out of the bathroom. He too is now dressed in his jeans. He wipes his hand over his head. "Fuckin' close, Josh."

"Too fuckin' close." I stand, staring at the man who's come to mean so much to me, but who I'm now going to have to push away, once again. "There can be…"

"…no more sleepin' over," he finishes for me. He steps closer while I'm still expecting an argument. "After yesterday, what we saw, how they treat traitors. Fuck, the Tucson Devils don't let a man go lightly, Josh. If they think we're betrayin' them by keeping our secret, or if you're right, and they feel threatened by us. Fuck, I don't know how far they would go." He pauses, his hand caresses my cheek. "I couldn't bear it if anything happened to you. I thought you were overreactin', when you wanted to keep what we have between us quiet. But now, fuck, I don't know what to think. Saw a different side of our brothers yesterday."

I think of Blade, Peg, Wraith and Drummer as I normally see them. Good brothers I'd want at my back. But yesterday showed me what they could do when crossed. "Need to stay on the right side of them, Scott."

His face is close to mine, he takes advantage, bringing his mouth down, brushing my lips with his own. "Doesn't change how I feel about you, but we've got to slow this right down."

There's nothing more to say. He's said it all. I don't want to lose him completely, hate the thought of not sleeping in the same bed. But better that than lose everything. When he walks out of my door with the rest of his clothes in his hands, my eyes follow him, settling for a moment on his door when it snicks shut. *We have to be careful.*

Club life starts getting back to normal with the exception that we're now missing two members. Lady's been dragged into arranging the poker run with Alex and Wraith. He spends so much time with them our paths don't cross much during the days, except when I'm called in in my role as Road Captain to talk about sorting out permits and shit like that. One day we witness young Tyler having an episode, which makes raising funds for his operation even more critical.

Fuck, it hurts seeing a six-year-old kid having a fit like that. There had been nothing for me to do, all I could do was watch as Alex dealt with him so competently, and young Paladin, his jaw tight, picked him up and carried him to his suite. The only contribution I can make is to do what I can to ensure the poker run is a success so we raise as much money as possible.

There's one thing that we need make no excuses for when we go off together. The club accepts that Lady accompanies me to the therapist without batting an eye. I've had a few consultations with her now, and today, we're going again.

"Here." Lady approaches, dangling keys in one hand, a letter in the other.

Post? For me? I take it, idly noticing it's been redirected from the Vegas club, but don't think much of it, simply slide it into my cut. Any letters I get are mostly demands for money or government shit I've no time for. "You ready?"

"Yeah," he replies.

I lead the way out of the door, not suffering anything like the trepidation I'd done on my first visit to Delia.

"Josh, Scott. Good morning." We return the pleasantries, then gravitate to our usual seats. Delia pulls out her tablet, taking a couple of moments to read through the notes of our last session. "So, Josh, how have you been?"

I think about her question carefully, taking a brief pause before I give my considered response. "Meeting Scott's family, as we discussed last time, was an eye-opener for me. It gave me an insight into a world where I could be accepted for what I am, not simply tolerated for what I'm not."

She looks at me critically. "Are you accepting you're gay, Josh? Or still wanting to be straight?"

I answer honestly. "I'm still pretending I'm straight to fit in. I, we," I point to Scott, "we have to in our situation. But I'm no longer resenting the fact I'm gay so much."

"And this situation you're in. You can't change that?"

I'm not sure what she's asking. "Do you mean leave? Go somewhere different?"

"Or take the bull by the horns and admit your sexuality."

Scott's usually silent, but this time it's him who replies. "We can't do that." He's so adamant, she can do nothing but accept it.

"I'm considering moving on, steppin' into something new." I lean forward. "To be with like-minded people, to not worry about hidin' anymore. That's startin' to look very appealin'."

Scott's gaze settles on me, there's a query in his stare. Yes, I know getting out might not be so easy. If we admit why we're leaving… Something to be approached very carefully. We might be risking retaliation in the same way as if we were simply found out.

She asks questions, I answer, then finally, she puts her tablet down. "You know Josh, you've come a long way during our sessions. Are you still having panic attacks?"

I haven't for a while now, I enlighten her as to that.

"What I see is a man who first came to me unhappy with his sexuality, but who's now closer to accepting what he is. But it's on you to find a place where you feel comfortable and belong. Which might well mean your changing your current situation, either by coming out or moving on."

I belong in the Satan's Devils. I'm comfortable there too. I try to explain that.

"Okay. We'll continue these sessions. I like the improvements I see, Josh. But at some point, the next stage will be up to you."

She's right. The ball is in my court.

When we get back to the bikes, Scott touches my arm. "You okay? Are these sessions helpin'?"

"She's right, Scott. Unless we change the environment, I, you, can't come out. Perhaps we need to do some serious thinkin'. Look into a gay club that might suit us." I stroke my chin. "Didn't want to think about that as I didn't want to be lumped in with a bunch of perverts," I raise my hand at his look of disgust. "Don't think that way any longer. We're different, but there's nothing wrong with that."

"Thank fuck for that," he laughs. "The way other people see us is on them, not us."

"I miss you, Scott." Miss the nights of him holding me.

His mouth curves. "Still want that ass."

In response, my cock jerks to life.

For a reply, I throw my leg over the seat, start my engine, and turn to wink at him before kicking it down into first.

CHAPTER 25

When they know I've been to the therapist, people normally leave me alone to process my thoughts. If they misread the serious expression on my face as I go up to my suite, they are perfectly happy to leave Lady to deal with whatever mood I've returned in. No one will be bothering us. We've got no church or anywhere else we need to be.

Scott pushes me inside his room, then with his hands on my chest, encourages me to the bed, putting pressure on my shoulders until I'm seated. Then he's on his knees behind me.

When his lips softly caress my neck, it starts as a tickle. Before I'm able to squirm, he moves his mouth until it's over a particularly sensitive spot which sends a shiver right through me. I start to turn my head, but his strong hands hold me in place as his teeth nibble my skin, moving gently back to where he started, then down to that pulse point in my neck once again.

Now he's using his left hand to gently tug the neck of my tee so it's exposing my shoulder, and his lips close in, applying small kisses as his mouth works its way down, then returns, then slides down again.

I throw my head back, wanting his lips on mine, but again, he moves me back into position, and continues the soft onslaught of just his mouth.

Tingles are running through me, my cock swelling in my pants. I raise my hand, placing it on the back of his head as he moves back to the other side, starting all over again. From below my ear to the pulse point, down my shoulder and back up. He nips, following it with a soothing lick of his tongue, sucking gently, but not enough to leave any mark.

My body becomes a riot of sensation, a shudder, a shake, a tingle, a tickle that I try to move away from. It's all adding up, increasing my desire, my arousal, sending even more blood to my cock.

When he moves his hand around to my chest and pinches my nipples through the cloth, my breath becomes ragged. *I want him so much.*

He's taking his time. My body starts to thrash in his hold, wanting, needing so much more from him. *He can do anything he likes.*

My hips start to thrust of their own accord, my hand goes to the base of my cock just trying to stop myself from coming from those kisses so expertly placed by his mouth.

His fingers find my chin, he's tilting my head up, finally bringing his lips down onto mine. At first he's gentle, a soft barely there sweep across, then his tongue probes. He doesn't rush, doesn't hurry. He chuckles against me, as I try to press harder, try to deepen the kiss. Then he moves his mouth away before I've had nearly enough.

He moves around in front of me. "Do you trust me, Josh?"

"Trust?" After all the months we've been close, I can't understand why he's asking me that. "Of course I trust you."

"But do you trust me enough?"

A momentary hesitation as I realise what he's asking. He wants to take the next step. To a destination that's known to him, but unfamiliar to me.

There's only one way to describe it. "I feel like a virgin."

"That's because you are," he says softly, into my ear. "Babe, I wouldn't do anything to hurt you."

Now in front of me, he tilts and lowers his head, starting that gentle kissing of my neck again. Fear of the unknown had made me tense, but his tender touches soon have me returning to that state of arousal. Again he takes my mouth, and I feel his hands taking hold of my shirt. I lose the contact for a moment as he pulls it over my head, then our lips are meeting again.

Half because I too want to participate, half because I'm desperate to feel his skin against mine, I move my hands down, grab a handful of his shirt and start dragging it upwards. He moves away, helping me tear it off. Our eyes meet. His flare with arousal, I suspect the same emotion's reflected in mine.

Seizing the opportunity, he gets to his feet, quickly divesting himself of the rest of his clothes.

"Want you naked, babe," he instructs. Then waits expectantly, standing tall, unashamedly showing me himself in all his erect glory.

I unfasten the buttons. Still sitting on the bed, I raise my hips slowly, and shrug my jeans down my thighs. As if I'm not moving fast enough, he brushes my hands away and crouches down, then slides them off himself.

Now he's stalking me. His knees one by one are placed on the bed. I scoot backward, my progress stopped when his hands take my biceps and he pulls me up so I'm flush against his chest. My legs fall to either side of his.

Another kiss. This one more determined. As our mouths move against each other Scott's skin slides against mine, I can feel the tight little buds of his nipples, I move mine to rub against them. That's not the only part of us touching, his groin is held a fraction of an inch above mine, our cocks knocking against each other like two swords preparing to do battle.

"Fuckin' want you, Josh," he gasps.

"Take me," I all but wail, my body primed, my cock ready for relief. My balls churning, so full it feels like they're going to burst.

His weight is gone from me as he reaches over to the side of the bed, opens a drawer, taking something out. "Fuckin' lucky I was a boy scout."

"Were you?"

"Fuck no." His eyes, bright and shining, seem to smile down into mine.

I watch as he fumbles with something, swears, then manages to extricate what he wants from the packaging, his eagerness making him clumsy. *Lube.* He applies a generous portion to his hand, then pulls a pillow toward him.

"Up." He taps my hips.

He leans back and half turns as he slips the pillow under my ass, raising it at an angle. Then he places his mouth over mine, using that contact to encourage me onto my back. While I'm responding to his lips and tongue I feel a finger probing where no one has touched before. There's pressure, I try to stop myself tensing, but it's hard, the alien invasion something I shouldn't be allowing. I...

"Stop thinking, Josh. It's me, and I want you so fuckin' much. But you tell me to stop? I will."

His voice grounds me. I try to shake my head, but don't want to lose the connection with his mouth, his tongue mimicking the small advances being made by his finger as he breaches my tight opening. There's a feeling of pressure, a slight burn. I start to become acclimated, my cock so hard as if anticipating the untold pleasures to come. Then he tries to add another digit, and it's too much. If this is just two fingers, how the hell will I take his dick inside?

"Relax, babe." His words echo around my mouth. Pressure, a popping sensation, then they must both be in, and then a strange motion. "Just readying you, Josh. You're going to be fine."

Without removing his fingers, he reaches with his other hand and picks up something else, opening the package with his teeth, then smoothing on a condom. One handed, he applies lube to that too. Lots of lube. He throws his head back and groans as he palms his own dick. I watch, intrigued as he tugs it a couple of times.

We don't speak, just lock our eyes as he at last pulls his hand away and positions himself at my entrance. An almost imperceptible raising of a brow, my miniscule, slightly nervous nod in return, then the real pressure begins.

I try to relax. I can't.

"Push back against me. Bear down." His voice is husky, the words staccato.

I attempt to follow his instruction, but fear starts to take hold.

"Open your eyes, look at me, babe. Stay with me."

I hadn't realised I'd closed them, my body shutting down against the invasion. When I raise my eyelids, and see the intense focused look on his beautiful face, I realise how much I want this, want this joining. Want to become one with this patient man.

"Oh fuck, I'm in."

His fingers caused burning, this is worse.

"Scott…"

"Just a bit more, babe. Stay with it, okay? Let me in, please. I want in you, babe."

Realising I'm holding my breath, I exhale, then remember to breathe in again, and try to relax my muscles.

"That's it, babe. That's it."

One of his hands has hold of my cock, when he took it I don't know, but I raise my head to see him stroking it, while looking down where his cock disappears into my body. A groan escapes my mouth at the sight.

"I'm going to move now."

Fuck. Yes, please.

He gently pulls out, then pushes back in, this time seeming to go further than before, hitting something inside me. He repeats his action, this time flexing his hips a little more sharply.

"Fuck!" I cry out.

"Does it hurt?" he gasps.

"So good," I rasp in reply.

Then he's increasing the pace, I watch his hips bucking, muscles rippling over his thighs, sweat drips from his forehead just like it is running down mine. Then, oh, the sensations, the feelings, my cock swells, I can't stop it.

"Lady, oh, fuck, Scott. I'm…"

"Me fuckin' too, babe."

As he swears loudly he loses his rhythm, now he's jerking inside me, tugging at my cock as it leaps in his hand, my cum shooting out in white ribbons over my chest.

I'd worried I'd regret it. That was why I'd put it off for so long. Expected to feel dirty, that the act was disgusting. What I hadn't anticipated was the emotional feeling that swells up inside as Scott's dick goes flaccid, and my cum starts to dry.

With one hand to his dick holding the condom, he leans over as he slips out. Once again, resting his forehead against mine, he asks, "You okay?"

Raising my hand I cup his cheek and answer honestly. "About the best I've ever been in my life."

"Me too, babe. Me fuckin' too." His words come out on a sigh that seems tinged with relief.

I sit up, wincing slightly. Keeping my hand on his cheek, I stare into his eyes. "Scott," I start, then I am unsure how to express all the emotion inside me.

Covering my hand with his own, he simply replies in a hoarse voice, "I know, babe, I know. You've become a fuckin' addiction for me." Then he's gone, going into the bathroom to deal with the condom.

While considering his words for a moment, knowing I feel the same way, I pull myself up and start gathering my clothes, pulling on my jeans. Since we were almost caught that morning, we don't sleep in each other's rooms, however much I'd love to spend the night with him by my side. I flinch as I feel an unaccustomed soreness. *Yeah, and once was probably enough for tonight.* My lips curl up, relishing the memory of him inside me. *Not dirty at all. Just right.*

As I pick up my cut, the letter I was handed earlier falls out onto the floor.

Scott, unashamed of his nakedness, comes back and lies down on the bed, his head propped under his hands. He nods at the envelope on the floor. "You gonna open that?"

Picking it up, it's fairly bulky, as if there's something else inside. I shake my head. "Won't be anything I want to read," I explain. "Probably a ticket or something."

"Give it here," he suggests. "I'll vet it for you."

I've no secrets I want to keep from him, so I chuck it across. "Have at it." I grin.

He leans over then pulls the knife out of the belt of his jeans, using it as a letter opener. I pull my tee over my head, not particularly interested in what I've been sent. No letter is ever good news.

"It's been sent on from the Vegas club," he informs me. "There's an unopened letter inside. Handwritten address."

I shrug. "Open it."

I brush my hands through my hair to get the worst of the *just fucked* look out, hearing the swish of the knife through paper, then a rustling as he looks through the pages. "It's from Simeon Wilkinson." The name makes me turn around, my eyes narrowing. "He a relative of yours?"

He certainly is. Momentarily stunned, it takes me a couple of seconds to reply. "He is. But I've not seen or heard of him for, oh, ten, eleven years?" My brow creases. "What the fuck does he want?" Scott starts handing the letter over to me. "Nah, you read it, Scott. Can't see anything good comin' from anyone in my family. And I ain't got no secrets from you."

Scott shrugs. "Okay." He peruses the first sentence or so. The letter's handwritten, I can see that from here, and presumably he's getting the hang of the script. He clears his throat. "*Dear Josh,*

What a lame salutation to start with, but that's the way letters begin, isn't it? But how else to address a brother I haven't seen in so long? I haven't the faintest idea where to start.

"First, I owe you an apology for not keeping in touch. The gap in our ages meant we were never close, and as I was away with the Army, I didn't come home much on leave. I think you'll understand when I say I preferred to spend what free time I had away from our bigoted parents. I assumed, from what contact I had with them, that you got along with them better than I ever had."

As Scott pauses, I move closer. Even more confused at the words he's reading out. *I'd thought Simeon was the one who was closer to them.*

Scott pulls me into his side, his arm slides around me. When I nod, he continues. "*I rarely made contact, but recently something happened to make me want to bury the hatchet. Couple of years ago I met a woman, well, she's become everything to me. We're married, Josh, and the day she told me she was having my baby was the happiest day of my life. It made me re-examine my thoughts about family. I decided to make a visit back home. A kid could do with grandparents, you know? My wife, Sara, is an orphan, so apart from you, they were going to be the only family my child would have."*

Scott stops reading, and grins. "Hey, Josh. You're going to be, or already are, an uncle? How about that?"

As I haven't seen my brother for so long, I doubt if I'll ever get to know my niece or nephew, but still… "Carry on," I request.

Another perusal, then he recommences. "*I barely got my foot over the threshold. Stupidly I'd taken Sara with me. I didn't consider our father's reaction. You see, Sara's black. I thought the fact we were married and expecting a baby would trump everything, but no. I was a disgrace to the family. Just like you, Josh.*

"*The hatred he spilled out was fucking awful. And that's when I found out. He wished there was a way to cure me as he'd cured you. He told me what happened to you, Josh. Proudly. So happy it had fucking worked.*

"*But I know it didn't, did it? Fuck, brother. I started to worry about you when I heard what he'd put you through. That stuff screws with your head. Knew I needed to find you to see how you are, perhaps even to act like a real brother after all these years.*

"*I'm afraid I used my Army connections to track you down. Found you'd joined a biker club in Vegas. Took me a while. Didn't know whether I could just turn up, so decided to write you a letter.*

"*I don't give a damn who or what you are, brother. I'm not our father, and let me say now, I wish the fuck I'd been there for you. Wish I'd been there to stand up to him and not let you go to that goddamn camp. No good can have come out of it. There is no cure for something that's not a disease.*

"*So, Brother. What I'm saying is that if you can forgive me for not being there when you needed support, I'd like to meet up. Like you to meet my wife, and your niece or nephew. Don't know which, don't care. We'll be happy with whatever we have.*

"My contact details are on this letter. If you don't get in touch, I'll understand. Some wounds never heal over. But I'll hope that you do.

"All that's left to say is, whatever you decide, I love you, Josh. Should have told you or shown you that before, then you might have come to me. That you didn't, tells me there wasn't much trust or love between us growing up. And that's on me, as I was the elder.

"Hoping to hear from you, your loving brother, Simeon."

As Scott's voice trails off, I place my head in my hands. It's too much for me to assimilate. All this while I thought my brother had hated me. Had felt the same disgust my parents had. Had known all about where they had sent me. That he hadn't a clue puts things into a different perspective.

Scott's arm tightens then releases. "You going to get in touch?"

"If I go see him, will you come with me?" It sounds crazy, that I, a big tough biker, feel reduced to a little kid in awe of his big brother who always seemed to be everything I was not.

"Of fuckin' course." Scott places a kiss to my forehead. "Just let me know what you decide and what you want to do."

At a loss for words, I take the letter from him. Deep in thought, I return to my own room.

CHAPTER 26

I remain undecided whether to make contact with my brother or not. I've got more than enough family now, brothers who'd have my back. I have Scott. Why would I need anyone else in my life? Someone who reminds me of what I'd rather forget, of how I grew up. Scott doesn't push or make suggestions, just gives me time to figure it out.

While I'm sorting it through in my head, there's a ton of stuff happening with the club which means I get distracted.

I'm really pleased to find out Alex's ex is dead, now she'll be freed from that shadow hanging over her. An accident as far as she knows, but Dart had been clever to make it look that way. Almost immediately after that news comes in, Heart returns to the compound. He's a changed man, and not for the better. I wouldn't have believed it had I not seen it with my own two eyes, but he refuses to have anything to do with his little daughter, Amy.

That poor kid, my heart bleeds for her. Okay, so she reminds him of Crystal, but surely he should be grateful he's still got her? He's surly, uncommunicative and unfriendly. Luckily Amy's already used to living with Drummer and Sam, and the prez's wife is amazing with her. Again she bounces back. Soon the kid gives up trying to get her father to pay her any attention. Each time I see Heart push her away it makes me angry. *How the fuck can Heart be so cruel?*

But she's not the only one to bear the brunt of his bad temper. Within a day of his return I doubt there's anyone Heart hasn't upset. Things progress rapidly from bad to worse. We'd all agreed he was going to take over from Dart as manager of the strip club. On his first night he does something no one expects; he tries to rape one of the strippers.

Shit breaks loose. Prez calls an emergency church. Dart's summoned back from San Diego to attend. It's hard hearing for all of us. The club treats its strippers well, that way we get and keep the best dancers. If we get a reputation for treating the girls badly, it won't do our business any good. Heart's not only gone against the code of our brotherhood, but could have harmed one of our income streams.

We've been at the Tucson chapter quite a few months now, but Lady and I both stay out of the discussion about Heart. Oh, we're present and listening, but leave it to the brothers who know him best to determine his fate after the eye witnesses give their statements.

When Lady glances at me in church, I believe I know what he's thinking. *How will they treat one of their own who's betrayed the club?* I listen carefully as Prez lays out the options. Out in bad standing, or sent to meet Satan. *Fuck. It was hard to watch our enemies being dispatched. What would it be like if it's one of our own?* Under the table, Lady's knee touches mine, just for an instant. Could have been a mistake, but I don't believe it was. Tactile encouragement during this hard discussion. *Out in bad standing or dead. For betraying the club.* I press my knee against Lady's. *Would that be the options for us?*

Things go back and forth for a while, then Drummer speaks. His voice sounding firmer. "I've got a proposal. I can't have Heart at this club, that's for sure. And he doesn't want to be here, we've already discussed that." As he pauses to take a breath, I give a worried look at my brothers. All eyes on Prez, all looking concerned. No one moving or interrupting, wanting and dreading hearing Drum propose Heart's punishment. "Man needs time to recover from a loss such as Heart's, and on top of that, fuck knows what effects his brain injury might be havin'. Yes, he went against our rules, and our moralities. Or that's how it appeared. You say he was stopped in time, Dollar, he didn't actually rape the woman. Was he bankin' on someone steppin' in? We can't know that answer. But I'm not proposin' we dispatch him to Satan on an intention we can't prove."

There's a collective sigh of relief around the table. I agree. Heart doesn't deserve death.

The prez hasn't finished. "If we send him out in bad standin', that's the end of him. He can never return to the club. Which brings me to Amy. I can't take away the chance that one day she'll have her father back."

Wraith taps his fingers against the table. "If he's out bad, he might take her with him."

"I don't know that he would, Wraith. And if he does, what kind of life could he make for a kid, with no home and no job?" Drummer shakes his head. "At the moment, Amy is better off with us. At least Sam and I can give her some kind of normality. But one day, I hope, Heart will wake up and remember what a great kid he has." Suddenly a look of determination appears on his face. "My suggestion is he becomes a Ronin. For six months. Then he returns and we re-evaluate at that time."

Ronin. I exchange a look with Lady. Yeah, I know what that means. It means Heart will be out alone on the road.

"He'd have to follow protocol, Prez. He can't expect respect in return if he doesn't abide by the universal rules that govern a biker's life. Could he do that? In the state he's in?"

"The old Heart would," Dart's the one who answers Blade.

But he's not the old Heart. How would the new one cope?

Drummer nods at Dart. "He's got a choice. Become a Ronin, or out bad."

"Why not just transfer him to another chapter?" Marvel asks, frowning. "If he's havin' difficulty copin', don't like the idea of him being on his own."

But Prez is adamant he doesn't want to transfer a problem. While I hate any brother being punished, thinking it through, becoming a Ronin seems the best option. Heart doesn't want to be here; we can't have him in the compound in the state he's in. Something's got to give. Drummer's proposal seems fair. Even if I have doubts about him ever returning.

After a bit more discussion, we vote on it. Prez's proposal wins out.

After a beat down—well, Heart couldn't get away without some form of punishment—Prez takes his cut and sends him away. For six months.

Scott knocks at my door that night. When he comes in, I indicate he should sit on the bed.

"Family's fragile," I start without preamble. "No one knows what's around the corner, or how they'll react."

"For a moment, I was worried about Heart," Scott admits. "Shouldn't have. Prez is fair."

"He is that. But Heart's out there without back up. No brothers to call on to help him. I worry it's a death sentence in any event."

"I hear you, Josh, but it's on Heart now. He's got a chance, whatever he wants to make of it."

I raise my chin. "Got me thinkin', Scott. Didn't expect Crystal to be killed. Would never have predicted Heart's reaction. Been hard times recently in the club."

He half turns, tilts his head on one side. "You've done something, haven't you, Josh?"

For an answer, I take out my phone, select email then pass it to him. His eyebrows rise as he reads. I wait for his reaction. His finger flicks the screen down, then up, then down again. Then one side of his mouth turns up, then the other. He passes the phone back to me.

"I think you've done the right thing, Josh. It can't hurt. You've got no expectations. You can't lose what you haven't got."

"It's Amy," I admit. "Can't believe Heart can walk away from her without a backward glance. Seems my niece or nephew isn't even born yet, but I'd like a chance to connect with him or her."

"Com'ere, babe." Now he's holding me. "Didn't want to influence you, but you've done good. Looks like he was waiting to hear from you. Your brother replied immediately."

Simeon had. He'd explained he'd rather not travel at the moment with Sara pregnant. But he's more than happy for us to go to him. Yeah, in the email chain I mentioned I'd be coming with Scott.

"Thank you." Scott waves toward my phone. "Babe, you can't know what it means to me that you've told him about us."

I shrug. "It's hard enough keeping our secret here, Scott. Don't want to rekindle a relationship with my real family on a lie."

"Looks like we're going to Ohio." Scott grins.

The club seems quiet, subdued, the day after Heart is sent away. There's other changes on the horizon too. Dart is making a permanent move to San Diego. He's grown into the VP role there, and good on the man. I reckon he's doing the right thing. I'll miss Alex, though, and little Tyler. Both have been great additions to the club, making it seem even more like family. But Tyler needs the treatment he's best off getting in California.

It takes me a while to get Prez on his own. Seeing his office door is open and empty, with only him behind the desk, I seize my chance.

"Prez?"

"Joker. Come in. Got a problem?" He wipes a hand over his beard, his tired eyes suggesting everyone normally has when they go in to see him.

I take the chair he's offered me. "I got a letter," I start.

"Well, go on, man. Summons or ticket?" Seems he expects the same as I had.

I shake my head while offering him a smile. "Nothing like that. Bolt out of the blue. It was from my brother."

"Real or imaginary? You don't need fuckin' excuses, Joker."

I deserved that. "Blood brother, Prez. We've been estranged for years. Seems he's married with an old lady about to pop a kid. Wants to get to know each other again."

He sits back, linking his hands behind his head. "You okay with that?"

I frown. "To be honest, Prez, I'm not sure. Could be a good thing. Could be a waste of time. Thing is, I think I've got to try. But as his wife's just about to drop, he wants us, *me*, to go to him." I hastily correct myself, but he doesn't miss it.

"Us?" His eyes narrow.

I continue as best I can. "He's in Ohio. I'd rather have back up with me, moral support so to speak. Lady has offered to come with me. I wanted to ask if it's okay if we take off for a few days."

Tapping his fingers on the desk, Drummer considers for a moment. "Can't see a problem with that. Sounds good you've got a chance to connect with your family. Bit of a closed book, aren't you, Joker?"

"To be honest, Prez, Simeon's contact came out of the blue. Didn't expect it. Wasn't lookin' for it. But now it's come, don't feel I can ignore it."

"When you plannin' on going?"

"Next week, if you can spare us. We'll be flyin' up. This time of year don't fancy ridin'."

"Hear you, Joker. Long way, winter weather. Not the best." Drummer raises his eyes, staring at a point above my head for a moment. Then he brings his focus back to me. "Don't see why not. Long as it's only for a few days. Still got that poker run to organise and Alex is leavin' so we'll be doing the work by ourselves."

"It's all in hand, Prez. I won't leave you short."

"Yeah, well, I'm thinkin' of assignin' the new prospect Fergus to do some of the legwork. 'Bout time we see what he's made of."

It's a good idea, so I nod. Dart had recommended we give Fergus, who'd worked at the strip club as a bouncer, a try. So far, he keeps to himself, but does what's asked of him without question.

After I make the arrangements the trip approaches fast. Before I know it, we're heading to the airport. The flight time is just under four hours, but the time difference means we arrive just one hour later than we set off. I've been quiet on the journey, realising I know next to nothing about my brother. He must be thirty-nine now, and I've no idea what he does for a living, his hobbies or anything else.

"You okay, Brother?" Scott asks me, having unsuccessfully tried to engage me in conversation.

"I don't know," I reply truthfully. "Half of me wants to turn around and go back home."

Scott squeezes my hand, just as a middle-aged woman is walking back down the aisle to her seat. She notices, her face tightens, and she gives a shake of her head. "Disgusting," she mouths as she walks past.

Scott growls, "Fuckin' bitch. Forget her, okay?"

I move my hand around so I'm now the one holding his. "Don't give a damn, Scott. It's just at the club I'd be worried about people finding out. Away from there? Proud to be with you."

I've made him smile. But the woman's reaction isn't so easy to put behind me. Sure, Simeon knows what I am, it's the reason he contacted me after all. But knowing and having it in front of you are two very different things.

Scott seems to read my mind. "You don't get on with him? You haven't lost anything but the cost of the airfare. You've got brothers enough at home."

"I've got you," I say.

"Sure have, babe."

CHAPTER 27

We hire a car. I don't want to be dependent on a man I don't know for anything, so refused his offer to pick us up. We program the GPS and follow the instructions, eventually drawing up alongside a nice-looking house in a decent suburb. I turn onto the driveway, pulling up and putting the car in park.

Scott opens his door and steps out. I take a moment longer, then do the same. Grabbing our small carry-on bags from the back seat, we approach the big double front door together. I'm just raising my hands to ring the bell when the door opens.

I'd wondered whether I'd even recognise him, but Simeon's not really changed. A bit wider than I remember, an inch shorter than me, features not dissimilar to those I see in the mirror. His signs of greying at the temples are slightly concerning as it hits me it probably won't be long before I have the same.

He's submitting me to an examination of his own. "Fuck, little brother. You're not so little anymore."

The last time we'd met I hadn't muscled up.

"Simeon…" I start to acknowledge him. Wondering how to move on past this awkwardness, when suddenly he steps forward and puts his arms around me.

"Brother, Josh. Fuck. It's been too long."

Tentatively I return his hug when my eyes fall on a very pregnant woman standing behind him. She's shifting nervously from foot to foot, her teeth worrying her lip. *My parents turned him away because of the colour of her skin. Does she think I'm cut from the same fucking cloth?*

I push Simeon away. "Hey, this can't be your fuckin' wife, brother," I tell him. His welcoming smile falls from his face. His hands drop to his sides. As I see his body start to tense I don't leave it too long before I push past him, approaching Sara. "What's a gorgeous woman like you doing with a reprobate like my brother?" I ask, as I take her hand, bringing it to my lips. I'm not lying. She's beautiful. Black, flawless skin, dark expressive eyes, and that big ripe rounded belly.

She laughs. "You didn't warn me your brother was a charmer, Sim."

He looks at me, relaxed again now. My eyes meet his. We both shrug. Truth is, we know nothing about each other at all.

"I'm Scott," a voice says from the open doorway. "Josh's partner."

It's a challenge. One they rise to. Without hesitation, Sara pushes past and goes to greet Scott, showing no problem at all with his announcement. "Well, come on in. Don't want you standing out there. Sim, you forgotten your manners?" She links one arm through Scott's, then her other through mine, and leads us away. "Hope you like Italian food? Sim only remembered you being a fussy eater, Josh. But I suspect you've changed over the years."

"Certainly have, ma'am. And I love Italian."

There's no formality with Sara. Instead of sitting us in the living room, she escorts us into a comfortable kitchen full of modern appliances, settling us down at a breakfast bar. As she busies herself getting a salad ready, Simeon follows us in, even he looks slightly bemused at the way she's taken charge.

"How long till…" I point to her bulging stomach.

"A couple of months," they both answer together. Simeon grins and waves, indicating she should continue.

"I can't wait," she tells us. "I'm fed up with peeing every hour of the day and night, and having the hell kicked out of me. Hey, come here, Josh."

Thinking she needs help with something, I get up and go over. Instead of asking for my assistance, she grabs my hand, resting it on her belly. Something inside gives a hefty shove against my hand. My eyes widen.

"Scott," I say over my shoulder, then to Sara, "Do you mind?"

"'Course not," she grins. "If perfect strangers think they've got a right to feel the baby kicking, it's all good for family."

Family. And she's included Scott too.

For a few seconds, Scott and I both stand like chumps, content to feel the strange sensation of a baby seemingly intent on kicking its way out. When I feel moisture prick at the corner of my eyes, I have to turn away, meeting the gaze of my brother. I shake my head, unable to speak. To meet my niece or nephew before he or she is even born? I never thought I could feel such emotion.

We eat, Sara excuses herself as she feels tired, then, with beers in our hands, Scott, myself and Simeon settle down. I realise I still know nothing about who he is or what he does.

"So, how you earn your living, Sim?" I've caught onto the shortened form of his name that Sara uses. It seems to suit him.

"Ah," he puts down his beer, and looks embarrassed for a moment. "See, in the Army I got into the intelligence stuff. So, I'm a fed now. Work out of the local office."

Scott and I exchange glances. "You know what we do, right?"

"Yeah, and I couldn't care less. You're my brother, okay? I researched your club before I contacted you. The Tucson chapter, especially, seems to be a clean club. Hear you helped the feds out a while back too."

We did. When we rescued Sam. "Uh huh," I reply, cautiously. "Nothing to interest your lot there." But I file the thought away. Good as it might be to reconnect with a blood relation, other brothers come first. Could be a problem there.

Sim goes to the kitchen, returns with three more beers. As he pops the top off one, he looks at it carefully. After a moment, he asks, "Was it as bad as I think, Josh? That fucking camp the parents sent you to?"

Scott's hand covers mine. "Worse," he tells my brother. "Screwed his head up, man. He's going to therapy now."

I'm glad Scott stepped in. It's not something I want to think, let alone talk, about.

"Motherfuckers," Sim responds, with a sharp look at me. "You've got us now, brother. No judgement here."

We spend that night and the next with them. The fact that Sim's co-workers, if not him, would see me and Scott as a criminal element involved in a gang stops us from bonding completely, but Sara's lovely, so easy to get along with. When we make ready to leave, it's with promises to keep in touch and to visit again, but I think both Sim and I know that we won't become close. But that doesn't stop me being pleased that there's someone on my side should I ever need it.

Just before we go, Sim calls me into his home office. He stands, tense, clearly uncomfortable. "Look, Josh. Let's not beat about the bush here." He waves me to a chair, and perching his backside on his desk. "Growing up, we were so far apart in age, we had nothing in common. As grown men, that hasn't changed much."

"Except our choice in music," I put in with a grin.

He grins back. It's almost like looking into a mirror. "No surprise there. One thing I can remember is you stealing all my CDs."

He's right. I did. A young boy with no music of my own, I'd listened to his. "Fair point," I reply.

He taps his fingers against the desk, another sign he's discomfited. "Josh, we're men. We don't do this touchy-feely shit, you know? Might not mind going to watch a game with you, might have doubts about the people you hang around with. But we're family, okay? What I wanted to say was, whatever Mom or Dad said or think, the man I see before me today is someone I can be proud of. To think of you going through what they put you through? Only thing that helps is seeing you now and knowing you're coping. That you're happy."

Fuck. I didn't expect him to say that. "I, I…"

A half-smile. "Told you men weren't good at this shit."

"I'm proud of you too, brother," I get out at last.

"And Scott?" he hasn't finished. "I like him. He's good for you."

"He is that." I don't hesitate to agree.

Now it's awkward. He's said his piece. I've said mine. I stand, then cross over to him, this time it's me pulling him in for a hug. "I want to know when my niece or nephew is born, okay? Send pictures too."

"You'll come up and visit then?"

I can't promise that. Bearing in mind his job, it might not do to get close. I'll have to take Drummer's views into account. "I'd like to. But I'll need to see how I'm fixed, brother."

He looks down, his eyes surveying some closed folders on his desk. He knows what I'm not saying. There might be familial love between us, but we're oceans apart in what we do. I can't afford to have close contact with someone in the FBI, and his superiors probably wouldn't want him to have anything to do with a man who's in what they term an outlaw motorcycle gang. Or might try to use him to bring us down. Our eyes meet, we both know the score.

It's into the evening by the time we arrive back at the compound. A party's already going on, but Slick, Drummer and Wraith are standing around the bar, meaning the old ladies are still around and the sweet butts haven't come down from their house yet.

Prez waves a bottle in my direction. "How did it go?" he asks when I'm within earshot. "Any blood spilt?"

"None," Lady answers for me. Taking a second bottle from Prez, he points it at me. "Joker here was quite well behaved."

"Good reconnecting with family?"

I better get it over with. "Thing is, Drummer. Wouldn't be good to get close. Sim, my brother, well, he's a fed."

"Aware of that, Joker." Drummer indicates Mouse who's talking with Road. "Looked into it."

I wonder whether it was a test to see if I was going to come clean. I cock an eyebrow at him. He laughs. "Just lookin' out for you, Brother." His amusement dies away to be replaced by a frown. "Can't choose our family, but admit I've been doing some thinkin' as to how it would play out if you'd become close. Turns out I don't need to explain anything to you." He salutes me with his beer. "You're a good brother, Joker."

Taking a beer from the prospect, I raise mine in return. "Club's my true family, Prez. A man I haven't seen in more than ten years and didn't really know before that? May be blood, but he doesn't come first."

"Hear you, Brother. I hear you."

"Made some progress while you were gone," Wraith addresses Lady, then proceeds to update him on some of the arrangements for the poker run.

Drummer starts his conversation with Slick again, so I listen to the VP, interested of course in the parts of the run which will involve me. While I do so, I look around. Yes, as I thought. Sam, Sophie and Ella are coming out of the kitchen, having an animated discussion from what I can see. When their conversation falters, I turn around, watching Jill, Allie, Pussy, Diva and Paige saunter in, looking like they own the place. Amused to see the old ladies go directly to their men as if claiming them.

Wraith smiles down at Sophie, then drains the last of his beer. "We'll be off then."

Drummer's eyes are on Beef who already has Paige on his lap, Rock's alongside tugging Diva onto his. "Yeah, Sam and I will be making a retreat too."

Slick's already half way out of the door with Ella.

"You have fun, boys," Drummer winks as he passes. "Don't do anything I wouldn't do."

The beer almost shoots out of my mouth.

I stay at the bar. Turning down Jill when she comes over. I've long gained a reputation for not going with the whores, so she doesn't take much persuading to leave me alone. The air becomes tainted with the odour of sex as Dollar takes Allie over the pool table. Then Tongue starts doing what he does best, going down on Pussy. Soon she's screaming. Knowing I've been sociable enough, I give a chin lift toward Jekyll minding the bar, and take myself off up to my suite.

Scott and I might have slept in the same bed at my brother's, but being in a strange house hadn't done more than hug. Whether it's the atmosphere I've just left, or the fact I've had to keep my hands to myself for a couple of days, I'm not sure, but whatever the reason, I'm in the mood for some loving from my man by the time I reach the privacy of my room.

I strip, and lie on the bed, my hand on my cock which swells as I think just what I'd like to do. Sim's easy acceptance of what I am, has made me feel brave. Tonight I'm ready to take that final step for myself.

It seems hours before Scott appears. My cock's more than primed when he walks into my room. I don't give him a moment.

"Need you naked," I rasp out as he closes the door.

"Like that, is it?" he smirks.

I don't reply, just feast my eyes as he gives me a show, removing his cut, then his clothes, with deliberate and agonizing slowness. It's only then I stand, crossing the room to him, standing chest to chest, skin against skin as I curl my hand around his head, my fingers tangling into his hair, pulling his face to mine.

My lips hit his with a blistering force. *Tonight, I'm the one in charge.* Our tongues meet, fight, duel. Teeth smash together. I pour every part of my need into his mouth. Eventually we part, but only because we need to breathe.

"Josh…"

"Want you tonight, Scott. You gonna let me have you?"

Pulling out of my hold he gives me his answer by going to the bed, kneeling first on all fours, then sinking his head to the mattress. Employing no subtlety at all, he waggles his ass in the air. "Take me, Josh."

Oh jeez. My cock, already like iron, swells even more. *I want him so badly.* It's all I can do to resist taking him unprepared.

I cross to the bed, climbing on so I'm on my knees behind him. The globes of his ass are tight and muscular and I can't wait to touch. But first I place my hands on his back, tracing his Satan's Devils patch back tat. His skin ripples beneath me, and he squirms as though ticklish.

"Need you, Brother," he all but begs.

But this is my time, he's not going to hurry me. Slowly I move my hands down, massaging his glutes, squeezing, then separating slowly until, at last, the tight puckered hole appears.

My eyes latch on as though seeing a tasty morsel. "Is this mine, Scott?"

"Yours, babe. All yours."

Very gently I place a finger to his most private place, circling it around. He twitches and his ass moves back. Raising my hand, I spank his flank, watching my handprint appear on his skin. Entranced I repeat the action on the other side.

"You're killing me here, man. Shit, I'm so fuckin' hard for you babe." His hips buck. I spank him again, loving the feel of my skin meeting his, hard enough to make my palm sting, loving the erotic sound of the slap, and the way his muscles move as he tightens and relaxes.

"You like that, Scott? Like my hand on you?"

"Too fuckin' much. Babe, I'm not going to last."

Taking mercy on him, not wanting to spoil my first time, I reach over to the lube I'd left close at hand, placing a generous portion on my hands. Then, with one hand to the small of his back, I probe with my finger, and push it inside his hole, feeling the resistance at first, then I'm in up to the knuckle.

"Another, Josh, please. Fuck. Feels so fucking good. Love you lovin' on me, man."

Another finger joins the first.

"Scissor them inside me, Josh. Babe, you're big, gotta prepare me first."

I'm thicker than him, so I do what he says. Wondering at how naturally this is happening. I'm in the driving seat, but I don't mind taking instruction. That this amazing man is offering himself to me, *trusting me*, brings emotion as well as arousal to the fore.

It's going to be my cock in there. Very soon.

With three fingers of one hand disappearing into his ass, I place the other to the root of my cock, pressing hard with the heel of my palm, knowing if I don't calm myself down I'm going to blow my load before I'm even inside.

Having gotten myself back under some semblance of control, I open the condom wrapper using my teeth. *Haven't thought this through. I'm right handed.* Can't do fuck all with my unpractised left, so I reluctantly remove my fingers, and fumbling with shaking hands, roll that fucker on.

"You ready for me?" I ask through gritted teeth. Applying the condom had nearly done me in. My fingers smell of him, I'm covered in his musk.

"I'm ready," he breathes out, and I see him making an effort to relax.

I don't want to hurt him. My eyes squint as I stare down at the rosette that looks far too small to take the girth of my cock.

"Just do it," he encourages.

"Tell me to stop if it gets too much."

He laughs. "It won't, Josh. I want you inside."

Neither of our voices sound normal. Both breathless. Me with anticipation, him with need.

I position my cock, still staring down in concentration, when an explosion goes off inside my brain. Blinding white light cancels out my vision, pain from my balls, dick, my head. My temple lobes throbbing. The agony so intense that with a scream I thrust myself off the bed, stumbling, relying on touch and memory rather than vision as I tear into the bathroom, somehow having the presence of mind to kick the door shut behind me. Then I'm leaning over the bowl and vomiting violently.

Only seconds later I feel a hand stroking the back of my head, a palm held against my neck.

Vomit rises again, then I spit out the remaining bile in my mouth. When I straighten a wad of tissue is held out, and I use it to clean my lips. A hand reaches around me, pulls the flush then closes the toilet lid. His other never stops stroking my back. *I feel so ashamed.*

"What the fuck, Josh?"

I can't turn around to face him. My cheeks blaze red, burning me from inside out.

"Just leave me."

"No way, babe. No fuckin' way." I'm kneeling in front of the porcelain, he slides down the wall so he's sitting, legs outstretched, alongside me.

"Talk to me," he instructs softly.

I don't want to admit what a fuck up I am, but he probably knows enough to work it out for himself. *What the hell type of man vomits when he wants to love on his partner?* Me, that's who.

Without turning my head, not wanting to face him, I try to explain. "They showed us porn. When we reacted, they'd apply an electric shock."

"Go on," he encourages quietly.

"Your, your asshole. It suddenly reminded me of that. I couldn't control my reaction. I'm sorry, so sorry…"

"Hush," he instructs. There's a touch of amusement in his voice when he next asks, "You saying my ass looks like that of a porn star?"

His unexpected comment makes me give a stunned laugh. "Must be your manscaping."

"Well, I do pay for the best."

He pays?

"Only joking, babe. No one sees this ass but you. But I might let you give me a trim sometime." He puts his arms around me, I don't protest when he pulls me to him. The trembling in my limbs starts to subside.

I allow him to just hold me. After a few minutes, he stands, pulling me up with him. I take the cup of water he's holding out and rinse my mouth. "How can I ever move past this?"

He turns my head to face him. "You will, babe. You will."

I mumble something under my breath.

"What was that?" he asks.

"You're a fool, Scott. I'm so mixed up in my head."

"Hey." He raises the chin that I'd dropped, forcing me to look into his eyes. "I'm your fool, Josh. And I'm not going anywhere."

CHAPTER 28

When you met your brother, you admitted you were gay?" Delia looks down at the notes she's just made.

"He already knew. But I didn't deny it. Scott came with me as my boyfriend. We didn't try to hide it. Weren't made to feel as though we should."

"How did that make you feel, Josh?"

"Good," I admit. "It was the second time in my life that I didn't feel dirty or ashamed. It felt natural." I nod over to Scott. "Much like when we were at Scott's mom's. Good, you know, to be accepted. Not to have to pretend."

"Hmm." Her teeth worry her lip. "There was no pressure then. But when you returned? That was the day you had your episode?"

I'd given her the gist. Didn't have to draw a full picture. She knew enough that being intimate with Scott had thrown me right back. I think about what she's asking. "I know I can't come out to my club. If we do, we may not have a club any longer." I glance at Scott who raises his chin in encouragement. "I was angry that once again we were havin' to hide."

"You didn't tell me," interjects Scott.

"Didn't know it myself until now." It's what Delia forces me to do, to analyse my reactions.

"Was that why…?" Delia seems content for Scott to ask the questions.

Was that why I pushed myself? Went for something I wanted for once in my life? Trying to convince myself I saw no shame in making love to another man. When I was playing the dominant role. They both give me space to get it sorted in my head.

This isn't a conversation to have in front of your therapist, however open she appears. I gather some more suitable words. "I came back from Sim's having gotten it clear in my head. I'm not dirty or disgusting, I'm not mentally ill. Yeah, there was some resentment against my brothers because I know that's how they would see me. I think I got over confident and my fuckin' brain saw fit to remind me."

"Remind you of what? You still see yourself as," she consults her tablet she'd been tapping on, "dirty, disgusting and mentally ill?"

"Nah," I shake my head. "Yeah. I'm not sure. Inside," I tap my forehead, "I know I'm not. When I'm with Scott's family, or my brother, I see myself being accepted. As me. Accepted whether I'm gay or straight. But when, when…"

She taps her fingers on the arms of her chair. "When you put yourself in a stressful situation, it came flooding back. Josh, like every PTSD sufferer you're going to have flashbacks. Things that remind you of the worst time in your life. Couple that with a highly charged atmosphere, your own thoughts of failure, I'm not surprised you had a violent attack."

"How do I move on, Delia? How do I fuckin' get past this? I want a relationship with my man. I don't want a violent panic attack when we try to get close."

Scott doesn't let her answer, instead jumps in asking a question himself. "If we were somewhere different. If Josh felt it was safe to come out. If we could live together openly and be accepted, do you think that would help?"

She sighs. "I'm going to lay it on the line for you. We live in more tolerant times. Homosexuality is known not to be a disease, gays can get married, and shouldn't be discriminated against. But we all know that's superficial. You're different, not wrong. But anyone who's outside of the norm risks prejudice, which can take many forms. You'll need to make your place in society, be accepted for what you are. I'd be wrong to mislead you and tell you it would be a bed of roses were you to come out." She pauses, removes her glasses, cleaning them on a cloth before replacing them on her nose. "From what you've both said, your current situation makes it impossible."

"But Josh accepting what he is, isn't that the hardest part?"

She stares at me. "Depends whether you have, Josh, deep down inside. How do you really feel? If I could take a bottle out of my drawer and give you a magical potion to make you straight, would you take it?"

Another question that provokes soul searching on my part. After a few moments have passed, I give a determined shake of my head. "I'm comfortable with what I am, more easy with it than I ever thought. Angry that people wouldn't accept me, but that's on them and their lack of understanding. Nah, I wouldn't take that potion. What I am, in here," I beat my fist on my chest, "is gay. Change that? Who knows who I'd become? But," I pause, as a muscled biker I shouldn't admit to this, "I'm also scared. I don't want to be faced with bigotry. I'm not strong enough yet."

She nods. "You've made great strides, Josh. Your panic attacks have lessened, and you've become accepting of who you are. But I agree. You get challenged by intolerant people, it could set you right back. You need to be more comfortable with yourself. Baby steps, Josh. Baby steps. Don't try to run the whole marathon at once."

Outside winter rain is falling. I get my wet weather gear out of my saddle bag and slip it on. Fuck knows why, the walk from the office means I'm already wet. As Scott's dragging on his, I catch his eye.

"Are there any one-percenter gay clubs?"

His eyes widen. "Yeah, in California. You suggesting we switch clubs?"

I shrug. It's an answer. Nice to know there's a place to go if I need to. Once again that seed of anger starts to grow inside. *Why should we have to? Why can't we just be accepted for what we are?*

As if he can read my mind, after sitting on his wet seat with a grimace, Scott looks across as I do the same. "Before we do that, we should give the Satan's Devils a chance."

A violent shake of my head. Images of the men I call brothers go through my mind. Beef, Tongue, Marvel. They're as straight as they come. I'd rather ride off into the sunset, into some unknown future without looking behind, than be left with memories of the disdain on their faces. Looks I grew up with from my parents. Or worse, they might not let us ride off. Not without retaliation for the dirty secret we kept from them. They might hurt us first. *Would brothers like Beef really do that?* It's so hard to fucking know.

In all honesty, I'm at home where I am now. The compound is great, there's not one brother I don't care for. Enough excitement to keep me occupied, that's for sure. Maybe I wouldn't be so satisfied if I didn't have Scott with me, but I do. The only bad thing is that we have to keep this thing between us quiet. I love my brothers, just don't trust them enough to be honest with them.

"Nah. Don't want to upset the status quo. And I don't want to change clubs." *Once a Devil, always a Devil.* That's what I've been for going on eight years now.

Scott puts his key in the ignition. "Well, we better be getting back then."

All the reasons why I want to stay with this club are illuminated in huge fucking lights on the day of the poker run. We end up with getting on for three hundred riders taking part.

Brothers from our other chapters, other motorcycle clubs as well as weekend warriors who come together to have a good fucking time, as well as to raise money for a little black kid they don't know, but who band together because he needs a lifesaving operation. The run's been planned to be about eighty miles in total, long enough to be interesting, but not so far as to put people off. They'll get a playing card at the beginning of the run, then pick another at the five planned checkpoints along the way. The person with the best hand at the end of the day will win a prize.

I, and the other Road Captains from the other chapters, will be making sure everything goes smoothly. Must admit, I won't be able to relax until everyone's safely rolled into the park which is the end point. There we've set up a beer tent, as well as a stage where a local tribute band have agreed to perform. Various catering vans and stalls will also be selling their wares.

As I look around at the masses of bikes, mostly Harleys but a good showing of other makes as well, I breathe in deeply, hoping there won't be any mishaps on the way.

"Got a good fuckin' turnout."

Swinging around, I pull Shadow in for a hug, slapping his back. "Good to see you, asshole."

"Back at yer," he grins. "Hey, Blaze. You gonna help out?"

Blaze, the Road Captain for San Diego, has strolled over to join us. "Yeah, Joker. Seems like you could use all the hands you can get."

"Won't be turning anyone away," I agree, as I reach out to shake his hand. "Got to get this lot safely through the check points."

"With Sparky and Piston, we can split ourselves up. Each follow, say, fifty, sixty bikes?" As Blaze mentions the Road Captains from Colorado and Utah, I nod. "Sounds like a good plan to me."

As if the mention of their names had summoned them, Sparky and Piston appear. Piston pulls up his sleeves as he comes over as if readying himself to get down to work. Another round of handshakes and back slapping is completed just in time before Drummer steps up to address the crowd. A quick discussion, then we're off. Piston follows the first groups out. I wait, slightly nervous, until the last man's ridden off, then bring up the rear myself.

At the second checkpoint, I've lost sight of most of the bikes in front of me, trying to keep behind the rear runner. I'm tapping my hand impatiently against the handlebars when the rider comes over to me. His face is lined and weather worn, he's shaking out his arms as if to remove the stiffness from them.

"I don't need a babysitter," he tells me with a grin.

"My job," I tell him, trying to un-grit my teeth.

"Nah," he points to his bike, an ancient Harley. "Me and this old girl go back a ways. We'll be fine. I can always call AAA if I get stuck."

I don't like it. Looking at the rattling heap, I have my doubts it will make it the whole eighty miles. However, the biker seems to know what he's up to, and has contingency plans if he breaks down.

"Look, you go on. I'll just putt along at my own speed."

I think for a moment, then nod, and hold out my hand. "I'll see you there, then."

"That you will," he agrees with another easy grin.

I leave him, twisting my throttle hard until I've caught up with the last group.

The park's heaving by the time I arrive. There's a good atmosphere as bikers, old ladies and a fair number of kids who've come with families in cars, all mill around with beers, soft drinks, burgers and hot dogs in their hands. All the stalls seem to be doing a roaring trade.

"Got here okay?" Lady approaches, his mouth stuffed around a bun.

"Yeah. Could do with a fuckin' beer." As I speak I eye up the long line for the beer tent.

"Here, have mine." He hands over his bottle. Taking a second to make sure there's none of the Tucson crew around, I take the half-drunk bottle from him gratefully.

"Want to take a look around?"

Might as well. So Lady and I wander from stall to stall, doing our bit, buying tickets for the raffle and spending time looking at what the vendors are offering. After a while we bump into some other Tucson members, and Lady and I split up.

"Will you fuckin' look at that?" Beef points behind me.

But the rattling and popping noises already have me turning, my face splitting into a grin. It's the old biker and his even older Harley. Catching his eye, I raise my, or rather Lady's, bottle of beer in salute. Then go over to talk to him.

Having found out his name I have a quick word with Drummer, who agrees with my suggestion. The last man in, Bob, will end up being given a spontaneous prize for completing the ride on the oldest bike.

It's a great day. Sunny, warm but not too hot for black leather, and the atmosphere is relaxed, even between rival clubs. As each man donates, buys a raffle ticket or places a bid in the auction, I'm pleased on behalf of young Tyler. *Looks like we'll be raising more than we thought.*

"You done a good job, Joker. Got everyone here safe."

"Thanks, Peg. Wasn't just me though. Had the support of the Road Captains of the other clubs." I turn to acknowledge the sergeant-at-arms.

"That's the thing about Devils. Doesn't matter what chapter you're in. We're all brothers."

We are. And it's that brotherhood I can't lose.

When Peg steps away, his place is taken by Lady. "Thought you could use this." He hands me a fresh cold beer.

I certainly could. I take it, go to thank him, when a tapping on the microphone gets our attention. As our prez starts to speak, Lady and I move closer to the stage. There's good natured cheering and laughing when Drummer hands Bob the money we'd decided he'd won.

Prez continues almost without a pause. "We'll be checking the poker hands for the winner as soon as we can. I hope you'll stay around and enjoy the day, and part with your hard-earned cash at the auctions and stalls which have been set up. Won't kid ya, we want to take as much from ya as you can afford to support our good cause."

Dart's here with Alex and Tyler, I'm close enough to see him nudging them toward the centre of the stage.

Encouraging them forward with a smile, Drummer turns back to his audience. "I'd like you to give a welcome to young Tyler."

Alex looks disconcerted. I doubt she expected to be called up. Putting two fingers to my mouth, I whistle loudly to show we're here to support her. Brothers from Tucson and San Diego all cheer them.

When they reach him, Drummer continues, "Tyler here is six years old and was born with sickle-cell disease. He looks fine today, but his health is failing. The only cure is an expensive procedure. And we all know about health insurance."

Lady and I join in with the jeering from the rest of the audience.

"His insurance would go for the option that may keep him alive, but wouldn't be a cure. Y'all know how companies wriggle out of payin' what they should."

Again I'm roaring in agreement and protest. Looking around me, I see Drummer's got everyone eating out of his hand. Then my attention returns to the stage.

"I hope y'all get a chance to meet young Tyler. He'll be judgin' some of the competitions today. And I think, if you do, you'll agree with me. He deserves to be given a chance of a good life."

More cheering from the crowd, now supportive. Drummer takes Tyler's arm and leads him to the front. "I won't keep you away from the beer much longer, but first I'd like to introduce Lost, the President of the Satan's Devils San Diego chapter. He's got something to say."

Lost? Didn't expect that. Lady and I exchange glances, then I watch as Lost comes to the stage carrying something in his hands. It's a small child-sized leather cut. *Oh no, they're not going to.* I feel tears of emotion prick in my eyes. If this is what I think, Tyler's going to be over the moon. What little boy wouldn't?

Drummer passes Lost the mic, Lost clears his throat, then starts to speak. "Satan's Devils' chapters are full of good men. And sometimes we transfer between chapters. Drummer here is our national president as you all know, but I have been lucky enough to wrangle Tyler from him and get him to California. From what we've seen, we've got a good member in the making, and following the vote of the San Diego club, today he's becoming a junior prospect for us."

He holds the cut up, I'm close enough to see if those exact two words are written on the back. *They fucking are.* I'm beaming, Lady's grinning, as Tyler stands completely bemused while Drummer and Lost both help him put his arms through the leather. I thought he'd been a happy little boy before, there's no words to describe the expression now on his face. Especially as Drummer picks him up and puts him on his shoulders. My hands automatically come together and I'm clapping and cheering along with everybody else, then give another loud whistle.

Lady nudges me. "What's Dart up to?"

Turning in the indicated direction, I see the new VP of the San Diego chapter stepping up onto the stage where Drummer puts Tyler down, and picks up the microphone again. "Now I think you'll agree, every kid deserves a daddy. So I'm passing the mic to my brother, Dart, VP of the San Diego chapter, and let's see if we can't do that today."

Lady grins at me broadly. I think we've both guessed what's going to happen next.

Dart steps up to the middle of the stage. *He looks a bit nervous to me.* I listen carefully as he speaks. "I'm not gonna take long," he pauses, giving a lopsided smile, "I hope. But I just want to say Alex is my ol' lady, and I want to make her my wife. And ask Tyler if he'll allow me to be his daddy." He gets down on one knee and holds out his hand to his woman.

"Alex, both you and Tyler mean the world to me. I want you with me and on the back of my bike for the rest of my life. Will you marry me, doll?"

"Yes!" she screams out. She might not have any means of amplification but in her delight she doesn't need it. Another nudge on my arm from Lady, and we both watch as Dart puts the most glorious, and big, diamond ring on her finger. We're hollering and cheering. Could this day get any better?

That's it. Show's over. Drummer disperses the crowd to their activities, saying the judging for the longest beard is going to take place next.

I stand, watching Dart, Alex and Tyler still hugging on the stage, unaware of the audience. *What would it be like to be able to claim my man like that? To have a family. Oh, I'm never going to father a child of my own, but there's other ways. Like Dart, I could adopt. I wonder what Scott's opinions are on the possibility?*

Finally pulling my eyes away, I see the man in question has wandered off. *Can't be too careful. Have to hang around with all the brothers.* I purse my lips then let out a sigh. *Foolish daydreams.* Yeah, ain't never going to happen. I straighten my back, pull my metaphorical socks up, and go off to catch up with my Vegas brothers.

Chapter 29

hurch seems to have a different dynamic now. Two chairs have been removed from the table, the one that had belonged to Dart, and Heart's, of course. We'd kept them empty until Dart's absence was made permanent, and out of respect for Heart while his recovery from his crash couldn't be assured—I think we felt to remove it would have been giving up on him. Once he was sent out as a Ronin, it no longer seemed appropriate to keep his space open. Who knows when he'll return, or maybe the more apt question is if. Or even if he does, whether he'll be able to take his place again.

Heart plays on my mind every time I see Amy. I can't help worrying about him, imagining myself in his place, cast adrift without the support of his brothers. It can't be easy out on the road on his own. That's if he's still above ground. As weeks pass during which we hear nothing from him, he might already be dead for all we know.

Scott and I jog along, continuing to be careful to hide our feelings for each other from the rest of the club, going out of our way to divert attention. I wouldn't say we've settled into an easy relationship, even in the privacy of our rooms we're cautious around each other, having reverted to heavy petting only. All down to me. My extreme reaction when we tried to do more had scared Scott enough that he didn't want to attempt it again. I couldn't blame him; it had frightened me too.

We become best friends first, lovers second, taking a step back until, *if,* I can get shit sorted in my fucked-up brain. I don't deserve him, expect him to give up on me, but no, he sticks around. When I repeatedly tell him he's a fool, that he ought to move on, he only smirks and reminds me he's mine. My fool. That he is. I don't deserve him.

When we have the opportunity, we escape from the club-house and just be ourselves in our rooms. We may simply talk, watch a film together or lie in each other's arms content to stay silent. Constantly I hope what little I can give him will continue to be enough, as I can't see it changing anytime soon. My flash-back has all but paralysed me to do much else. The effect on our relationship, the strain it must be causing Scott, well, slowly my fear turns into something different. Instead I become angry at the strength of the hold my past still has over me.

I continue to see Delia, sometimes alone, sometimes with Scott. When I'm there, everything she says makes sense. It's when I'm back on the compound it seems harder.

"You're a fool, Scott," I tell him again one night, as we're lying on my bed watching TV.

He grasps my hand harder, and I hear the smile in his voice as he replies, "Yeah, but I'm your fool. And don't you forget it."

I get the news my brother and Sara have had their baby. A little girl called Maya. We're invited to meet her, of course. But having a biker's innate wariness of the feds, I'm reluctant to visit them again. Sim's still little more than a stranger. It's my brothers here I know I can trust, but him? They say blood's thicker, but what do I know about him? I can't risk relaxing my guard, and saying something that could bring harm down on the club. Sara keeps in touch more than he does. She sends pictures, tons of them. Maya's first smile is the one I love the most, it's now the background on my phone. It's the closest I'll ever come to having my own child.

"Hey." I smile at Scott who's just walked in, breaking into my reverie.

"Hey yourself, babe. Got more photos then?" He nods at the device I'm holding, his comment offered when I barely look up from the screen.

Yeah, he reads me well. For an answer I pass over the phone. He puts in my code and opens it. "Fuck, what a mess." He chuckles. Yeah, apparently my niece has some difficulties with eating custard. She's wearing most of it. "Apart from the yellow stuff, she's a cute little bean, isn't she?"

Cute she is. And from the accompanying text, has her parents wrapped around her little finger.

We might have lost two members from the table, but the club has otherwise increased in size. Sam's given Drummer a baby boy they named Eli, and Sophie's given Wraith his pride and joy, Olivia. Prez is how you'd expect him to be, proud as punch of his son. But I'm certain I see Wraith already sharpening his knives in preparation for when boys start sniffing around his daughter. What chance has that girl got? She'll have him, me, and the rest of the brothers all watching out for her. A whole club of over-protective uncles. It's strange having babies in the clubroom, but I find myself enjoying it. Uncle Joker, that's what I am. And, as all uncles, it's good to be able to hand a baby over when it poops or begins to cry.

"Amy's buzzing around on that bike Prez got her." Scott ruefully rubs his leg. "He's told her not to ride it inside."

"Bet he didn't tell her off though." Prez has a soft spot for the three-year-old they're still looking after. Reckon the girl has probably forgotten her real dad by now.

"How can he be so scary to us, and a total marshmallow with her?" Scott shakes his head, wonderingly. "Kids fuck you up, don't they?"

I frown, his words suggesting he doesn't see any in our future. Probably just as well. If we can't come out, there's no way in hell we could consider having a family. I dismiss the strange thoughts in my head as a whim needing to be locked away. Out loud it's easiest to simply agree, "Sure do."

Days, weeks pass. One day Beef approaches me, a Harley parts mag open at a page. "Thinking of getting these, Brother. What d'you think?"

My initial thought is that I've lost count of the times Beef's added or replaced shit on his bike. He's probably rebuilt it a dozen times. But I look over to see what he's pointing out, offer my opinion, adding the suggestion I'll make time to give him a hand.

Finally, Prez hears from Heart. We're all pleased as fuck to find out he's still alive. Even happier when Drummer announces at church Heart's made the decision to come back at the end of his six months. The intervening four months seem to have flown by. There's only a couple more until he'll be home. I'm not the only one to give a sigh of relief, or a grin when Drummer confirms he sounds like he's got his head screwed on right now.

"Good fuckin' news." Wraith looks pleased. "Miss him."

"Like that he's on the mend. Seems you made the right call, Prez." Tongue's nodding his head. Then he yawns widely without covering his mouth, making that stud in his tongue glints. It's not hard to see why all the sweet butts and hangarounds love him.

Prez raises his hand for silence. "Been contacted by the agents managing his house. Heart's arranged for a friend to stay there. Told them to give him the key."

"Friend?" Blade's eyebrows rise.

"Yeah, goes by the name of Mark."

"That's good news, isn't it, Prez?" Beef suggests. "He's thinking of someone else."

I jerk my chin toward him. It does sound like it's a step in the right direction. I just wish he'd start thinking about his daughter.

I only hope he's different with her when he returns. *Will she even recognise him?*

Wiping his hand over his beard, Drummer's eyes do that thing that lets you know he's deep in thought, slightly unfocused as though he's looking at but not seeing what's in front of him. After a moment, he speaks. "Mouse, that house is rented through a shell company, isn't it?" At Mouse's nod of confirmation, he carries on. "Don't know who Heart's met on the road, so we'll have a stranger livin' on what is essentially club property. Probably best if we keep our ownership quiet. At least until we know more about the fucker who'll be stayin' there."

Wraith's frowning. "It's been left just as it was that morning. No one's been inside. Fuck, wouldn't be surprised if there's shit growin' in the fridge."

"Don't even like to think about that." Blade shudders, going slightly green. *Christ, I can understand burning a tat off a man's back gets him puking, but a bit of mould?*

"What you suggestin', Wraith?" Peg interjects. "Should we get it cleaned for Heart's friend?"

Prez gives him a look, then sighs and nods. "It is in a state. Sam and I went, picked up some shit for Amy, clothes and toys, but otherwise it's how Crystal and Heart had left it the day of the accident." As he drums his fingers on the table, I close my eyes briefly, the reminder of how much we'd lost unwelcome. "Heart didn't ask us to tidy it, and we don't know the fucker so on one hand I'd say we leave him to walk into whatever mess there is. But on the other, we're dealin' with a stranger. Need to check Heart's personal stuff, make fuckin' certain there's nothing lying around that would link the house to us."

Peg frowns. "I'll get the prospects to go around. Sort it out for this Mark fella. Get some beer in the fridge. No harm in being friendly if it's a friend of Heart's." He pauses, tugging at his beard. "Haven't liked the thought of Heart being out there alone. Know it was right, but the times I've thought of him dead… Well, if this friend has helped him, a small gesture wouldn't go amiss."

Personally, I'm glad it's the prospects who'll be cleaning out the rotting food, trying to clear the vision of just what they might find in that fridge from my head. My eyes go to Drummer, hoping he'll confirm it.

Prez thinks for a moment, then raises his chin. "Good call, Peg. Organise it, will you?"

"Sure thing."

We might have agreed the prospects would take point while we were sitting around the table. But our decision doesn't count for much once the women get wind of what is going on. Sam and Sophie, babies in tow, end up going to Heart's old place to direct the prospects in the proper way to clean a house.

Hyde is white faced when they return, the six-month-old contents of a fridge, as we'd expected, not being at all pleasant to clean out. I hear him mumble something about exploded eggs.

"How did it go, Prospect?" Drummer asks Hyde as he walks into the clubhouse.

Hyde waves to Jekyll who's walking in carrying a box. Fergus is following them with more shit in his hands. "Got Heart and Crystal's personal stuff here."

"Put it in Heart's suite, will you?"

As Jekyll nods, he thumps Hyde's arm. "You stopped puking yet?"

As Hyde looks sheepish and steps away, Slick shakes his head. "I knew the fucker couldn't handle shit," he says pointedly to Prez.

I think he's being a bit unfair on the man. I'd probably have felt ill myself, but I stay out of it. Slick's problems with Hyde go way back. I doubt he'll ever get his vote and be patched in.

Heart's house, I hear later, has been stocked up with the basics, beer and condoms. That sounds about right. What more could a man want? Heart hadn't left any specific instructions, or given us any information about any requirements for this Mark who'll be staying there.

It's a week later that we find out we've all been wrong, I have to stifle a laugh when I first hear. Heart's guest isn't a man, but a woman who goes by the name of Marc, or Marcia. She comes to us out of sheer desperation when she can't make contact with her friend. *Heart.*

Then, when it becomes clear exactly who she is, I begin having doubts about Heart's sanity all over again. She's no stranger to us, and Heart goes back down in our estimation for letting a cop stay on club property. Her full name being Marcia Hannah, the fucking detective that stood by and did nothing while her cop friends smashed up the club.

While dealing with the mess the cops had left had been a pain at the time, in a sense they'd done us a favour. The girls had got together doing the shit they do best. Now in the clubhouse we sit on matching, comfortable leather sofas—easy to clean, I've overheard Sophie say. We drink at new tables and chairs, and the whole room's been freshly painted.

But it's the principle of the matter that concerns us all. A cop? *What connection has she got to Heart?*

When Marc, *Marcia,* meets with Drummer and brings him up to date, her worries about Heart transfer themselves to the prez. Immediately she leaves the compound, Prez, Peg, Wraith and Mouse come tearing out of his office with only a quick shouted call for volunteers. Heart, it seems, may well be in trouble. I get to my feet, but Blade and Slick are the ones picked which Drummer seems to think is enough, even Wraith's staying behind. Soon after, the other six fire up their bikes and take off.

"Fuckin' hell." Wraith walks into the clubroom a few hours later, shaking his head. He looks around to see the women have stopped their conversations. "Church, Brothers ."

It's a depleted group who sit around the table, but knowing Dollar's got news, we wait to learn what's going on with bated breath.

"Okay." The VP isn't going to draw this out. "Heart was taken by a club called the Demon Sons." He glances up, "If that name sounds slightly familiar, it was a club started by the Rock Demon that got away. Good news is Slick's got his wish now. Havin' taken him out, all the Rock Demons are gone."

As we all start thumping the table and stamping our feet, Wraith holds up his hand. "The bad news," he barks, "is that Heart wouldn't have made it if they hadn't gotten there on time. He's in a bad way in the hospital. Oh, he'll make it. But it will take time. Poor fucker's had enough of being cooped up in bed, I expect."

Collectively our mouths drop open. Wasn't what we expected to hear at all. I give a sideways look at Lady in time to see him mouth, "Poor asshole."

He's not wrong.

Wraith shifts in his seat, looking uncomfortable. "Probably hear more from Prez later, but it seems Heart owes a lot to Marcia. He was suicidal when he was out on the road, seems she talked him down. That's why he's taken a likin' to her."

"A fuckin' cop?" My cheeks glow as I think how I'm steering clear of my brother because of his job, turning down the chance to get to know my niece. While Heart's cosying up with the enemy.

"There's nothing between them. Leastwise, that's what both of them say. But Heart's tryin' to persuade Prez to let her stay in his old home, and he's of the mind to agree. Heart, understandably, doesn't want to set foot in there again. It seems she really does need protection. Someone blew up her house, almost killed her. Heart thinks he owes her for keepin' him alive."

Beef's drumming his heels under the table. "Protecting a cop? Don't like it, VP. Why can't her own people give her a safe house?"

Viper shoots him a look. "Agree with you, Brother. Something doesn't smell right."

It seems Dollar doesn't have all the answers. "Just tellin' you what Prez has relayed."

Unable to give it up, Viper's face is like thunder. "Like to know that's going to be the extent of our protection. Givin' her a place to hole up. Fuck knows what kind of shit it will bring down if we get involved with a cop."

I hear him loud and clear. Again, it reminds me of why I'm keeping my distance from my brother. Too easy to become too relaxed, end up saying something you didn't mean to. Cops and feds would leap on the slightest whiff of wrongdoing, be like a dog with a bone. Nah, I don't want anything to do with the bitch. Sooner the club—and Heart—cuts her loose the better.

"Why she come onto Heart? Isn't that suspicious?" Tongue asks. I nod. Exactly what I was thinking. Heart's been in no frame of mind to think straight. She might be working him, just like I'm worried Sim would dig to find my secrets if I got too close. There's too much shit we've done recently, too great a risk we'd inadvertently let something drop. Especially Heart, who can't be thinking straight.

"Nah," Wraith thinks for a moment, then shakes his head. "Prez seems to think she's legit. She's investigatin' Heart and Crystal's accident. Got in touch to update him they haven't got anywhere."

I frown. "Doesn't that make it more fuckin' dangerous? Who knows what she could find out?" Slick had made sure the man who ran them off the road isn't going to be talking to anyone anymore. Detective Archer is very much dead.

"Slick killed a cop, ain't none of us are gonna apologise for it. But," Wraith points to me, "He covered his tracks. Not too worried anything will surface."

"Why does she need protection anyway?" Lady looks puzzled. "She a dirty cop?"

"Doesn't seem like it. But there's a smell that's not right, Prez said."

Turns out I was right to have my suspicions. In her determination to sort out a mystery, Detective Hannah starts digging too deep. How the fuck she joined the dots, I don't know, but though it's just her theory, she's linking the explosion last year that took out some of the Herreras, and the explosion that had her looking for new accommodation and ending up at Heart's house. Slick was responsible for the first, but not the second. How she could find a connection I don't know. But when Prez comes home, retaking his place at the head of the table, he makes a good point. Keep your friends close, your enemies closer.

When Heart's released from the hospital a couple of weeks later, he returns to the club. It's fucking good to have him back again. Even more so when I find out he's decided to be a proper dad to sweet little Amy. We greet him properly at church, I zone out a bit when Peg talks about helping him get his strength back, and then perk up again when we're discussing a replacement bike for him. *I could give him a few suggestions. There are a couple of models I'd recommend.*

But it seems my input isn't needed, when Heart says, "Prez, if it's okay with my brothers, I'd like to keep ridin' Adam's. Sort of got used to it while I was on the road." He pauses, looking around. "It's only a single seater, might keep the bitches from getting ideas."

Remembering a discussion Scott and I had last night about how careful we need to be, I put in mainly for effect, "Good fuckin' idea, Brother. Might fit one to mine. Fuckin' hangarounds keep on about me taking them for a ride." They do. I just always tell them no.

Catching on fast, Lady bumps fists with me. "Might do that myself."

It's an easy decision to allow Heart to keep our deceased brother's ride. I suspect Adam will be pleased the bike he no longer needs is staying in the family. Then, after lighting a smoke, Blade enquires without pussying around, what's between Heart and the cop.

At last. Something I want to know too.

I'm not the only one sitting forward to hear Heart's answer. In amongst the assurances that there was only ever one woman for Heart, and now she's gone, he doesn't want anyone else, the explanation again of how Marcia kept Heart alive sends chills down my spine. My thoughts voiced by Tongue.

"We should have been there for you, Brother."

Tongue's right. It never sat easy with me. I dip my head to him.

But Heart blasts that thought down, though he still gives credit to Marcia. Again, Drummer confirms we'll help her out, but forbids Heart to have any contact with her himself.

At Prez's instruction, I find myself eyeing Heart carefully, wondering whether he's told us the truth. Oh, he probably thinks he believes it, but that woman's done so much for him, I can't see how he can't have some feelings for her. It's down to her that he's here living and breathing and no doubt, made it possible for him to be slowly coming back to himself. I hope he's right and she means nothing to him. She's been his lifeline for six months. How would I feel if the prez forbade me to have any contact with Scott? If he split us up, put him in different accommodation, or heaven forbid, sent one of us away from the club. Yeah, I hope Heart's not lying. If he is, it's to himself as well as the club.

Turns out Heart's cop is one feisty lady. Ends up she not only thinks she's been partnered with another dirty cop, but that her sergeant could be on the take as well. When she links them both to the Herreras she only goes to try to meet with Leonardo, the head of the family by herself. Luckily, suspicious of her, we have a prospect tailing her. Knowing the crime family have no love of cops who are not in their pockets, to keep her out of their way, she ends up at our compound. A cop. On the fucking compound. If she hadn't kept our brother alive, we'd never have sanctioned it.

Me and Lady were out on a run when they had an emergency meeting to agree to it. Good thing, else I might have had more than one word to say. Prez warned me about getting too close to Sim, now he's letting the police inside our sanctum? But word reaches me Prez isn't too happy about it, he's made Heart responsible for ensuring she behaves and keeping her away from anything she shouldn't see or hear. He's put her in the suite next to his.

"That could be interesting." Scott nods at Heart's suite that night as we pass. It's adjacent to Dart's old one, and where they've put Marcia. A convenient arrangement, if you want to get close, as Scott and I are well aware of.

"You reckon there's more between them than they admit?"

Scott pauses, kicking at a stone. "I followed you from Vegas, had nothing to hope for, just thought I'd nothing to lose. Wasn't going to let you get away, not without at least tryin'. Have to ask yourself, what made Marcia put herself in danger to rescue Heart? You don't do what I did, or what she's done, if you're just friends."

I chuckle, "Don't recall we were friends at the time."

Scott looks at me carefully. "I think we were already more than that."

"Fool," I tell him, smiling.

"Your fool," he responds with a wink. Then, Heart and Marcia clearly gone from his mind, his look becomes heated as he leans over, murmuring into my ear, "My room or yours, Josh?"

Chapter 30

"How long, Scott?"

"What the fuck you askin'?" Raising his head from the pillow, smirking, he looks down his naked body. "Nine inches as you very well know already."

Picking up my tee I throw it at him. "Not what I meant."

"Well, what then?"

We've just had another jerking each other off session. I'm still too scared to go further, or even for him to take my ass again. But how long will he be content with just that?

"Com 'ere." His hand held out in invitation, I walk back over, half dressed, and perch on the edge of the bed. Propping himself up on his elbows, he looks at me earnestly. "I'm here for as long as it takes, Josh. I'm going nowhere. I'm willing to try again; we can always stop…"

"Not that easy. Can't stop. Didn't get no warning last time." I shudder as I remember how that light and pain blindsided me.

"Doesn't mean it will happen again." He shrugs. "If it does, I'll do the same as last time, hold you while you puke."

I purse my lips, that's just what I don't want him to do. "Can't ask my man to do that."

"Your man, eh?" He shuffles closer, his arms looping loosely around my neck. "You're mine too, if we're claimin' each other. You know that, don't you?"

Leaning my head back so it rests on his shoulder, I wish we really could make that commitment, just like our brothers claimed their old ladies. Lately I've been considering, if we were somewhere we could be accepted, just be ourselves, maybe I wouldn't have so many worries. Scott doesn't know how often I've jerked off in the shower just to prevent myself going to his suite. It's a temptation I'm finding increasingly hard to resist. If I knew I could follow through, I'd be opening that door. But I've no way of knowing how it would turn out. He might make a joke of it, but if the same thing happened again, I don't think I'd be able to risk a third time.

I want to tell Scott how I feel about him, but I know I'm not being fair. Not when I can't move past this block between us. A block which my fucking past put there.

Forcing myself to stand up, I pick my jeans up from the floor and continue getting dressed.

"Stay tonight, Josh."

Without turning, I shake my head. Since that early morning visit from Dart, it's true no one else had turned up unannounced at the bloc. Even so, we were lucky that time, can't take the risk again.

Biting my lip I swing around, deciding to let him in on the thoughts I've been having. It would kill me to lose him, but I'm not being fair. "Scott. You should leave the club. Go somewhere you'll be happier. I can't ask you to stay with me. I can't be what you need."

In one quick movement he's off the bed and standing in front of me. His hand's around the back of my neck as he growls, "Not going anywhere. Not without you. I can wait as long as you want. It's not just sex, it's everything, Josh. You're the one that I want."

A wave of relief floods through me. Followed quickly by concern. *He says that now. But how long will my limitations satisfy him?*

It shouldn't be surprising that when I return to my room, I have a restless night. While I spend the small hours contemplating, when I wake with sore, red eyes in the morning I have no answers to how I can deal with my problem. *Perhaps I should leave. Let him get on with his life. Maybe I'm damaged beyond repair.*

It doesn't become clearer over the next few weeks.

As it turns out, Scott was spot on about Heart and Marcia not being able to keep away from each other. Heart got her pregnant before doing some stupid shit that sent her running from the club. It was a complicated story which I hadn't known at first. But apparently, Marcia thought she'd never be able to have kids as a result of a nasty accident when she was eighteen. The news came as a surprise to them both. They had difficulty accepting it at first. But now they're both happy, but worrying and hoping she'll successfully carry, what we find is, two babies to term. I keep my fingers crossed for them both.

When Marcia returns to the club she seems to have adopted a scraggy pup she calls Grunt. Heart seems amused that she picked it up from the side of the road. Tongue, of all people, takes to the beast, and I must admit, apart from when it peed on my boots, I've taken a liking to the mutt myself, though I'd deny it if anyone asked me. Grunt, it seems, takes to the club. Darn dog soon is accepted as a permanent, if unruly, fixture.

Kids. It all seems to be about kids recently. Stories of missing children abound in the news. Marcia's working with Mouse, both doing some digging. Ends up the kidnappers are stealing kids to sell at a fucking auction. At church we discuss how we can infiltrate it and bring the whole fucking ring down. Devil, the security consultant from England, who helped us free Sam from the slave trafficking ring, is in the meeting as well. Road, patched in shortly before Heart returned, sits listening with his mouth falling open. It's the first time he's been around the table discussing such serious business.

Then things get dire when we find a list of the 'items' on sale, which includes a description of Amy, and Ella's sister, Jayden. Watching Heart lose his shit I can well imagine what he's feeling. *What if it was Maya? How could I even contemplate it? A young kid sold to be abused? Not on my watch.*

The thought makes me ready to volunteer for whatever my club wants me to do. As I sit listening for an appropriate time to offer my services, a name familiar to the others, but not to Lady or myself is discussed. A Sheikh Nijad from the Arab state of Amahad. He's trying to get an invite to the auction and needs someone to be his representative.

Drummer raises his chin toward Devil. "Firstly, we need to choose who will go in on Nijad's behalf. It will be one of us. Who wants to volunteer to get dressed up in a posh suit?"

I sit forward, interested to see who'll be chosen, inwardly chuckling. That's one part I couldn't put my hand up for. I'd never be able to pass myself off as a respectable man of society.

"Got to be someone clean looking." *Yup. That rules me out.*

As I'm looking around my brothers wondering who could fit the bill, when I notice all eyes are staring down at this end of the table, I know they're not looking at me. Nor Shooter or Paladin as they're too young, and the heavily bearded Marvel wouldn't be a good choice. No, everyone's focused on Lady, who shuffles awkwardly in his seat.

Fuck no. Not Lady. I send him a worried look, then before he can speak, step up for him. "Fuckin' dangerous going into a place like that. They suspect anything, a bullet to the head would be the least of his worries."

"I'll do it," Lady says without hesitation, throwing a nod at me. A nod which means he knows we'll be having words later. To the rest he continues, "I'm about the only clean-shaven one out of all of us here. And I don't look like a fuckin' body-builder." He elbows me in the ribs. I glare back.

I don't want him exposing himself to danger. But it's not the time or place, not in front of my brothers, to try to dissuade him. Around this table I'm unable to verbalise my reasons why I want to keep him close. I'm the one who's insisted our relationship stays hidden. By not speaking up now, I might have sealed his fate.

"So, we'll have a man on the inside. Devil will brief you on what to expect." Drummer looks pleased.

Devil's peering over at Lady as if making his own assessment of whether he'll be able to play the part. I hold my breath waiting for him to say why it won't work, but as a crooked smile slowly emerges, it seems he agrees Lady will pass. "I can give you a run down. I've been to auctions like this before. Can't show my face now as I'm too easily recognised."

Man's got a huge fucking scar on his face. It would be impossible to disguise that.

As I sit listening to the details being discussed, my gut's already churning with worry. Wondering how I can have Lady's back, wondering if there's some way I can get inside as his bodyguard. Then things get worse. Not only will I not be able to go with him, but none of us will. Everything will be handled by the feds and the cops.

I'm not the only one incensed. Drummer's fists thump down on the table as he thunders out, "Ain't gonna leave a brother with no one at his back."

My own shouts join the general uproar around the table. Devil's voice is even louder than Drummer's. "Quiet. I've addressed that." Gradually the objections die down. He attempts a grin, which doesn't work because half his face doesn't move, his contorted expression, though, suggests he's trying to convey amusement. "When I spoke to the sheriff I explained he wouldn't be able to keep you out of it. Your man inside will have all of you at his back. He didn't like it, but could do with the extra numbers. So he's agreed to have you work alongside the cops for the night."

I'll be close by. But working alongside the cops? Never heard the like.

The incredulous silence is broken by Prez. "Well, fuck me," he says, showing this was news to him too. "No tricks?"

Devil shakes his head. "They'll be grateful for all the manpower they can get. As you say, you want to keep tabs on your man. I feel the same way too. Seth and Ryan, two Grade A protection officers, will be flying out to have Sean's back."

"Hey, we going to be deputised or somethin'?" Tongue's stud flashes as he jokes.

"Not in a fuckin' western, Brother," Beef admonishes him.

"Do we get cop medical cover if we're hurt?" Tongue tries again.

Peg's not looking amused as he tries to keep things on track. "Not going to try to arrest us if we have to take action?"

Ignoring the more inane questions, Devil raises his chin toward Drummer, but appears to answer Peg. "Complete amnesty. You'll be on the same team as the cops. Not going to try to pull the wool over your eyes. This will be dangerous, and bullets will fly. What happens at the auction will be sanctioned. Soon as you leave, you'll be on different sides again."

Nothing that's been said makes me feel happier. I try to pay attention to the discussion continuing around me—seems Heart's about as happy with Marcia taking part in the raid, as I am about Lady's role—but I find it hard to concentrate.

While everyone else is talking across each other, I lean in toward the man who means the world to me, asking quietly, "You sure you want to do this, Lady? Don't like you puttin' yourself at risk."

"Of course I fuckin' do, Brother. I'll have you watchin' my back." He shoots me a loaded look.

"Course you fuckin' will," I growl. "Try to keep me away." But by the sounds of it, I'll be outside. Lady will be on his own taking all the risks.

The meeting goes on and on. Words become meaningless to me as they float around in the air. The buzzing in my head drowns out all the individual voices. I try to nod and shake my head along with the others, while all the time wanting to get out of here to claim my man the way I should have done long ago. Needing to be as close to him as I can possibly get.

He's putting himself in danger. Doing something so brave he might not be coming back. *He knows this.* He's doing it anyway.

Doesn't he care about me? About my feelings? Shouldn't we have discussed this together first? Isn't that what couples normally do?

Are we a couple?

"Need to talk, *Brother.*" I grab hold of his arm when the meeting finally finishes and Lady is making a beeline toward the bar with Tongue.

"Can it wait?" One eyebrow rises in challenge.

"No, it fuckin' can't," I hiss. Momentarily my fear of being found out is overwhelmed by my concern about Lady.

"Later, Tongue, okay?" As Lady signals above his head receiving a 'no worries' gesture in return, I make my way across the clubroom.

"Discreet, eh, Brother?" Lady's almost jogging trying to keep up with my pace.

I keep my mouth shut, discretion the least of my worries right now. Keeping my man safe is far more important. I open the door to my suite, all but dragging him inside. "Leave the club," I say, huffing a little from the fast pace I'd set. "We leave now, join one of the gay clubs you always wanted to."

He crosses to the bed, sits down, and stretches out his long shapely limbs. Only when he's got himself comfortably situated does he raise his eyes. "And that would do what? Make them see me, *us*, as cowards? Unable to do what we signed up for? What we'd sign up for in any one-percenter club? To lay our lives on the line for our brothers."

I wouldn't care if it was me laying my life on the line. But his?

I cross the room and fall to my knees, putting my hands on his thighs. "Scott, the way you talk… You can't act the part of a sheikh's representative. You'll scrub up well enough, I don't deny that. But to talk proper? You're a biker, Scott. You sound like what you are."

"So I'll keep my mouth shut. Won't speak unless it's essential. Then I'll just have to do my best. Ain't backin' out, Brother."

I study his eyes, see the flare of excitement in them, then know his decision is made. There's not a chance in hell that he'll be backing down. A couple of days is all I may have left with him. Two days when I have him as mine. What he's going to do is so fucking dangerous, showing him what he means to me now, before I risk losing him, overrides every other thought in my head.

Pushing his knees until they're bent, I then pry apart his thighs, pushing myself between them. Rising up I place my hand around his head, taking a firm hold. I stare at him, seeing his pupils dilate. "I fuckin' love you," I admit for the first ever time. "Love you, Scott."

Taking my free hand he wraps his fingers around it. "Loved you for a long time, Josh. Just didn't think you were ready to hear it."

"I'm ready now," I respond. I'm oh, so ready.

Our kiss starts gentle, emotion pouring from him to me, then gradually begins to heat up, mouths opening as though we are trying to outdo each other. Our tongues dancing, advancing, retreating, teeth nipping.

My lungs heaving for air, I slide my mouth away, moving down his neck, sucking his tender pulse point between my lips, hard enough to mark. I don't give a fucking damn. Using my body weight I all but slam him back onto the bed.

"Need you naked. Now."

I stand, ripping off my cut and my tee, then strip off the rest of my clothes fast. Only moving slightly slower than me, he rises from the bed copying my actions. When we're both undressed, I take a moment to study him. His chest is lean, muscular with no fat, his waist narrowed and that glorious V leads to his beautiful erect and straining cock. I feel his eyes burning into me, as though we're both trying to burn each other's images onto our retinas.

I crawl over the bed to the opposite side, sliding onto my feet, pulling myself up so we're standing nose to toe.

"No going back," I growl. "I'm taking you tonight. All of you. Understand me?"

For a response he pushes me backward hard, I fall on the bed, he comes over me, trying to hold me down. I use my bulkier muscles to shove him off, rolling him over onto his back. "You're fuckin' mine, Scott. In every way you're going to be mine."

"You're mine, too," he grunts. "Mine."

I reach for the lube and condoms I haven't touched in so long. No doubt in my mind that tonight there's only two of us in this bed, nothing else will intrude. No memories, no conditioning. My fear of losing this man, these next few days being the only chance I might get, overriding any other thoughts.

I only hope I can be gentle. I want to imprint myself on him, so he'll walk into that fuckin' place full of my cum, feeling me every step. I'm wound up like an overwound clock. *Nothing is going to stop me doing this.*

Scott's got an amused smirk on his face. *I'm going to wipe that right off. Give him the pleasure he gave me, make him scream as he comes.* And, at last, understand how he had felt inside me.

"How d'you want this?" he asks me.

"You, on your front. Ass up."

A shadow passes over his eyes. "Are you sure?"

It's the same position as before. *I can do this.* My expression must provide my confirmation, as he turns, positioning himself as I'd requested.

I drop the tube when I go to get lube, swear, then locate it on the floor. This time taking a firmer hold I squeeze a good dollop out. I'm shaking as I reach for his ass, feeling those tight globes under my hands. My cock's throbbing and jerking all by itself, pointing toward Scott's ass as if to show me where its target is.

I push in one finger, not needing the words to tell him to relax, Scott knows more about this than I. I add another, then three, pumping them in and out, scissoring them inside.

"Need you, Josh."

Fucking need you. My brain responds, and my cock jumps. My balls feel heavy as they hang down, full of the cum I'm going to fill him with.

"Want to take you bare," I cry out.

"Do it," he responds.

Ignoring the condoms, I put more lube on my hands, then smother my dick. *Has it ever been this hard before?* I'd surely remember if it had.

Impatient, I delay no longer, positioning my cock at his entrance. As I start to push in there's more resistance than I expected, causing rational thought to return. However much passion is driving me, I worry about hurting him.

"I'm fine, man," he gasps, as though sensing I need encouragement.

Gritting my teeth, I continue into the unknown. I feel him bearing down to help me. Once I'm past that initial ring, I grip his hips with my hands, and with gentle thrusts gain ground.

"Oh fuckin' God, Josh. Feels so fucking good."

He's so tight. Jeez, he's right it feels so good. Better than that. Feels fucking fantastic.

I move one of my hands around him and taking hold of his cock, stroke him in time with my thrusts.

"Harder, Josh. Harder."

I'm not sure what he means, but taking both options, put more strength in my thrusts, my hips bucking against his while tightening my grip on his cock. Remembering how good it felt when he did it to me, I slide almost all the way out, then hammer home. I repeat the action again and again.

My balls are tingling, churning. I feel his cock swell in my hand.

"I can't hold off, I'm gonna…"

I'm right there with him. "Come for me, Scott. Come all over my fuckin' hand. Let me feel you *come*."

At my final instruction I lose control, all rhythm leaving me as the pressure of the cum rising through my cock takes over and I'm pumping, pumping my all into him while at the same time jerking him off, feeling the burst of his semen flooding over my hand.

The air smells of musk, beads of sweat run down my face and into my eyes, Scott's back is misted with perspiration. The only sounds are the hoarse pants coming from us both.

As I remove my now flaccid cock from his ass, Scott collapses face first to the bed, then he turns on his side. I reposition myself next to him.

Cupping my cheek with his hand, he says, "Still ain't changing my mind." Then he pushes me over onto my back and sits astride me. I watch as his cock begins to lengthen in front of my eyes. He looks down and chuckles, palming it, stroking it and tugging. "My turn," he says.

Betraying the strength of his deceptively strong muscles he manoeuvres me onto my front, mimicking the position I'd had him in, I'm almost winded with the speed he uses.

CHAPTER 31

I didn't think I'd be able to get hard again so fast, but with Scott's hands on me, pushing my ass cheeks together and massaging my flanks, my cock does more than stir, it leaps back into life as blood pulses through the veins, rushing south, swelling it once more.

Leaning over me, Scott puts his lips to the side of my neck, trailing kisses from the base of my ear, across the pulse point which has me uncontrollably jerking. His mouth now meets the skin between my shoulders, his tongue comes out to trace my Satan's Devils tat. He takes his time, his haste gone now. Tremors of expectation rack my body, as my skin ripples beneath his touch. Goosebumps rise in the wake of his kisses.

Now he moves lower, his lips on the small of my back causing my nerve endings to twitch. At last he parts the globes of my ass. He exhales, I can feel his warm breath. Then his tongue is there, tracing my puckered hole. As if to test how ready I am, he snakes a hand around taking hold of my cock. A gentle stroke, then he tightens his grip and tugs it. I let out a groan.

"Scott, I…"

"No, you won't. You don't come until I do."

If he keeps up that delicious torture, I've no idea how I'll hold back.

His other hand cups my balls, his thumb caressing gently. I'm so close… Removing his hands, I feel his weight shift, a pause, then the coldness of the lube trickling down the crack of my ass.

"Gonna fill you up."

God, please, yes.

Now the intrusion of one finger, quickly followed by the second. I writhe at the sensation. It burns like it did the last time, but on this occasion, there's no fear, just the expectation of the pleasures to come. I push back against him, wanting more. Needing his cock.

His fingers are gone to be replaced by a different sensation. A pressure, something that feels too large for my small hole. I try to relax, try to bear down. He's relentless, giving me no option but to take him.

Then there's that strange popping feeling as he makes headway, passing through that tight ring of muscles.

"You feel so fuckin' amazing, Josh. So good."

He advances and retreats, gaining ground each time, until I feel his balls against mine. After just a moment to give me time to adjust, he pulls out, then slams in again. The feeling of him moving over my prostate is incredible. I push back, wanting him to repeat the sensation. I'm not disappointed, as he picks up a rhythm. All I can do is submit, to give myself over to him.

He controls me absolutely. In this position I can't touch him, hold him, or even see the look on his face. My own is scrunched up. My hands have a death grip on the pillow as an unstoppable whine comes from my mouth. Being in him felt good, him being in me is different but just as amazing.

He fists my cock, his hand mimicking his dick hammering in and out of my ass. The dual sensations almost too much. But I can feel him swelling inside me as he tightens his grip. I give myself over to him, let my body feel nothing but the combined pleasures of his hand and his cock. My brain empties of everything.

As he plunges into me, I thrust into his hand. The pressure starts building, I'm unable to do anything but give in completely, now impossible to stop or delay the inevitable.

I grunt as the cum shoots out of my cock, he moans, then roars his own release. For a second we're a frozen tableau, then his weight is once more on my back. His hands, sticky with my cum, come around my chest.

Lungs heaving in unison, I feel tears at the corners of my eyes. *What we've done isn't dirty. It's the most natural thing in the world. I've made love to, and been made love to by, the man I adore.*

He rolls to his side, taking me with him. I feel a loss as his cock slips out. We're lying with my back to his chest, his lips nuzzling my neck as though he can't get enough of me. I turn my head, his hand's there to support it, his lips find mine.

It's a gentle kiss, one full of emotion. When I open my eyes I see his glistening like my own.

He turns onto his back, his touch a signal. I turn over, snuggling into his side, my head resting on his arm.

"Fuckin' love you, Josh."

"Back at you, Scott."

It must be the hitch in my voice signalling the reason, the drive that led me to taking this final step, committing to him completely that makes him say, "I'll come back. I promise, babe. You, me, this. Nothing can keep us apart when we're so good together. Never felt anything like this before. This," he doesn't explain what he's alluding to, but I know exactly what he means, "is so incredible between us. We fit, we work. Not giving you up, Josh. Ever."

"You can't promise you'll be safe, Scott." I frown against his skin. "Not when you're going into such a dangerous situation. I'll get Drummer to agree I'll come with you, have your back. Pose as your bodyguard or something."

Propping himself on his elbow, he looks down at my face. "How do you think I feel about that? Think about it for a fuckin' minute, will you? I won't be able to do what I'm there for if I'm worried about you. Works both ways." His features tighten. "I can't afford to put a step wrong. Even if Prez agreed, you'd probably be putting me more at risk."

Damn it. He's got a point. As he settles back down again, I know that he's right. Knowing he cares about me as much as I do about him, everything I fear for him, he's got the same concerns about me. I have to play whatever role I'm assigned, trust him to keep himself safe. The one buoyant thought is that he's got as much to lose as me. What we've got between us? Well, that's worth fighting for.

"Stay here tonight," I suggest.

"Too fuckin' tired to move, babe," he replies, with a soft laugh.

My own eyes are closing. "When this is over, Scott. Let's talk about the future. Where we might go. I don't want to hide anymore."

"Best fuckin' thing you've ever said, Josh. And don't worry. We'll sort it out."

Satisfied and exhausted, I'm just dropping off to sleep when my phone pings with a text.

"Maya?" Scott chuckles as I reach over, picking it up to check.

"Maya," I confirm. "Fuck, she's as cute as a button." I show him the screen. She's sitting up, sucking the ear of a teddy.

Then I put my phone down, snuggle in against him. And know nothing more until morning.

We know when the auction is. We don't know where. The final day in the clubhouse, the atmosphere is subdued. Brothers are checking and cleaning guns, knives are being sharpened. Devil is sitting with the two men of his who've arrived, clearly going over their plans. Lady goes over to join them. Another of Devil's men, Sean, is, like Lady, posing as a buyer at the auction, but he's already acting the part staying at a hotel in Phoenix.

Looking over, I suspect Lady's getting some last-minute advice, going over everything for the hundredth time. Fuck, I'm not going to interrupt them. While I want to spend every moment with him, the more he can do to ensure he comes out alive, the better.

When Mouse appears from his cave, all eyes flit to him, but he shakes his head, confirming there's no news yet. I start to hope the auction's been cancelled, but Mouse knocks my fleeting optimism on the head.

"No need to worry yet, Prez. They'll leave it right to the last minute. Just enough time for people to get there. Not enough to involve the feds." Mouse answers Drummer's question as though he can see into my head.

Then another of Devil's people who's been working with Mouse over the last few days, an information analyst called Nessa, summons Mouse back to work. Only seconds later, they return. The location is now known.

A phone dings.

"Got a text, Prez." Lady, still looking at the screen, stands, brushes off his smart suit which has been tailored to fit, and goes to compare notes with Drummer. I can't help my eyes landing on his trim figure, showcased spectacularly in his posh clothes.

I get to my feet. I'm not alone. Everyone is waiting in readiness. Lady gets a hug and a word of support from Drum, then gets slaps on his back as he walks through the assembled crowd of brothers. He gets to me and hesitates.

I can't help it. If this is the last time I'm going to see him alive, I'm not going to let him go without him knowing, once again, what he means to me. My arms go around him as I pull him in close enough to say into his ear quietly so only he can hear, "Love you, Scott. Be safe."

It's inadequate, but the brief tightening of his arms around me, as he responds, "Back at you, babe," has to suffice.

We may have held each other too long, but I don't give one fucking damn.

"Let's give Lady a moment to get movin', then we'll get rollin'," Drummer's voice booms out. Reluctantly I let Lady go. *It's time.*

My eyes linger on him, drinking in every movement as he walks, without turning back, across the clubroom and out of the door to his expensive hired car waiting outside. *He looks the part. As long as he remembers not to open his mouth, he'll pass for a representative of a rich sheikh.* He'll be fine. *He might not.*

I take the bulletproof vest that's handed to me on auto pilot, slip it on, then go to my bike as the tail lights of Lady's car fade into the distance. There's a hole in my chest as though he's taken part of me with him.

Then I wait for Prez to pull out in the lead, Wraith and Peg behind him, then Dollar, Blade, Heart and Mouse. When all the rest of my brothers have passed, I take my spot at the rear, just in front of the crash truck driven by the prospect Hyde with Heart's woman, Marcia, in the passenger seat. She'll be the liaison between us and the cops tonight.

We haven't a clue what we're heading into. Lady, and Devil's man, Sean, are wearing tiny undetectable two-way communication devices. Once they gain entry we'll be able to hear what's going on inside the auction. It's only then that it will be possible to put the final touches to our plan of attack. Lady's doing a fucking important job for us tonight. *But if he's found out. If that device isn't as discreet as we hoped...* I try to concentrate on the ride and to dismiss the feeling of dread that's settled inside me.

Then we're at the hastily arranged meeting place. There's a large police contingent, and a whole bunch of feds. Parking up I exchange an amused look with Tongue. Fuck, what a joke to think tonight we're all on the same side. Marcia leaves the truck, going to join her old colleagues, then it's a waiting game.

Ah, hang on. Prez is walking over. With a man I recognise. Fuck, it's the fed who set us up for a fight he didn't expect us to win. *Bet he's still wondering how we survived.* The shuffling around me shows I'm not the only one to be uncomfortable in his presence.

"Agent Haughton, you'll probably remember," Prez tells us, impassively.

The agent nods then begins, without hesitation and certainly not the deserved apology, "Your main job is to concentrate on getting your man out. We're going in heavy. The bidders won't want to be taken, and the organisers will want to get away clear. But we do want some still alive to question, you hear me?"

All I hear is that our job is to get Lady out. I don't give a damn who I kill in the process. I growl, eager to get on with it.

Devil comes over and begins handing ear pieces out. Mine is larger than the one Lady's wearing, but then it doesn't need to be discreet. Awkwardly I get it in place over my ear, anxious to hear Lady's voice.

"I'll be turning the receiver on and off. I'll be in control of what we're transmitting. Don't want Sean or Lady to be distracted by voices in their heads until we start giving them instructions. Got it?"

I certainly do get Devil's drift. Don't want anything to draw attention to Lady, or to the other brave man, Sean, for that matter.

Fuck! That's strange. Men go quiet around me as voices start sounding in my head. Lady's inside already, Sean just entering. A fleeting smile comes to my face as Lady's offered a glass of champagne and he accepts with just one word. *Probably would have preferred beer, but sensible enough not to ask for one.*

Sean's the one who politely asks when the auction will get underway giving us the info we need. *Within the hour, when the last guests have arrived.* I shift one foot to the other, anxious to get going, but knowing it will feel like a long wait. *Just want him back. Safe.*

Tongue's talking to Heart. Beef, like me, looks like he'd prefer to get moving. Rock's standing still, deep in thought. Other quiet conversations go on around me, I don't get involved, my focus only on one thing.

Then at last we're given the instruction to move. I'm with one of the groups going in the main entrance, while Heart, Blade, Peg, some cops and some feds, are aiming to go in via the rear to get out the children. At least they didn't ask me. I'm going in the front whether they told me to or not and will be heading straight for my man. I'm patting my side pocket with my spare weapon that I'm going to put straight into his hand.

"On my count." Devil's voice comes over clearly. Then, as he's obviously switched Sean and Lady's earpieces onto receive, "We're coming in five. As soon as we come in, cover your faces."

Devil's two men, Seth and Ryan, quickly and silently deal with the guards standing outside by slitting their throats. Bloody, but necessary. As police run up with a battering ram, I slip my mask on. The door gives way easily. A gas canister is thrown inside.

Immediately shouts and screams come from the interior. Men and women try to flood past us, tears streaming from their eyes. Shots start firing. Handcuffs come out, yeah, I'm carrying them too. A blinded man, coughing, barrels into me. I snap those fuckers on his wrist and push him behind me, then head further into the room.

Where is he?

There! He's scrapping with a man. *Fuck, he should have kept up the pretence.* I see a knife rise but I'm there in fucking time. A bullet to the forehead and the man goes down. Immediately I slip my spare weapon out of my vest and into Lady's hand, then hand him the spare mask clipped to my belt.

I'm not the only one heading for Lady. Tongue's got his back, Road's on his other side. Slowly we start making our way across the room out to safety. Through the haze I see Rock go down. *Fuck.* Lady starts to change direction, but I hold him back. Rock's taken a bullet but Shooter's got him up, now they too are making their way to the nearest exit. Beef and Bullet have his six.

We push on. The numbers around us are fading, but we're stepping over bodies now.

"Jesus. Joker!" Lady's agonised shout and quickly fired shot has me swinging around. *Tongue's down.* Fuck. He's landed face down with a huge fucking hole in his back. Lady's firing indiscriminately hoping to take out the man who'd shot him.

Quickly assessing that the remaining enemies are being corralled and taken away, Lady seems to have got the last men standing. I shout at Road. "Go get him some help."

As someone approaches I raise my gun, then recognise her. *It's Marcia.* Shit, Heart will be going apeshit if he knows she's in here.

With that thought in mind, I snarl out, "What are you doing here?"

She indicates around. "It's contained and controlled now, Joker. Let me have a look at Tongue." She starts trying to lift him, I help, both of us getting his blood on our clothes. There's an exit wound on his front, he's lying in a puddle of his own blood. Gently she nods, and we put him back down. Shaking her head, she places a finger to his neck. Her face falls. "He's gone."

Tongue's dead. He died protecting Lady. It could have been me if I'd been in a different position. My eyes meet Lady's, he's as shocked as me.

Outside it appears to be organised confusion. Police piling protesting auction goers and racketeers into trucks, dead bodies being brought out. I stand stiffly as I watch Tongue's body being stretchered away, the cops treating him as reverently as though he was one of their own. He died beside them tonight.

Rock can't ride. I supervise both his bike and Tongue's being loaded onto the crash truck, then nod to Lady who'll be driving his posh rented car back home. Brothers go to their bikes and peel off into the dark night in formation, a space in our ranks where Tongue should have ridden.

Tongue will never be riding with us again.

CHAPTER 32

an't we put something in about how he used that stud in his tongue?"

"For fuck's sake, Pussy. This is a eulogy to celebrate Tongue's life." Prez, who'd been sitting at a table in the clubroom, puts down his pen where he'd been jotting down some notes.

The sweet butt shrugs, unrepentant. "It was one of his talents."

Allie, standing next to her, nudges her. "He was the best."

Lady, quieter than normal, meets my eye. I lead him away from the group, going to stand by the bar. "It probably wasn't an attempt to kill you. It was indiscriminate shooting. Just bad luck Tongue was in that place."

"If he hadn't been there, it would have been me. He was right behind me."

I hate that Tongue died. But the thought that we might otherwise have been preparing for Scott's funeral chills me to the bone. I shudder. Scott's been in a bad place since that night. Though he and Tongue weren't particularly close, he was a good brother. We all miss him like fuck. Noting Allie and Pussy have given up with Drummer, I frown. Seems the sweet butts will miss him as much as anyone.

Turning back to Lady, I see him staring morosely down into his beer. I put my hand on his back. "Fuck, Brother. You know the score. Any one of us would give up our lives for anyone wearin' the same patch. That's a given as soon as we get a seat around the table, if not before. You think if Tongue was here and it was someone else dead, he wouldn't be sayin' the same?"

Lady looks around, and seeing no one close, leans in. "You think any more about leavin' the club?"

I do. But I know Lady's guilt is making him think about it for different reasons. "Lady. This life. Comes with risks. No guarantees. But fuck, would you really want to give it all up?" I'd put down my bottle, now I pick it up and drink from it. Wiping my hand over my lips, I continue, "If we left the Devils behind us, I'd want to find another club. Couldn't live the citizen life."

Lady drains his own beer. "That's the only alternative, isn't it? Nine to five and livin' in suburbia."

Sounds like I'm getting through to him. "Sure is. I think that would kill me. Maybe slower than a bullet, but I wouldn't survive."

He's quiet for a moment, then he raises his chin. "You're right. That adrenaline rush when I went into that auction. Being part of the team. Playin' an important part…"

"It was vital," I interrupt him. "Without you inside we wouldn't have known how or when to attack. Could have lost more brothers, more cops or feds. The children might have been hurt."

"Culling the feds wouldn't be so bad."

I laugh along with him. The fleeting thought of my brother crosses my mind. *Would I be able to take him out if we got caught up in the same mess from different sides? If one of my Devil brothers' lives were at risk?* I have no answer.

"Fact is," I address Lady again. "You did what you had to. Up to the moment Tongue was shot, I reckon you fuckin' enjoyed it."

He salutes me with his bottle. "Truth right there," he admits. Then he frowns. "It could have been you, Joker."

"I could come off my bike tomorrow," I snap. "And there's no way I'm giving ridin' up. Life's a risk, Brother. From the moment a baby starts breathin'."

He's quiet. I give him space. It's a few moments before he next speaks. "So we stay Devils?"

"As long as they still want us."

Our bottles clink together.

When the day of the funeral arrives, Tongue's given an incredible send off. Brothers attend from all the other chapters, Patriot Riders turn up, and the police not only provide an escort for the trip to the graveyard, but also for the coffin to the grave. Everyone he fought beside and lost his life for that night, stands up for him as he is lowered into the ground. Tongue died a hero.

Once Tongue is buried, Scott starts to come back to his normal self, which includes us sleeping together once more. It just progressed naturally without conscious decision or discussion. We've become more relaxed, prepared to take things as they come. If we slip up and are found out, we'll deal with the circumstances whatever they bring us.

Lady having volunteered to go into the auction seems to have changed the brothers' views of us both. I couldn't put my finger on anything in particular, but no longer do I feel I'm being treated like an outsider. I even begin to think that while they probably wouldn't accept gays in the club, I don't think repercussions would be as bad as I once expected. Or so I hope.

One thing we have talked about is how much we love the brothers here, the women, fuck, even the babies. Now there are two more of those on the way, Heart and Marcia's twins. We don't want to leave.

I've done some hard thinking about myself. Looked at things in a different way. I'm a biker, a Satan's Devil, first and foremost. The fact that I'm gay is incidental. It might guide who I want to spend my life with, but it's not the main thing that determines who I am. Becoming more comfortable with myself enables me to fully give to the brotherhood, whereas I expect I used to hold something back. With the one exception they don't know about, I feel fully accepted here.

Life settles down, rumbling along without incident after the auction. I'm just happy to have some peace and quiet in my life. What more could I want? Good brothers around me, money in my pocket, great location to live in, the man I love by my side. As the weeks turn into months, my worries about the Devils finding out what Lady and I do behind closed doors starts to fade.

We have church on Fridays as normal, all routine, going through the businesses. Bullet and Viper's construction business is really taking off. Jekyll gets patched in, but we don't change his road name. Hyde, well, Hyde's got a lot of bridges to mend before he gets his patch. Though listening to the way Slick and Heart talk about him, he never will. He tries hard, the poor fucker. Fergus is still an unknown quantity, thought he seems to fit in.

We've all prospected for a year or more, putting up with everything thrown at us, proving ourselves worthy of wearing the patch. Trust is the key. Brothers have got to know they can rely on each other, that they'll have each other's backs in every situation. It's a hard and gruelling twelve months or more, some don't make it. It's the failures I feel sorry for.

"Heard a whisper Peg's been talkin' to Slick and Heart about patching Hyde in," Scott informs me one night. He points to his door, then mine.

I shrug. It makes no difference to me as long as we're together. Both rooms are identical. When he opens the door to his, I follow him in. He goes to the mini fridge, taking out a couple of beers, then, when he indicates the balcony, I nod.

When we settle ourselves outside in the warm, spring evening air, me leaning back on the chair with my feet perched on the railing, I respond. "Been thinking about him. Man lives for the club."

Scott puts his beer down on the table between us. He looks out at the view, letting out a sigh. "Fucking good place here. Still don't take it for granted. Would hate to be Hyde."

"I wonder what he'll do if he has to prospect for much longer."

"Don't think it will come to that." His comment makes me look at him in surprise.

"What d'you mean?"

"Overheard some chatter. If he doesn't get the patch soon, he'll be out. He's been here eighteen months, if he can't prove himself in that time, word is he never will."

I reach for my drink. "Good point there." I frown. "Fuckin' hard thing. Reason we're still flying under the radar. I hate to think what would happen if they forced us to leave the club."

"Me too, Josh. Me too." His hand reaches across the gap between us, but falls before it lands. We're too exposed here. Brothers have got used to us being friendly, but as far as they believe, it's just because we patched over together. Hand holding where we might be seen is definitely out.

We both go silent. Yeah, we could find another club, but they wouldn't be Devils. We may even have to start at the bottom again. I shudder at the thought, thinking of all the shit we put the prospects through, same as I had taken in my day. Wouldn't want to go back there again. No, switching clubs is not something I'd do lightly.

I bring my feet down and sit forward, my eyes looking in the direction of the setting sun. "Being gay doesn't define me." I let Scott in on thoughts I'd kept private up to now. "Being a Satan's Devil does."

Now it's his turn to frown slightly. "You know my feelings; I'd much rather we were able to come out. But yeah, the thought of not being a Devil any longer is what frightens me. So much to give up. This place is my home and my family. That I've got you, babe, is just the icing on top."

I throw him a quick smile. No need for me to confirm I feel the same way. He knows it.

But in the same way we daren't come out, we can't progress our relationship. Hell, if I had my way I'd marry him. Make it official. Tie him to me. Not that that would provide any guarantee, but it would prove a commitment.

Scott finishes his bottle just as the sun dips under the horizon. The crickets are chirping—too early for cicadas—and the gnats are coming out. He stands, waving for me to do likewise. Collecting the empty bottles, I follow him inside.

He draws the blinds, then lets out a sigh and reaches for me.

During the day I have to keep my distance, have to pretend he's nothing special. These moments, these nights, are precious. My lips meet his with no hesitation. Our hands act in unison as we push each other's cuts off, then tangle as we try to take off our tees. A quick grin, then we're reaching for each other's jeans. The months together mean our movements are practiced.

Chests rubbing, our mouths caressing, I'm drinking in the flavour while breathing the unique perfume of my man. Two hard cocks duelling together. Tonight I let him take the lead, let him take me how he wants to.

Later we'll shower together, washing the sweat and cum off our bodies.

This is my life, and I fucking love it. The only thing missing is that I can't publicly claim him.

As Lady had predicted, at the next church, the prospects come up on the agenda.

When Prez gives him the floor, Peg begins, "I'll throw it open, but want to give you my thoughts first. Let's start with Fergus. He's been here getting on for a year, but I'm not recommending we patch him in yet. We need a prospect to do the shit, and while he's probably close to earning his patch, I don't think he's quite ready to bring to the table. Anyone think different?"

"Like the man," Wraith puts in. "But we've not had to put him to the test yet."

I suppose that's right. He wasn't involved at the slave auction. We kept him out of that shit. I nod to show I agree, others do likewise.

Peg takes another breath. "Which brings me to Hyde."

I don't find it surprising that Jekyll's the first to support him. They came into the club together. "I've got a couple of things I'd like to say. I know I'm the newest member at this table, but I worked alongside Hyde for a year. He's hard working and dependable, and I, for one, trust him. Don't know if my view counts for anything, but he never turned down even the shittiest of jobs."

"Your view's as valid as any other," Prez tells him. "Anyone else got anything to say?"

Peg has. "Hyde's been prospecting for longer than anyone else. We either patch him in, or part ways. He's been here eighteen months dealing with all the shit that we've thrown at him." He pauses, then slams his fist down on the table. "And never once have I heard him complain. Unlike you, Jekyll."

Jekyll shrugs, giving a quick grin. Paladin, sitting beside him, places a playful punch on his arm.

Prez raises his eyebrow at Peg, who shrugs when no one else speaks. "Right," Drummer starts. "Let's go around the table. And I don't need to remind you, one nay and Hyde leaves the compound tonight."

I risk a glance at Lady, my look conveying that if they ever found out, this could be a discussion they'd be having about us. His slight chin lift in return shows me he knows exactly what I'm thinking. Just like this, they could be going around the table, deciding our fate. Whether we'd leave or stay, or worse. *Christ, I wouldn't be able to bear it.*

Wraith starts us off with a yay. Dollar echoes him. Bullet's quick too, another positive vote. Blade thinks about it, a snide look thrown in Peg's direction then he votes yay too. Now Slick. I'm watching him carefully, wondering which way he'll go. Also wondering which brothers would be for or against us if we got careless and were outed.

Slick's staring down at his hands. "Hyde fucked up when my old lady first came here. Fucked up good." He pauses, and raises his head, receiving the chin lifts of acknowledgment. I nod. Can't deny that. "I'll leave Heart to talk about what happened later." Heart growls from two seats down. Then an unexpected grin comes to Slick's face. "I'll miss givin' the asshole shit, but I'm not averse to bringin' him to the table. He's gotten things straight over the past months. My vote's aye."

Well, I didn't expect that. I raise my eyebrow toward Lady.

The voting continues, I say 'aye' when it's my turn, as does Lady. Then it gets to Paladin. The youngest brother raises his hand. He talks for a moment about the hardships of prospecting, his description confirming I never want to have to do that again. Then, at last, he gives his nod for Hyde to get his patch.

Jekyll shrugs. "I like him, Aye from me."

Viper's quick, he says aye. Shooter and Rock don't take much time. Road gives his vote, another plus for Hyde. Then it's Heart's turn.

Heart clears his throat. I listen as he manages to extol Hyde's virtues, as well as to reference the excellent ability of his old lady, Marcia, in handling her bike. Finally, he leans forward, looking Peg straight in the face. "I vote aye."

After that it's quick. Mouse doesn't take a minute to give his positive answer, Peg's an obvious yes, but Prez seems to hesitate before saying, "I don't have a problem with the fucker. Think he'll do good things for the club. It's a unanimous vote, Peg. Let's call him in."

I wink at Lady, pleased that Hyde's not going to suffer the fate we'd talked about. Anticipating welcoming a new brother to the table, I force the grin off my face as he walks in.

Well, of course he might hope, but he's no idea what he's here for. From the expression on his face, he thinks he could well have been voted out. He pulls back his shoulders, standing tall gazing straight at the prez.

The silence seems to last forever. A pin dropping would be louder than any noise we make. Every brother staring down the table, but to Hyde's credit he takes it, and doesn't try to look away.

Eventually Drum speaks. "You've been prospecting for us for eighteen months now. Came in with Jekyll, but we gave you longer as you needed a few second chances."

Hyde doesn't flinch, doesn't show any reaction. Doesn't try to defend himself for the mistakes that he made. In the light his eyes glisten. My face goes tight, imagining if it was me standing there, expecting to be told I was no longer in the club.

Prez can be canny. Instead of continuing, he gestures to Slick. "Slick, you've had problems with Hyde. Anything you want to say?"

The patches are passed discreetly down the table. Hyde's shoulders slump further as he realises the man who he's wronged the most probably has been given the honour of throwing him out.

Slick has his say, ending with, "Welcome to the table, Brother." He brings out the patches he was holding. The Satan's Devils insignias that Hyde will now be able to wear with pride, as a fully patched member.

I stamp my feet and bang my fists on the table along with everyone else. Then we're all up on our feet, slapping Hyde's back, welcoming him as a member.

Beside me, Lady yells out, "Patch in party!"

Hyde's still not cracked a smile, he seems bemused. Peg's last to congratulate him.

As he looks up at the sergeant-at-arms, he wipes away a tear, and then, at last, his face cracks. "Thanks, Peg." Then louder, he calls out, "Thanks, everyone. I won't let you down."

His reaction, his emotion gets to me. He worked his ass off to get to this place. *This is precisely what I can't lose.*

Careful to let Lady and a few other brothers walk out before me, I follow Hyde as he's hustled toward the bar. Then crack a smile as, after shaking Fergus's hand, with obvious delight, he asks the prospect why he hasn't got a drink in his hand yet.

"Way to go, Brother," I call out.

CHAPTER 33

"Well come in, you two. I was thinking you'd forgotten me."

"Mom," Scott admonishes, "We speak every week on the phone."

She swats him. "You've been keeping this gorgeous man of yours too much to yourself. Josh. How are you?" As Rachel puts her arm around my waist and leads me away, I see Scott wink at me over my shoulder.

This time no other relatives appear, and Rachel seems more than happy to have us to herself. The women at the clubhouse do their best to create good meals for us, but having one home cooked by Scott's mom is something else. *Just a pot roast* she'd told me, but that title didn't do what she served up justice. Once again I envy how Scott grew up.

Scott and I are on clean up, he's insisted she sit down and relax. When we've finished, he takes a couple of beers out of the fridge, then calls out to ask if her wine needs topping up.

"Does a bear shit in the woods?" she yells back, making me laugh.

He carries in the bottle, fills her glass, then takes the bottle back to keep it cool. "Yeah, Mom. And the pope wears a funny hat," he says drily. Their exchange sounds practiced.

"Josh, come here. Sit beside me." I do as she asks. "Now," she starts seriously, "how have you two been getting on?"

Scott returns, taking the chair opposite. Picking up the remote, he clicks on the TV.

"Scott. I want to talk to you both."

With a sideways look at her, he sighs, then turns it back off. "Mom," he starts, but she stops him with a huff.

"I don't see enough of you. Wanna see your faces, not the back of your heads."

Scott grins. "So, what's it you want to know, Mom?" He settles back, folding his arms.

"What I want to know is when Josh here is going to make an honest man of you."

It's a shame I've just taken a mouthful of beer. Her question coming right out of the blue makes me choke and quickly need to put my hand to my face to stop spitting my drink out.

"Don't get your hopes up, Mom. We won't be getting hitched." Scott gives a shake of his head which I interpret is an apology to me.

"Why not?" she asks defensively. "It's legal now, you know."

"Quite aware of that, Mom. But remember, we haven't come out."

Her lips thin. "Scott. I brought you up to be proud of what you are, not to pretend to be something you're not. I don't like the idea of you feeling you have to hide your relationship."

"Rachel," I step in. "Scott and I are happy where we are, but we don't want to rock the boat. The men we ride with, well, we don't want to make them uncomfortable."

Now she rounds on me. "Whether they are or not is on them, not you." Again she huffs, and folds her arms over her chest in a gesture exactly the same as her son's. "I see the both of you together, hear about you every week, Josh. You make a perfect couple."

Scott looks exasperated, sends another look of apology toward me, then tries to justify where we stand. "We make the perfect couple whether we're married or not, Mom. Same as straight folks. They don't always tie the knot."

It's true, they don't. In our world claiming someone as your old lady is even more important than a piece of paper signed by a judge. *But I can't claim Scott, and he can't claim me.* Much as I want to. As Scott and his mom continue the discussion, it comes to me how much I'd love the world to know we're together, then recall all the reasons why I can't.

Having made it clear that she'd love to see us make things official, Rachel at last changes the subject. Instead of the TV, the board games come out again, and the rest of the evening passes swiftly.

It's only later, when I'm lying in the double bed with Scott, that it hits me the extent to which I'm able to relax here. Rachel doesn't give a damn about our sexual preferences, she's just pleased to know her son's found someone to make him happy. I don't need to watch what I say, worry if I'm unable to resist touching Scott in a way others might think inappropriate, holding his hand or placing a kiss to his cheek. In fact she glows when we demonstrate what we feel for each other.

In Tucson it will be different again. Always feeling on edge, being wary of giving myself, and him, away.

But there's no use wishing things could be different. I've made my decision which Scott's agreed with. We're Devils. If we want to stay in the club, keeping our relationship secret is the only way we can do it.

But this, this couple of days when I'm allowed to be me, is refreshing. In the dark of the night I pull a sleeping Scott closer. I try to concentrate on what I have, not what I haven't. Whether or not we can admit to it openly, I'm one lucky fucker to have him any way that I can.

We return to the compound and our version of normality. I'm not blind to what's going on around me. Since the last church when Hyde patched in, I've noticed that just one over-worked prospect can't handle everything here. As Fergus, without uttering a word of complaint, tries to split himself into three, I take pity on him, helping myself to my own beer. When the time comes that kid will deserve his patch, no doubt about that. I make a note to raise it tonight in church.

Lady comes alongside to join me. "Reduced to getting your own drink?" He bumps his fist to mine.

"Look at him," I nod toward Fergus. "Lad's run off his feet."

"Heard you get a text earlier."

Pulling my phone from my pocket, I grin. "Nosy asshole." None the less, I put in the code, swiping to the picture I'd just received. Another of Maya. She's in a swimming pool with Sara.

"Can they really start swimming that young?" Lady tilts his head.

"Suppose so." I'd thought it strange myself. "Some mother and baby bonding shit, I expect." The one thing that kid has is loving parents. It's clear to see the love shining out of Sara's eyes.

Lady looks down at his bottle, then at me. "Want to take a trip up there, sometime? See the kid? It's been quiet here for a while, nothing for the feds to take an interest in."

"Only the fact we exist," I grumble. Unlike my biker brothers, Sim hasn't earned my trust. I'm not sure he ever will. We spent too many years apart.

"Looks like we're on." Lady nods toward Drummer who's calling everyone in.

Positive updates again at church. Then they're discussing the houses being built at the top of the compound. I knew Heart was having one built next to the Prez's, but I didn't realise Wraith wanted one too. Fuck, they've got a good spot up there. I risk a sideways glance to see almost a look of longing on Lady's face. *He, we, deserve a home too.* At least we could adapt the two suites we've got into an apartment like Peg's. But for that, we need to come clean.

I give an almost imperceptible shake of my head. *Not for us, Brother.* Not yet, maybe not ever.

As does everyone else, I offer my help in getting Heart sorted out and his and Marcia's stuff moved in, in preparation for their imminent new arrivals. Then with that finished, take the opportunity to raise my hand. When Prez gives me a nod, I point toward Hyde. "We're down to one prospect now our new brother's joined us at the table. That's leaving us short. Any plans what we're going to do about it?"

Drum looks at Peg who responds. "There's a man who's been hanging around at the auto shop. Came in with his bike, and has been visiting a lot. Talking about our life here, and indicating he's interested."

"Background?"

The sergeant-at-arms shrugs. "Not got that far, but Blade," Peg nods at our enforcer, "called me down to meet him one day. What I saw, I liked."

"Good guy, from what I can tell." Blade returns.

"Okay. Get his name and what you can to Mouse, and Mouse, you know what you gotta do."

Good plan. Mouse can find anything out. Make sure the man's got nothing in his background that could put us at risk.

"His name's Matt Gore," Blade tells him.

Mouse notes it down. "I'll get Marcia's help too. Well, if she's able." His head tilts to query Heart.

Marcia's old man shrugs. "Better do it soon, or she'll have her hands tied. But sitting at a computer screen won't tax her none."

Prez bangs the gavel. "Okay. Let's hope we get something sorted. And keep your eyes open for anyone else. We need someone to tend bar. And someone who won't give my whisky away."

Lady waggles his fingers. "Just a thought, Prez. While we usually have a prospect behind the bar, why don't we get one, or all, of the club whores to be bartender? Means we're not a man short all the time."

Always happy to take an opening when it's offered, I elbow him in the ribs. "'Cause the sweet butts have better things to do with their hands." Looking around I see single men nodding in agreement, but Peg's giving me a strange unreadable look. He continues staring long enough for me to feel uncomfortable.

Prez is stroking his beard, taking a few seconds before slowly nodding. "Sounds like a good idea to me. Who wants to find out whether any of them got skills in that direction?"

Beef nods his head. "I can have a word." I grin. Rather him than me. I can imagine that going down like a ton of lead.

Heart records the vote. I raise my chin toward Lady. It was a good fucking idea.

Church over, my brothers are in the mood to party. I'll have a few beers to be sociable, maybe try to win my money back from Rock at the pool table if he's up for it, then go to my room and wait for Lady.

Getting a drink is my priority, so I head for the bar, rapping the wooden top to get Fergus's attention. Beer swiftly in hand, turning I survey the room. Nah, won't be winning much from Rock tonight, he and Beef are already heading off with Diva and Paige. Guess they'll be occupied for a while. Ah, but… over in the corner I see Dollar, Viper and Shooter starting to deal cards. Yeah, a game of poker sounds pretty attractive.

"Got room for another?" I ask, as I near the table.

"Sure," Dollar smirks. "If you want to lose some cash."

I almost change my mind. Playing with the treasurer maybe isn't the best idea, but at least it isn't the card shark Rock. Pool I can beat him at. Cards? Not so much.

Dollar deals, I check my hand. Not fucking good. But I'm in, I'll take my chance. I throw away three cards, then check the replacements I'm dealt. Hmm, a pair. Can't expect very much with that, but maybe I'll bluff. Raising my eyes from my hand, I scan the faces around the table. There's a glint in Viper's eye, which could mean he's holding something good, or nothing at all. Young Shooter, now, his face is completely impassive, I can't read him at all.

Taking a chance, I raise, swapping out another two cards. *Fuck. Complete crap.* With the gods certainly not looking down on me kindly tonight, I fold. Turns out fucking Viper's got the winning hand, so he takes the pot.

It's not my night. I call it quits when I'm more than a few dollars down. Needing another beer, I wave to Fergus. While I'm waiting, someone comes up alongside me. It's the prez.

"How you doing, Joker? Not heard much from you lately."

Prez doesn't normally single me out, but maybe he's just being sociable. "Doing good, Prez."

It's quiet for a moment, so I fill it in my normal way. "Heard a story about a badass prez once."

Prez raises an eyebrow, but his mouth twitches. He knows where I'm going with this.

"So," I continue. "Prez wakes with a huge hangover, can't remember a fuckin' thing about the night before, so he knows he has to have tied one on. He's alone in the bed, his first thought is about his old lady. Fuck, she's gonna give him some shit. He wishes he could recall what he did so he can cover his ass, but it's all a blank. But when he sits up he finds Advil and water on the table beside him as well as a note from his wife telling him breakfast is in the oven.

"Now, Prez is fucking confused. He was expectin' to get shit thrown at him, not a hangover cure and breakfast. Wonderin' whether it will be poisoned, he staggers to the kitchen, finding it spotless and his son sitting eating without a care in the world.

"What the fuck happened last night? he asks his son. Son replies, oh, just the usual. You came in at dawn, drunk off your ass. Puked everywhere, smashed the place up.

"Prez is confused. He looks around. Everything's in its place though there seems to be a few less plates on the counter. He knows his old lady would be fuckin' mad about that. So he asks his son cautiously, what's got into your mom? He waits to hear she's out smashing up his bike.

"His son smirks. Well, Mom woke up, dragged you to bed. But as she was takin' your pants off, you told her to leave you the fuck alone as you were married."

A pause, then Drummer chuckles. Okay, so maybe not one of my best ones. Companionably he drains his drink, then waves at Fergus to bring him another.

I try again. "Okay, so an old wizened biker, with his bitch-pullin' days far back in his rearview, draws up at a bar, noticin' the menu outside. Plain burger, one dollar, cheeseburger two dollars, hand job, fifty bucks."

I pause, glancing at Drummer, see I've still got his attention. "Eagerly he gets off his bike, in his haste, almost forgettin' to put the stand down. He all but runs inside."

Taking a breath, I leave another gap, and see my companion shifting impatiently. "Inside he finds this really attractive bartender, fuckin' gorgeous she is. Thinking of what's to come, his tongue's hanging out through the gaps in his teeth. When she approaches him, he's all but salivating as he asks, You the one who does the hand jobs? Yes, she purrs. Well, he tells her, go wash your damned hands really damn thoroughly and bring me a fuckin' cheeseburger."

It's not often you see this relaxed side of the prez. He barks a strangled laugh. It can't be the first time he's heard a version of this one, but at least it's made him chuckle.

As his mirth fades, I notice Prez is subjecting me to a type of scrutiny. "'Sup, Prez?"

He shakes his head. "Nothing. Just wonderin' if you and Lady are settlin' in now? Took you a while to get comfortable here."

"Been here, what, two years now? Yeah. This is home." I turn, leaning my back against the bar. "It's strange changin' clubs. Brothers are the same all over, but all got their little quirks. Takes a while to get to know them."

He raises his bottle. "Yeah, we've all got quirks." Finishing the beer, he puts down the empty, slapping me on the back. "Even patched in members need time to earn trust. That goes both ways. You and Lady are good men, Brother. A good fit for the club."

What does he mean by that? As he walks off, a weight settles in my stomach. *Nah, he was just being friendly. He couldn't know...* Then I examine his words in a different way. *I've got approval from my prez.* The dread inside me vies with my pride. *If he did know, he probably wouldn't be saying that. If he did know, I'd disappoint him. Just like I've been disappointing people all my life.*

I give up on my idea of playing pool. For one thing, I'm no longer in the mood, for another, the table's already in use. Marvel and Jekyll are fucking Allie on it. I look around, and see Lady chatting to Hyde. I catch his eye, jerking my head toward the door. He grins, holding up one finger.

He catches up to me as I'm walking up the incline to our bloc and follows me in through the front door. I take hold of his hand, pulling him into my room.

"Well? What did Prez say? Saw you havin' words."

"Just shootin' the shit. Gave us the seal of approval as brothers. Told me we fit in."

"Good. 'Cause I'm not plannin' on leavin' anytime soon."

"Nor me."

The light from the bulb overhead shines on Scott's face, putting his features into relief. *This man is so beautiful.* Suddenly, I don't want to talk. I want to touch him, hold him. Make love to him. *My man.*

"Josh?" Scott looks confused at my short answer.

I step close, crowding him. Placing my hand to his chest I push him backward. The back of his legs meets the bed, and still I apply pressure. A smirk comes to his lips as he allows me to push him down.

It doesn't matter how often I have this man in my mouth, my ass, my hands. Every time is as good as the first. As I undo his zipper, my hands no longer shake, or if they do, it's with anticipation, no longer from nerves. He tries to pull me up, to give me pleasure at the same time. But tonight's for him.

Kneeling on the hard floor, I reverently extract his cock, relishing the feeling of it growing in my hands, watching it lengthen, seeing the pearl of white glistening at the tip. My tongue flicks out to taste him, and I groan as I inhale his musk, knowing I'll never grow bored of him or this feeling.

He growls at my teasing, collapsing back on the bed, giving himself over to the ecstasy he knows I'll bring him. It's only then I take him in my mouth, my tongue tracing those pulsing veins, my hands clasping his balls, fingers knowing exactly where to touch and what pressure to apply.

I take him in as far as I can, swallowing around him. Moving my head up and down, my lips, tongue and throat muscles quickly work to bring him to the point where he swells, almost choking me as he comes down my throat with a roar.

I lick him clean, then wipe my mouth on the back of my hand.

I feel his hand on my head, gently stroking. "What did I do to deserve that?"

"You're just you, Scott. That's more than enough."

His fingers toy with my hair. "Your fool," he says with a smile in his voice.

Later, after he's reciprocated, we lie together on the bed. Tonight my arm is around him.

CHAPTER 34

For appearance's sake, we usually stagger our entrance to the clubhouse in the mornings, but today we're walking down together. When we're almost there, Lady puts his hand on my arm stopping me, before removing it sharply.

"Don't like that." Lady points to what has caught his eye, the smoke rising in the distance. As I watch in the direction of his outstretched finger, it's possible to even make out flames.

I'm not keen on the look of it myself. "Think there's any risk to the club?" I know fuck all about wildfires. Never been this close to one before.

Apparently, neither does he. "No idea, Brother. Fuckin' hope not."

"Peg's new ol' lady's a firefighter. Hopefully she'll warn us if we're in any danger. Heard that's how the Devils got hold of this compound. Original place was burned out."

He doesn't need to tell me, I'm fully aware of that. The thought makes me shift my eyes warily toward the burning mountain again.

Prez isn't ignoring the fact either. An emergency church is immediately called. Lady and I find ourselves around the table discussing how to fireproof the compound. Brothers have been called back from all other jobs, any construction work is halted as we work our damn asses off to protect the club. Then both Lady and I are assigned to clear a firebreak outside the back of the compound along with Peg, Marvel, Slick, and Dollar. Peg at times seems distracted, looking at the fire burning in the mountains above.

"His ol' lady might be up there." Lady nudges me.

Realising he's probably right, I decide to cut the sergeant-at-arms some slack. If that was Lady up there firefighting, I'd be out of my mind with worry.

It's fucking hot. The wind blowing heat from the fire adds to the hot rays of the sun. As pieces of ash fall around us, we don't need Peg's terse instruction to double our efforts. My tee comes off, now used for wiping away my sweat. When Lady takes his shirt off, I'm side-tracked, but only for a second, when my eyes catch sight of his glistening torso. Reluctantly I drag my gaze away, going back to clearing scrub again.

As the hours pass, the fire seems to have us in its sights, approaching mercilessly. I know the situation is growing serious when Drummer tells us to get all the valuables stored in safety in what's normally our armoury, under the old swimming pool. *Fuck, I hope it changes direction.* Would be a fucking shame if fire took the compound for a second time. I put my few things I wouldn't want destroyed, documents and shit, in the safe place, then resume toiling at the front line again. The air's thick with smoke. When Lady hands me an extra bandana he'd picked up when sorting his stuff, I tie it around my nose and mouth with relief.

To many of us, the fact that we have a neighbour takes us by surprise. Her name's never been mentioned as long as I've been in Tucson. Viper's worried when they can't raise her on the phone, so he and Peg decide to be neighbourly, going to check up on the elderly woman they call Ma Jones.

Despite the efforts of the firefighters doing what they can, by the time the pair get back, bringing the old lady with them, along with her great-granddaughter, the fire's taken on a life of its own. Now it's not only heading straight for us, but flames have looped around the compound, cutting us off from the road. It's become not only a fight for our possessions, but a fight for the club, the people within it. The evacuation had been left too late. Women and children are unable to leave the compound.

"Look at that." Lady points to the edge of our firebreak. For a moment I just stand watching as firefighters seem to be setting their fire line up right behind the compound. *Fuck. That fire's coming close. Too close? Will it reach us?*

I raise my chin toward Lady. No need to say anything. Just need to keep working.

Time zooms past as if in a blur. The firefighters want us out of the way, so we retreat inside the gates. A burning piece of tree, blown by the strong winds, lands on Drummer and Sam's veranda, all hands rush to put that out. Then we're tackling any small fires started by windblown burning ash that lands our side of the fence. I'm only vaguely aware that in the midst of fighting this relentless enemy, Heart and Marcia's babies are born. Thank fuck mother and children—Jacob and Isabel—seem to have come through safely. *Now to keep that fire back.* I rake, stamp, kick over without pause. Seeing shit for myself and putting it out, running to help others when I've missed something. I'm working on automatic pilot, not even thinking of the heat, the smoke or the encroaching flames, just doing what I can mechanically.

Suddenly there's a tap on my shoulder. "What? Where?" I swing around, but can't see anything burning.

"Wind's dropping," Lady yells over the roar of the fire. I look up. The first thing I realise is he hadn't needed to shout. I can hear him clearly for the first time in hours. Without the gale behind it, the fire is being tamed. Now I stop, I realise the air is easier to breathe, ash is no longer falling from the sky. Any flames still flaring seem in the distance now.

"Have we beaten it?" I ask in wonder.

"They have." He points to the firefighters, some of whom are already standing down and returning to their fire trucks.

Then there's the thwacking sound announcing a helicopter, the winds have dropped sufficiently to allow it to land. I watch, a lump in my throat, seeing Marcia and her twins being transported to get proper medical care. *Thank fuck for that. Heart and Marcia have been through too much to lose those kids.*

The helicopter's only just disappeared into the lingering smoke when Prez appears, waving us and the other brothers toward him. "You can stand down now. Fire Chief is sending some of his men home, only a skeleton crew will remain to keep an eye on things. We've done it, Brothers." He pauses, wiping his hand across his face. I doubt he cares he's only served to worsen the streaks of soot that cover it. "The compound's lived to see another day."

We cheer, but half-heartedly. Now the adrenalin has faded, most of us are too tired to even pump our fists in the air.

"You want any of us to stay up here to keep an eye on things, Prez?"

"You volunteering, Lady?"

If he is, I won't be leaving him alone. "If you need us, count me in too, Prez."

Drummer looks around, his eyes lingering on where small fires which had been burning all now seem to be put out. "Think it should be alright now, but I was going to ask someone to stay to keep an eye out for flare ups. If there's any trouble, give us a shout and brothers will be right back."

Then, having given us another one of those curious looks, which gives me a feeling as though someone's walking over my grave, Prez slaps us on the back as he passes on his way back down to the clubhouse. "Thanks, Brothers."

In the end there isn't much to do. A sudden gust of wind fans a small fire into life just inside the gates, but our boots and stamping feet are enough to smother it. Lady rakes some dry grass away, then uses a hose to damp it all down. When that's out, we perch on a log, and see the night through by watching the remaining flames gradually die away in the forest behind us. Lady dozes while I keep watch, then we swap.

Stumbling into church the next morning, I raise my chin when the first thing Prez does is thank us for watching out. Stifling a yawn, I reply, "No problem, Prez."

Then Drummer's attention snaps to Peg when he asks if the fire is out. As sergeant-at-arms he should be on top of that shit. Now it dawns on me he hadn't come up to check during the night. Strange for the man for whom the protection of the club is paramount. Narrowing my eyes I take in the state of him. Fuck knows what happened, but Peg must have really laid one on last night. I wonder why. *Has anything happened to his old lady?*

Once Peg's belatedly reassured the club's now out of danger, brothers continue giving updates. But one thing's not mentioned. They probably already know, but Lady and I have been left out of the loop. I ask, "Anyone heard from Heart?"

"Yeah, he got to the hospital no problem," Rock informs us. "Babies and Marcia all doing good."

That's good fucking news at least.

It's so hard to keep my eyes open, I didn't get more than an hour's rest last night, and only that lying up against an uncomfortable log. After the busy day prior, I'm about to drop. I perk up when I hear them discussing the old lady, Ma, whose house, it seems, has been totally destroyed.

Apparently she's already causing havoc, telling brothers off right left and centre. Their stories make me laugh. But I'm happy to give my vote, agreeing to let both her and her great granddaughter stay on the compound until their accommodation is sorted.

Then, at last, Lady and I are free to go to our beds to get that much needed sleep. It's all we can do, lying, or rather collapsing down, fully clothed on the bed in Scott's room.

It's late afternoon when we venture out, amused to find that although the woman's indeed got a sharp tongue, there are benefits to letting Ma stay on the compound. Seeming like she's enjoying herself for the first time in years, she cooks great fucking food, and plenty of it. I'd go so far as to say her recipes rival Scott's mom's. I take a plateful, then go back for seconds. Lady does the same, his eyebrow quirking at me.

We've fought fire and beaten it. Surely we deserve some peace and quiet now? But that's not what life is like in Tucson. Peg's old lady has been attacked and left for dead on one of our construction sites. Viper and Bullet having pulled the workers off to repair the tarmac on the approach to the compound, meant she wasn't found until it was almost too late. Peg's beside himself with worry, but fuck knows what's going on there. I get the feeling she's blowing hot and cold on him, but he doesn't let on. One thing he's determined to do is to find and take out the fucker who hurt her.

A routine Friday church. As Lady and I walk in, I notice we're late, everyone else already in their seats. I suppress my grin knowing it was my fault we were delayed, well, I had to have my man's mouth before we left the suite.

But as I take my seat I notice Blade narrowing his eyes at us, and Peg and Drum exchanging a look. I push thoughts of what delayed us out of my head, hoping my recent release doesn't show on my face, instead making a show of giving my attention to the meeting.

Mouse has an update that brightens Peg up. Seems the computer guru has found out who gave Peg's old lady's assailant an alibi, now they're making arrangements to go pay this Cherry

Orchard a visit. Won't involve us, though I'm ready to volunteer my services if they need me.

Okay, so the meeting is about to wrap up. I'm thinking of returning the favour Scott paid me. Feet are shuffling, people getting ready to leave the table, when Prez gets our attention again. He's leaning back in his chair, his arms casually folded across his chest.

Doesn't seem like anything important.

"Before we get partying," Prez starts, "Just want to remind everyone that old ladies need to be voted into the club. Ain't much of a stretch to say that goes for any partner."

Okay. I look around, unaware that anyone else here has a woman they're serious about. *Is he talking about Peg? What have I missed?* Like me, everyone seems mystified.

That's when I notice Prez is looking straight at me. The enforcer's knife that he's always twirling suddenly spins faster on the table. Blade stops it when it's pointing directly between Lady and myself. *Fuck.* I feel as though a cold hand has gripped my heart and stopped it beating.

They can't know. We've been careful, haven't we? My thoughts make me shift uneasily in my chair. I try to return Drummer's stare, but I can't. I look away quickly, pretending to be as confused as everyone else. Out of the corner of my eye I see Lady intent on inspecting his hands which are resting on the table.

Prez gives it a moment, then his steely gaze becomes more menacing. When he speaks there's no doubt the question's targeted at myself and Lady. "Got something to say, Brothers?"

Now everyone's looking at us. There's no mistaking or pretending we're not the subjects they're interested in.

Oh, fuck. As I return hard stares from around the table, it's clear we haven't been as discreet as we had thought. Chills ripple through me. In little ways, everyone is giving themselves away. Slick looks awkward as though he wishes he wasn't here. Wraith's looking resigned. Beef, Rock and Marvel have sly grins on their faces, Jekyll, Hyde and Road just look puzzled. Dollar's nodding his head, and Blade and Bullet are giving us probing stares. Viper, Shooter, and Mouse are the only ones looking like they haven't a clue what's going on or couldn't care less if they have.

I look at Lady, he meets my eyes, his expression is guarded, then he shrugs. Probably only I can see his slight nod of encouragement. Taking a deep breath, prepared to leap into the unknown, knowing it's time, that now we have to man up and face the consequences, I put my hands on the table, palms facing upwards and open, take in a breath and seal our fates. "Lady and I are together."

"And?"

Marvel punches Shooter on the arm then says adding emphasis, "They're *together.*"

Shooter's mouth opens into an O.

Drummer bangs the gavel. His face is impassive as he says, "Joker, Lady. Thank you for being straight with us."

Peg bursts out laughing at his choice of words, a real belly laugh at our expense. His head falls onto the table. The others are outright chortling or have their hands to their mouths.

Drum snarls, "I'll fuckin' rephrase that. Thank you for being upfront. Now could you fuckin' leave us for a moment as we've got things to discuss."

Lady looks like he wants to say something as he opens his mouth, then shuts it. There's nothing we can say. Our dirty secret is now out in the open. Taking his arm I give him a supportive nod. *We're in this together, Brother. I've got your back.* In silence, we exit through the door.

Scott goes straight to the bar. No one's behind it. Athletically he leaps over the top, takes a bottle of whisky and pours two shots, pushing one toward me. His eyes meet mine. "Shit's out in the open now, Josh."

"How the fuck did they guess?" I snarl. "We've been so fuckin' careful. Who gave us away? Did anyone see us? Did they go running straight to the prez?"

"Hard to tell," Scott's face is tight. "But it's done now, Josh. Whatever happens, there's no more hidin'."

When I thought about this day, while hoping it would never come, I hadn't thought how I'd take it. Now it's here, and so unexpected, I feel completely numb.

"They already suspected," he continues. "You could tell. Most of them weren't surprised."

"No one said anything before."

"Don't ask, don't tell," he shrugs. "Maybe it would have been better to have stayed that way."

"And now they've got to deal with it. Deal with us. What the fuck are they going to do, Scott?" Visions go through my head. Will they let us pack our bags or just send us out with the clothes we're wearing? Will they burn the tat off my back? *Will they hurt Scott?*

Scott pours another couple of shots, I down the second automatically. "Whatever happens," he reaches over the bar, taking my hand, "we'll be together. Don't worry, Josh. We'll sort it out."

The hand he's holding is shaking as the ramifications hit. "We might not be Devils any longer." Fuck me, that thought hurts. When I'd woken this morning, I never thought this would happen today. "Right now, Scott. They might be discussing takin' our patches."

Scott jumps back over the bar, bringing the bottle with him. Glancing around I check no one else is here, then realising it doesn't matter now anyway, I put my head against his chest, feeling his strong arms close around me.

"Together, babe," he murmurs reassuringly. "Always together. You and me, against the world. Whatever happens, whatever they decide. You got me, I got you. Together. Ain't gonna hide any longer. You and your fool, Josh."

"Me and my fool," I say back, automatically. But first it will be him and me against the club. "How long they going to take, Scott?" I can hardly bear it. We've lied to our brothers for two fucking years. How are they going to take it?

I stand, his arms around me, my legs are quivering, in truth I need him to keep me upright. I feel like sinking to my knees and howling. *Everything has been lost.* It's quiet in the club-house. The door to church opening sounds like a clap of thunder to my ears. I pull away from Scott, and we both turn together.

"You can come back in."

I try to read Shooter's face, but can't get a damn hint of the result of any discussion they've just held behind closed doors. Lady pulls back his shoulders, I make a concerted effort to straighten my back as together we step back into church for what might be the last time.

There's laughter and joking, but as we walk in Prez waves for everyone to be quiet and they quickly settle down. I try to read the mood, but it's impossible. Lady and I stand, unsure if we'll ever be allowed to sit around the table again. But Drummer points us to our seats.

When we're sitting, me with relief as my legs feel weak as a newborn kitten's, I wait for the expression of disgust to come. Wait for the pronouncement we're no longer members. Wait to hear what punishment will be handed down.

Prez, his face set, his steely gaze fixed on us, commences, "You've probably had thoughts on why I sent you out of the room, but what you're thinking is wrong. You're members of the

Satan's Devils Tucson Chapter. Whatever your personal inclinations are, they have fuck all to do with that."

What? We're still members? Suddenly the air seems easier to breathe. My heart starts beating again, hammering in my chest. *Thank fuck!* I swipe at my eyes feeling moisture starting to pool there. One look at Lady shows he's as relieved as me.

"Now," Prez only gives us a moment with hardly enough time to come to terms with his pronouncement before he continues, his tone deadly serious. "We always vote in ol' ladies. What we need to know is which of you will be wearing a property patch."

Air's sucked into lungs all around the room. Lady's face goes completely white. Blade obviously can't hold it together, his head collapses to the table, his body shaking with laughter. Shooter's wiping tears from his eyes.

I feel my lips twitch. The laughter, the teasing mockery. In that moment I know they really don't give a damn. *This is family. These are my brothers. They might be having a joke at our expense, but there's no malice in it. That's what family does, isn't it?*

Rock's pointing at Lady. "I guess that look on your face shows you're the bottom in this relationship."

Oh, these straights don't understand a thing. This time I glance toward Lady, he's also got over the shock, now he's starting to grin.

Beef screeches through his belly laughs. "Bottom! Did you need to say that?"

"I guess you're the taker not the giver." Slick's trying to hold back his mirth but failing.

I frown, another glance at Lady, he raises his chin. His eyes are twinkling. The table's gone quiet as if worrying they've pushed us too far. *I'm going to enjoy this.* I let the silence string out before explaining. "You're all wrong," I tell them. "We take it in turns."

"Oh fuck, man. We didn't need to be given that visual." Marvel's shaking his head. I give a wicked grin and wink to Lady. *They mess with us; we'll mess right back.*

Mouse is looking confused. "Thought your full handle was Lady's Man." It's a statement posed as a question.

Lady shrugs, and gives his own explanation. "I'm bi. Or at least I was, before I met Joker." And fuck me if he doesn't take my hand and squeeze it, right there at the table.

If I didn't think it was pushing it too far, I'd kiss him. I leave my hand in his, unable to stop smiling, feeling lighter like a massive weight's been lifted from me. The last of my worries disappear when Marvel slaps Lady on the back, then Shooter does the same to me.

Turns out our sexual preference doesn't matter one fuck to these men seated around this table. Proving they're my true family, unlike the one I was born into. All my worries were for nothing. I'm grinning like a fucking loon. I just can't stop.

Drummer bangs the gavel. "Guess this calls for a party."

Lady's sharp intake of air from beside me, and the pleased look on his face, shows he too is realising that far from being disappointed, annoyed or even angry, like us, everyone is pleased to clear the air. A party. For us. Lady whispers into my ear, "A coming out party."

He's right. I sit, stunned, as the rest of the brothers get up and leave. Lady stays beside me. His face is working as if he's thinking something through. Just when Peg's walking past, Lady hisses to me, "I'm not fuckin' wearin' a property patch."

This time I'm the one laughing.

The room's empty now, except for us.

"I've no words," I tell him quietly. "No words."

His arm comes around me, pulling me close. "Me neither, babe. But I tell you this. If anyone's wearing a property patch, it's going to be you."

"No patches," I shake my head, not rising to the bait. "But a ring's not out of the question."

Chapter 35

It's like I'm living in a dream world after our outing at church. No one looks at us any differently when Lady slings his arm around my shoulder, or we join hands. Respectful of our brothers, we're not over-demonstrative in public, but enjoy the relief and freedom from the constant stress of having to hide what we mean to each other. At first, I was hesitant at any outward expression of our relationship, but gradually, over the next week, since we're treated with no awkwardness, I start to relax.

Another Friday's come around, and we're waiting for church. "You're smiling," Lady points out.

"Am I?"

"Yeah, babe. You are." He puts a beer in front of me then takes a seat next to me on the couch.

"So?"

He gives me a considering look before he replies. "Just realised I've never seen you truly happy before."

My lips press together as I give careful thought to his words. "You've always made me happy, Scott."

"Nah. I always reminded you of someone you'd rather not be."

That's not true. Thanks to him, his family and my brother too, I'd accepted myself months ago. "I have been happy," I tell him. "It's just feeling I had to keep what we mean to each other under wraps that ate away at me. Now I feel like I've got the fuckin' world handed to me on a platter."

"You deserve it."

"I'm sorry." I look into his eyes.

"What the fuck for?"

"You were right all along. That they wouldn't have minded. Wasted a couple of years trying to pretend this wasn't happening." I bite my lip as I consider the time we've let go by, and all the unnecessary worry.

"Nah, babe. You weren't wrong. We needed to find a place here, gain the trust of the brothers. If we'd come clean when we'd arrived they would have seen us as two gays looking for a home." He sighs, "What we did was let them see the men underneath. That we were brothers they could trust. Then when it all came out they couldn't give a damn. Because we'd already proved ourselves." He glances around, Rock and Beef are playing pool, Drummer's deep in discussion with Sam. "You said it yourself. Being gay is just what we happen to be, doesn't take anything else away. Isn't the be all and end all of everything."

Breaking off, he points to Blade just walking in. "Blade's the enforcer. Fuck, I couldn't do his job. Does it make me look at him differently? Nah, he's just able to do shit I wouldn't want to touch. It's who he is, but not *what* he is. Man's a good fucker to have at your back."

I grin. "What about Mouse?"

"Now he's just a fuckin' weirdo."

I can't hold back my laugh.

Drummer's started to make his way into the meeting room. Lady and I stand up to follow him.

As bikers we don't do things the same as in the civilian world, seeking our own forms of retribution. If someone harms us, we hurt them right back.

I know Peg was worried how Darcy, his old lady, would feel after she killed the man who raped her, but firefighters don't seem much different to bikers when it comes down to it. Far from setting her back, it seemed to bring her closure. And tomorrow the sergeant-at-arms and the firefighter who gives him a run for his money are tying the knot. Church tonight will probably be quick. It's Peg's stag party later.

As brothers walk in, Blade's knife spins, stopping when it points toward us. "I suppose you fuckers will be next."

"What?" Lady's arm, which had been around my shoulder, drops and he looks confused.

"Getting hitched."

As he cocks an eyebrow my way, everyone cracks up. *Hmm.* They think Blade made a good joke. Perhaps we'll end up having the last laugh.

I've developed a soft spot for the sergeant-at-arms. I'm sure it was him who forced the issue that made us bring everything out in the open. There's nothing that makes me see him as a snitch, so grateful he brought us out of hiding. As such, I'm gutted for him when during church, Mouse breaks the news there's been an explosion and Peg's fiancée's crew were caught up in it. I feel even worse when he ends up spending the night before his wedding at the hospital worried sick about his soon-to-be wife. But luckily Darcy's not badly injured and even makes the wedding on time. Yeah, what they'd hoped to be a quiet wedding with just the two of them ended up with City Hall filled with his brothers and her firefighting crew. Well, he should have expected it.

As I stand up watching them make their commitment to each other, my eyes glisten with emotion and I turn to look at Scott. "Us next?" he mouths.

"Why not?" I whisper back. There's nothing I'd like more than to shout our commitment to the whole world.

I suppose it's natural that such an emotional occasion makes anyone in love want to cement their relationship. After joining in the reception that Ma and the old ladies had planned for a respectable time, Scott and I sneak out from Peg's celebrations as soon as we can, seeking the privacy of our suite.

Beef smirks as we pass him, miming thrusting his hips, but I show him my middle finger and ignore him.

Taking my hand in his, Scott pulls me up the incline to our suites. Slamming the door shut behind us, Scott's mouth crashes down on mine. His hands trace my body, landing on my ass, pulling my hardness against his. As our tongues mate, we both start to writhe.

Our coupling is frenzied. Even though I thought it couldn't get better, our familiarity with one another, the emotional charge of the day, means when I come I see stars. From Scott's shouted completion, I wouldn't be surprised if he had too.

When we've recovered our senses, I realise it's time. His eyes narrow as I pull him off the bed and make him stand in the middle of the room. My mouth suddenly feels dry. Despite the vague promises that we've made to each other, my legs shake as I drop to my knees and take hold of his hand. I swallow a couple of times, trying to get enough moisture to get out the words. "Ain't got no ring, Scott, but… will you marry me?"

Instead of giving me a verbal reply, he drops down beside me, raises my hand to his lips, and briefly places them on it. Looking straight into my eyes, he replies, "Will you marry *me*?"

A moment passes, then together a yelled, "Yes."

No more words are necessary. A quick glance down shows both our cocks are hard again.

Later, sated and satisfied, while Scott's holding me, he huffs a laugh. "This is going to make my mom so fuckin' happy."

I grin broadly, thinking of Rachel's reaction. "Women love an excuse to buy a new dress."

"She'll want the full ceremony," he groans.

"Just want something quiet, myself. Just the brothers and your family."

"Your brother?"

My laugh is strangled. "Not if the reception's here on the compound."

"We could always elope. Go to Vegas."

It's an idea, I suppose.

Fuck. Me getting hitched. Who would ever have thought it? And instead of keeping it quiet, I want the Satan's Devils to witness it. How my life has changed in the course of a few short months. As my eyes close and I fall asleep, snuggled up to the man who's just made a commitment to me, I realise how much I've grown into the body and mentality I was born with. And that I haven't had a panic attack in months.

The next morning I awake early, already feeling like I'm on cloud number nine, but it's impossible to wake Scott. When I shook him he mumbled a complaint, rolled over, going straight back to sleep. *Must have worn him out good and proper last night.*

The thought still has me grinning as I walk into the club-house to find Fergus is clearing up from the wedding party. Being in such a good mood, I call out a cheery good morning.

"Hey, Fergus. What gives?" He'd acknowledged my greeting with a jerk of his head, but not in his normal *I'll do anything to get my patch* manner.

He doesn't respond to my query either. Intuitively seeing something must be wrong, I approach him. "Hey, talkin' to you, man."

"I'm alright."

But now I'm looking straight at him, I'm sure that's a lie. His eyes are rimmed red, and look dull. "Anyone upset you?" I ask through gritted teeth. Fergus is made of stern stuff; it would take a lot to get him off balance. I wouldn't be surprised if he got his patch before long, he's certainly proved himself.

When he shakes his head, I take the garbage sack from his hand putting it aside. "There's something botherin' you, man. Come sit down and let me help." Kicking out a chair I forcibly push him down on it. "Now spill."

He looks up, swallows, then starts to speak. "I'm this close to gettin' my patch." He's holding his forefinger and thumb fractionally apart.

"That you are," I agree.

He gulps, swallows, wipes a hand across his eyes, before saying, "I've going to have to leave the club."

Reeling back, my eyes widen. "What the fuck?"

"My mom." There's more, so I don't fill the silence with questions. "She's all I've got. And I'm all she's got. She's been diagnosed with cancer. She's terminal, Joker."

Oh, fuck. "Fergus…"

"No, don't say you're sorry. I'm going to have enough of that. I'm fuckin' sorry enough as it is. But that doesn't help. She spoke to me last night."

Fuck, while the brothers were partying and Scott and I were proposing, he was dealing with this shit.

"She's known for a couple of days, didn't know how to tell me. But she's going to need help, Joker. There's no one else but me, so…" He waves his hands despondently. "Losin' her is going to be bad enough. But losin' the club too?"

"It might not come to that." I can't make him any promises. "You need to talk to Drummer. How, how long's she got?"

"Hopefully months, but no more than a year."

I'm optimistic Drummer will let him come back. He'll need us. He's losing the only parent, *the only family* he apparently has. "Talk to Drummer, today," I insist. "Then get yourself home to your mom."

"Don't want to leave you short…"

"That's not your priority. We've got Truck, and Matt will be joining us soon." Darcy's firefighter colleague had joined as a prospect a few weeks back.

At that moment Drummer walks in. Not giving Fergus a chance to back out, I call out, "Hey, Prez. Have you got a moment?"

He swings around. "Yeah, Joker. What's up?"

I fix my eyes on the prospect. "Fergus here needs to speak with you." Then I turn my gaze on the Prez.

He narrows his eyes, then gives a sharp nod. "Okay, Prospect. My office. Now."

I knew Drummer would sort it out. Fergus leaves that same day, Prez updates us on their chat. Seems he's agreed to leave the position open for him. When, or if, he decides to come back, we'll discuss whether he'll have to start all over again, or pick up where he left off.

Rather than anyone being upset he was leaving, there are offers of help. Even the idea of a fundraiser if money was needed to make his mother more comfortable. Mentally I think we'd already promoted him to brother.

As if the universe wants to keep life in balance, after Peg's wedding yesterday, him finding out his old lady's pregnant and will be giving him the family he always longed for, and my own slice of heaven when Scott agreed to marry me, things take a downturn the next day. First Fergus's news, followed by the death of Ma. That she went peacefully in her sleep was a blessing, but we'll all miss her around the club. Her acerbic tongue a source of amusement, her sharp words usually belied by a twinkle in her eye. That she returned our fondness for her became apparent when the club found we'd been named in her will. I cross my fingers hoping there won't be a third thing to go wrong. Luckily, there's not.

Having decided Scott's mom should be the first person to hear the news that we've decided to get married, we keep our secret to ourselves until we can find time to go visit her. With one thing and another we are kept busy around the club, for a while we can't find the time to take a couple of days off to go to Flagstaff. As Lady says, brothers are still getting used to the idea of us being a couple, it's probably best not to spring the news that we intend taking the ultimate step right away.

There is one thing we want to address. I raise it at the next church.

"Er, Prez. Any objections to Lady and I changing our accommodation around a bit? Like to convert our suite in the same way the sergeant-at-arms has. Turn one of the rooms into a living room."

"Makes sense if you're only using the one bedroom," Wraith observes. "I haven't a problem with it."

Prez gives us a considering look. "Don't want to make changes on a whim. This thing is serious between you two? Not going to change your minds or want your own space?"

Lady sits up straighter. "Might not have come out and put it on the table using the right words, but I've claimed Joker, and he's claimed me. It's as permanent as you can get." My hands are clasped together on the table. He covers them with one of his. I give him an appreciative smile.

Viper sighs. "Suppose you want my boys converting a bathroom to a kitchen."

"We've still got the plans from when we did Peg's," Bullet reminds him. "As long as they don't want anything much different."

"Whatever is fine with us." I know I speak for us both. We might be gay, but we're both men. Won't be spending much time in the kitchen. Especially as Ma, God rest her soul, left the women her recipe book.

"I don't see how anyone can object," Prez starts. "Don't see why we need to vote on it. So I'll just say go ahead." Marvel's looking at us with narrowed eyes, Prez notices. "You got something you want to say?"

Marvel shakes his head. "Still wondering which one we call the ol' lady."

I roll my eyes. "Neither," I reply. Seems while they don't seem bothered by it, brothers still are having difficulty sorting our relationship out in their heads.

Lady raises his head from his hands. "See, you're trying to put us in straight boxes where we don't fit. Neither of us is dominant, neither submits. We're just two guys getting along."

Blade sits back, crossing his arms over his chest. "Doesn't one of you take the feminine role?"

I bark a laugh. "You've seen Lady in the ring. And I know there's a few of you won't take him on…"

"I do," contradicts Rock.

"And me." Beef and Rock reach across the table and give themselves high fives.

I glare at them. "If anyone wants to check how feminine I am, I'm ready and waiting."

Blade's head's cocked to one side as though he's thinking.

Prez looks impatient. He picks up the gavel and bangs it. "If no one else has got anything else to say other than dissecting our brothers' love lives, I suggest we bring this meetin' to a fuckin' close."

"Who wears the trousers in your house, Prez?"

Oh fuck me. Beef did not just go there, did he? When he winks at me, I know he's done it on purpose. Relationships are private. Whoever they're between.

"Knowing my daughter it's probably her."

At Viper's comment, the table erupts in laughter, while our prez turns a lovely shade of red.

Then everyone's moving, standing and exiting the room as though they've suddenly remembered there's somewhere else they urgently need to be.

<h1 align="center">CHAPTER 36</h1>

Walking into the suite I see Scott looking at his phone, his mouth pursed, his eyebrows drawn down.

"What's up?" Going over to where he's sitting, I bend, placing my hand under his chin, and turning his face to mine. A gentle kiss of greeting. My actions briefly transform his face into a smile, then he's frowning again.

"Just a text from Sarge."

I plop myself down on the bed, leaning back against the pillows. "Everything alright in Vegas?"

"I'm not sure," he replies, throwing a quick glance in my direction. "Remember the restaurant that set up shortly before we left? Got burned down last night."

Now it's my turn to crease my eyes. "Anyone hurt?" I remember the nice woman who'd owned it, and the food she used to serve. What was her name now? Emily, Elaine… Erika. That was it.

"The waitress, Regan. She was locking up, got caught in an explosion. She's got quite bad burns apparently."

"Fuck." I remember her too. "Deliberate?"

"First reports are a gas explosion, but Erika was pretty hot on all the safety and fire stuff. Our lot suspect the gang."

"Damn. Sarge say they want help?"

"Nah. Red's handling it. Looks like it was a message to leave that fuckin' gang alone."

His words make me remember my time in a different club, and the brothers I used to hang with there. "I wonder," I think aloud, "What would have happened if I'd been brave enough to come out back then? Would we have wasted these last two years?"

Scott swings around. "Two years haven't been wasted, and who the fuck knows or cares? You weren't in a good place at that time. You needed your therapy sessions to get yourself on track." He pauses, looking down. "Nothing against the brothers in Vegas, not that I knew them as well as you did, but fuckin' love my brothers here. Love Arizona too."

His views are the same as mine. I've never regretted changing chapters. "How's Red going to deal with it?" I go back to the original topic.

Scott taps his phone. "He's looking into employing security guards rather than using the brothers. Money from the businesses will need to go up, but they'll probably be willin' to pay. After last night."

"Makes sense."

Barking a laugh, Scott brings his eyes back to me. "Just as life here is quietin' down, it's heatin' up in Vegas, typical, eh?"

"I'm all for a quiet life," I tell him. "Booze, ridin' and sex. That's all I want."

"Sex?" His eyes light up.

"Yeah, give me some loving, babe."

I don't need to tell him twice.

But quiet and the Satan's Devils Tucson Chapter seems to be a contradiction in terms. We have perhaps a couple of months after the wildfire when nothing distracts us from the good things in life, before shit hits the fan once again.

None of us expect it when we walk into church that Friday night on a wet autumn evening. Recently Drummer seems to have mellowed a bit, so it takes us by shock when he snarls for quiet as he bangs the gavel to start the meeting.

Turns out we'll be butting heads with the Herreras again. They're pitting us against a new club setting up in Tucson.

Gun running. Yeah, I was involved in it for a stint until Vegas, like the Tucson chapter, got out of the trade. It's risky. Too damn dangerous now I've got something to lose, Scott. One look at his face shows me he's on the same wavelength.

Prez's next words have me back paying attention. "If the Chaos Riders carry guns for the Herreras, part of their payment is they'd get help takin' us out. Seems they've got their eye on this compound."

I'm on my feet, leaning over, slamming my fists on the table, same as everyone else. We're all shouting. "Fuck that," comes out of my mouth. *Take this compound? Never!*

Peg's equally incensed. "Then we wipe them out. Before they get their fuckin' feet under the table in Tucson."

Too fucking right we will. Protecting our property trumps my wishes for a peaceful existence.

Suggestions, ideas, calls to arms are thrown around the table. I've been a biker long enough to know how things work. Clubs don't just come in and set up in another club's territory. Not without getting permission from the dominant club, and in Arizona, as in most of the south-western states as well as others, that club is the Wretched Soulz. If they've not asked permission from them, nor satisfied them they're doing it all right, it might not need to be us who slaughters them.

"What does the dominant think?" I ask.

Drummer shakes his head. "Had a word with the Wretched Soulz' local chapter prez, just to see if they'd had warning of a new MC. They have. The Chaos Riders did it all polite. Got their permission to set up in Tucson. How we settle any difference that might arise between us, they're leavin' to us. Won't be gettin' any support in that direction. Unless it starts reflectin' on them. Then they'll decide who they wish to fuckin' side with."

I glance at Lady, we both shake our heads. *No help from that direction.* Sounds like we're going to war.

Turns out we've got a month to prepare. A month while the Chaos Riders get settled in Tucson.

"I need a fuckin' beer," Lady tells me as we walk out of church. I jerk my chin and follow him. "Didn't fuckin' expect that."

"Me neither," I reply, with a shake of my head as we step up to the bar and put in our request.

Jill, tonight reluctantly on bartending duty, hands us two beers. Almost dropping the bottles in front of us as if they're dirty to touch. Catching her eye, Lady holds it, then reaching his arm around me, places a kiss to my forehead. Her look of blatant disgust is almost palpable. *Yeah, most here don't turn an eye now our relationship is out in the open. She's the exception.*

"You ever tap that?" I ask.

"Nah. Not that one. Nasty mouth on her, didn't want my dick anywhere near it."

He's got that right.

Picking up my bottle, glad I watched her open it to make sure she didn't spit in it, I shudder as I return to what we'd been discussing. "Don't like this threat to the club."

"Me either. Guess we put the wedding plans on hold until it's all over."

Until we know there'll still be two participants at the wedding. I put my hand on his. "Whatever happens, promise me you'll take care, Lady. Don't take any chances you don't need to."

"Back at you, babe. We've got too much to live for."

It's going to come to a fight, I know it. There's not a man here prepared to walk off the compound and give it up to a bunch of motherfuckers who've got their eyes on it. But gun running isn't an option either. I start to wonder how things will play out.

When Drummer calls an emergency church a couple of days later, I'm not surprised. Guess we've got a fuck ton of things to discuss. In the meantime, we've all been talking it to death among ourselves. Now it's sunk in, we're slowly drifting into battle mode.

Lady and I arrive early. I follow Heart in, almost being knocked over by his fucking dog, that little pup Grunt who had surprised everyone by growing into an over-large wolfhound cross. Heart throws me an apologetic grin as he turns to send it back to Marcia. Reckon the dog thinks it's a fucking member now and can join us in church. As I take my place, I notice the room's still half empty.

I try to lighten the mood. "Little girl wanted to walk her mutt." The mention of a canine gets Heart's attention. He starts to grin. "Her dad won't let her, as the dog's in heat. Kid keeps on and on and fuckin' on, so he thinks about it. Decides if they pour gas on the dog's ass the scent will be hidden and she won't attract the males. That's what they do, well, it shuts the kid up." I look around, keeping my face straight. Lady's smirking. I can't remember if he's already heard this one. Beef is staring at me. Bullet and Shooter too. I continue. "Half an hour later, kid returns but without the dog. Dad asks where the fuck the pooch is. His kid pipes up, 'Guess she ran out of gas half way round.' Dad's just about to ask again where the fuckin' dog is when the girl continues, 'But it's okay, the neighbour's dog is pushin' her back home'."

As I finish the punchline I hear Rock laugh, Heart and the rest of them groan. Lady's shaking his head at me. I shrug. Can't come up with gems all the time.

The table's filled up since I've been speaking. The only person missing is Mouse, he's off doing cultural things so I've heard. Drummer bangs the gavel, which signals the beginning of one of the most shocking meetings I've ever attended.

Rock's stolen from the club? Lady grips my hand under the table. He mouths, "This is bad, man."

I shake my head in disbelief. *He's taken the money Ma left us in her will? Lost it gambling? The money we were going to use to buy a new business?* Fuck. I can't comprehend what I'm hearing. *Not Rock.*

Beef, the man who Rock's closest to, shares my incredulity. But Rock confirms it. The words condemning him coming out of his own mouth. We all feel betrayed. Viper reacts physically, managing to get a punch in before Drummer orders him back to his seat. *I hope that fucking hurt.*

Prez's beard seems suddenly to have gone greyer. "Can't believe this of you, Rock. But I tell you, it's fuckin' serious." He lets that sink in for a moment, then points toward me. "Joker, escort Rock to the clubroom and get a prospect to stay with him. Rock, you gonna give me your word you'll not be a problem?"

As Rock stands, I get to my feet. This is the last thing I expected to be doing this evening.

"I won't be a problem," Rock says, before following me out of the room.

I'm eager to get back to the meeting. But with Fergus gone, we're down to two prospects, and one of those works his firefighter shifts. Matt's the only one here, he's currently manning the gate. Deciding it's more important to have eyes on Rock rather than standing sentry at a locked entrance, I select my phone from the box where I'd left it, and give him a call.

It's only a couple of minutes before he appears. He's only a prospect, so I don't explain anything.

I point to Rock. "Make sure he stays put. He's not to leave under any circumstances until a member comes to collect him."

Rock sits down, looking at ease and comfortable, though fuck, that must be a front. *How can he think he'll get away with this?* However long he's been in the club, he'll be feeling some punishment. I eye him carefully; he's giving no signs that he'll go back on his promise to the prez.

But before I return to the table, I narrow my eyes at him. Rock nods reassuringly.

Satisfied as best I can be, I return to the meeting.

As could have been expected, there's people talking over each other. The crime admitted by their brother is hard to take in. Looks like Prez had been waiting for me to come back, as it's only when I'm seated that he bangs the gavel. It takes more than a moment before there's quiet again.

"This is shockin' news, Brothers," Drummer starts speaking. "Never had to deal with this shit before. Not from such a long standin' member."

"He's gotten too comfortable. Confident we'll overlook this shit," Blade suggests. He spins his knife, stopping it at Rock's now empty chair.

"Could be, Blade. But we can't brush it aside. It's too fuckin' serious." All eyes look to the prez, who sighs loudly. "I know no one else wants to voice it, but I see no other option than lettin' him know how much we don't like it, then turnin' him out bad."

"You're takin' his patch?" Beef's eyes widen. "Fuck, Prez."

"You think we can do anything else?" Prez snaps. "You think this is easy? Rock was around in my father's day. Got patched in after doing a twelve-month stint for something that another brother had done. He's been a solid member." He pauses, steadily moving his gaze, one by one, to all of us sitting around the table. "Who can honestly say they'll ever trust him again?"

Beef grimaces, but even he can't say that he could.

"Trust, Brothers, is everything. Don't need to remind you, it takes a year or more to earn it. Once lost, it can't be restored. I'll listen to you, but my proposal stands." He nods at Wraith.

"Much as it hurts to say it, out in bad standing is the only option I can see." The VP looks as though he's been struck by lightning. "Just never expected to hear something like this."

Blade takes his turn. "Out bad. Ain't no other option."

Dollar sitting next to him agrees. "Couldn't believe it when I saw the figures. But there's no doubt in my mind. That there's a man I can no longer trust."

Viper shakes his head. "This fuckin' hurts, Brothers. He's lucky we don't despatch him to meet Satan. He's betrayed the club, betrayed us. Betrayed the brotherhood we stand for. Out bad."

"Out bad," Bullet says.

"Oh fuck," Beef wipes his hand over his face. "Man, this is hard to hear. I wouldn't have believed it if I hadn't heard him admit it. Made fools out of all of us, a fool out of me. All the years we've been friends, and I never suspected. You feel betrayed, Viper? Goes tenfold for me. Out bad."

Shooter, Marvel and Paladin just say the two words. Their faces are white, the seriousness of their decision with its outcome for Rock not lost on them. Jekyll, Road and Hyde do likewise.

"So fuckin' sorry. Wish this had never happened. But it has, and we need to deal with it. Out bad."

I nod at Lady as he makes his pronouncement. There's only one way this can go. "Out bad," I say.

"Nothing else we can do," says Slick. "Out bad."

"Why the fuck didn't he come to us, Prez?" Heart sounds distraught. "Why the fuck didn't he ask for help?" But Drummer just stares at him. "Out bad. Can't do anything else."

There's one last vote before the prez makes it final. That man seems deep in thought.

"Peg?" Drummer prompts him.

"Never thought I'd see the day. But the hurt he's done, is doing to the club, can't go unpunished. We're a clean club, earn our money honestly. Now he's taken a chunk of our future away. He's out bad."

Prez nods at the sergeant-at-arms. "Mouse isn't here, but I ran it past him. He's given me his vote should it come to this. Out bad if we're agreed Rock's guilty."

"No doubt about that. Heard it from his own mouth," Wraith states.

Drummer picks up the gavel. "My vote's out bad too. It's unanimous. Heart, record it."

Heart looks like someone's killed his dog as he reluctantly picks up a pen to write down the result of what has probably been one of the hardest decisions ever made by the club. I over-hear someone saying Rock's been a member for sixteen years. *Sixteen fucking years.* If it had been someone with a more recent patch, maybe we could better understand it. What the fuck did he think would happen? We'd give him a pat on the back and say all's forgiven? When he's lost our trust and messed with our livelihoods?

"Joker, bring him back in."

Lost in my thoughts, Prez's words take a moment to process. But not so long that he needs to repeat them. Composing my face, with a heavy heart, I leave the room.

The clubroom is empty.

What. The. Fuck? No, not empty. Just one man missing. A groan alerts me to Matt who's sitting on the floor, looking dazed and rubbing his neck.

"Prospect!" I snap, going over to him. "Where's Rock?"

"Rock?" Matt says, his eyes unfocused.

"Yeah. Rock. The man you were supposed to prevent from leaving." But the answer's staring me in the face. Instead of staying to take his punishment like a man, he's fucking run away.

Reaching down, I yank the prospect to his feet, then propel him in front of me into church. They're expecting Rock, they've got the prospect instead.

"What the fuck, Joker?"

"Rock's fled," I say shortly. "Think he took the prospect down then ran off."

"Shit!"

"Fuck!"

"Fuckin' coward." The same expressions of disgust voiced in various ways come from every direction.

Prez's voice barks over the rest. "What the fuck happened, Prospect?"

When my hand falls away, Matt's unsteady, he places a hand on the back of a chair to help himself stay upright. "I don't know, Prez. I'm sorry. Last thing I remember Rock was sitting, looking relaxed. He asked me for a beer. He seemed friendly, I had no idea why I was supposed to be watching him, but he didn't seem worried. So thought there'd be no harm in getting him a drink. I was leaning over the bar… Then Joker was there."

"Fuckin' pressure point. Rock's lucky he didn't kill him."

"Not lucky, Peg. He's signed his death warrant by running away," Prez sounds and looks grim.

I hold my hand up. In it is the cut Rock obviously threw down. Drummer's eyes narrow as he looks at it.

Blade, noting what I've brought in, is furious. "I was dreading burning off his patch. Now I'm fuckin' lookin' forward to it."

Wraith starts getting to his feet. "Let's go after him."

"In a moment, VP," Prez snarls. "I want to make this clear. Rock's no longer a member. He's out in bad standing, he'll know that whether we had the chance to tell him to his face or not. Anyone sees him? I want him back here, don't care what state he's in as he'll be dead soon after. But for this, he's going to hurt."

No one around the table disagrees. He had our sympathy as he'd been a member for so long. But by not staying, he's incurred our wrath.

After a few seconds, Prez continues. "I want his name to be dirt in Tucson. I want all chapters alerted. All friendly clubs. No one takes him in. They treat him how they want, then return him. He'll find no other home, no club to give him a home. Any of you see him and attempt to help him, you'll suffer the same fate as him." He glares at Beef. Beef jerks his chin. *Fuck, this will hit him the hardest.*

"Let's burn his cut," the VP suggests to roars of agreement.

"Nah," Prez beckons with his finger to me. "Bring it here, Joker. I'll take care of it." He takes the cut, folding it carefully. Might have belonged to a disgraced brother, but it's still Satan's Devils' leather. "Now. Think where Rock could have gone to hole up. I doubt he'll have taken time to go to his room, so he'll have only the clothes on his back and the money in his pocket. Beef, any friends, women you know of in town. Go visit them. Everyone else get out there searching." He pauses for breath, then spits out, "I want the motherfucker found."

Those first few days we're all out trying to find him. Asking around, going to any and all sleazy establishments where he might have found shelter. But there's no sign of Rock or his bike. As time moves on, we pull back on the men allocated to searching for him. Then as weeks pass, the instruction changes to just keeping a lookout.

"Reckon Rock might have headed out of town," Lady says one evening when we return empty handed. No sight nor sound of the man we used to call brother.

"Depends how much gas he had in his tank, and how much money in his pocket."

"You reckon he might have been prepared? Got money on him?"

I think about it, thinking back to that meeting. "Unless he's a fuckin' good actor, his exposure took him by surprise. Nah, I don't think he left with much, Scott."

"Then he could be dead."

"If he is, he'd have gotten off easily." I want him back here so I can take a shot at him myself. There's not one of us who harbours any sympathy for him. Man ran, he should have stayed.

CHAPTER 37

As time goes on, Scott and I aren't the only ones assuming that Rock is dead, his body lying rotting somewhere undiscovered. It's dangerous for a lone biker on the road, any number of ways for him to have been taken out.

We're just finishing up church, everyone despondent that we haven't had eyes on the traitor, when Drum raises the gavel, then pauses. "Something unrelated. Wraith's had word of a girl who needs our protection…"

"Another one, Wraith?" Bullet interrupts. "Isn't one bitch enough for you?"

The VP's not upset, "Yeah, and how Sophie needed our protection is precisely the reason I'm proposing we help this girl out. She needs somewhere to hide. I'll be bringing her back to the club."

"Who is she? Who does she need protecting from?" Shooter asks.

"Need to know basis." Drummer shuts him down. "You trust me that I've got the best interests of the club in mind. But what you don't know, you can't speak about. Remember Chrissy?"

I don't, but the others do. But I know the story. Sweet butts get to know things, Chrissy nearly got Wraith killed with her loose mouth. Lost her life for it too.

Peg nods. "Okay. We'll look out for her while she's here. No questions." His eyes narrow, "But don't like things being kept from the brothers, Prez."

"I hear you, sergeant-at-arms. Just trust me on this, okay? All will become clear in a couple of weeks."

Another bitch on the compound doesn't mean much to me or Scott. It's each other we're interested in, not the opposite sex. But a day or so later, I see the lady herself.

Wraith's collected her from somewhere, and when he brings her through the clubroom, my questions about why Doc was around got answered. Christ, whatever that girl's been through has been bad. I've never seen such a sorry state. Neglected for certain, malnutrition, sores running down those legs which are exposed by the short skirt she's wearing. She looks dead on her feet. And terrified.

So much so, none of us hinder her progress into the back rooms for Doc to check her out.

Beef's staring after her. "Don't need Prez's instructions to protect that little girl. She looks like a refugee from a war zone. Not gonna let anyone hurt her."

I think it's how we all feel. Traits common to all bikers are their dedication to their club and their protective nature toward club property. By placing herself under our protection, she's become one of ours. Beef is right. Having seen her, any one of us would have taken her under our wing.

Thoughts of Becca's predicament fades as our focus needs to be on how we're going to deal with the Herreras, as well as decide what we're going to do about the Chaos Riders who are gunning for us. Drummer and Wraith spend hours holed up in the president's office, presumably working on some plan. We're updated on the details at another hastily arranged church.

"I've requested a meeting with Chaos, the president of the Chaos Riders."

That sounds like a good plan. Drummer waits for us to settle again. "VP's coming with, Blade, I'd like you there too. And Beef. Want some muscle along."

There's good-natured laughter. Beef's easily the biggest man amongst us. Good in the ring, though both Lady and I have taken him down. But with his height and his muscles he certainly looks the part.

Wraith nods at Blade. "Prez has got a plan. That includes misleading Chaos as to our state of readiness. So you and Beef, keep your mouths shut. You hear something that gets you surprised, don't even twitch to give us away."

"Got it. Dumb fucks." Beef grins. "I can play that part. Fuckin' lookin' forward to seeing Chaos face to face."

"When's the meeting, Prez?"

"Tomorrow. We'll feed back after."

The next day is the day when Viper's crew starts work on adapting Scott's bathroom, making it into a small kitchen. We've already moved his stuff into mine. When I first saw his clothes hanging up next to mine, a lump had come into my throat. Somehow seeing his stuff there made it real. *We're a couple. And everyone knows it.*

Viper shoos us away, saying his team know what they're doing, our presence would be more hindrance than help. We take the hint. Using one of the club trucks, we leave them to it, going to a mall in Tucson. Fuck me, I'm walking around with *my man*. Shopping for a couch, table and flat screen TV, the essentials that we can think of. A place to sit, table for our feet and drinks, and something to watch the game on. What more do men want?

To everyone else, we're just two bikers. Parents shield their children from us, others shy away giving us space. We're treated with suspicion as if we're going to take out our guns and start shooting the place up. I straighten my shoulders; prejudice is what I'm used to.

We go into the furniture store, see a leather couch that is comfortable when we sit on it. That'll do. No point wasting time looking around. A low coffee table is next, a place to store Harley mags under it. Yup, we'll take that as well.

We spend the most time in the electrical store, trying to discover which TV has the best picture, and whether we should pay out for one that's curved or flat. We end up with a decent sized one, paying out for a sound bar to be thrown in. Well, the deal offered was sweet.

After we load the truck, Scott pauses with his hand on the passenger door handle. I tilt my head to the side as I watch.

He nods back into the mall, shifting a bit awkwardly, before looking up and saying, "Saw a jewellery store in there."

I catch up immediately. "Yeah?" One corner of my mouth turns up.

"Yeah." He peers at me through his eyelashes, as if he isn't sure of my reaction. In truth, we haven't spoken about our future plans since the Herrera business arose.

"You're talking rings?" My voice gives nothing away.

He kicks at a stone. "Just a thought."

I let him out of his misery. "A fuckin' good one, too. Come on. I'm all for it."

The man at the counter looks panic-stricken as two burly bikers walk in. I can see his hand hovering, presumably over a panic button. Ignoring him, I lead Scott over to the showcase containing wedding rings for men.

Eventually the assistant comes over, asking timidly, "Can I help you?"

"Wedding rings," I tell him.

He relaxes a bit. "And which of you gentlemen, is getting married?"

Scott looks at me and grins. "Both of us," he replies.

The assistant rubs his hands, probably wondering how much we're good for. "I can show you some beautiful wedding sets that would make the women in your lives very happy."

I look him straight in the eye. "We need two matching men's rings."

He's clearly not on the same wavelength, his creased brow shows he doesn't understand. Scott sets him right. He points to himself, then to me. "We," he states confidently, "We're getting married."

The penny drops. So does the man's face which starts to grow red. He pulls himself up, his mouth thinning. "I don't think we have anything that will suit you in this store. I'm sure you'll find somewhere else to help you."

I hear Scott's indrawn breath as I ask casually, "Is your manager around?"

His eyes flit behind him, then back to us. "I'm not sure if she's available."

Scott puts a snap in his voice. "Well, I suggest you find out." The hand he puts on my shoulder grips with tension.

I think the man's forgotten who he's speaking to, as suddenly he hisses, "I think you should leave. I don't have to serve your sort if I don't want to. I don't believe in your way of life. It's immoral…"

I move fast. I'm not stupid, don't want any trouble with the cops, but shaking off Scott's touch, I press my body against the shop assistant's which moves him back so he's trapped between a tall, muscular biker and the counter. "Funny, that. I don't give one fuckin' damn what your fuckin' beliefs are." For good measure, my finger comes out, prodding him in the chest. "What I do believe in is not forcing my thoughts on others. Your God might judge me, but that's his fuckin' right not yours."

The assistant gulps. "Maybe I was being hasty…"

"Maybe you've lost yourself a sale," Scott says, deceptively lazily. I hear the emotion under his tone. This should be a joyous purchase for us, a promise of our future together. I'm not going to let it be ruined by one judgemental man.

You're dirty, disgusting, immoral. No. I shake my head. Not letting those thoughts invade. Not today, not now. I'm what I am, this man's got no right to censor me.

"Maybe you've lost yourself a job." A woman appears from out the back. "Can I help you, gentlemen? Matching rings, right? I'm Marnie, the manager." Tossing a glare at her employee, she beams a megawatt smile at us.

I stand, undecided.

"I'm sure we can do a deal that will benefit us both. Saul, go wait for me in my office."

As the assistant sends me a look of disgust, I move back, letting him get free. He brushes his clothes down then turns to his boss, informing her petulantly, "Arizona law says I shouldn't have to do anything against my religious beliefs. You can't fire me…"

"I can fire you for not acting with human decency," the manager responds. "Now get out back while I serve my customers."

"You can't get away with this," Saul hisses his parting shot as he leaves the front of the shop.

"Sorry about that." The manager watches him go, then turns back. "When's the big day? I love a wedding. Of any kind." Her mouth broadens again. Then she looks us up and down. "Something plain, not fancy I presume given your, occupation." She seems to know it's the wrong word, but I let it go. "Working on bikes, you don't want anything that will catch."

"That's right, ma'am," Scott agrees. "Plain wedding bands."

"But we'd like the inside engraved." Well, I would. From Scott's quick grin, he also seems keen on the idea.

She shows us several, we try them on. Both agreeing on a couple we like the look of. I look down at the ring which will need to be resized, and see Scott admiring the identical one on his hand. I can't help it. Reaching out, I curl my hands around his neck and kiss him. Right there. In public. In a jewellery shop.

Marnie just smiles as though we were any other couple. She rings up our purchases, jots down the wording for the engravings we want, gives us our receipt and information as to when they'll be ready.

I feel on top of the world as I walk out. Scott's moving into my room, and we've bought the rings now. Nothing, except perhaps the Herreras, can pull us apart.

Back at the compound we find most of the work has been completed. The shower and stall ripped out and replaced by a sink, worktops and even an oven ready and hooked up. Viper explains they'll be back tomorrow to finish the tiling and painting. At least they've left it tidy.

We start bringing our new furniture up. Once it's in place, Scott looks at me and laughs. "Feel the need to christen our new sofa. But we've got that meeting, we can't be late."

"Prez might turn a blind eye to our activities, but don't think he'd accept us fuckin' as an acceptable excuse we missed church." I laugh.

Scott looks at his phone. "They should be back at the clubhouse anytime now. Best be makin' our way down. We'll have to pick this up later." The promise in his eyes shows me we're on the same page about what exactly *this* is.

Arm in arm, feeling about as happy as I ever have done, thinking nothing could spoil it, we enter the clubhouse. We've only just got beers handed to us by a scowling Jill, when Blade and Beef push inside.

Blade stops just inside the door, his face red, his chest heaving. "Rock's a fuckin' traitor!" he yells. "Fuckin' joined the Chaos Riders!"

Everyone stops what they are doing, frozen in tableau. My beer's halfway to my mouth.

"Fuckin' what?" Lady hisses beside me.

Then everyone's shouting at once. Prez pushes past Blade, throwing a furious look at him. "We'll discuss this in church," he throws at him. Then, to the room in general, "Church, now."

It's like a stampede. Brothers rushing in to find out what's happened. Blade glares at Drummer, bouncing in the chair as though he can barely hold himself back. Beef's face is as black as thunder.

Wraith's looking more composed, exchanging looks with the prez. When the sound of chairs scraping over the floor as they're pulled into the table dies down, Prez takes a deep breath.

"As you've probably all gathered, Rock was at the meeting. He's a patched member of the Chaos Riders now."

Shouts of disbelief go up from all directions.

"Should have killed the fucker," Peg declares, then asks hopefully, "Or did you take care of it?"

The VP sighs, "Blade gave it a good shot." He exchanges a look with Drummer which I can't interpret.

"He saw it coming," Blade rasps, his nostrils flaring. "He jumped back. Sliced him open, but doubt I hit anything vital. Motherfucker." He slams his fist on the table.

"I tried to hit him, but the fuckers were protecting him. Stopped me."

"We were there to talk, Beef, Blade. Not kill."

"Did you know Rock would be there?"

"How the fuck would I know that?" Drummer's eyes open wide. After asking his question, Blade shakes his head at the answer.

"So Rock's turned traitor?" Heart interjects. "I can't believe that."

"Heard it and saw it with my own eyes," answers Blade. I notice the enforcer's doing a lot of talking today. Strangely Prez seems to be letting him get away with it. Maybe he feels it's not good for him to keep all that rage inside.

Beef's nodding, he looks drawn. "Wouldn't have believed it unless I'd seen it for myself. But Rock's turned on the Devils. He's giving Chaos all the shit he needs to bring us down."

"If I fuckin' see him…" Peg begins.

But Viper doesn't let him finish. "You'll do the same as any of us. Finish the job Blade started. And this time, do it right."

"You…!" Blade's out of his seat.

"Sit the fuck down, Blade," Drum thunders.

Blade does so reluctantly, then shakes his head. "What was that crap you fed them, Prez? About the other clubs."

Prez shares a quick grin with Wraith. "It's part of the plan we've been working on. I've reached out to the other presidents, got rumours going around that they aren't supporting us anymore. Worked like a charm. Chaos has obviously soaked that shit right up. He thinks we'll be on our own."

"While in fact they're all onside, ready and waiting for us to call them in," the VP finishes for Drummer. Prez and VP exchange satisfied glances. So they should. It is a good plan.

Now we get into details, discussing how we're going to play it and arranging the timing.

CHAPTER 38

ach time I see the newcomer in the club, Becca, she seems a little stronger. But she's got this peculiar thing of having to ask permission for everything she does. It's clear she's unnerved and worried by the men, even though we all try to behave around her, ensuring we do nothing to make her feel threatened.

Sam seems to have found out a little more about her, and lets us know she was kept as a slave, never allowed to make decisions for herself. It makes me more patient when I'm behind her in the food line. Lady, copying Sam's example, sometimes makes suggestions to her, not so much to hurry her along, but to help.

One morning, I'm eating breakfast with Lady and Marvel, when Becca appears. Normally she'll leave if there's no women present, so seeing her in the clubhouse alone is unusual. But then I recall Peg saying he was going to help her get her muscles strengthened up in the gym. *She must be waiting for him.*

But no, she comes over. She's shaking.

Marvel is the one who asks, "Becca. Need anything?"

She replies timidly, "Er, I'd like to see Drummer. Please, can you tell me where he is?"

With narrowing eyes, Marvel probes, "Why?"

"Um, I've something to tell him." Her trembling worsens.

Marvel jumps in. "Prez is a busy man. You shouldn't interrupt him unless you've got a good reason. Perhaps we can help instead." Marvel's eyes rake over her, then he cocks his head to one side. "Want to keep me company for a while?" Always the asshole, he pats his lap in invitation.

"Oh." She looks undecided, not sure whether to sit on Marvel's lap or not—he's pushing it in my view—then from somewhere she finds a bit of strength as she insists, "I need to see Drummer."

"What's this?" a voice barks. "You givin' Becca a hard time, Marvel?"

"Nah, Peg. Just messin' with her. But she wants to see Prez. I've been tellin' her she shouldn't bother him."

I tune out a little as Peg and Becca go back and forth. I'm just leaning forward to have a word with Lady when I hear Prez's snarl.

"What the fuck is going on?"

Becca's face fills with relief. "Drummer," she cries out. "I need to speak to you; I think Rock might be in danger."

Marvel, Lady and I stand as one.

"You fuckin' what, bitch?" Marvel shouts. Peg's got her tight, her back to his chest, arms holding her prisoner and roars, "What the fuck do you know about Rock?"

Drummer's staring at Becca, then his eyes go to the sergeant-at-arms, saying wearily, "Let her go, Peg."

"Prez, she might know something about what Rock's up to." Peg's hold is tight and he's not letting her loose. "We need to question her."

Drummer snarls out, "Let. Her. Go. Peg. I know exactly where Rock is and what he's doing." He doesn't even let those words sink in before pointing to the three of us. "Get everyone in church now." Then he indicates the woman. "Come on, Becca. You're coming in too. Might as well get this all over with at once."

As they walk away, the three of us are on our phones, each of us repeating the word Rock incredulously time and time again, accompanied by variations of *that bitch, Becca, knows what he's up to, Prez knows where he is, Church, now!*

As I walk into church I see Becca, *a bitch*, seated at the bottom of the table, Peg standing behind her as though on guard, his arms crossed over his chest.

Having ascertained there's just two of us missing, Road and Bullet who are making their way back, Prez asks Becca what was so urgent that she had to tell him. *Yeah.* I glare at the girl sitting between me and Shooter, *what do you know about Rock, bitch?*

She's scared and shaking, but right now I don't have an ounce of sympathy. If she's in contact with Rock, she'll have probably betrayed the club too.

Prez, noticing how frightened she looks, gentles his voice and gives her encouragement. At last she speaks.

"I think, well, there's a chance he could be in trouble."

Startled laughs bark from all directions. "I don't give a fuck," I shout. Similar versions of what I've said are repeated from many seats.

Banging the gavel, roaring for us all to be quiet, Drummer shoots the bitch another compassionate look, then wipes his hand over his beard. Then gives us an explanation, followed by Becca, which means my thoughts on Rock do a one-eighty.

Rock didn't steal any money, and he didn't betray our club. It was all a plan to get him where Prez needed him – undercover with the Chaos Riders, giving us updates on their plans while feeding them bullshit about ours. A disgraced, bitter ex-Devil was the only kind of Devil they'd take on. So Rock volunteered to be an outcast. But by now, it's more than likely the Riders have learned the truth.

It's like I'm taking a ride on an emotional roller coaster. The stunned expressions around me show I'm not the only one. We've all been lied to, but for a good reason. An accidental slip would have meant our brother's death. My hand wipes over my face as my thoughts rapidly change from wanting to kill Rock on sight to doing everything I can to rescue him. Thing is, I also have to accept he might already be dead.

We put a plan together. Prez starts making phone calls fast. By evening the other clubs start to arrive. Marvel goes off to greet his brothers from San Diego who arrive first. I have a quick word, just to be polite, with Dart asking about Alex and Tyler who I discover are doing well. Then another roaring of bikes from outside, and fuck me, in walks Red, Crash, Twister, Petty, Roller and Sarge.

"Joker, Brother, how's it hanging?" Sarge punches me playfully on my arm, before pulling me in for a man hug. "And you, Lady? What the fuck have you got yourselves into this time? Always comin' to Vegas for help. Pussy club Tucson, can't even wipe your own asses without callin' on us."

As Lady's nostrils flare, I put my hand on his arm, my fingers gently squeezing. "He's just fuckin' with us." I realise both of us are now Tucson boys, our affiliation with Vegas ended.

"Hear you've been havin' some trouble yourselves," I remind him.

"Yeah, but we're handlin' it."

"And any more shit comin' out of your mouth, *Brother*," Red's overheard and clipped him around his head, "will mean we won't get help when we need it."

"Ouch," Sarge rubs the back of his head. "Only foolin' with them. And since when have we ever needed Tucson's assistance?"

A glare from Red has him shutting his mouth.

Twister and Crash come across. Without thinking, I put my arm around Lady and step forward to greet them. They come to a full stop, inches before they get to us. *Oh shit.* I've become so comfortable here in this club, I don't even think about giving demonstrations of our relationship out in the open. I hold my breath. The air becomes full of tension. I feel Peg and Blade taking a step closer, Heart is standing at my back. I've the comforting knowledge my Tucson brothers will have our six if this starts to get physical, but I hope, *oh, fuck I hope*, my old brothers, my old friends, the men I prospected for and fought beside, will accept it.

Twister barks a laugh. "So that's how it is, is it?" He reaches out his hand, shakes first mine then Lady's.

Sarge is shaking his head, his eyes creasing. "Never would have fuckin' expected it. You and Lady, Joke? Didn't see that coming."

I glance at Crash to see him smirking. *Yeah, no surprise to him.* What is surprising is all this time he must have kept it quiet. *Wasn't important to him. Only to you.*

Suddenly there's another hand on my shoulder. Turning I see Red behind us, his other fingers resting on Lady. Gently he bats our heads together. "Was this the reason you left Vegas?" he growls. "You didn't trust your brothers to have your backs?"

"Red, you old fucker."

Red's pulled away from me as Wraith pulls him in for a hug. I remember hearing they prospected together ending up with a special bond. After a lengthy greeting with much slapping of leather, Wraith pulls away indicating me and Lady. "They didn't trust us, either, Red. Only came out a few months back." Both Vegas prez and Tucson VP glare at us.

What can I say?

Sarge pipes up, "Which one of you's the ol' lady?"

"I'll take bets it's Lady," Twister puts in. He's shaking his head. "You hid that shit well, brothers."

Lady quickly asks Twister about his new bike, and just like that we're, *thank fuck*, off the more personal subjects. *Why do people always give a damn about who's the top? They wouldn't ask a straight couple questions about their relationship.*

"That was bad fuckin' luck, Brother. Christ, on a new bike?"

"Yeah, Lady. Harley ended up doing a recall on nearly sixty thousand bikes. But the problem showed up on mine before they found it. Fuckin' clamp on the oil cooling system. First I knew of it was oil leaking out over the rear tyre. Fuckin' lucky Crash here spotted it."

It was. That's dangerous shit. Had he ridden it without it being noticed, he could have lost control. "So you bought a lemon?"

In response, I get a growl.

Suddenly there's a commotion the other side of the room. Everyone turns.

"Fuck it," Red snarls, pushing past me. My cheeks puff as I see it's got something to do with Petty and Roller, the two newest patches in the Vegas club. They're being confronted by Beef who's yelling at the top of his voice.

"You watch your mouth, Petty. She ain't for you. She's Rock's." At his shout, the room falls silent. Someone's cut the music off. As brothers part to let Red through, I see Becca's there, Roller's hand on her shoulder, seeming to be pulling her back.

What the fuck is he doing?

Roller yells back, "That fuckin' traitor? If she's his and he left her behind, that makes her fair game."

"Rock's no fuckin' traitor," Beef roars, his loud voice easy to hear over the commotion. "As you'll find out yourselves when Drum updates you."

Twister, Crash and Sarge look at me as if for an explanation. I shrug. "Beef's right. But best you hear it from Drummer. I'll tell you this, though. Rock's a fuckin' hero."

Beef pulls Becca up into his arms. *What the fuck have they done to her?*

Red's angrily questioning Roller and Petty. After a moment he comes back, his head shaking at Crash. "Can't afford to lose two men right now, we'll deal with this back in Vegas."

He's barely spoken when the door to the clubhouse bangs open, the sound echoing with the force. *Beef's back.*

Looking around he makes straight for the pair he'd just left and without hesitation, raises his arm.

Fuck me! I wince. *That must have hurt.* I've been up against Beef in the ring, know what a powerful punch he's got, and Petty's just had that to his jaw. Roller quickly goes down, oh, now Petty's on the floor too. Both men having the sense not to get back up.

"Tomorrow you fuckin' apologise to her. You hear me?"

Both men clearly hear him and quickly agree.

Lady and I stay drinking with our old and new—well, not that new nowadays—brothers until the small hours. When bodies drop on any horizontal surface around us, or those lucky enough to nab a room, normally just the officers, we decide it's time to leave. Seeing Sarge looking for a spare space to spend the night in, I wave him over.

"Want to sleep on our sofa?"

"Fuck yeah."

Having jumped at the chance, he follows us up the incline, his eyes widening when we open the main door to our suite then the door to our living area. He stands in the middle, his arms open wide, turning in a full circle. "What the ever lovin' fuck?"

With a grin, Lady informs him, "Bathroom's off our bedroom. Kitchen's through there."

He doesn't seem able to take it in. "You have it fuckin' cushy, here, don't you? No wonder you prefer this to Vegas."

Lady's arm comes around me pulling me into his side. "Wouldn't change a fuckin' thing, Brother."

We leave Sarge to make himself at home on the couch, then in our room, I pull Lady to me, my palms cupping the sides of his head. "Tomorrow, Scott. Take fuckin' care. Ain't gonna lose you now."

He lowers his forehead to mine. "Back at ya, babe. That goes for you too."

Scott strips off, gets into bed, and seems to have no problem falling asleep as illustrated by the gentle snores coming from his direction. I lie awake, worrying about the day ahead. Hoping we rescue Rock, hoping we lose no one at all, especially hoping I don't lose Scott. Rolling over, I pull his sleeping body into my arms.

I'm still restless when the door opens, and someone noisily stubs their toe against the chest of drawers, swearing loudly.

"You okay, Brother?"

"Jesus. Fuck. That hurt. Sorry to wake you. Need a piss."

"Put the light on. Lady sleeps like the dead."

He does, and now able to see clearly, he goes into the bathroom without further mishap. I grin. *He hadn't turned a hair seeing me and Lady in bed together.* Why had I worried for all those years?

CHAPTER 39

ock's woman? Huh. She looks more like Beef's woman the way he's sticking to her like glue. But then, Rock's his best friend, and his guilt for ever thinking the worst of his brother is written all over his face. When Beef leads Becca into the crowded clubroom, I notice he's putting his body between her and the men. I turn away, grinning. The scowl he's wearing is more than enough to make everyone keep their distance. Beef's not someone you want to get on the wrong side of.

Drummer gives an inspiring talk, pepping us up so we're all bouncy on our toes, eager to get on our way and bring our brother home.

Beside me, Lady's as tightly wound as everyone else.

"Fuckin' hope Rock's okay," I say to him out of the corner of my mouth.

"Me too, Joker." He points at the woman who Beef's now leading away. "And her too. Fuckin' brave girl."

"Watch out. Trouble?" I point to Petty and Roller, both suffering from having their faces rearranged last night.

Lady spies them, then says, "Nah, reckon they're going to apologise after all. Don't envy them when they get back. Red's going to have their hides for disrespecting another chapter."

Too fucking right he is.

The other chapters are going to pull out first, so they're already walking out while we're still waiting for our signal to get going, giving them a chance to get into position. As the Vegas boys pass, I overhear Petty talking. "Stuck in my gut havin' to apologise to a bitch. How were we to fuckin' know?"

Last time I saw him he was still a prospect. From his behaviour last night, in my view, that's what he should have stayed. Placing myself in front of him, I get right into his face. "She tell you no?" I growl.

Petty's eyes widen as he notices me. I don't miss the way his hands clench at his sides. While it's hard to make the transition in my head, I have to remember he's been patched in. Doesn't mean I won't fight for what's right.

"Well, if it isn't the resident queens," he sneers.

Lady's quick to move, his hand around Petty's neck. He's pushing him back to the bar.

"Leave it!" Red and Drummer, who I hadn't noticed approaching, say together. Lady stops but doesn't let Petty go.

Red addresses my man, "Lady, stand down." Then to Drum he says, "I've got this, Brother. We need to focus on the job ahead of us now. Will be havin' words later, I can fuckin' assure you of that." His tone leaves nothing to doubt.

Red's meaty fist lands on Petty's back, his other hand curls around Roller's shoulder. "Out, now. Fuckin' assholes. We're the fuckin' visitors here. How d'you think your behaviour reflects on Vegas?"

My fists itch to have at them, but Red and Drummer are right. Got enough to focus on for now. The paling of their faces as they begin to realise the extent of their crime has to be sufficient.

"Take care, Brother."

"Be safe, love you man."

Around us, everyone is preparing to leave. Having hugged or back slapped all of my brothers, I pull Lady into me, holding him as tight as I can. "You keep safe, you hear?"

"You too, man." Lady's hugging me back, keeping hold for a moment as if not wanting to let me go.

Then we're off. Riding, I lift my face letting the wind clear my head. What happens after we get there becomes a blur. I go into automatic mode, firing at anyone not wearing a Satan's Devils cut. Just as fast as it began, it's finished. All the Chaos Riders appear to be down.

While the air still echoes with the sound of gunshot, Drummer waves us to him. "Need anyone not wanted back at the club to stay to clean up. The other chapters are getting out of here before anyone clocks there are too many bikers in Tucson. I'm getting Rock and Beef to the compound to see Doc."

Lady and I have no reason to leave, so obviously, we stay to help. Our first task is to drag all the bodies into the clubhouse. It's not a nice job, but needs to be done. When we've finished, Slick's going to be setting explosives.

Peg's looking around, pointing out where we should put the dead Riders. We're all wearing gloves, positioning guns and hands so it looks like a shoot-out amongst themselves.

"Jill's dead. In the cellar." Slick's expression is unreadable as he comes up the stairs, his hands brushing over his bald head. He could be feeling sorry for the slut, glad she'll no longer be a problem, or a combination of both. His face hardens as he tells us, "Fuckin' bad shit. If that's where Becca was kept, I don't know how she survived three months."

Lady makes as if he's going to see for himself, but Peg stops him. "We need to get out of here. Can't afford to be caught anywhere close. We've done everything we can. Slick, you ready?"

Slick's bouncing a device in his hand. "Yeah, I can set this off remotely. Fuckers were messing about with meth. Careless, could cause a fuckin' explosion." He grins.

"Okay," says Blade. "Everyone back to your bikes. Let's get this shit done."

Half a mile away, I hear a loud boom from behind us. Guess that's the end of the Chaos Riders in Tucson.

Back at the clubhouse, Beef is in one of the crash rooms, Rock in another. Doc's dividing his time between them. Initial news is that they're both going to be okay, so what else would we do, but party to celebrate our win today?

I talk, joining in as hyped up brothers go back over today's events. Revelling in Chaos going down. Totalling up individual kills. The bloodlust, our brush with death… Like the rest of my brothers I'm on a high, my blood pumping. When my eyes find those of Lady, my cock throbs, urgently needing relief.

Brothers are already fuckin'. Blade and Allie on the couch, Shooter with Diva on the pool table. Marvel has Paige up on the bar, and Dollar has Pussy against the wall. Single brothers not at present occupied, are queuing up to take their turns. Those with old ladies have long since disappeared. Guess dancing with death needs a reaffirmation of life.

I drain my beer and ask huskily, "Ready to get out of here, Lady?"

"Yeah." The heat in his eyes accompanying his response suggests he's on the same wavelength as me. My confirmation comes when I look down to see the bulge tenting his pants in a direct correlation to mine.

We stride to our suite. Scott barely gives me any warning, once in our bedroom, he pushes me back against the door, at first taking time to stare into my eyes. His eyes flash with arousal, then close briefly. *We made it again. We're both safe.*

Neither of us want to delay. As our mouths meet, I unzip his jeans, he unzips mine, then we're pushing them down over each other's hips, freeing our cocks. My hands are on his waist, pulling him close, his gripping my shoulders. My lips move over his, my tongue pushing into his mouth, as we pull each other close, our cocks rubbing against each other. Hips bucking we get into a rhythm, mutual stimulation, as those frenulum nerves rub, the tight hold sufficient to provide pleasurable friction. *God, it feels so fucking good.*

His tongue slides against mine, our hips grind frantically, our cocks push hard together.

"I'm close."

"Me too."

Jesus. I can't hold back. He feels too good. Already overstimulated and tense, simultaneous grunts and groans come out of our mouths. Still locked together, I swallow his sounds, as he muffles mine.

Now with shorter, but more determined movements, our cocks try to get closer. My fingernails bite into the skin of his back as his dig into my shoulders.

"Fuck…"

"Oh shit…"

Warm cum covers us. When I come back to my senses I realise gravity's making it trickle down, and remember I haven't removed my jeans. Pulling my mouth away from Scott's, I murmur, "Shower?"

"Fuck yeah. Just let me catch my breath."

A few minutes later, we're both squeezed into the too small shower. "One day," I promise him. "We'll have a house of our own. Get a shower big enough for us both."

His hands, covered in soap, start wiping my stomach clean. "What about here on the compound?"

"Here?" The idea takes me by surprise, but as I let it filter into my brain, I start to realise what a brilliant notion it is. Here, on the compound, where we're accepted. Alongside Wraith, Drummer and Heart's houses. "There's more than enough space." There is. This was a huge fucking resort back in the day.

He glances up eagerly. "Let's bring it up at church."

"When it's a good time," I agree.

It's surprising the turns things take, and what Rock's become involved in. Herreras, gun running.

"You ever wish we'd stayed in Vegas?" Lady speaks into my ear.

"What? Miss all the excitement?" I whisper back.

In amidst everything else, we decide to expand our businesses, using Ma's legacy to set up our own tattoo shop.

Rock's well onboard with the idea, I can't help teasing him. "You could always have Becca's name tatted over your heart," I suggest to him during church.

For my pains I get an empty pack of cigarettes thrown, quite accurately, at me.

As well as a thump on my arm from Shooter. "You could volunteer to have Lady's there instead. Oh, fuck me, yes. Lady could get a tramp stamp!" He bends over the table belly-laughing at his own joke. Rock's lips twitch. Lady gasps beside me. But I sit with my face completely straight. The talk of a tattoo shop brings something else to my mind. *Hmm.*

But instead of being able to broach my idea with Lady, the very next morning we're having to face the possibility that there's a bomb on the compound. We find it in the auto-shop. While Slick tries to disarm it, Lady and I work alongside our brothers trying to get anything flammable out.

I'm scared shitless, but trust Slick knows his stuff. I keep close to Lady, my reasoning being if anything does explode, it would be better to take us out together. From the way he stays glued to my side, I reckon that's his thinking too.

"You think Slick can disarm it?" Lady asks me quietly, once we've done all we can.

"If he can't, there's no one else here who could."

"Brave fuckin' man," Lady watches admiringly.

Then a sudden shout as Slick yells a warning. "Get back! Get back now!"

I'm pushing Lady, we're in front of the rest but still get knocked to our feet by the blast. When the dust starts to settle I see to my horror, Slick's down.

"Got to get him out of there," Lady says grimly, pointing to the burning ashes raining down.

"Here!" I run over, grabbing part of a door that's been blown off its hinges which can be used as a board.

Careful of his injuries, we roll Slick onto it, then, accompanied by Road, take him up to the clubhouse.

Later that afternoon, we're all at the hospital where two members of our chapter are being treated. Slick's been in surgery for a while now, Beef having already been transferred here when his injury had become infected.

"Probably still trying to find his brain," I offer, my usual retreat under pressure is levity. But even I have to admit now's not the right time, unsurprised when I receive a cuff around my head from Lady.

"Joker," Wraith takes me to one side. "Mind taking over from Blade, watching that fucker's place?"

Mouse had discovered the address the car containing the bomb was registered to. With no other leads, we'd decided we should check it out. The car may have been stolen, but if it had been sold, the previous owner may have details of the buyer. Anything we can find out to lead us to the bomber would be useful. Blade's been waiting for someone to come home so they can be questioned. As I'd rather be out doing something than hanging around here, waiting for news of Slick, I'm quite happy to take over from him. Even though what is essentially a stake out isn't the most thrilling thing I could be doing. "Yeah, VP. I'll go. Text me the address."

Lady's overheard so I don't need to explain anything. He just raises his chin as I leave.

I'm still trying to process everything that's happened today, the bomb, the tension before the explosion, the worry and concern following. I push my bike to its limits, forcing myself into the mechanics of riding to try to clear my head. To some extent, it works, I'm feeling more settled when I draw up my bike alongside Blade's, then walk to where he's watching a house.

"Joker," he greets me.

"Blade. Any movement?"

"Nothing."

"I'll take it from here." As Blade leaves the vantage point he'd chosen, I settle in for a long wait.

It's actually not long until someone draws up at the house. I stiffen as I notice the guy's black. *It couldn't be, could it?* He's getting something out of the back of the truck. *Turn and face me, will you? Fuck, what are you doing in there? Come on, come on. Got you!* At last he turns. He's a short guy, young. Quivering with excitement, I call up the picture on my phone that Mouse had sent all of us. *I was right*. He's the fucker who planted the bomb himself. *It's him. It's actually him.*

With shaking hands, I call a number. We'd expected it would take longer to trace him, that he'd stolen or bought the car from the man who lived in this house. That it was actually registered to him at his home address is beyond crazy. Fucker must be mad.

A voice sounds in my ear. "Prez? Someone's come home. I'm pretty certain it's that Bo fucker." I hold the phone away from my ear at his loud exclamation, then answer him, "Yeah, I'll stay put."

It's another waiting game. Seeming far longer than it is in actuality, but at least the asshole stays put. Finally, Matt and

Blade join me. Matt takes the back to stop any escape, while Blade and I approach the front door.

We don't ring the bell. Blade just kicks that shit open.

"What the hell?" The man comes running up, initially consumed by the door hanging from its hinges.

I look at Blade, his grin reaches from ear to ear. "Got him."

Now he's noticed who's come calling. Of course, he tries to make a run for it, but I'm ready for him. I've got the height and weight and soon have him zip-tied ready for transportation. Matt brings the SUV up onto the drive, Blade and I bump fists as we take the asshole back to the clubhouse.

My mind goes back to a conversation I had with Lady, as I watch Blade prepare him to be questioned in the Satan's Devils' way. *Even the enforcer doesn't enjoy doing this shit.* So rather than staying in the background, this time I step up to help him.

When we're ready and the other brothers appear, Lady stands at my side. Man, some sick shit goes on, but we have him singing like a fucking canary. I find I'm not so sensitive if I remember Slick lying in that hospital bed, maybe never to get out of it.

CHAPTER 40

We're all at the hospital. Beef's taken a turn for the worse. He's in septic shock and has slipped into a coma. That he's unconscious doesn't stop all the brothers taking turns to go inside to say goodbye. Lady and I are waiting, facemasks on and gowned up, though at this point, that seems just a technicality.

We go inside. Leaning over I kiss Beef's forehead, taking hold of his limp hand. It's hard to believe he's still with us, but if there's a chance he can hear me, I'll take it.

"Beef, come on big fella. Your bike's waiting. Your brothers too. We need you back, man." My intention had been to say a final farewell, but I just can't do it. I squeeze his hand, hoping for, but not expecting a response. I get none. I step back, leaving the floor to Lady.

"Been good knowing you, riding with you, Brother. You're one of the fuckin' best." Lady's voice breaks. "Come back to us, Brother. You can fight this."

But the man lying still in the hospital bed looks like he's losing his final battle.

We step outside, Marvel's waiting to take our place. Before returning to the waiting room, Lady sighs, and turning, bangs his head gently against the wall. "Couldn't do it, Joker," he says. "Couldn't fuckin' say goodbye."

I can't stay away; I press my back against his chest. "It's not right. He shouldn't be dying like this. Shouldn't fuckin' be leavin' us."

We return to the waiting room. Time ticks past. Hardly anyone is speaking. What conversation do you have when a brother's slowly slipping away in a nearby room?

Suddenly there are multiple footsteps in the corridor. Wraith goes out to see what's happening, as I glance at the clock. *Six-thirty.* Is this it?

Wraith pokes his head back inside the room, his features drawn. "Doctor's with him. They're putting him on a ventilator. He's no longer able to breathe on his own."

You could hear a pin drop. *He's going.* Lady takes hold of my hand and squeezes it. I look at him, see tears glistening in his eyes as they must be in my own.

Now there's commotion outside. Doors opening and shutting, people running around. A glance at the clock shows it's nearly twenty to seven. Wraith steps out again. But he doesn't come back. Not for a good few minutes.

At last the VP appears in the doorway, his hand holding onto the doorjamb as though holding himself up. His jaw is slack, his eyes open wide. As we all watch, a big fucking grin splits his face.

Blade stands. For some reason, I do too. Then Lady.

"Beef's woken up," the VP begins. Then his voice grows louder. "He's fucking woken up!"

For a moment there's silence, then such shouts and hollering the nurses come in and threaten to throw us out if we don't keep it down. But they admonish us smiling, well aware of the reason. Lady and I hang around for a while, but we're no longer keeping a vigil. Beef's a fucking miracle, now he's fighting, he's got a good chance.

As if Tucson is agreeing it's a great night, the stars shine bright in the clear overhead sky as Lady and I ride back to the compound. I'm high on the events of the evening, so goddamn happy our prayers were answered. So pleased my brother's got the chance to come home.

After having a celebratory drink in the clubroom, I drag Scott up to our bloc.

I have him naked in minutes flat, and lying on the bed. I gaze into his face as I start to play with his nipples. He squirms, he's really sensitive.

"Nipple clamps," I tell him.

"What?"

Twisting his nipples, I feel his cock jerk against me. "Yeah, gonna clamp these little buds." I pinch them again, it's like I'm controlling his dick.

"Oh, fuck, Josh. Yeah, that gets me every time."

Now seems the right time to introduce the idea I'd had when we were talking about the tattoo shop in church. "Get them pierced. Nipple rings, eh?" I close my fingers on the tight nubs again.

His head presses back on the pillow, his eyes widen, then gradually a grin appears on his face. "Man, yeah, okay. But you've got to get something too."

"No way. I'm not sensitive like you."

As I keep up my play, toying with his nipples, he gasps, "Not your nipples. Cock piercing."

What? Fuck no. My denial must show in my expression.

He smirks. "Only fair. You make me get needles—and I hate fuckin' needles—poking a hole through my nips, you've got to do the same."

"I bought you a wedding ring, for fuck's sake," I grumble. But I find myself considering the idea. *Hmm. A Prince Albert perhaps.*

My hand goes down and surrounds Scott's shaft. As I start to move my fingers up and down, Scott grunts, "When are we going to get married? No use having a ring if I can't fuckin' wear it."

"After Christmas," I suggest. "Once Beef's out of hospital, we'll mention it at church."

"Mid-January," Scott confirms. Then he puts his hands on my chest, pushing me up. We end up, me sitting between his legs, mine either side of his hips. He takes my cock in his hand, gently starting to stroke it. "We actually going to do this, babe?"

"Fuck?"

He squeezes tight, then relaxes.

"Get pierced?" I try once more.

He strengthens his grip to the point it almost makes my eyes water. "Get married. Of fuckin' course. We've got the bloody rings." He grins at me.

His free hand brings my face nearer to his, our mouths touch, our hands work in rhythm. I still can't believe this man says he'll be mine. *How the fuck was I so lucky to find him?* He's a fool. *My fool.*

"If you will, I will."

"What?" I'm in our tiny kitchenette cooking breakfast the next morning when Scott comes up behind me, planting a kiss to that sensitive spot behind my ear. There's not much space, but I'm enjoying being self-sufficient to some respect, and not always having to go down to the clubhouse to eat. I've also found cooking to be a pleasure, maybe not so much the eating of my first few experiments, but at least I can cook bacon and eggs which are at least edible now. To his credit, Scott pretty much consumes everything I put before him without complaint. Along with that big shower, I'd like to have a large kitchen installed in that mythical house we keep discussing.

"Piercings," he clarifies. "But if we're going to do it, let's get it done today. Before I lose my nerve."

I start to plate up, pushing him back out of the doorway to give myself elbow room. Words said in the dead of the night come back to me. *Having a stranger put a needle through my cock?* I shudder. *This was a very bad idea. Why the fuck did I suggest it?*

Scott takes his plate putting it on the coffee table. He looks ridiculous leaning over to eat. I sit with mine on my lap. A *dining table, chairs... When the fuck did I get domesticated?*

"I've been looking it up. Nipple rings can increase sensitivity. You're right. I love you playing with my nipples." He swallows a piece of bacon, turns, and places salty lips over mine, before tackling his food again. "And the Prince Albert? Apparently, that makes for incredible orgasms."

"Well, you get yours fuckin' pierced then," I reply grumpily. Though in the back of my mind, I start to wonder exactly how the perfection I achieve with him could be enhanced. Fuck, I'd black out for certain. Suddenly the idea doesn't sound so unattractive.

He ignores my objection. "Been looking at places in Tucson. There's a shop which has great five star reviews."

"Shame we haven't got our own tattoo place." We'd had to abandon that idea when the money instead was earmarked to repair the auto shop.

"Babe," he places his hand on my arm. "Would you really want one of our employees to go to work on your cock?"

He's got a point. "You sure this place knows what they're doing?"

"Looks like it from the write ups."

I pout. "I wouldn't do this for just anyone," I tell him.

"You and me both, babe." He shudders, then chuckles. "But you came up with the idea first. I just happen to want to go along with it."

Yeah, but I thought of adorning him, not myself.

I finish eating in silence. Scott collects the plates taking them to wash up. As I watch his ass flexing while he walks to the sink, it hits me how domesticated we've become, and how natural, how good, it feels. I lean back on the couch. We're already like an old married couple. I can see nothing wrong in that.

"Okay," I call out, after a moment's reflection. Then I stand. Now it's me interrupting him with a kiss under his ear. His skin ripples beneath my touch. "Let's do this before I chicken out."

To say I have second thoughts on the drive down to Tucson is an understatement. I have third, fourth… must be nearing my fiftieth by the time we arrive. I'm of half a mind to tell Scott to forget it, but when we arrive the shop looks clean from the outside. As if he knows I'm on the verge of bailing, Scott pushes me in through the door, and I see that inside it seems sterile enough. *Guess I'm doing this. Can't back out now.* As Scott talks to the receptionist, I wander over to look at pictures of piercings, intrigued at the types you can have done.

"They've got two piercers. One is free," he tells me quietly. "I've booked us both in."

Something disturbs me. "If they're as good as you say, why aren't people queuing up?"

"Babe, it's early afternoon. They do most of their business at night. Drunks walking in off the street."

Being drunk for this sounds like a very good idea.

"Mr. McKenzie? Would you like to come with me?" *Shit, that was fast.*

And no, I fucking wouldn't. Why hasn't Scott gone first? I glare at him, then not wanting to look like a pussy, follow the girl to a cubicle in the back. The door shuts behind me, and my torturer awaits. She's a girl whose face is covered in metal. *Guess she's no stranger to piercings herself.* The thought gives me a grain of comfort. Unless she's a masochist, she knows what it feels like. Surely it can't be too painful if she's had all that done to herself?

"Mr. McKenzie? It's a Prince Albert we're doing, isn't it?"

"Yeah." I try to sound positive. *I'm a biker for fuck's sake.* I strut nonchalantly over to the chair.

"Hmm, you'll have to remove your jeans, or push them down over your hips to give me space to work." She grins.

"Um, do I have to be, er, erect?"

"No. I can work with whatever you've got."

Good. Because I'm so far from being hard at the moment it's a joke.

"You've said no to an anaesthetic?"

Have I? I'm going to kill Scott when I get out.

"Does it take long?"

"Nah, it will all be over quickly."

I undo my belt, then the button, then my zip. All the time thinking *what the fuck am I doing?* Then smile secretly. This will be the first time a female has touched my cock. I shrug down my trousers, and lie back in the chair, squeezing my eyes tightly shut, wishing I was anywhere but here.

Her hands feel sure. I don't watch. Don't want to see that fucking needle. *That doesn't feel too bad…*

"I'm just cleaning the area," she informs me.

I thought that might be the needle going in. People have piercings all the time. It can't hurt that much else they wouldn't go back for more…

Fuck! Fuck! Fuck! I clamp my mouth shut to swallow the scream but I can't stop my eyes watering. The pain is intense. Jesus H fucking Christ! I'm never having sex again for the rest of my life. She's killed my fucking cock.

Resisting the urge to curl up into a ball, or to take her by the throat and shake her, I only just hear the words through the rushing sound in my ears.

"That's done. The worst is over. You'll feel a dull throbbing for some time. Any acute pain, you need to get it checked. Take ibuprofen, but avoid aspirin as it can cause you to bleed. You've got a bent barbell at the moment, but once it's healed you can change that if you like."

I'm never touching my fucking cock again. Nah, that thing's dead now. Completely useless.

I realise there's something I should have asked before. "How long, how long 'til…"

"It should be healed in four to six weeks. The first time you have sex, you should use a condom in case it opens back up."

Four to six weeks? But we're getting married in a month.

She talks me through aftercare, then, after giving me a piece of paper to remind me—I'm going to hang on to that shit, don't want a fucking infection in my dick—she turns away while I dress. *Fuck! Fuck! Why didn't I wear looser jeans today? Oh fuck, we should have brought the truck. Scott's dead for suggesting this. I'm going to kill him with my bare fucking hands.*

I open the door, gingerly stepping out. Doing a good John Wayne impression as though I've just got off my horse.

Scott stands, his face full of concern. "How did it go?"

I'm not giving him a chance to back out. "Piece of cake," I tell him, forcing a smile onto my face.

As the receptionist leads him to face my torturer, I very carefully take a seat. Sitting pulls my jeans tight over the sore area, so I quickly stand up. Then try to adjust myself to a more comfortable position. *I can't find one.* Christ, this hurts. *Maybe I should suggest piercing to Blade, as a good method of torture to get answers…*

"Are you okay?" the receptionist asks when she comes back. "Can I get you a glass of water?"

"I'm okay," I answer gruffly, but my voice sounds weak.

I sit again, this time making sure to lean back. I study the woman's face carefully as she goes back behind her desk, expecting to see her smirking. She doesn't. But then, she probably sees this a hundred times a day.

Should I have warned Scott? Nah, let him suffer like I'm suffering.

It's not long until he appears. His face has gone white, he's shaking as he comes over. "Never doing fuck like that again in my life," he spits into my face. "Next time you have good ideas, fuckin' keep them to yourself."

"Painful?"

"They haven't invented a fuckin' word to describe it," he hisses. "You know how long they're going to take to heal?"

"Weeks?" I suggest.

"At least three fuckin' months!"

Three fucking months? Damn. Sounds like our wedding night will be completely fucked. I won't be able to play with his nipples, and won't be able to stand him anywhere near my cock.

"You're lucky you're not a woman." The receptionist has overheard. "It's double the recovery time for females."

Scott shakes his head, ignoring her. He's leaning over me, one hand braced either side of the chair. I go back on my plans for killing him, looks like he's suffering enough. I watch his face carefully, his features are drawn, pain lines crossing his forehead.

"What the fuck have we done, Josh?" One side of his mouth turns up, then the other. Then he starts to laugh.

Chapter 41

Having left the shop, I stand for a moment, eyeing my bike without my usual enthusiasm. Scott's standing next to his, looking about as keen as myself.

"Could always call a prospect to come pick us up with the crash truck," I suggest.

He raises an eyebrow at me, then sits astride his bike, leaning forward awkwardly. I throw my leg over the seat with none of my normal elegance, and again try to adjust myself. I grimace at him as I start the engine.

The journey back to the compound from Tucson seems far longer than normal. The vibrations of the engine beneath me playing havoc with my sore dick. By the time we get back, sweat is pouring off my face even though it's a winter's day. While the sun is shining, the temperature isn't that high. Thankfully, but again very carefully, walking my bike back into the parking space, I see Scott's not in a much better state than me.

As though we're a couple of old men instead of bikers in the prime of life, we walk slowly up to our bloc. I rip off my jeans, he takes off his cut and tee, then we both gently lie down on the bed, identical groans coming out of our mouths.

"Fuck," he exhales the one word.

Fuck indeed.

"I never want to go through anything like that again," I tell him forcefully. "Might love the fuck out of you, but not even for you I don't."

"I hear you, I hear you." He's quiet for a moment, then says, "Think we need to delay the wedding."

He's echoed my earlier thoughts. "I'd rather wait until we can enjoy the wedding night."

"No hurry, babe. I'm not going anywhere." We're both lying on our backs, the only comfortable position. He reaches out, fumbles for my hand, and squeezes it. "We're together, nothing matters but that."

I feel tired, exhausted. Slowly I drift off to sleep, only waking when a call of nature demands I get up. Not looking forward to using my abused cock, I walk that John Wayne stride into the bathroom, take aim gritting my teeth.

"Oh shit!" I cry out.

"What, babe? What's the matter? You got a problem?"

Yeah, I've got a fucking problem. And now I've started, I can't stop. Piss is going everywhere, I'm unable to control it. It doesn't help that Scott's laughing his head off. "You gotta sit down."

"Sit? I'm a fucking man! And how the hell do you expect me to turn around? This shit's going everywhere already."

"Er, that's not shit, babe." He's laughing so much he's sliding down the wall onto a dry bit of floor.

Eventually the stream, or rather, two streams, dries up, and I'm able to bring it under control. The activity has me throbbing again, though not as badly as before. Now I'm on my knees trying to mop up the mess. First I glare at Scott, his mirth isn't helping. Then I'm chuckling myself.

"You think that my masculinity is gone? That I'll always have to piss sitting down like a bitch?"

Scott shrugs. "Could be."

"Then you know what's going to happen, don't you? I'll be bitching for you to leave the seat down."

Which strikes us both as funny, and again we crack up.

When it's time for us to walk down to the clubhouse for church, neither of us are looking forward to putting on clothes. I choose my loosest pair of pants; he puts on a tight supportive tee. Then we nod bravely at each other, and step out into the evening air.

Prez's chair is empty, so brothers shoot the shit until he comes in.

Viper's eyes are fixed on us; he seems to be examining us critically. "What's up with you two? You both look as though you've seen a fuckin' ghost."

Lady and I look at each other, then we shrug. "We're fine," I tell him. "Nothing out of the normal."

"You don't look fine." Blade's knife is pointing at us. "You look ill."

Bullet leans forward. "What's that?" He points at Lady's tee. "Oh, fuck." He begins to chuckle. "You've gone and got your nipples pierced. I can see them through your shirt."

Lady looks at me with eyes wide open. We hadn't thought of that.

Brothers start laughing at his expense, then Peg stops mid chortle. "That might explain Lady, but what's going on with Joker?"

"He's just pale in sympathy," Shooter suggests.

"Nah," says Peg. "It's more than that. Well, you ain't had your nips done, so what are you hiding, Brother?"

"His cock," Viper suggests as a joke, but my face must give it away. He slams his fist on the table. "You have, haven't you? You've gone and got jewellery in your fuckin' dick."

While the others can't stop poking fun at us, Peg and Blade exchange looks. "That fuckin' shit hurts, Brother," the enforcer sympathises.

"Sure does."

"You're pierced?" I ask, seeing they have more sympathy than the rest.

"Prince Albert for me," says Blade proudly, then casts another glance my way. "It wasn't so bad, was it? That anaesthetic dulls it right down. Didn't take more than a moment, nothing much more than a bee sting." He must read something in the glare I send Lady, as his eyes open wide. "Tell me you didn't have it done without that?" I can't, so I stay quiet. "Oh shit, Brother. That must have fuckin' hurt." My suffering seems to be another source of amusement, as they all start laughing again.

"That's nothing," Peg smirks at Blade as he proceeds to top his choice of adornment. "Jacob's ladder here."

"Apadravya," puts in Mouse. Which is unusual. Recently he's not been contributing anything he doesn't have to.

Prez has come in at the end of the conversation. "You lot stopped discussing your dicks yet? Or are you going to get them out and compare piercings? Or shall we get down to business?"

"Business," I offer, firmly. Sending a scowl at everyone else. *I'd thought we'd be able to keep our personal shit private.*

Dollar runs through our finances. When he finishes, Rock holds up his hand. "Becca asked me to bring something to the table, Prez." He waits for Drummer to raise his chin before going on. "I've explained the club doesn't want her thanks for dealing with her ex and the Chaos Riders, but she insists…"

Peg interrupts. "Had to deal with the Chaos Riders in any event, and finding out what Hawk had stashed away got the Herreras off our backs."

"I've told her that, Peg, but she wants to do something. As we had to use Ma's money to repair the auto shop, she wants to give us enough to set up the tattoo place herself."

There's an audible intake of air around the table. Girl's good to think of that.

Prez gives what for him passes as a wide smile. "That's good of her, Rock. I know you'll have tried to dissuade her, that money's hers fair and square. But if she's determined, we'll start looking for premises again. Blade, you able to do that?"

"Sure am, Prez." He sends a look toward me and Lady. "We'll look at getting a piercer too, as our brothers enjoyed the experience so much."

He gets dual middle fingers from Lady and myself.

Paladin shoots up his hand. "Any updates on the Herreras, Prez?"

Drummer shakes his head. "Nothing so far, Paladin. You and Slick will be the first to know if we hear anything more."

"We're still keeping a close eye on Jayden," Slick confirms. "Not taking any risks." Glancing across at Slick, I'm glad the Tucson crime family, for now, seem to have removed the target on his old lady's sister's back. After months, years of trying, she's at last pregnant. Neither of them need more pressure heaped on them.

Mouse clears his throat and looks slightly sheepish as he announces, "I'm going to need to take off for a bit, Prez. Got some personal shit to sort out."

Again? Prez's eyes narrow, but if he knows more than the rest of us, he doesn't let on. "Come see me later, Mouse. Tell me how long you're proposing to be gone."

The meeting wraps up. No drama. No one coming for us. Just how I like it.

Christmas comes and goes. Lady and I exchange small gifts consisting of shit for our bikes, but we do take time trying to find something suitable for me to send to Maya, in the end asking the toy store shop assistant what she recommends. Apparently a battery powered motorbike will be too advanced at her age. Peg's old lady, Darcy, is getting enormous, her baby is due in a few weeks. I find myself envying their excitement, and not for the first time, wonder what Scott's views are on adoption. Not that it would be easy, we're gay, and bikers. Two strikes against us before we even start.

The benefit of having piercings done together is that we're both determined to keep the sites clean. I do his, he does mine. After a couple of weeks my dick starts growing when he gently takes it in his hand. Something that makes me sigh with relief. I'd begun to think the damn thing was dead.

We agree to have the wedding in March, when hopefully both of us will be fully healed. A couple more weeks and we mutually give each other hand jobs. My cock is fully functional and pain free, and wow, the intensity of the feeling. But that could be down to the fact it's not been used for so long. So we do it again to make sure. Yup, the pain I went through was worth it.

At church Lady holds my hand as we announce we're getting married. A small, quiet affair. That is, until the old ladies get wind of it. Fuck knows what they're going to prepare, but it's easier to let them deal with it than argue.

Peg and Darcy's new arrival takes the heat off us for a while, a bouncy boy to the sergeant-at-arms' obvious relief. They've called him Noah.

"Joker! I was coming to see you."

"Prez?" I walk across to join him at the bar. "What can I do for you?"

"My office. Now. Bring Lady."

Turning around, I beckon Lady over. His facial expression similar to mine, a 'what have we done now' look.

"Know what this is about?" he hisses quietly as we follow in the footsteps of Drummer.

"No fuckin' idea," I reply, running shit over in my head to see if I can think of any reason for the summons. I come up blank.

Prez holds the door open for us, then waves us to the chairs in front of the desk. Walking around, he sits behind it. My eyes view the huge flag behind him, the same picture as that on our cuts. The grim reaper hovering over three grinning devils.

"What's up, Prez?" I prompt, when he seems reluctant to speak.

"A lawyer's been in contact with Alex."

Alex? It takes me a moment to place her. "Ah, Dart's ol' lady." She's taken over as the lawyer for the club. I sit forward. Contact from a lawyer is never good. Not in my experience anyway.

"That's right," he confirms. He wipes his hand over his beard, his steely grey eyes burn into me. "Joker, there's no easy way to tell you this. So I'll just spit it out. I'm sorry to tell you, but your brother and his wife were involved in an accident. Head on collision. His wife died immediately, your brother hung on for a couple of days, but died from his injuries."

Oh fuck. Of all the things I could have anticipated, I never expected to hear that. I feel Lady edging closer, then placing his hand on my knee, his fingers tightly squeezing. "Maya?" I ask quickly. *Sim gone?* I shake my head, unable to process it.

"Their daughter is fine. She wasn't with them. She was with a babysitter for the night."

"Who are we killing?" Lady asks grimly.

"The other driver was killed outright too. Drunk as fuck apparently."

I drop my head into my hands. *Fuck, fuck, fuck.* All the reasons I hadn't returned to see him seem weak as shit now. Why did our chosen occupations have to separate us? Surely, if I'd tried a little harder there would have been a way to overcome that? Now I've lost my chance to ever get to know him. We might not have been close, but I feel his loss keenly.

"What happens to Maya?" I wonder aloud. As far as I know Sara had no family. What the fuck happens to that little girl? All the pictures Sara had sent me seem to appear in my head.

"That's why I called you in to speak to you, what Alex needed to contact you about." Drummer takes a sheet off his printer. "Your brother knew he was dying, but managed to dictate a new will and sign it. You're his sole heir, and the guardian of Maya."

What the ever-loving fuck? Me? Her guardian? I look up. "What does that mean, Prez?"

He taps the paper, then hands it over. "Read that."

Dear Josh

I know we were little more than strangers, but I know I've not got long left. The doctors can't stop the bleeding. Thing is, I never expected Sara and I would go more or less together. Part of me is glad, I don't want to live without her, I'm pleased I'll be joining her soon. But I'm leaving behind a precious baby girl, and I need to make provision for her.

In between the pain meds, I've given this some thought. I investigated the Satan's Devils, and know they run a clean club, well, as far as one percenters are able to. Yeah, I was checking up on you, little brother, but looking out for you too. I'm glad you've made a home there.

Thing is, I don't trust many people with my angel, but I certainly couldn't go happily knowing I was leaving her with a stranger. The only other kin she's got are her grandparents, our parents, and they probably wouldn't have her in the house.

So, Josh, I'm asking you one favour. It's my dying wish that you take Maya and bring her up.

I'd say more, but the doc's hovering again. Next time I sleep I might not wake up. Just trying to keep breathing to sign everything and make it official.

Look after my Maya.

Love always, Simeon

Wiping tears from my eyes, I pass the letter over to Lady. The feeble scrawled signature makes my gut clench.

Prez passes me a box of tissues, I take one, blowing my nose, then dabbing the wetness from my face. "She'll be welcome on the compound, Joker, if you're going to comply with your brother's last wishes."

I hollow my cheeks. "How the fuck do I look after a baby, Prez? I haven't a clue where to start." My hand reaches out, fumbling for Lady's. When I find it, I grip it hard.

"We," Lady squeezes my fingers. "We, Josh. It's not just you anymore."

Turning, I try to read his expression. "You wouldn't mind?"

He smiles. "Fuck no. Always wanted a kid. We'll give her the best life we can."

He did?

"Do we know who's lookin' after her at the moment?" Already taking on my responsibilities, I want to know that she's safe.

Drummer's face sets into a scowl. "Your parents. They came and took her from the babysitter." He points to the note in Lady's hand. "Seems your brother was wrong about that. It was their Christian duty apparently, or so the lawyer told Alex."

Christian duty. Yeah, to fuck kids up like they had me and Sim. I stand. "I've got to go get her."

Prez narrows his eyes. "Lookin' after a kid ain't something to do on a whim, Joker. It's a fuckin' lifelong commitment. Now you know family is takin' care of her, wanna take a minute to think whether your parents might be better placed to do a good job?"

It's Lady who stands so fast, his chair rocks backward. Putting both palms on the desk, he leans over getting in Drummer's face. "They're fuckin' child abusers, Prez. Fucked Joker up. Toughened him up by getting his ribs broken. I've seen the fuckin' x-rays, they're not fuckin' pretty." He wipes his hand over his face, then sends a quick glance my way. I shrug. Prez knows what I am, won't be any harm in him hearing anything else Lady wants to say. I leave it to his judgement.

Lifting one hand, resting it on my shoulder in support, Lady looks again at Prez. "They tried to change him, Prez. Sent him to undertake fuckin' conversion therapy. That place was no fuckin' summer camp. Another boy, Joker's age, killed himself while he was there. Made Joker believe being gay was dirty and unnatural."

"Sit down, Lady," Drum says sharply. When he's obeyed, his eyes soften as he looks at me. "Heard about those places, Joker, what came to my ears wasn't good." His hand toys with his beard. "Explains a lot. Why you didn't fuckin' trust us for two years." It's Lady he peers at for confirmation, before turning his eyes on me. "I knew there had to be something behind your lack of faith in your brothers. Christ," he pauses again, shaking his head. "Your family rejected you when the therapy didn't work?"

It's time for me to speak up. "They thought it had. Broke off contact with them. Thought no one would accept me unless I was straight."

Drummer nods. "So you pretended for years." He sighs. "Noticed a difference when it all came out into the open. You've been far more relaxed." Leaning forward, he places his hands on the desk. "I'm sorry you felt under such pressure. I'm not going to blame you for assumin' you had to pull the wool over our eyes. You'd already lost one family, couldn't afford to lose another."

He's summed up exactly how I'd felt. I feel some relief he now knows the whole story.

"Getting back to your brother and his daughter, I understand now why you want the kid with you." Drummer's mouth thins. "Don't know how to describe a perfect childhood, doubt many people could say they'd had one. But I know this. Here on the compound your niece will want for nothing, have other kids around to grow up with. And no fuckin' one will try to force her to be something she isn't, or that she doesn't want."

"Prez," I start, then stop. My throat feels swollen, my eyes glisten.

He waves off my unspoken thanks, his eyes grow steely. "You've got to go get Maya."

I have, I nod. But the thought of facing my family… I shudder.

My reaction doesn't go unnoticed by Prez who's looking at me sharply, then both hands cover his face as he thinks. Nothing is said for a moment. He looks up. "Alright, how about this? You've never met the kid, and it's likely your parents might give you some fuckin' problems. How about Sam and I comin' along for the ride? Sam can help you with Maya."

My mouth drops open at his generosity. "I can't ask…"

"You didn't. I offered." The way he says it, his mind's made up. Why would I argue? It gives me any backup I need with my folks, and what the fuck do I know about looking after a baby?

Choking up again I manage to get out, "Appreciate it, Prez."

He looks first at me, then at Lady. "This is a lot to lay on you. A lot to come to terms with for you both. But from what you've said, you've got no option. I'll get the tickets booked. We'll fly up as soon as we can."

As I stand to leave, I reach over the desk holding out my hand. "I'm," I look at Lady who nods, "*we're* going to do the best we can for the kid. And for your help? I don't know how to thank you. I owe you, Prez." I owe him a lot, so bemused at the moment, even arranging flights is probably beyond me, I'm grateful he's taken that burden as well.

He gets to his feet, takes my hand and holds it. "Sure you do, Joker." He sighs. "You and Lady have done whatever we needed you to for the club. Time the club gave you something back."

But the club's already given me everything. The freedom to be who I am. Can't top that.

CHAPTER 42

"Y"ou sure about this, Scott? It's one fuck of a lot to ask you to take on." I'm conscious this is life changing for us. Sure, my dream has always been that I've wanted a child, but with all the obstacles that would have been in our way, I hadn't seen much point in discussing it with him.

I hate that my brother died, but at least he didn't have to live without Sara. That hole he's left inside me refuses to close up. While there were things that kept us apart, he was the only one in my family that accepted me for what I am. Though we didn't stay in touch, he'd been a lifeline I could have used. Someone who'd be there for me had I needed it. Now he's gone, and he's left an orphan behind. All I can do for Sim now is to make sure Maya's well cared for. That means I'm not going to leave her with my fucking parents, or strangers to bring up. However, I'm all too well aware taking on a baby might put a strain on my relationship with Scott.

He leans against the chest of drawers. "How long have we been together, Josh?"

I answer his odd question, "A couple of years?"

"Yeah. I think we're about as settled as any of the brothers with their old ladies. We're getting married. You're it for me, Josh, I hope the same's true for you."

My brow creases. "Of course, it is."

"Seems a good time to add a child into the mix."

"It's not like getting a dog," I object. "This is a lifelong commitment. Once she's with us, that's it. No turning back."

"You're going to take her whatever I say, aren't you?" He steps forward. "The question isn't whether you're going to give that kid a home, it's whether that home will include me."

I freeze. There's no way on this earth I'm not going to take her, love her as my own. My heart skips a beat thinking it could put a strain on our relationship, I could lose Scott.

His hand touches my face. "Haven't I already said I'm in this with you, Josh? Fuck, it's hard to get my head around that we'll have a kid. But fuck me if that doesn't feel right. I'm in this with you, Josh, one hundred percent."

At last my muscles are able to relax. "You sure?"

"Never been surer of anything in my life." There's such promise in his eyes, I can do nothing but believe him. He leans in closer and whispers, "How's your cock? Want to take it for a trial run?"

The tone of his voice, the way it resonates in my ear, has me rock hard in seconds. "My cock's fine," I manage to stutter out.

"Just avoid my tits, man. They're still fuckin' sore."

If I was in love with him before, that he's willing to take on my niece and bring her up as his own makes me feel like a huge bubble of happiness has settled inside me, slightly marred by mourning the loss of my brother. But I love this man so much. He's my family now, him and Maya.

Placing my hand to the back of his head, I close my mouth on his, careful not to push my weight into his chest. It's not a hurried or frantic kiss, it's as though the thought of being truly family takes away the urgency. This is an outpouring of love, one to the other.

As our lips move, we begin to undress each other, me stepping back to let him pull up his shirt, still careful not to catch the barbells he has in while he's healing. The sight of his pierced nubs making my cock come alive and twitch as though it's got a mind of its own. *Yeah, can't fucking wait until I get my hands on those.*

Connected again by our mouths, but now without the barrier of clothes, I push him until the backs of his knees meet the bed. As we've done a hundred times before, he sits then lies flat. I follow him down, straddling him, taking my weight on my thighs, rubbing my cock against his.

His eyes look down, flaring as they settle on my piercing. "That looks so fucking hot," he rasps. "Can't wait to feel it inside."

I reach for the lube, remembering the instructions, the condoms I'd bought in anticipation. I pull his legs up, my fingers rim that puckered hole. Our gazes meet as he gasps in pleasure as I gather up lube then push one, then two, fingers inside.

Freeing the condom from its wrapping, Scott takes it out of my hands. "Let me," he suggests.

Gritting my teeth, so primed I'm afraid his hands could trigger a premature ejaculation, I try to think of the things I need to do to my bike. Try to picture the parts of an engine, but when his fingers trace my piercing I'm almost gone, having quickly to press the heel of my hand to the base of my cock.

The asshole grins. "Close, are we?"

"Fuckin' close," I gasp. "Just get on with it, will you?"

To taunt me he pumps me a couple of times, his calloused hand feeling so good against my cock. "Scott…" I wail out, knowing I'm on a hair trigger.

At last he rolls on the condom. His hips jerk against me, his pupils dilated, his breathing coming in gasps. Pre-cum is leaking from the tip of his dick. All signs he's as close as I am.

"Not going to last long," I tell him as I get myself into position. I'm impatient, I can't take this slow or be gentle.

Inhaling a sharp breath, he bears back down as I work my way inside, once past that initial ring that's reluctant, his sheath feels slick and warm and oh, the sensations from the Prince Albert, stimulating nerve endings which hadn't been brought into play before.

"Can you feel it?" I ask breathily.

"Fuck yeah. Feels different."

"Good different, or bad?"

"Good, fuckin' good. Get on with it, man."

I don't need encouragement. I pull back, then slam in. Then do it again. And again.

Lady pushes back against me, his hips bucking in time. The muscles in my loins expand and contract as I give this man I love everything I've got.

My breath catches, my spine tingles, my balls draw up as I start that journey to its inevitable ending, the piercing amplifying everything I've ever experienced before. "I'm coming."

I grab hold of his cock, my hand wet from the pre-cum that's pouring out, it's all the lube I need as I mercilessly pump up and down. Then I feel it swelling.

I come with a shout, he's there with me, white ribbons of warm cum simultaneously pulsing out over my hand, running down to where my cock joins his body.

Oh my fucking God. My lungs struggle for air, my eyes close. *What the fuck was that?* I feel like I'd fucking died.

Unwilling to lose the connection, I rub his cum into my pubes, then onto his stomach, massaging it in, then rubbing it into my own skin.

Suddenly our eyes lock. He smiles, then gives a quick shake of his head. "Never been so fucking good, babe. That was fucking out of this world amazing."

Careful to keep my weight off his chest, I lean forward and take his mouth. "Love you, Scott."

"Love you too. Fuck, I love you, babe."

Drummer doesn't hang around, somehow managing to get tickets for the next day. I'm pleased as fuck. I think hearing who was looking after my brother's, *my* little girl, and the reasons why they shouldn't, had spurred him on. That I was unwilling for my parents to have that sweet little girl in their hands any longer than necessary he seemed to understand. He's also booked return flights the same day. In all a six hour or so journey, changing flights at Dallas Fort Worth.

We leave early, getting there mid-morning local time. I'm dreading the thought of seeing my parents for the first time in almost a dozen years. During the flight, I fear on seeing them I'll regress to the man I'd been then, suppressing my identity, trying to pretend that fucking conditioning had worked. Unable to challenge them with my sexuality, running and hiding rather than addressing it head on.

"You alright?" Scott's sitting next to me.

"Not really. I never thought I'd go back."

He glances at me suspiciously. "How are you going to play this? Want me to stay in the background, pretend that you're straight?"

Surprisingly, now he's challenged me, despite my concerns, I realise that's the last thing on my mind. "Not going to be someone I'm not, Scott. Never again." I try to put my thoughts into words. "You know how screwed up I was, trying to function as het. I've never been happier since we came out, and I can relax and be the man that I am."

"It would be easier…"

"Huh!" I laugh, but mirthlessly. "Look at me. I can't pass for an upstandin' citizen. They'll have enough problems with me being a biker, let alone anything else. I don't want to hide anything. Who you are, what I am."

He hisses air in through his teeth. "We'll have a fight on our hands."

"What they did was unconscionable, Scott. How they tried to force me to change. How they condoned the treatment, me conforming to what they believed more important than my mental health. How I appeared to other people, how they wouldn't let me shame them. They're the ones at fault, not me." It had taken me hours of therapy to understand that. For a fleeting second I see Grant's body, swaying gently in the breeze. They'd nearly driven me to suicide. If I hadn't found Lady, hadn't had therapy, I might not be here today. "I'm not going to force myself into a box just to make things easier. Best face it now or get caught in a lie further down the line. They want to make waves? I'd rather face it head on."

He doesn't seem convinced, but doesn't disagree.

I'm not helpless, could do things myself. But Drummer, used to being in charge, goes off to hire an SUV, Sam first having whispered something in his ear.

After a short wait, he's handed the keys. We go out and I grin as I see what Sam had obviously suggested. A baby's car seat is waiting inside. *Damn it. I wouldn't have thought of that.*

Prez gets into the driver's seat, I get in the passenger side to direct him. Before starting the engine, he turns, examining me. "You okay, Brother? You ready for this?"

"Truth, Prez? Nothing would get me to go back there. But I can't leave Maya with them. I need to do this."

"I don't know everything you went through, Joker. But where there are gaps, I can guess well enough. It was child abuse, plain and simple. You're a good man, and you've got another good brother at your side. That kid deserves better than your parents can give her. I've got your back, Brother. Whatever you need, okay?"

Once again, I've got watering eyes.

Then we're off. A one hour journey that takes me back to my childhood. Now we're passing the church that's so important to my parents. Then into the residential area where I was brought up. Finally, pulling up outside the house which holds nothing but bad memories.

My hands shake as I open the door and step out.

"We're with you. You've got this." Sam steps up alongside me. "That little girl is all that matters, right? Focus on that, Joker."

I walk up to the front door, noticing there's now a block paved driveway, and the house has been painted a different colour, but everything else is much the same as when I'd walked out of that door for the last time. I hadn't flounced out, simply returned to go on deployment, never said a final goodbye. I just hadn't had the strength to go back.

I ring the doorbell, an unfamiliar action. I'm here as a visitor, not a resident. *Neither this house nor the people inside hold any power over me.* They've got something of mine that I'm here to collect.

There's movement inside, then the door opens a fraction, an unfamiliar face peers out. Oh, I recognise it, but the hair's gone grey now, and there's far more wrinkles than were there before.

"Millie." I refuse to call her Mom. She gave up all rights to that title long ago.

Her face tightens at my form of address. "Josh. We were wondering what became of you."

There's the sound of a baby crying. I'm no expert, but the hiccups sound like it's been going on for some time. The noise gives me impetus to get on with the reason I've turned up.

"I'm here for my niece, Millie. Please let me inside."

The door opens a little bit further, her eyes roam over my companions. Then light on Sam. "Is this your wife?" she asks hopefully.

"No. A friend who's knowledgeable about children. She's here to help me get Maya home." I nod at Sam, who I notice is cocking her head to the side as though listening. She's looking concerned. Then I put my hand out to Lady. "This is Scott. We're getting married soon."

"Oh my dear God! Heaven help us!" She tries to shut the door, but my boot prevents her. "Art, Art! Come here, quick!"

"What the hell is it, woman? Who's at the door? And when's that kid going to shut up?"

"She'll cry herself to sleep soon, Art. You know what we agreed. It's attention she wants."

"My niece is going to get what attention she needs." Drummer was right in his assessment. They are abusive. From the inside I hadn't realised, now grown up looking in, it's plain as day. Ignoring Millie's growl of protest, and Art's attempt to stop me, I push my way inside.

I'd built him up in my memory. Art, *my father*, was a big man. A man who worked out, a man who boxed. A man who could easily overpower a child. *A man who stood by watching my ribs get broken, just to toughen me up.* It's only now I realise I'm as big, no, bigger than him. As my biceps flex, I see a flash of fear in his eyes. *Not so powerful now, are you, Art?*

But he tries. Placing himself in front of me.

"He's still a queer," Millie snarls. "We can't let him take Maya."

"You've got no choice. I'm her legal guardian."

"Your brother signed that paperwork on his death bed. Were you there? Did you force him? Perverts like you, heaven knows what you're going to do to a child. Millie, call the police."

Drummer steps up. "I suggest you don't do that," he says calmly. "I think you should take a look at this." He passes over an envelope I hadn't noticed him carrying.

My eyes widen as Art opens it up, and I see what's inside. *How the fuck?* I mouth at Scott.

Prez goes toe to toe with Art. He looms over him. "Lawyer says this proves that Josh was abused as a child. A medical expert can tell when the breaks happened. Something about how children's bones grow. I think that tops any complaints you might offer about Josh's sexuality. Seeing this, no judge would let you have custody of a child."

Art now looks at me. "You needed toughening up," he spits without apology.

"I needed love and support. Got none of that."

"It was for your own good, Josh. And now you've gone back to, to…"

"Being myself. And comfortable with it."

All the time we've been talking, Maya's been sobbing in the background. I've had enough. The sound tells me where she is. *In my old fucking bedroom.* I push my way past, no one's going to hold me back.

"Josh, Joshua!" Millie comes after me, tugging my arm. "You can't take her."

"Just fuckin' watch me."

"Language!" my father shouts, which makes me want to laugh.

I'm there, opening the door. The girl I know only from photographs is standing in a crib, her face red, tears flooding down her cheeks. Her real family left her, she must wonder what hell she's come into. I don't stop, my feet carrying me straight over, pulling her up into my arms, giving her perhaps the only comfort she's known for days.

As if hungry for any human contact, her little hands clasp onto my jacket, holding me as though she doesn't want me to let her go. "I've got you," I tell her. "I've got you." Under my breath I make a promise I'll hold her, keep her safe, forever.

Turning I notice Lady and Drummer positioning themselves in front of my parents, giving me clear passage to carry her out.

"Duh da." Her hands pointing over my shoulder, she repeats herself. "Duh da." Sam steps forward and picks up the only toy in the crib, a soft well-worn teddy. She gives it to Maya who grasps it in her hand, then brings it to her mouth, sucking an already wet ear.

"Leave everything else." Sam's looking around with her mouth pursed. "We can get you set up on the compound. There's nothing worth taking here."

Leave her bad memories behind, is what she's suggesting. Make new ones for her. Make a new life. I nod.

"Where are you taking her?" Millie accompanies her words with a wringing of her hands. I can't work out whether me taking her means she's failing in her duty, or whether she's got any real attachment to the little kid. *She left her crying.* Probably did the same to me. Started to fuck me up from the moment I could breathe.

"Tucson," Drummer informs her.

"You can't take her. That's our grandchild," Art tries again.

Speaking quietly, mindful of the child I don't want to upset now she's settled, but none the less firmly, I tell him, "Your grandchild who you wanted nothing to do with while her mother was alive. Because of the colour of her skin. What will you do? Try to beat the black out of her? Like you tried to beat the gay out of me?"

"What do you do, Josh? What can you offer her? You're a fucking pervert."

"Language, Father," I can't resist throwing back at him. "I'm a biker, I have all my brothers around me. Men who'll watch out and make sure no harm comes to this child."

"A biker? Huh! And you think I'll beat the black out of her? What are your *brothers* going to say when you go back with a half caste child?"

Drummer draws himself up to his full impressive height, his steel eyes turn deadly. "Don't give a fuck about skin colour in our club. What we do care about is children being mistreated." As if to emphasise the point, he pulls Sam in beside him, pointedly laying a hand on her rounded stomach.

Art's still holding the x-ray. He glances down at it and shrugs. I reckon he's weighing up whether it's evidence that would sway a judge. After a moment, he seems to conclude it's not worth the bother, when he suddenly says, "Just take her. I never want to see you or her again. Perverts can bring up the cross breed."

I see Prez's fists clenching. I shake my head. Yeah, I want to hit my father, want to lay him out on the ground. But words can't hurt me, and I don't want violence in front of my niece. The girl I'll be adopting officially. *My daughter.*

"Art, we can't…"

"Oh for God's sake, Millie. You didn't even want the brat. We just took her on because it was expected." He glares at his wife, then turns to me. "Just get out. You're dead to me. I have no sons. No grandchildren."

"You don't fuckin' deserve them," observes Prez.

"Come on, let's go." As Scott puts his arm around both me and Maya, Art and Millie shield their eyes as though they could be infected by something we carry.

"Wait," says Drummer. "Paperwork. Birth certificate." He holds out his hand, palm up, in front of Art.

My father huffs, but goes into his den, opens a drawer, coming out with a folder. Drummer takes it, skims through it, then says with a nod, "Looks okay, Joker."

"*Joker?*" Art barks an incredulous laugh.

I don't wait to explain it's my road name, I just start carrying Maya through the house I'll never be entering again. As I step into the sunlight my father's last words reach me.

"That's all you ever were. A fucking joke!"

The car ride doesn't faze Maya. Strapped in her car seat she looks around with wide eyes, then dozes for a while. At the airport I have my first awakening of what it means to be responsible for a child. Lady grabs a highchair when we decide to fill our stomachs. Sam—and I'm so glad she's here—chooses some age appropriate food which Maya ends up wearing. Opening the bag she brought with her, Sam takes out some wipes and wordlessly cleans her up. I exchange a glance with Lady. *Got one fuck of a lot to learn.*

The flight. Well, the sooner I can forget about that the better. The air pressure must hurt the kid's ears. Her screaming sure hurts mine. She's sick too, just after take-off. Thankfully the second flight's shorter, as it's a repeat of the first. Sam stoically helps, but even her tricks can't quiet Maya down. I find myself sending apologetic glances to the passengers in our vicinity.

At last, in the car back to Tucson, Maya falls asleep in the seat Drummer gets out of the trunk. *I didn't think to come prepared with anything like that.*

CHAPTER 43

Scott stands over the crib, watching Maya sleeping, his hands brushing his hair back from each side of his face. As he turns to speak, I hold a finger over my lips then indicate the room we use as a living room.

Following me through, he sighs. "Fuck, there's more to this than I thought."

"Nightmare journey, for sure," I agree. He's right. I don't know what the hell I've taken on. What I do know is I've now got full responsibility for that tiny human in there. I've got to man up and face it.

"The ol' ladies came through."

They had. Sam was right not to take anything from the home of the people who'd brought me up. While we'd been gone, a crib had been purchased, along with clothes suitable for an eleven-month-old, diapers, changing mat, toys, the lot. I might have my work cut out learning how to care for her, but one thing's for certain, there's no end of people willing to help.

A sniffling from the bedroom. Scott catches my eye. We already know what's going to follow. Fuck, that kid's got a set of lungs. "I got this," he tells me, drawing back his shoulders.

He disappears, reappearing with a wriggling, giggling bundle. I bite my lip to suppress my grin seeing his face scrunched up in an expression of disgust and the way his nose is wrinkling.

I'm unsuccessful holding back my chuckle. "You said you'd do it next time," I point out.

"Fuck, man. You're enjoying this." And fuck me if I catch myself telling him not to swear in her hearing. *Just like my old man.* Okay, so there's maybe one thing I now understand, why he told me to watch my mouth.

I stand back, arms folded, watching with a stupid smile on my face as Scott lays her down on the mat, kneeling beside her. Tickling her, making her giggle even more, then attempting to get her out of the clothes she slept in.

"You're a stinky one, aren't you?" She thinks it's a game as he coos to her, turning over on her tummy, then does the same thing again after he rolls her back. "You're making it worse," he admonishes her. When he takes off her onesie, I see what he means. Crap, literal crap, is pushing out of the sides of her diaper. *Jesus!* How much shit does a small body hold?

Scott's trying to keep her in place, while pointing at the bag that's just out of reach. Taking pity on him, I move it closer to hand.

Fuck. That smell. Scott's face is turning a shade of green, my stomach churns.

"Want help?" I offer.

"I got this," he says firmly. By fuck, he has. The dirty diaper is off and placed into a bag, now he's lifting her legs in one hand and quite expertly cleaning her up with some wipes. Lots of wipes.

The new diaper takes a few moments to put on, but at last he manages it. This time, when she rolls over, he lets her go. She's crawling across the floor. Quickly I assess whether there's anything that shouldn't have been left lying around. Sophie told me she'd done her best to childproof the suite, but there could be something I've missed.

"I need a shower, babe." Scott's eyes are twinkling as he glances at me, then over to Maya with a look of pride.

"You did good. I'll get her dressed while you get ready." I'm proud of my man, the way he's stepping up, wondering how the fuck I got so lucky when… *Oh fuck.* "Maya, Maya. No, sweetheart." I'd forgotten the old muffler I'd left behind the couch. Now I need a wipe to get the grease off her hands.

Sweeping her up I take her into the bedroom, clean her hands with baby wipes, then start to sort through some clothes. Ah, yes, this will do. Someone's bought an adorable pair of jeans and a tee shirt with 'Biker Girl' sparkling on it. *Yeah. That'll do for my girl.* I wonder if we can get biker boots in her size? But for now, I'll have to go with the sneakers one of the girls must have supplied.

Not everything is new, Sophie must have given us some of Olivia's hand-me-downs, but there's nothing wrong with that. Probably where the Biker Girl tee came from. I could see Wraith buying that.

I'm tossing her into the air, making her squeal with glee when Scott reappears, a towel around his waist when normally he'd walk out naked. "Like that," he says, pointing to me holding Maya. "Suits you."

As he approaches, putting his arms around us both, I suddenly get the feeling this is going to work. Already I love this little girl, and from the softening in his eyes, Scott does too. My *family.*

It's not all plain sailing. Maya has her ups and downs. At night she cries inconsolably, I know it's for her parents who she must miss like fuck. Sometimes it's hard to comfort her, but either Scott or I sit with her, rocking her in our arms until she goes back to sleep.

In the clubroom she quickly becomes everybody's darling. Beef seems particularly taken by her, and strangely, she by him. The women love her, taken by her coffee coloured skin and dark brown eyes.

Maya, herself, is fascinated by the toddlers in the clubhouse, trying to crawl after them. Screaming impatiently when she can't keep up.

"You're going to have trouble on your hands." Beef raises a beer in salute. "When the boys start sniffing around… She's going to be fuckin' beautiful."

"I'll have my gun ready," I butt in. I have no fucking idea how I'll handle that. But first I've got to get through the next few years. Fuck, the next days, weeks, months will be hard enough. But Scott and I are learning more every day.

"Joker! You watching this?" I swing around to where Lady's pointing. Little tyke has crawled over to a couch and pulled herself up, and fuck me, for the first time she's let go of it. Lady gets down on his knees a few feet away, holding his arms out. There, in the middle of the clubroom, she takes her first steps.

"Got it!" Becca yells happily, holding up the phone she always keeps close at hand. "Got it on video. I'll send it to you, Joker. You too, Lady."

I turn away to hide the moisture in my eyes. *Sim and Sara should have witnessed that.* Maya's first steps. It's bittersweet. I feel honoured to have been here to see it, but I still have the feeling I've been given something I don't deserve. A pleasure borrowed, but one I can't give back. *I'll do my best for her, Sim. She'll never want for anything.*

The clubroom's filling up with brothers. All the old ladies and children are here. Drummer saunters in. I catch Lady's eye. *Something's up.* Brothers gather around, beers in their hands as if waiting. After getting a shot of his whisky from Allie, Drummer turns and looks straight at us.

"Joker, Lady. Come 'ere."

Raising my eyebrows at Lady, we cross to the prez. He takes something out of his cut, tossing it in his hand. I can't immediately see what it is. We're now in the middle of a circle of brothers and old ladies. *What the fuck's going on?*

"Last year we adapted the house that we kept for visiting officers for Ma. Equipped it to make her comfortable. While the young kid there's been keeping you busy, Viper and his crew have been changing it around again." He takes my hand, putting in it what he'd been holding, folding my fingers around it. "Reckon with young Maya there you need more space. So here it is. The key to your new home, Brothers."

I look at Lady, he looks at me. Cheering starts all around us. Maya, upset by the noise, comes crawling over to me. I pick her up in my arms. "Prez," I look around, "Brothers. I don't know what to say."

"Thank you," Lady steps in. His arm around me. "Christ, we can't thank you enough."

"Just in time for the wedding!" Sam steps up. "Two weeks' time. I've got your tuxes ordered."

My face drops. I'm not wearing a fucking tux. Clean jeans will be enough for me. *How do I tell Prez's woman I won't be wearing that shit?* I glance first at Sam who's beaming as though pleased with herself. *Fuck! How can I say no?* Then I look toward my man, seeing Scott's as bemused and shocked as me.

Suddenly Prez is laughing, clutching his stomach. "You should see your fuckin' faces," he roars. Of course, that sets everyone off. "She's fuckin' jokin' you assholes."

Thank fuck!

When it quiets down, Lady approaches Sam. "We don't want any fuss. We're thinkin' of just going to the courthouse, then comin' back and having a party here."

"Good luck with that," Peg calls out. "That's what Darcy and I tried." He's balancing his own bundle of joy in his arms.

Raising my eyebrows I shake my head at Lady. Might as well give in. The women will do what they want. And, fuck, if my brothers want to witness our legal union, why should I have any issue with it? In fact, I'm proud as fuck. It was all I'd ever wanted, but part of me had been afraid to ask.

"Leave it with me," Sam suggests. "I'll sort out the arrangements. Unless there's anything special you want?"

"They could arrive on a horse and carriage," Blade calls out. My answering glare is as good as any from the prez.

But that gets everyone making inane suggestions, so Lady and I leave them to it, going up to check out our new accommodation.

Having a house makes all the difference. Maya has her own room, so Scott and I can sleep by ourselves. That first night we make up for the time we spent keeping our hands off each other, unable to relax with a baby in a crib next to our bed.

Maya gets used to us, we get more expert with her, and gradually we settle into a routine.

The wedding day approaches fast. I buy a new pair of jeans and polish my Harley, Scott's preparation is much the same. Peg was right. There was never a chance of us going to City Hall unaccompanied. I pinch myself, wondering whether this is all a dream. A year ago I never imagined my brothers would accept my sexuality, let alone wish to celebrate with us. With Maya, Scott and my brothers, I've got everything I could ever want.

I didn't think I'd be nervous, but when the day dawns, I'm tense, overcome by what's going to happen today. I'm officially committing to Scott in front of everyone. Taking him as my husband as he's taking me as his. There's no doubt in my mind that nothing will prevent us getting hitched. Maya's arrival has only cemented the strength of our relationship.

At the clubhouse I'm surprised to see who has arrived, and who is already huddled with the group of old ladies.

"Rachel! What the fuck? Thought you'd be joining us at City Hall." I walk over, kissing her on the cheek.

"Told you I'd adopt you the first time I saw you," she replies with a laugh. "Just here to make sure you're not backing out. And where's my grandkid?"

Scott's behind me with Maya in his arms. She's quickly taken over by her grandmother. "Well, aren't you a cutie pie? I'm your gramma and we're going to have such good times." She's bouncing her on her lap, Maya's giggling away. "Sam," Rachel turns to Prez's old lady. "Shall we go get her dressed?"

What?

"She is dressed, Mom," Scott points out. Very nicely I think. Another biker girl tee and jeans. I don't try to stop his mom who appears to be on a mission, but Scott tries to protest, "Mom..." Rachel just shushes him with a look and disappears with Maya and Sam.

We look at each other and shrug. Then grin.

"You ready?" Blade walks over. "You really doing this? Both of you fart and snore, you know. Really want that for life?"

I punch him on the arm. "We're ready."

"Has that fuckin' horse and carriage arrived yet?" Blade shouts to no one in particular.

Scott's face is a picture, mine probably mirrors his, as he hisses, "They wouldn't have, would they?"

Knowing my brothers... My eyes fill with horror as I think that they might. Luckily when the enforcer's loud guffaw puts us out of our misery, we realise he's been pulling our legs.

Blade's holding his stomach, laughing loudly. "Almost got you there. You really thought..." This time he bends, puts his hands on his knees still chortling.

But the jokes at our expense haven't yet stopped. "Hey, Lady. Where's your dress?" Shooter yells out. To a chorus of cheers.

"Will you be an ol' lady?" Marvel asks. "Think Carmen's waiting to do your hair, and Sophie said something about makeup."

"He's not, and never will be, my ol' lady," I growl, rising to the bait. "He'll be my husband."

"As Joker will be mine." Scott's eyes gleam. Then he swings round on Marvel. "Got time. I'll take you down to the ring and show you exactly how feminine I am."

Marvel raises his hands, his eyes open wide. "Was only joking around." Hmm. He would back down. Last time Lady laid him out with one punch.

"We doing this then? Or have Joker and Lady come to their senses?" Drummer's voice booms out.

"No fuckin' chance," my husband-soon-to-be shouts back, as we lead the way out of the clubroom. We go to our bikes. Old ladies and children, including Maya who I get a brief sight of bundled in Rachel's arms, situate themselves in the trucks. When they're sorted, Drummer goes to the front, Lady and I riding at the back of the pack.

The roar of Harleys sounds loud as we drive en masse through the streets of Tucson, heading for City Hall. Each bike looks like it's been shined to perfection.

"Joker. Will Lady be riding bitch on the way back?" Beef gets my middle finger flipped in his direction.

Then there's more sounds of Harley exhausts reaching my ears. Bewildered, I turn. Well, fuck me. Red's in the lead, I spot Crash and Twister riding behind him. Then Indian. Blow me, there's Fox with Tiffany up behind him. Keys is there, he's got a bitch on the back. Sarge, well, he too has got a girl riding pillion. Reckon there must be some stories there.

Who else? Those deviants Rope and Cuff, followed by Cobra and Hammer, and bringing up the rear, Petty, Roller and Shadow. There's Titch, he's driving the crash truck. It's the whole fucking Vegas chapter.

Scott sucks in air beside me. I straighten my back as a wave of emotion crashes through me. "Give me a moment."

He gives me a sharp look, but then nods with understanding, as I take myself off around the side of the building. Leaning over, I place my hands on my knees.

CHAPTER 44

The vision of Grant's body, the rope holding his neck at an unnatural angle, his face a strange shade of purple fills my mind completely as the streets of Tucson disappear around me. I'm back there, envying him, at that time only able to see pain and hurt in my future. Just as he had. The reason he'd felt he had to take his own life. *He should have waited. Not given up.*

There, on my wedding day, I say a prayer for his lost life, so fucking grateful for the chances that have been handed to me. Fuck, it wasn't easy. Forced to man up, abused by my parents, sent to that fucking camp, only able to escape it by pretending to be something I'm not. Hiding my sexuality like it was shameful, trying to fit into a straight world. Meeting the man who made me face up to myself, until eventually I could accept and be comfortable in my own skin and with my inclinations.

Perhaps that's why I hadn't expected anyone would want to witness what we're doing today. Still there in the back of my mind is the thought we're doing something we shouldn't be advertising. I'm so proud of my brothers, from both chapters, all turning up to share in our special day.

I'm not filthy, dirty or abnormal. I'm a brother. *You should have stuck it out, Grant. If you only knew how close I'd come to following you…*

But I didn't. I'd resisted that bullet. Now I've got a wedding to get to. *I'm getting married today.* My eyes fill with tears, I wipe them away. Then take a deep breath. *Time to do this.*

When I go back out front, Scott's standing alone, waiting. His sharp eyes look over me, I raise my chin. He nods back. He doesn't have to ask, I've no need to explain.

Hand in hand we enter the building and walk up the aisle, side by side.

Now my focus is on him. *How the fuck did I get so lucky?* He and Maya are my life. I've got no qualms committing to him. The officiant is saying something I don't hear, my attention purely on Scott.

Shit. Focus. What's he saying? *Vows?* Fuck. I haven't written anything.

"Josh McKenzie. Josh?" My name brings me to my senses.

Taking Scott's hands in mine, I look into his eyes. "Lady, Scott, today I take you as my husband." *What the fuck can I say?* My mind goes blank. "From this day on, I promise to cherish and love you as much as my Harley."

One of his eyebrows goes up, as a roar of laughter comes from our brothers. The officiant waits, but I can't think of anything else.

"Da da. Da da da." A wail goes up. I look round to see a pretty as a picture Maya, struggling in Rachel's hold.

Instead of immediately saying his vows, Scott walks over, taking her from his mom. She immediately quietens. The girls have dressed her in a pretty bridesmaid's dress, flowers in her hair for fuck's sake. He returns to my side, now with our wriggling daughter in his arms.

"I, Scott (Lady) Flintstone, take you, Josh (Joker) McKenzie as my husband. I promise to cherish and love you as much as my Harley. And ride you as often."

The congregation erupts. Maya's laughing but thank fuck she doesn't understand what he's just said. I'm chuckling myself. The officiant looks like he's trying to hide a grin.

We exchange the rings we bought so many months ago, the officiant seems to rush through the rest of his spiel having cottoned on no one's really interested, pronounces us legally joined, then we're walking out. Rock's got Becca in front of him, her phone at the ready as she starts to snap pictures. Maya, so fucking beautiful, poses with us, smiling ear to ear, seeming to know today is something special.

When phones are put away, enough photos taken to fill several albums, Scott gives Maya back to his mom, then we head for the bikes. Drummer waves us into pole position, then my prez positions himself behind us.

I feel proud as punch riding back to the compound. Not, perhaps, so thrilled about the white ribbons hung from my handlebars. But then it's not so bad. My *husband's* bike has been adorned the same way.

Fuck me, what a reception. My throat hurts as I've been talking so much, catching up with old friends from Vegas. The women have gone to town with the food, they must have been cooking all night. Probably using Ma's recipes as the dishes are so tasty. There's a fucking cake, two bridegrooms on top.

The room starts to quiet as Drummer stands up. He bangs his hands on the table, then there's silence. "Brothers," he starts. "Today we've witnessed something special. A wedding between two brothers. I'm proud as fuck that Satan's Devils welcome any fucker into the club. Providing they can ride and stand up behind and beside their brothers."

Tables are banged and feet stamp at that.

Prez's eyes find me. "Peg once told me that we were family. A dysfunctional one, but that's what we are. Not one of us here fits into a mould. We're all different. Today's a celebration of that. Now, raise your glasses to our new couple. Husband and husband, Joker and Lady."

Glasses are raised, then there's shouts of congratulations together with certain suggestions that I might be tempted to act on later. But for now, I'm too busy yet again wiping tears from my eyes. Scott's own are glistening as he pulls me in for a hug.

"Kiss! Kiss!"

Oh fuck, yeah. It had to be Rachel. But others are soon taking her cry up. I swear I hear an echoed, "is, is," from Maya.

With a quick grin, Scott proceeds to do just that. In the club-room, in front of all my brothers.

As he sweeps his tongue into my waiting open mouth a voice calls out, "Get a fuckin' room." That's from Beef. It would be.

Neither Scott nor I feel the need to make a speech, except to thank everyone for the presents we're inundated with. There's a huge pile in the corner which Maya takes great joy in helping us unwrap. Brothers with old ladies give us stuff for the house, those still single, shit for our bikes. We're grateful for everything, as well as bemused by their generosity.

Finally, a slightly tipsy Rachel informs us she's staying the night with Drummer and Sam, and that she'll be taking Maya for us. To give her the chance to get to know her granddaughter better, she says with a knowing wink, her gaze flitting between us. Then, at fucking last, Scott and I feel we can sneak off.

"We've done it." In the bedroom in our *house*, Scott takes off his cut, then holds his hand out. The light catches the plain wedding band he's wearing.

"We have," I confirm, looking at my matching ring, the weight feeling good on my finger.

He comes nearer. "Feels like it took a long time to get here. Sometimes I didn't think we'd make it."

"I was stuck up my own ass," I agree, taking full responsibility.

He leans in. "Prefer you to be stuck up mine. Or, tonight, me up yours."

His dirty words go direct to my cock. "Or both." Feeling like I do, I could go all night. We've no Maya to worry about. We should take advantage.

"You healed now?" I ask, my hands going to the bottom of his tee.

"Fuck yeah," he replies, breathlessly.

A mischievous grin appears on his face as I raise his shirt up. "Well, fuck me," I say, gazing at the rings he's replaced the studs with. *Just as I'd always imagined. Just as I'd hoped.* My fingers almost have a life of their own as they touch and gently turn the rings. "Does it hurt?" Carefully I watch the expression on his face.

"Fuck no," he exhales.

Experimentally I take each ring between forefingers and thumbs and tug, making his nipples protrude from his chest.

"Fuck," he gasps, sliding his hand down to his jeans. "Fuck Josh, keep that up I'm going to come."

"You're so sensitive."

"Fucking right. I've been half hard all day."

I know what he means. I've been walking around with a partial hard-on too, just thinking about tonight. *It's special.* The first time I'm making love to the man who I've fucking married.

Dragging myself away from those rings, momentarily I leave him, going to the drawer beside the bed, taking out something I hoped I'd be using tonight. His eyes alight when he sees what I'm holding. With a gleam in my own, I attach the chain to each of the rings, leaving it loose and dangling. Next I lower myself to the floor, unbuckle his belt, unfasten the buttons, then slide his jeans over his hips. As expected, he's forgone underwear. Once freed, his cock bobs up, pre-cum glistening. Reverently I place my mouth to the slit, sucking that delicious drop into my mouth. Cupping my hands around his balls, I slide my tongue up the underside of his shaft, feeling the veins protruding. His hand rests on my head as I open allowing him to thrust inside.

With one hand I reach between us, grab the end of the chain, and give it a small tug. When he doesn't protest, I apply more pressure. His cock jumps in my mouth, his hand fastens on my hair and he pushes my face down as he thrusts up.

Another tug. He groans. He thrusts.

I swallow around him, pulling that chain at the same time.

"Josh, babe. Josh. Josh…"

I pull away, standing up. "Need to be inside you."

His face is red, his lungs heave as though with exertion. Then he sinks to the floor and removes my jeans in the same way I did his. His lips around my cock come as no surprise, and his tongue toys with my piercing. Each flick over it amplifying the response of the nerves. It feels fucking fantastic. If I'd teased him, he's now getting his own back. My balls seem to be pulsing, growing impossibly heavy. He sucks the head of my shaft into his mouth, curling his tongue around the barbell. I'm lifting up on my toes, almost unable to bear the extreme sensations. My hips are jerking, trying to get him to take more. I'm so fucking close…

He pulls away, leaning forward to softly kiss my frenulum.

Curling my hands around his biceps I jerk him to his feet growling, "On the bed, now."

Not waiting to be told a second time, he leaps on the bed, rolls to his stomach, then groans, "Oh fuck."

He must have been close. "Scott," I say with disappointment, eyeing the sticky mess on his thigh.

To my surprise he starts laughing, so much so, he struggles to get the words out. "I… I…," he howls with laughter, then tries again. "I rolled on the fucking lube."

My first thought, thank fuck, my second… Well, I'm chortling too. Collapsing down beside him. But it's not long before my throbbing cock has my brain back in the game. My hand slips through the lubricant useless on his leg, sliding it around to his puckered hole where it should rightfully be. I use the rest to smother my cock.

It's the first time I haven't used a condom since I had the piercing done. The feeling of being inside him, skin to skin, is amazing. As he arches his back off the bed, I sweep my hands over his flanks, feeling his muscles clenching.

I slide in and out, relishing the feeling.

"Feels so good. Oooh. There. There, Josh, don't stop."

I've no intention of stopping. Sliding my hands across his slick thigh, I put one hand on his cock, tugging in time with my movements. Then I take that chain still attached to his nipples, pulling at first gently, then a little harder.

"Babe. Babe."

I want to make this last, don't want to finish too early. I try to slow my pace, but Scott's bucking back against me, groaning out loud each time I jerk that chain.

"Josh, Josh. I can't last. Your piercing, my nipples, fuck babe."

We both want this. Need it, now. I change the position of my hips and start to hammer in.

"Babe. So good. Soooo fuckin' good."

"Are you there?" I hiss, more than ready myself. Unable to hold back.

"Yeah. Josh, Yeah…"

I'm coming, my cock jerking, spurts of cum filling him as his fills my hand. "I fuckin' love you, Scott."

He gasps air into his lungs, then reaches back his hand and finds mine. "Love you too. Husband."

Once we've come back to our senses enough to stumble to the bathroom, we can't keep our hands to ourselves as we clean up in the shower that Viper had installed, large enough for two men. Soaping each other's cocks only leads to a natural conclusion, then we have to get clean all over again.

As if it's the first time, we spend moments exploring each other's bodies. Me, with reverence. *This is my husband.* I take his left hand, hold it in mine, then position it so I can see both rings as though to confirm the events of today actually took place.

"Married," Scott breathes out, looking at our joined hands. "Done it now, Josh. No going back."

But I don't want to go back. Forward is the direction I'll be taking.

Eventually, when we're both drained and lying in bed, Scott curls into my side.

"What bothered you today, Josh? Before the wedding? Were you havin' second thoughts?"

"Never." Having reassured him, I give him the truth. "I remembered Grant. How I envied him that day. Thought for someone like me life wasn't worth livin'. But I realised, he might have put the rope around his neck, but he didn't take his own life. Society did it. Society fuckin' killed him."

"We've come a long way. Middle of last century, being gay was still a crime. Moved way forward since then. But there's still far to go, Josh. We've got to keep fighting. Got to keep holding our own, educating the ignorant, putting up with their looks of derision. There's still far too many that think being gay is a choice, or worse, a mental illness."

Raising myself on my arm, I look down at him. "If I had a choice, I'd choose you. Someone offered me a pill to make me straight, I wouldn't dream of taking it. It's not just the sex, it's the privilege of knowing you, being with you, sharing everything with you."

His hand caresses my face. "Isn't that what love is? In whatever form it takes?"

I nod, then lie back down again. "I've been thinking of Maya. Whatever she is, we're going to love and support her."

"Too fuckin' right we are. Together. We can do anything together." He yawns, snuggling into my side again.

He's right. We can, and we will. Riding together. Riding alongside my fool through life. I go to sleep with a smile on my face.

EPILOGUE

So, Josh, Scott. Congratulations." Delia smiles as she taps on her tablet, then looks up. "I count your treatment as a success, Josh."

Quite naturally, I take the hand of my man. "You're right to," I reply to her, while looking into Scott's eyes.

"When you first came to me, you used some harsh words to describe yourself. Tell me now what description you'd use?"

Switching my focus back to her, I give serious weight to her question. "I'm a biker. I'm married. I've got a family. That I'm not considered normal has nothing to do with that."

"Normal?"

I've not said it quite right. "That's wrong. I don't mean I'm not normal, just that my path is different to most others."

Her fingers start flying again, as a satisfied smile appears on her face. "You remember the six stages we've spoken about? Well, the last we call identity synthesis. That's where your sexual orientation just becomes a part of your whole, not your total identity. As you said, you're now a family man with responsibilities. That you're gay is no more than the other aspects that make you who you are. A man, a biker. A husband. A father." She replaces her tablet on the table. "It won't all be clear sailing, Josh. Sometimes it will be harder, there's still discrimination you will face. But you've accepted yourself, and that's been one hell of a journey for you."

Leaning back, she gives a satisfied smile.

I think back to when Scott first suggested the sessions. When I thought nothing and no one could help. I owe a lot to Delia, having to admit it was her guidance, her understanding, her pointing me in the right direction, that's helped me become who I am today. I try to thank her.

"Josh," she begins, sitting forward again. "And you too, Scott. I'd like to say you are both well-adjusted homosexuals. Which is true. But out there," she waves her hand toward the window, "there are people who won't recognise your marriage, who won't think it's right your daughter has two fathers and no mom. Who call you names, who might even be violent toward you. Some religious zealots would even like to see gay sex a crime once again. That's unfortunately the world that we live in."

"That's on them, not us," Scott puts in, his brow creasing.

"Indeed it is. But it does mean there's more external pressure on you than on people who fit societal norms. I'm happy to bring these sessions to an end, but my door's always open. To talk, to vent. You've got to a good place, Josh, but you may still need help to stay where you are."

I look at Scott, he stares at me.

"The good news," Delia continues, "is that society has come a long way. Still got further to go before we win the war. May even have to face some backward steps first too." She frowns, I wonder if she's thinking as I am, about things such as people being able to refuse to serve us, just because they've got different views. Then she shakes her head. "Just bear that in mind. It's not weakness to ask for help if it gets too much."

I shake hands with Delia, knowing I could well be going back. Therapy's got me grounded, if my head starts to get fucked up, I don't rule out the need to go get pointed in the right direction again. But for now, it's goodbye.

We leave, me taking a moment to look back one last time at the building where I'd received so much help, considering how

I viewed myself when I'd first come here, unable to break free of my conditioning, comparing it to the man I am now. Scott looks at me knowingly and takes my hand, leading me over to the bikes. We're almost there when we hear an incredulous shout.

"In daylight? Perverts!" Two men, getting out of a car, throw us twin expressions of disgust, the speaker's voice drips with derision. "Shouldn't be allowed. You're both going to hell."

Scott pulls me closer, raises an eyebrow, whispering, "Seeing as we're Devils, I expect that we are."

I grin at him, ignoring the men staring after us, and get on my bike. I wait for him to start his engine, then start mine, drowning out any further insults with the roar from our exhausts.

Then, side by side as we'll always be, we return to the compound, our daughter, back to the men who couldn't give a fuck what we are.

Mouse Trapped

SATAN'S DEVILS #9

Mouse

I rescued Mariana. Then I found I wanted her.

To keep her family safe, she can't let a man like me into her life. A man who rides with an MC.

I couldn't have her, I have to stay away.

But no matter how hard I try, I'm drawn to watch over her, like a guardian angel. This isn't like me.

Why do I care? When she finds herself in trouble again, why am I prepared to sacrifice everything I am for this woman?

*I've been careful. Done everything I've needed to.
Obeyed every law.*

*I even gave up my chance to be with the one man who
interested me.*

*I'm in trouble, again. I've no one to call, except the one man
who came to my rescue before.*

*But would Mouse help me again? Why would he care?
What could he do?*

This time I don't think it's possible for anyone to save me.

SATAN'S DEVILS #9: Mouse Trapped

OTHER WORKS BY MANDA MELLETT

All books can be read as a standalone.

Blood Brothers

A series about sexy dominant sheikhs and their bodyguards

- *Stolen Lives* (#1 – Nijad & Cara)

- *Close Protection* (#2 – Jon & Mia)

- *Second Chances* (#3 – Kadar & Zoe)

- *Identity Crisis* (#4 – Sean & Vanessa)

- *Dark Horses* (#5 – Jasim & Janna)

- *Hard Choices* (#6 – Aiza)

SATAN'S DEVILS MC

- *Turning Wheels* (Blood Brothers #3.5, Satan's Devils #1 – Wraith & Sophie)

- *Drummer's Beat* (# 2 – Drummer & Sam)

- *Slick Running* (#3 – Slick & Ella)

- *Targeting Dart* (#4 – Dart & Alex)

- *Heart Broken* (#5 – Heart & Marc)

- *Peg's Stand* (#6 – Peg & Darcy)

- *Rock Bottom* (#7 – Rock & Becca)

- *Joker's Fool* (#8 – Joker & Lady)

Coming soon:
- *Mouse Trapped* (#9)

Sign up for my newsletter to hear about new releases in the Blood Brothers and Satan's Devils series:
http://eepurl.com/b1PXO5

GLOSSARY

Motorcycle Club – An official motorcycle club in the U.S. is one which is sanctioned by the American Motorcyclist Association (AMA). The AMA has a set of rules its members must abide by. It is said that ninety-nine percent of motorcyclists in America belong to the AMA

Outlaw Motorcycle Club (MC) – The remaining one percent of motorcycling clubs are historically considered outlaws as they do not wish to be constrained by the rules of the AMA and have their own bylaws. There is no one formula followed by such clubs, but some not only reject the rulings of the AMA, but also that of society, forming tightly knit groups who fiercely protect their chosen ways of life. Outlaw MCs have a reputation for having a criminal element and supporting themselves by less than legal activities, dealing in drugs, gun running or prostitution. The one-percenter clubs are usually run under a strict hierarchy.

Brother – Typically members of the MC refer to themselves as brothers and regard the closely knit MC as their family.

Cage – The name bikers give to cars as they prefer riding their bikes.

Chapter – Some MCs have only one club based in one location. Other MCs have a number of clubs who follow the same bylaws and wear the same patch. Each club is known as a chapter and will normally carry the name of the area where they are based on their patch.

Church – Traditionally the name of the meeting where club business is discussed, either with all members present or with just those holding officer status.

Colours – When a member is wearing (or flying) his colours he will be wearing his cut proudly displaying his patch showing which club he is affiliated with.

Cut – The name given to the jacket or vest which has patches denoting the club that member belongs to.

Enforcer – The member who enforces the rules of the club.

Hang-around – This can apply to men wishing to join the club and who hang-around hoping to be become prospects. It is also used to women who are attracted by bikers and who are happy to make themselves available for sex at biker parties.

Mother Chapter – The founding chapter when a club has more than one chapter.

Patch – The patch or patches on a cut will show the club that member belongs to and other information such as the particular chapter and any role that may be held in the club. There can be a number of other patches with various meanings, including a one-percenter patch. Prospects will not be allowed to wear the club patch until they have been patched-in, instead they will have patches which denote their probationary status.

Patched-in/Patching-in – The term used when a prospect completes his probationary status and becomes a full club member.

President (Prez) – The officer in charge of that particular club or chapter.

Prospect – Anyone wishing to join a club must serve time as a probationer. During this period they have to prove their loyalty to the club. A probationary period can last a year or more. At the end of this period, if they've proved themselves a prospect will be patched-in.

Old Lady – The term given to a woman who enters into a permanent relationship with a biker.

RICO – The Racketeer Influenced and Corrupt Organisations Act primarily deals with organised crime. Under this Act the officers of a club could be held responsible for activities they order members to do and a conviction carries a potential jail service of twenty years as well as a large fine and the seizure of assets.

Road Captain – The road captain is responsible for the safety of the club on a run. He will organise routes and normally ride at the end of the column.

Ronin – A biker who travels alone, sometimes wearing a patch denoting he's Ronin. Not affiliated to any club, but often bearing a token which will help ensure safe passage through territories of different clubs.

Secretary – MCs are run like businesses and this officer will perform the secretarial duties such as recording decisions at meetings.

Sergeant-at-Arms – The sergeant-at-arms is responsible for the safety of the club as a whole and for keeping order.

Sweet Butt – A woman who makes her sexual services available to any member at any time. She may well live on the club premises and be fully supported by the club.

Treasurer – The officer responsible for keeping an eye on the club's money.

Vice President (VP) – The vice president will support the president, stepping into his role in his absence. He may be responsible for making sure the club runs smoothly, overseeing prospects etc.

Brothers protecting their own

ACKNOWLEDGEMENTS

I was asked to write Joker and Lady's story a few books back, but I didn't feel confident in doing so. I've read some excellent M/M MC books. My problem was, I didn't think I had anything different to offer.

But as characters do, they stayed at the back of my mind, and ideas began to germinate. I decided I'd write a novella, I mean, there wasn't much for them to say, was there? Well, when I gave them free rein, I found they actually had quite a lot to tell me, and the novella became a full-length book.

I have a gay son, and some of our conversations got, well, quite interesting, when I was checking some of the detail with him, especially when sharing a bottle of wine. My first thanks must go to him. Thank you, Michael. And thank you for all your support and encouragement.

I can't express my gratitude enough to Maggie Kern who's become my editor. "Send me the rough draft," she said. So I did, even though it must have been torturous to read. Her attention to detail, especially in helping to match up scenes from the other books, has been invaluable. I really enjoyed knocking this book into shape with her help. Loved working with you, Maggie.

What can I say about my beta readers? Nothing more than again extending my heartfelt thanks to Danena, Colleen, Sheri, Terra, Zoe, Nicole, Alex and my husband Steve. Each of you pointed out things that were really useful. Couldn't do without you, beta team.

I've been working with Lia Rees since the first book I've published. Up to now she's designed my great covers and done the formatting of all my books. On this occasion she's also been my proof reader. As always, I'm in awe of her work. Thank you, Lia.

I started off by saying I was asked to write this book. Every time a reader tells me how much they enjoy any of my books, especially when they ask for more, it spurs me to continue writing. So please keep in contact, I appreciate every review, message or comment that you give me.

Thank you for reading the words that I write.

To anyone asking the question, the Satan's Devils have a long way to go yet. There'll be another Devil along very soon.

STAY IN TOUCH

Email: manda@mandamellett.com
Website: www.mandamellett.com

Connect with me on Facebook:
https://www.facebook.com/mandamellett

Sign up for my newsletter to hear about new releases in the
Blood Brothers and Satan's Devils series:

http://eepurl.com/b1PXO5

ABOUT THE AUTHOR

After commuting for too many years to London working in various senior management roles, Manda Mellett left the rat race and now fulfils her dream and writes full time. She draws on her background in psychology, the experience of working in different disciplines and personal life experiences in her books.

Manda lives in the beautiful countryside of North Essex with her husband and two slightly nutty Irish Setters. Walking her dogs gives her the thinking time to come up with plots for her novels, and she often dictates ideas onto her phone on the move, while looking over her shoulder hoping no one is around to listen to her. Manda's other main hobby is reading, and she devours as many books as she can.

Her biggest fan is her gay son (every mother should have one!). Her favourite pastime when he is home is the late night chatting sessions they enjoy, where no topic is taboo, and usually accompanied by a bottle of wine or two.

Photo by Carmel Jane Photography